BARELY BREATHING: A DARK BULLY ROMANCE

AN ACADIA PREP NOVEL

K.G. REUSS

A STANDALONE NOVEL

Copyright Barely Breathing © 2021 by K.G. Reuss

All rights reserved.

No part of this book may be reproduced in any form or by any electronic or mechanical means, including information storage and retrieval systems, without written permission from the author, except for the use of brief quotations in a book review.

Cover Design: Moonstruck Cover Design & Photography, moonstruckcoverdesign.com

Editing: N-D-Scribable Services

Formatting: Books from Beyond

WARNING

READ ME

Dearest Reader
 You're here because you love to read. I'm here because I love to write. Together, we should make a great team. Ah, but nay nay. It doesn't always work out the way we plan.

That being said, once you turn the page, you will be sucked into a dark world filled with abuse of all natures, violence, and heartbreak. If you have ANY inkling that you may be triggered, please navigate away. Barely Breathing is NOT for the faint of heart.

I'm not joking. Authors sometimes say there are dragons between their covers.

That's not me. We have more than dragons 'round these parts. There's fires. There's devils. Demons. Evil and heartache lurking around every corner. Whips, chains, and all the things that could make a woman squeal. Or scream. Dirty, depraved fucking. Yes, not just sex. It's downright fucking. Non-con. Dub-con. Ugly little things that can take its toll on those with heightened emotions.

All of these things ride on the backs of horned dragons, prepared to lay waste to everything you thought you knew.

So. Are you staying? If so, grab a cozy spot, get some wine, and get ready to get your emotions fucked.

Because where's the fun if there aren't any tears?

Happy reading.

-K

ONE
ASHA

I wrapped my fingers around the edges of the dingy, porcelain sink in a death grip as I tried to hold myself up. My reflection stared back at me from the dented-up metal screwed to the wall in the place of a mirror as the pulse of the thumping music outside the room blared on. Each thud felt like a hammer fall, driving the nails into my coffin.

Thud. Thud. Thud.

I drew in a shaky breath. My blue eyes were glassy with the threat of tears I refused to let fall while nerves worked my stomach over. It felt like it was doing flips, end over end. Acid burned its way up my throat, and my mouth watered, my stomach demanding to empty. I willed it away.

I knew what I had to do.

With a heavy sigh, I stood up straight, my legs wobbling on the ridiculously high heels that were thrown at me moments ago. They came along with a black, leather G-string that was studded and a matching bra. Looking down at my body, I wish I could've said I didn't even recognize myself, but that would've been a lie. It wasn't the first time I'd been manipulated, used, and treated like trash by my stepfather, who ran the illegal sex trafficking ring in the basement of a night club.

It was the perfect place to entertain his criminal friends. There were drinks and drugs galore. Plenty of women to fuck or buy. And all the noise was concealed by the loud club above. Nobody noticed if someone stumbled out onto the sidewalk fucked out of their skull. Nobody paid attention to a man carrying a girl away. Only the scum in the club knew she'd been drugged and sold against her will. Any innocent bystander would just assume some dude's girlfriend had a little too much fun.

Gio, my stepfather, claimed I was one of the lucky ones. I was never to be sold, not as long as I went along with whatever fucked up plan he had for me. His term was more like *borrowed*. I'd been passed around his circle far too many times to count. Even he'd had his fun with me, the man who swore to care for me as his own. He never fucked me though, which was a surprise really, considering what a piece of shit he was. But I still knew what his mouth tasted like and how rough his fingers could be and how *hard* he got when I cried.

I glanced around the dirty bathroom and took in the grimy, white-tiled walls and the stained, concrete floor. The smell of mildew and mold wafted up my nostrils and made my stomach roll. I couldn't figure out how to get out of this. I considered faking sick, but even I knew it wouldn't work. There'd been plenty of times over the years where I was forced into bed with a man I didn't know when I had been sick. The deal was I had to put out and shut the fuck up.

Gio was my real father's sworn enemy in the dark world of mobsters, drugs, and violence. Mom walked out on my father, Nicolai Reznikov, leader of his own bratva, when she caught him fucking some stripper in their bedroom. Her revenge was to fuck us over by marrying his enemy, a feat easily conquered once Gio realized how much of an embarrassment it would be for my father. Gio wanted to hurt my father any way he could, whether Dad knew about it or not. And what was the number one way to get to my father? *Me.*

Gio's revenge on my father was owning me, my father's most

prized possession. *The kicker?* I couldn't speak to my father anymore either. I'd played the silly, little game of being the angry, spoiled daughter who was betrayed by Daddy's indiscretions. My father assumed I'd sided with Gio's syndicate—a blow to both his ego and heart.

I never told my mother or father about the things Gio made me do. He'd threatened to kill them if I didn't do as he demanded, and I knew he'd hold true to his word. My father wouldn't come for me. He knew if he took my mother to court, her anger would let loose everything she knew. Surprisingly, there was *some* honor among thieves since Mom had not spilled the beans to anyone, at least that I knew of. Perhaps my father didn't love me the way I thought he did. Or maybe he made a deal with my mother I didn't know about. It didn't matter though. None of it did. *This* was my life now, protecting people who didn't protect me.

And so there I was, eating shit to keep myself and my mother alive. Trapped with no way out.

I was jolted from my morose thoughts when the old, wooden door flew open, crashing against the filthy, cracked tile behind it as Gio sauntered through. His shiny, expensive shoes scraped across the grit on the floor, the sound sending a chill up my spine. He smiled around a toothpick clenched between his teeth as he reached behind him and closed the door. His black hair was slicked back. Women fell at Gio's feet wherever he went. *Handsome. Powerful. Wicked.* The only reason I ever dropped to my knees for him was because he put me there.

I felt like cowering as he erased the space between us, but I resisted the urge, knowing any sign of weakness would only lead to more trouble. I pushed my shoulders back and held my chin high as he stopped inches away. His thick, musky cologne washed over me and made the urge to vomit stronger.

His dark eyes narrowed in on mine, making deep lines appear around them as he took in my appearance. "Mmmmm, you're looking beautiful tonight, Asha. All this blonde hair is going to drive the men mad," he said, pushing a lock away from my face.

I wanted to flinch, but I planted my feet and refused to move.

Both of his hands moved up to cup my cheeks as he forced my gaze to his. "You're nervous, yes?"

I wet my lips and nodded my head as a long breath escaped me. I didn't even want to think about having to go out on that stage and remove my clothes for those men.

His smile returned. "I have just the thing to take the edge off." He reached into his pocket and brought out a small, golden container. He flipped the lid back. Inside were tiny, white pills. The long fingers on his left hand took out two pills as his right hand closed the case and tucked it away. He removed the toothpick from between his teeth as he popped one of the pills into his mouth, then raised the other to my lips.

I didn't open for him. I didn't want the pill. There was no telling what the hell it was. I should've known that refusing wasn't an option. His right hand roughly grabbed at my chin as he pushed me backward until my back pressed against the cold, metal divider of the stalls.

"My guests want to have a good time tonight, and you're going to give it to them. They love young, pink pussy. Nobody wants to watch a woman dance who looks scared out of her mind. Now, take this. It'll make you feel good."

He pressed the pill to my lips again, but something wouldn't let them open.

"I said *take* it, Asha, or you'll be the one being sold tonight," he ground the words out between his clenched teeth.

I knew he wasn't lying. He'd sell me just to teach me a lesson. Sure, he'd probably come a week later and buy me back, but a week was more than enough time for some man to do whatever he wanted to me. It was bad enough Gio loaned me out by the hour.

Slowly, I opened my mouth.

His facial expression shifted from one of anger to one of pleasure as he placed the pill directly on the tip of my tongue. "Now, swallow," he whispered.

I closed my mouth and swallowed the bitter pill. His lips pressed against mine a moment later. His tongue demanded entrance as his hands yanked my body against his. My blood ran cold as he squeezed my ass and breasts a little too roughly. When he pinched my nipple between his thumb and forefinger, I cried out.

He pulled back with a menacing laugh. "Oh, the boys are going to love you," he said, his eyes skimming down my body as the tips of his fingers followed along between my breasts and down my stomach, between my hipbones and into my panties. His long fingers forced their way between my folds. When he found nothing but dryness, he removed them. "The pill will help that. Nobody can have fun with a dried-up pussy. You're on in five. You'll need to get home after you're done with your clients. You have school in the morning. Wouldn't want my pride and joy to miss classes." He let out a laugh at his sarcasm before he turned and exited the bathroom the same way he'd appeared.

A long breath left my lips with his absence as I moved to stand back in front of the mirror, having to start the process of calming myself all over. The seconds ticked by like I was waiting for my death sentence to be delivered. My heart raced, and sweat beaded up on my skin. My hands began to shake. I rolled my neck in an attempt to loosen myself up. I closed my eyes and felt the dizziness take over as the pill worked its way into my system.

Someone pounded on the door. "You're up," a man called out.

My eyes popped open, locking in on the blurry image of myself in the metal sheet on the wall. I took a deep breath and pushed forward. The longer they had to wait, the worse the punishment would be.

I clutched the cold, metal handle of the door and jerked it open. The loud bass hit me as I made my way through the crowd of men and onto the stage, each one of them grabbing handfuls of my ass, breasts, and hair along the way. The booming music helped drown out my thoughts as hate consumed me. Self-loathing coursed through my veins.

The crowd of men before me roared with excitement as the music shifted from one song over to "Tainted Love" by Marilyn Mason. My vision began to blur as I stared out over the sea of men. My heart started to calm. My hands shook less. The pill was doing its job. I wasn't sure if I was happy about that or if I was even more afraid of the things it could make me do.

I reached for the pole in the center of the stage and wrapped my fingers around it as I walked a slow circle, giving the men a nice look at everything I had to offer. Hate coiled in my stomach like a snake ready to strike, but I remembered Gio's words from earlier when he'd informed me of his little plan: *Be cute, be flirty, be a fucking tease on the stage to lure them back, then do what you do best. Be a fucking whore. Seventeen is a tender age. Let them eat you up.*

With that thought, I shut off my mind and let my body do what it did best: perform. I swung around the pole. I crawled across the stage. I took my clothes off and touched all the places on my body the men were dying to touch. When the song wrapped, I grabbed my things and rushed from the stage. Gio was by the bathroom door, waiting for me with a wide smile. He pushed the door open as I approached. I walked straight by him. In the center of the bathroom floor, I tried to dress, but he plucked the panties from my hand.

"You won't be needing these the rest of the night," he said, tossing them over his shoulder.

I immediately took a hesitant step back.

"You're going to go out there and do your job, Asha. I want you servicing man after man in any way they see fit. I don't give a fuck if you have to drink a gallon of come." He leveled his eyes on me, and my stomach threatened to spill over. "These men are *very* important to my business. If they're not happy, I'm not happy. And you know what happens when I'm not happy, yes?"

My gaze dropped to the floor as I nodded my head.

His hand moved up to cup my chin, and he tilted my head back until my eyes found his. "Good girl," he whispered as he pushed my back against the stall. His chest pressed against mine as his hand slid down between my legs. Thanks to the pill from earlier, his fingers came back glistening. "That's better," he breathed out as he took a step back. "Now, go get to work," he said, smacking me on the ass as I walked by.

My heart cried out at what my life had become. My stomach wanted to empty with the thought of being forced to become a whore who was pulled off the shelf whenever men saw fit. They always returned me back to my rightful place, but I was never the same. I was always bruised, bloody, broken—an empty shell of the person I once was. I longed to escape. I dreamed of an end. But I knew there was no happy ending for people like me. I'd be used and broken time and time again, only ever mended, never fully repaired. Until the day came along when there was nothing left to mend. Then I'd be tossed out like the trash I'd been forced to become, never finding love, never finding happiness. Only finding more destruction.

I knew I wouldn't want to remember the night—hours of being touched, raped, beaten, and abused—so instead of heading to the ringleader of the men in the group Gio aimed me at, I strode straight to the bar for a few quick shots. I didn't know how the alcohol would affect the pill in my system, but I didn't care.

What's the worst that could happen? I'd die? Even that seemed better than the life I was forced to live. In my eyes, I had nothing to lose and everything to gain. Might as well push myself to the limits.

I had just tossed down my third shot of tequila when a hand wrapped around my throat. I was pulled against some man, my back pressing against his chest as his mouth moved toward my ear.

"You're mine, princess. Now, let's get busy," he said, dragging me away from the bar and back to the private room.

The old, wooden door opened inwardly, and he shoved me through, my heels scraping along the dirty floor as I rushed forward, trying to regain my balance. My outstretched hands found the cinder block wall, righting myself. The man had the door shut and locked by the time I turned around. His fingers moved back to my throat, and he threw me onto the mattress. He loomed over me as he freed himself from his expensive suit. The one hanging bulb in the center of the room lit him up. His face was old, covered in lines and wrinkles. His hair was falling out. The strands that were left were gray and greasy. Just the sight of him made my skin crawl.

"Touch yourself," he demanded as he slid a condom on his unimpressive length.

At least, Gio demanded that of the men. They had to wear condoms in order to keep me clean enough to use again.

I shut my eyes, not wanting to see the man before me, and allowed my hand to drift down my stomach to the junction between my legs. My finger slid between the folds with ease thanks to the pill, but it didn't help settle my mind or calm the hate raging inside of me. I prayed the shots kicked in quickly, not wanting to remember the way the man touched me, moved inside of me, or the disgusting grunts he made when he thrusted into me while squeezing his hands around my throat.

"Take it, you little cunt," he rasped as sweat beaded on his forehead. "Fuck. That's a tight, little pussy. So young. So sweet." He let out a low groan as he squeezed my throat tighter.

Let me die. Please. Let this be over.

I didn't fight his tight grip as sparkles popped off behind my eyelids. In fact, I embraced the darkness. But nothing lasted forever, and I was brought right back to my personal hell as he rammed into me breathlessly, droplets of his sweat raining down on me. Then the blackness returned as he squeezed my throat again.

I prayed I'd get lucky enough that every man I had to be with would treat me the same and give me an out from their abuse with the brief dance with death. But I wasn't that lucky.

I never was.

TWO
LIAM

The bell rang, and I started toward my locker. I glanced down at myself and shook my head at the stupid ass tuxedo shirt I was wearing. Normally, I wouldn't have been caught dead in a dumbass shirt like it, but that was what I got for losing a bet while playing history trivia against my best friend, Max.

Max was good people as far as I was concerned. He was another scholarship kid like me. He couldn't just walk down the halls and have people fall at his feet. He was at this school to work. He and I had become quick friends the day I started freshmen year. All of us scholarship kids stuck together. We had to. If we were on our own, we'd have to deal with Lucas and the rest of his rich, prick friends without backup.

Putting up with Lucas and his crew was just part of surviving the halls of Acadia Academy. Taking them on as a group made things much easier for us. There was no way of escaping them, and telling a teacher only made the next encounter worse. None of Lucas's crew ever got in trouble for the shit they did. Their parents donated too much money to the school for that to happen. I'd seen an ambulance pick up a student due to Lucas's hazing, and all he got was a smack on the wrist. No, when it came to Lucas and his buddies, we were on our own.

I arrived at my locker and quickly put in the combination. It opened easily, and I got a flash of myself in the mirror stuck to the door. My dark hair was shaggier than most of the guys kept it around there, but it was still fixed to have that perfect messy look about it. Dark circles rimmed my green eyes because I'd stayed up too late the night before, finishing my writing assignment. But other than that, I looked OK given the heavy workload school forced upon us. The tuxedo shirt was a bit tight. I'd been working out more after school in the gym. I needed to look like I could handle myself, or else I'd end up like Mickey Westcott, a skinny, scholarship kid who got stuffed into a garbage can every Friday before lunch. My size was probably the only thing that kept me from totally getting my ass handed to me. Not that I didn't get pushed around by the rich pricks. I just didn't end up in the trash can.

Everything about me looked fine in my reflection—everything but the stupid fucking shirt. It even had a fake rose on its fake lapel.

I deposited my books inside my locker just as Max, Andy, and Sofia came to a stop behind me.

Max bumped his shoulder into mine with a smirk. "Looking good today, Liam. Love the shirt. What do you guys think?" he asked, looking over at the other two.

Andy ran his hand through his brown hair and laughed. "Nice, man. I never thought you'd go through with it."

Sofia shrugged and offered up a flirty smile. "I think you look good in anything, Liam. You know that," she said, her slight Spanish accent coming through as she batted her long, dark lashes at me. She brushed her black hair away from her face and gave my hand a quick squeeze.

I laughed and rolled my eyes. "Yeah, right. I've gotten all kinds of looks today. Remind me to *never* bet against you," I told Max as I held up my middle finger.

He laughed harder before pulling his fist back and sending it flying toward my bicep. It landed with a solid thud. "Don't bet against me when it comes to what I know best. Now football or something stupid like that, you'd win every time."

I grinned at him, grabbed the library book out of my locker, and slammed the door shut. "I gotta return this book now that I've finished my essay. I'll meet you guys in a few." I held the book up.

Max and Andy both waved before turning and striding down the hall toward the cafeteria.

Sofia lingered a bit longer. She fluttered her eyelashes and peeked up at me from beneath them. "I'll walk with you if you want."

"And miss nacho day?" I scoffed. "No way. Go get lunch. Grab me some too, and I'll see you outside."

She looked let down until I asked her to grab some for me. When I added that on, her smile was back full force.

"Okay. See you in a minute," she told me, rushing away, her hair swinging from side to side as she went.

Our friendship had been getting complicated. At first, there was nothing between us but friendship. But then the two of us went to a party at one of the townies' places—public school kids— where I'd had a little too much to drink and probably a little too much to smoke. The next thing I knew, we were making out. We'd made out a few times after that too, but nothing had ever come of it. Since then, she'd been looking at me with big doe eyes, batting her lashes and shit. Sofia was an awesome girl, but she wasn't really my type. I didn't want to fuck up our friendship, so I had no intentions of letting the relationship develop.

I pushed my way through the door of the library and made my way to the center where the drop box was. The library was deathly silent as I dumped the book in. It landed with a thud. Satisfied I had that shit over with, I left and strolled down the hall. I heard a clicking behind me. I turned to find Lucas and his crew coming toward me. Lucas was flicking his Zippo lighter open, then closed, then open again.

"Well, well, well. Look who we have here," he said, eyes moving over me like he was sizing me up.

I raised my hands, showing them my palms. "I'm not looking for trouble," I told them. I'd fight Lucas one-on-one any fucking day of the week. In fact, I'd love to. *But fight him when he had his whole crew to back him up?* I wasn't that fucking stupid.

Hudson and Jude were on either side of him, both of them big, stupid, and rich. The girls stood off to the side—Tiffany, Marcie, Heidi, and Asha—arranged in order from bitchy to bitchiest. My eyes lingered just a bit longer on Asha, and she noticed. She shot me a coy smile as she peered up at me from under her dark lashes, pushing a strand of blonde hair over her shoulder. Asha was Lucas's girlfriend. Nobody got away with looking at her, and I was no exception.

Lucas stepped closer. "You checking out my girlfriend, douche bag?" he asked, bumping his chest against mine.

I pulled my gaze away immediately and ran a hand through my hair. "Nah, man. She ain't my type," I told him, trying to play it cool.

His chin jutted out as his dark eyes landed on mine. "Yeah? Why not? You into dudes or something?"

I let out a huff of a laugh and shook my head. "No, not into dudes. But I'm not into whores either."

His hands moved faster than I thought possible, and within a second of saying that last sentence, he pushed me hard. I had no choice but to topple back, my back smashing into the locker behind me.

He pointed his finger in my face. "If I *ever* hear you talk about my girlfriend like that again, I swear to God, you'll regret it. You think we're bad? Let these girls get ahold of you with their claws."

"Fuck the claws," Asha spoke up. "I say we cut his tongue out. I bet his little girlfriend, Sofia, wouldn't like that since he's the only one brave enough to go down on her." She offered up an evil smile, making the rest of the girls giggle. Asha turned to look at her bitch squad. "You see her arm hair? I bet her snatch is ten time hairier than that." That was enough to have them cackling.

"Oh, Asha, you're evil," Tiffany said, combing her fingers through her naturally red hair. Her green eyes held a glint of evilness to them that made chills race up my spine. Something about that girl had always gotten under my skin. She was the type who'd skin you alive and laugh as you slowly bled out. She was hot as hell though, and she knew it. Everyone knew it.

I shook my head, wanting to clear it. "Sofia and I aren't a thing," I told Asha. The last thing I wanted was for poor Sofia to be pulled into their harassment.

Asha's blue eyes cut back to me. They were striking in comparison to how darkly she had them lined. "You're not screwing the geeky girl?"

I shook my head. "Nope."

She smirked. "So even she won't let you near her." She shook her head, tsking me. "What a shame. It must suck having all the girls puke with the thought of you touching them. Or maybe it's because you have a tiny dick." She moved toward me until her face was a fraction from mine.

I had to admit, she was breathtaking—probably the most beautiful girl I'd ever seen. But the fact she was a raging bitch nullified it.

My breath hitched in my chest as she reached out and cupped my manhood, rubbing her hand against me. My cock didn't know the difference between a beauty and a bitch, so it did the only thing it knew how to. It got hard.

"Wow," she breathed out softly in a shaky voice so only I could hear her. "I guess it's *not* a dick problem. Who'd have thought you'd be packing this?" She caressed me again.

I squeezed my eyes closed and tried to keep my shit together.

She let out a soft laugh and moved away from me completely before proclaiming, "His dick *is* the problem. I couldn't even feel it."

"Shrimp dick," Jude snorted loudly as everyone laughed. "Hastings has a tiny cock!"

I ground my teeth together but held my tongue, knowing if I got into it with Asha, I'd get into a fight with the whole fucking crew.

And seven against one weren't good odds. Asha had been on my shit for a long ass time. It seemed she sought me out to mess with. It wouldn't surprise me a bit if she'd encouraged this interaction. My dick softened immediately as they catcalled to me, making fun of me.

Lucas started flicking his lighter open and closed again, getting my attention. "What? Nothing to say? She right? Do the girls puke with the thought of you touching them? Is your dick really that small?" he asked, cocking his head to the side. "I bet pussies dry up whenever you're around." He snorted like he'd told joke of the year.

His guys joined in.

"Your pussy dry, Marcie?" Jude called out, grinning like an asshole.

"Ew, Jude. That's disgusting," she shot back, frowning.

"Mine is," Heidi giggled.

Hudson waggled his brows at her. "I bet I can get it wet for you."

She giggled again, and he moved toward her. I looked away as they started kissing. As far as I knew, they weren't a couple, but everyone in their group probably fucked one another.

I looked back to Lucas to answer his stupid question. "I don't know, man. I guess so," I agreed, wanting this shit show over.

He smirked and then had me by the neck a second later. He managed to spin me around as he slammed my head against the locker. He held me there. I could've kicked his ass, but again, he was a bitch and I'd have to fight them all. *Pick your battles, Liam.* That was what my dad always told me. The advice came in handy at Acadia.

"Keep your mouth shut around my girlfriend, and keep your eyes to your fucking self. Or else," he snarled.

I wanted to ask him *or what*, but I heard the Zippo open again, only this time, it lit. He moved the flame toward my face. I felt the heat of the flame dancing only millimeters from my nose.

"Got me?"

"Yes," I agreed tightly, understanding what the *or else* meant.

He'd toast my ass. Literally.

He held the flame there a few seconds longer, but they felt like minutes slowly ticking by as the end of my nose started heating up. Suddenly, he pulled it away and released me.

"Come on, guys. Let's get some lunch," he said, leading them away as I straightened up and watched them go.

Lucas was first while Asha was last. Before she walked through the door, she turned to look at me. She wore an evil smirk and licked her lips seductively. Her eyes though, they held a slight shimmer of remorse. It was only then I noticed the dark circles beneath them. I wondered if she stayed up late finishing an assignment like I did. In reality, she was probably just up too late partying and living the perfect life.

The door slammed between us, and my anger bubbled over. I pulled back my fist and sent it flying toward the locker my head had just been slammed against. My ears were ringing, but I didn't know if that was due to my head hitting the metal so hard or if it was because my blood pressure was through the roof. Pain shot through my hand, but I ignored it. I ignored the blood left behind on the locker too.

I hated those mother fuckers. Hated their self-entitled bullshit. Hated that they couldn't get into trouble because of who their parents were. Hated they thought of themselves as gods who ruled the school. And I hated her. *Asha Blake.*

I fucking loathed how breathtakingly beautiful she was. I despised her blonde hair which looked like silk hanging almost to her waist, her blue eyes that were icy and cold, her perfect body that I *knew* would fit perfectly beneath mine. But most of all, I detested her because I knew I'd never get a chance with her. No matter what I did, I wouldn't be good enough. I was a poor, scholarship kid. I didn't have money, an expensive car, or a trust fund. I was beneath her in every sense of the word, and there was nothing I could fucking do about it.

Of course, I hated myself too. It was my desire for her, knowing what I knew about her. She'd rubbed my cock in front of her crew and had gotten me hard. I'd enjoyed her touching me. It had to shriek volumes about how fucked up *I* was, especially since she'd told everyone I had a small cock after she knew it was a damn lie.

I finally made my way out to the courtyard and found my group of friends sitting under the same oak tree we always sat under. Sofia had her back against the trunk as she picked over her nachos. I took my place beside her, which made her smile as she handed over my portion.

"Thanks," I grunted, not exactly in the mood for the flirting shit anymore.

"You're welcome," she told me sweetly.

I picked up a chip covered in cheese and jalapeños and stuffed it into my mouth.

Sofia crossed her legs beneath her and leaned forward. "So...this weekend, my parents are taking off. I thought that maybe you and I could—"

"Can't," I blurted out, not giving her the chance to finish. "Got plans."

She nodded her head once and sat back, clearly annoyed with my rejection.

I took a deep breath and cleared my head. "I'm sorry. I didn't mean for that to come out all..."

"Dickish?" she finished for me.

I forced out a laugh. "Yeah. I just... I really do have plans."

Her face smoothed over, and she looked much more at ease.

"Look at them, man," Max said to nobody in particular.

I followed his stare to the elite table where Lucas and his crew sat —talking, laughing, fucking around. Lucas had his arm around Asha, and he was whispering something in her ear that made her tip her head back and laugh. A pang of jealously shot through me. I wished it was my hands on her, that I was the one making her laugh. *What the fuck was wrong with me?* Girl had just insulted me and rubbed my cock to embarrass me, and I still wanted her?

She may have been the evil queen bee around the school, but I was clearly fucked in the head for even looking at her, let alone, wanting her.

"Don't let them bother you, man," I told Max.

He hated them just as much as the rest of us.

"Could you imagine being one of them?" he asked, peering from me, to Sofia, to Andy, and back. "What it must be like, huh? I bet Lucas could demand Mrs. Wheeler drop to her knees and suck his dick, and she'd do it. Even the teachers treat them like gold."

"I wouldn't mind Mrs. Wheeler dropping to her knees for me. Bitch is like forty and still hot as hell," I joked, noticing the way it made Sofia squirm.

Max and Andy laughed at my joke and only added to it, getting dirtier and dirtier with their remarks until Sofia got up and left completely.

"Oh no, someone is mad," Max joked.

I shook my head. "Cut her some slack, man," I said, watching her retreating back.

I wished there was a way to get out of this situation with Sofia, but I didn't know how to give her what she wanted without making things even worse for myself. I didn't have eyes for Sofia. I only wanted one person. Asha Blake.

Talk about being a masochist...

THREE
ASHA

I was tired, had a headache, and I was grouchy. My hangover was holding on tight, not letting up no matter what I did. When I woke this morning, I took some Tylenol. I knew the three shots of tequila from the night before wasn't what had me feeling so badly. It was the pill Gio had given me. Remembering how I spent last night with a man I didn't know on top of me only added to my bad mood. I always tried *not* to remember those times when I was at school. I liked to keep my two lives separate. Otherwise, it only reminded me I wasn't good enough. It made me feel out of place walking the halls like any other normal teenage girl when I was anything but. No one knew about my secret life. Not even Lucas. I didn't need anyone else looking at me in disgust. I did it enough for everyone.

After we left Liam in the hallway, a few of us gathered around Lucas's locker while he dug around looking for the joint he'd hidden. Jude stood in the middle of the hallway, watching and waiting impatiently while I leaned against the locker beside Lucas. I couldn't get the thought of Liam out of my head. *How he'd hardened in my hand. How the motion had made my heart pound harder. How long and thick he'd been.*

"Found it," Lucas said, holding it up for me to see.

I smiled in return, hoping the joint would give me some kind of relief from the pounding in my skull. Lucas slipped it into his pocket and closed his locker. His hand found my hip, and he pulled me down the slick metal until I was standing directly in front of him. Slowly, he leaned in and pressed his lips to mine.

Kissing him was the last thing I felt like doing, but I knew if I pushed him away it would only cause a fight. I was in no mood for his high school drama bullshit, not after the night I'd had. So, I let him kiss me, praying he quickly got it out of his system. Acting like a dick and bullying kids around school always gave him this high, and when he was riding the waves, the one thing he always tried for was sex. But that was also the one thing we never did.

After having it stolen from me for so long, it was not something I gave freely. It was the only power I had left, and I planned on holding onto it.

The kiss turned heated, and I did my best to pretend I was into it, but when his hand moved up to grab my breast, I broke the kiss off and pushed him away. He quickly looked back at Jude to see he wasn't paying any attention before stepping up close to me again.

"What *the fuck* is your problem, Asha?" he whispered, his lips nearly touching mine because he was so close.

"You really think I'm going to let you feel me up with Jude watching?" I spat back.

Lucas ran his fingers through his blond hair and rolled his eyes. "He's not even paying attention. Besides, it's not like it would be the first time he's seen me kiss you."

I shrugged. "I'm not a toy you can play with whenever you feel like it, Lucas." I crossed my arms over my chest, making him take a step back.

Anger flared in his dark eyes as he cocked his jaw. "No, you're a fucking tease, and I have no idea why I even waste my time with you," he said, turning and storming away.

I glanced at Jude, and he just shrugged before loyally following his leader.

I stuck around a moment longer, needing to push the memory and torment of last night away. At school, I wasn't the same person. In that dirty, disgusting club, I was weak and powerless, but at school I was strong. I held all the power. I was untouchable.

I took a minute to mentally apply the crown back to my head. After that, I sauntered down the hallway with my head held high and my shoulders squared.

I stopped by the cafeteria and grabbed some nachos before going out to the courtyard to sit with the rest of my friends. They must have smoked without me, but it was just as well. They liked to go to an empty classroom that was just used for storage and light up. It was on the way to the commons, so the convenience alone made it easy. I peered around to find students sneaking looks at us. It was always this way. Wonder in their eyes, lips parted like they wanted to greet us but were too scared. I hated it. But I loved it. It was the control I needed.

After a few bites of lunch, the nauseousness passed, and my headache eased as well. The tension began to ease away as I took a few deep, relaxing breaths. My back wasn't so tight, my shoulders nowhere near as tensed. My stomach growled, ready for more food. I picked up a nacho and shoved it into my mouth. The warm cheese tasted amazing as I chewed and swallowed. It had been over twenty-four hours since I'd eaten solid food. Between the hate and depression brought on by my *loving* stepfather, I'd lost my appetite and with it, weight.

Gio thought I looked even better skinny, so he demanded I keep up the good work. *Asshole.* He couldn't see that my dramatic weight loss was a cry for help or hopefully, a painfully slow path to escaping him. No, he thought protruding hip bones and ribs were sexy. To him, it probably just meant I was too weak to fight anyone off.

As everyone around me talked and laughed and had a good time, my eyes found Liam sitting across the courtyard from us. He was with his scholarship friends under the big oak tree. I couldn't help but to feel a little jealous as I watched them. They were all laughing and talking, seeming to be having the time of their lives. The Mexican girl, Sofia—the one I thought was screwing Liam—looked pissed. After shaking her head, she got up and strode back into school, leaving the three guys alone.

Tiffany noticed me watching.

"Can you believe that shirt he's wearing?" She snorted.

I nodded. "Who wears stuff like that?"

She shrugged. "I don't know, but someone seriously needs to teach him how to dress. He'd be pretty hot if he wasn't so poor."

I smiled at her jab. He *was* pretty hot, even for a poor kid, and I wondered how he could be so happy. He had no standing at school. He didn't have money. He didn't have a nice house or an expensive car. *Why did he get to be so happy? And why couldn't my life be that way?*

Even though I had more than enough money, I'd trade places with him in a second.

Jealousy began eating at me, and it turned to anger as it bubbled in my stomach. He had nothing, yet he had it all. I had everything, yet nothing at the same time. My gaze dropped to the plate of nachos in front of me, and an idea hit me.

"Hey, Lucas," Tiffany said, getting his attention and nodding toward Liam. "Asha and I were just talking about Liam's shirt. I think we should get you one." She offered him a flirty smile, making me scowl.

Lucas threw his head back and laughed.

I narrowed my eyes on him. "What? You don't like it? I think it's kind of sexy," I said, watching as he processed my words. I could see the jealously filling him. "Sure would be a shame if something happened to it," I added on.

A smirk cut Lucas's lips up as he caught my meaning. My friends tittered with my ill intentions.

I leaned closer to Tiffany and whispered, "Watch this."

I stood with my plate in my hands and walked across the courtyard, hips swaying. As I passed him and his friends, I pretended to trip. The plate of nachos went flying out of my hands. I watched in slow motion as they soared through the air. Cheese splattered, covering his face and shirt as the chips fell to his lap.

"Oh, oh no. I'm *so* sorry," I said in my overly sweet voice as I smiled and did my best to hold back a giggle. It did no good though. Giggles bubbled over. The sounds of my friends laughing filtered across the yard.

Liam looked from me to his shirt then over to my friends, all laughing and talking about him. He took a deep breath and stood up. "It's fine. I hated this fucking shirt anyway," he said, reaching behind him.

He yanked it off, and my mouth dropped open. Standing before me was something I never expected. Muscles upon muscles greeted me. His biceps were big and bulging. His pecks were toned, and he had a rock-hard six-pack. His dark hair was disheveled from removing his shirt, and it only made him sexier. And God, the V that disappeared into his low hung jeans. His angular jaw tensed then relaxed as his green eyes lit up with anger. He offered up a tight smile before turning and striding toward the school.

It took me a moment to pull myself together. That was something I never expected. I didn't anticipate he'd act so cool. I never thought he'd take off his shirt in front of everyone. And I most certainly didn't anticipate what he was hiding under that shirt. I shook the image from my head and returned to my table. Everyone was talking quietly about what had just happened. I sat across from Lucas and next to Tiffany.

She instantly turned to me with wide eyes and her mouth hanging open. "What the fuck was that?" she asked.

I forced out a laugh and shook my head. "I'm just as surprised as you are," I said, trying to remain cool about the whole thing, while I was anything but.

I was pissed he was able to one-up me, and I was livid when I thought about how my heart betrayed me when he removed his shirt. It started beating out of my chest, acting like my life was full of cute boys, romance, and love, when in reality, I was never going to have any of that. My heart was hopeful. But my brain, it knew better.

"Boy is mighty fine." Heidi fanned herself and giggled, her eyes sparkling. "*Now* my pussy's wet."

"You're so bad." Marcie laughed.

"Don't let a good pussy go to waste." Hudson grinned and winked at Heidi who giggled back.

Lucas scowled and went back to talking to Jude about football. Lucas was quarterback, so his life was money and football.

Everyone around me carried on like nothing happened, but I was still stuck thinking about Liam and my fucked-up life. In a perfect world, I'd be a normal girl with a normal boyfriend like Liam. I wouldn't be dating Lucas, who was always pushing for sex. I'd have friends I actually liked and who liked me. Instead, we were all together because of our families and how much their bank accounts totaled. My life was fucked up, and what was even worse was I was hoping that by humiliating Liam, it would make me feel better, right the scales if you will. I was pretty and popular. I had money and nice things. I should've been happy. He had *nothing*, yet he was always smiling. *How fucked up was that? Was I really so rotten that I thought hurting someone else would make me feel better?*

To my surprise, my brain decided to ponder it. I felt twice as bad about what was going on with Liam. Liam didn't deserve the shit he got from us. But on the other hand, I didn't deserve the shit I had to deal with either.

Or maybe I did. If I hadn't been born the daughter of Nicolai Reznikov, notorious crime boss, I never would've been put into this position. That was the only reason Gio forced me to be what I'd become.

I thought back on the first night Gio approached me. It was the end of the summer, shortly after his and my mom's wedding.

I was sitting in the library at home. The room was dark, only lit by the raging fire in the fireplace in front of me. I was in the brown, leather chair directly in front of it with a blanket thrown over my legs as I wrote in my diary. Even though it was nearing the end of summer and the weather was hot, that house always remained unusually cold.

The door opened, and Gio walked in, dressed in his pressed black suit. His shiny dress shoes tapped on the wooden floor as he drew closer to me. The flames lit up his face, and for the first time, I noticed how menacing he looked. Gio was in his mid-forties and was a rather good-looking man, if you liked older men. His skin was deeply tanned, with not a mark on it. His eyes were big and dark and reminded me of thick, warm chocolate. His hair was raven black and always styled nicely. But seeing him in the dark, I saw the silent threat he held.

"Asha," he started.

I sat up and closed my diary.

He pulled his brows together. "You want a drink?"

I frowned. "I'm only fifteen."

He shrugged as he turned and walked to the drink cart. "Suit yourself. I just thought this news would go down a little easier with whiskey poured on top."

"What news?" I asked, fearing he was about to inform me I was being sent to some fancy boarding school where I'd be out of his hair.

He poured his drink, took a sip, and strode back over before sitting in the chair across from me. He rested his elbows on his knees as he held his whiskey glass with both hands. "I've watched you with your mom," he started. "You seem close."

"We are," I said, nervousness rising in my stomach.

Giovanni Valetti was a scary man.

He nodded, seeming to take in this information. "And I know you're a daddy's girl."

I swallowed and nodded.

"As you probably know, your father and I have several things in common when it comes to our businesses, but we also disagree on many things."

I didn't speak. I didn't move. I just waited.

"One of those things we disagree on is you."

"Me?" I asked.

He nodded and took another sip. "Your father thinks of you as his little girl, someone pure and good. But I know the truth. You're nothing more than his spawn, a whore who needs to be taught her place."

My mouth dropped open.

"That's why, the best way I can get back at your father is to put you to work…for me." He waited to let that sink in. "I have a guest here, and he's interested in buying your virginity. You are a virgin, yes?"

It felt like I had swallowed a bucket of sand. My throat with thick with the threat of tears. I couldn't talk. I shook my head no, but in all reality, I was a virgin in every sense of the word.

He laughed. "Don't lie to me. I've gone through your files."

"What files?" I managed to get out around the lump.

He shrugged as he stood and walked around the chair. "All of them. Your school, your doctor's notes, and at your last exam, your doctor noted you weren't sexually active. That was only one week ago. And since you've been here since then, I'm going to go out on a limb and say nothing has changed. Antonio?"

The door opened, and a man walked in. He was tall and muscular. Small wrinkles lined his dark eyes. His hair was black as night. A fancy suit hugged his body. As he took me in, he pulled his jacket away from his chest, tucking his hands into his pants pockets.

"What do you think?" Gio asked the man.

"It's hard to see when she's all bundled up," he said in a thick Italian accent.

Gio looked at me. "Stand. Undress."

My eyes cut to him, and I gasped. Shock at the situation reverberated through my body. "What?"

"You heard the man. He wants to see you. Stand. Undress," he ordered again.

I pulled the blanket up higher on my chest and shook my head. Tears prickled my eyes.

Gio took a few steps closer, and he grabbed my bicep, yanking me up out of the seat. My diary and blanket fell from my lap as he pulled me to his chest. His mouth moved toward my ear. "I said undress. This is my deal, and this is a lot of fucking money. You'll do as I say, or I swear to fucking God, Asha, your mother will pay for your defiance. Your father and his syndicate only live because I allow it. I could go to war with him right now, and not a single soul would survive. Don't. Fucking. Push me."

I swallowed as my tears fell over the edge of my lashes.

"You know, without a mother or father, I'd be your guardian, and I promise, there'd be much more pain in your future if that was the case."

I peered into his dark eyes and saw a flicker of the fire dancing in them. I knew my father's business and how brutal it could be. My father had me take my mother's last name so I wouldn't be a target. I was Asha Blake for a reason. If Gio was anything like I knew my father could be, he was telling the truth.

"Now, are you going to do as I ask?"

I sniffled as I nodded my head, fear tearing through me.

He pushed me toward the man, and I stumbled but caught myself. There I stood before two men—one who'd vowed to protect me—and undressed. My hands shook as I unbuttoned my long sleeve flannel pajama top. Since I was getting ready for bed, I wore no bra beneath it. I pushed the top down my arms and let it fall onto the floor. Heat flooded my body. I was sure if I looked down, I'd see the paint of red from the shame washing over me. I'd never shown myself to anyone before.

Gio smiled when he took in my naked breasts. Mine weren't small compared to the other girls. I took after my mother in that way. She'd always been very shapely, something that got her attention from men and women everywhere she went.

My thumbs slid below the waistband of my pajama pants, and I pushed them down my legs along with my panties. No sense in *drawing it out. I kicked them away from my body and stood straight, letting the men inspect me.*

My pulse roared in my ears as I stared at my feet. How had it come to this? Why had it come to this? What could I do? Gio would make good on his word, and my family would be caught in the crossfire. I was. . .stuck.

Gio walked up behind me and brushed my hair off my shoulders. He leaned in close as he inhaled my scent. "Go on. Come closer. Feel the firmness of youth," he urged the man.

The man swallowed, and his jaw flexed as he took me in, but he stepped forward. His hand moved up and wrapped around my breast, squeezing, kneading. I sucked in a breath and held it. My body trembled, and nausea twisted through my guts as I waited for him to be done.

"So?" Gio asked the man.

The man took a step back and nodded once. "A hundred thousand," he offered.

Gio scoffed. "One hundred? I can get at least three times that when I bring her to the club this weekend. Put your clothes back on, Asha," he ordered.

I jumped to move, quickly gathering my clothes to yank them on.

"Wait," the man spoke up before I could even get my arm into my sleeve. "Two hundred thousand," he offered.

"Two and a half," Gio countered.

The man ground his teeth as he thought. I stood frozen, waiting.

"Asha, lie down on the desk and spread your legs."

I couldn't move. I just stood motionless, watching the two men.

"Now, Asha. Remember what we talked about," Gio reminded me.

With a silent sob, I dropped my clothes and moved around them. I sat on the desk and lay back.

Gio marched over, grabbed my ankle, and bent my knee upward. He did the same with the other, so I was lying on the desk with my legs spread before them. Tears burned my eyes. I clenched them shut, my breathing ragged.

"See that? Completely untouched by anyone," Gio told the man. "Nice and pretty and pink. I bet she's tight too. If you want, I can slide a finger in. I'll be the first," he said a twinge of excitement in his voice.

I heard his shoes on the floor as he took a step toward me. My stomach churned.

I tensed at his impending approach. Help me. Someone help me!

Gio's hand touched my knee then slowly slid down to the junction between my legs. His hand cupped me, and his fingers spread, opening my folds.

"Wait," the man spoke up. "Two and a half. We have a deal."

Gio pulled his hand away, and my eyes opened in time to see them shake.

"I'll be back for her this weekend. Do not take her to your club, and don't touch her yourself or the deal is off."

"You have my word," Gio agreed, sealing my fate.

I shook the ugly memory away and rubbed my arms, wanting more than anything in the world to go back in time and die before any of this stuff had happened to me.

But this was reality. There was no going backward. *But death?* I was holding out hope, my greatest one of all that one of the sick bastards would put me out of my misery since I was too scared to do it myself.

Liam Hastings didn't know how lucky he was. And for that, I hated him.

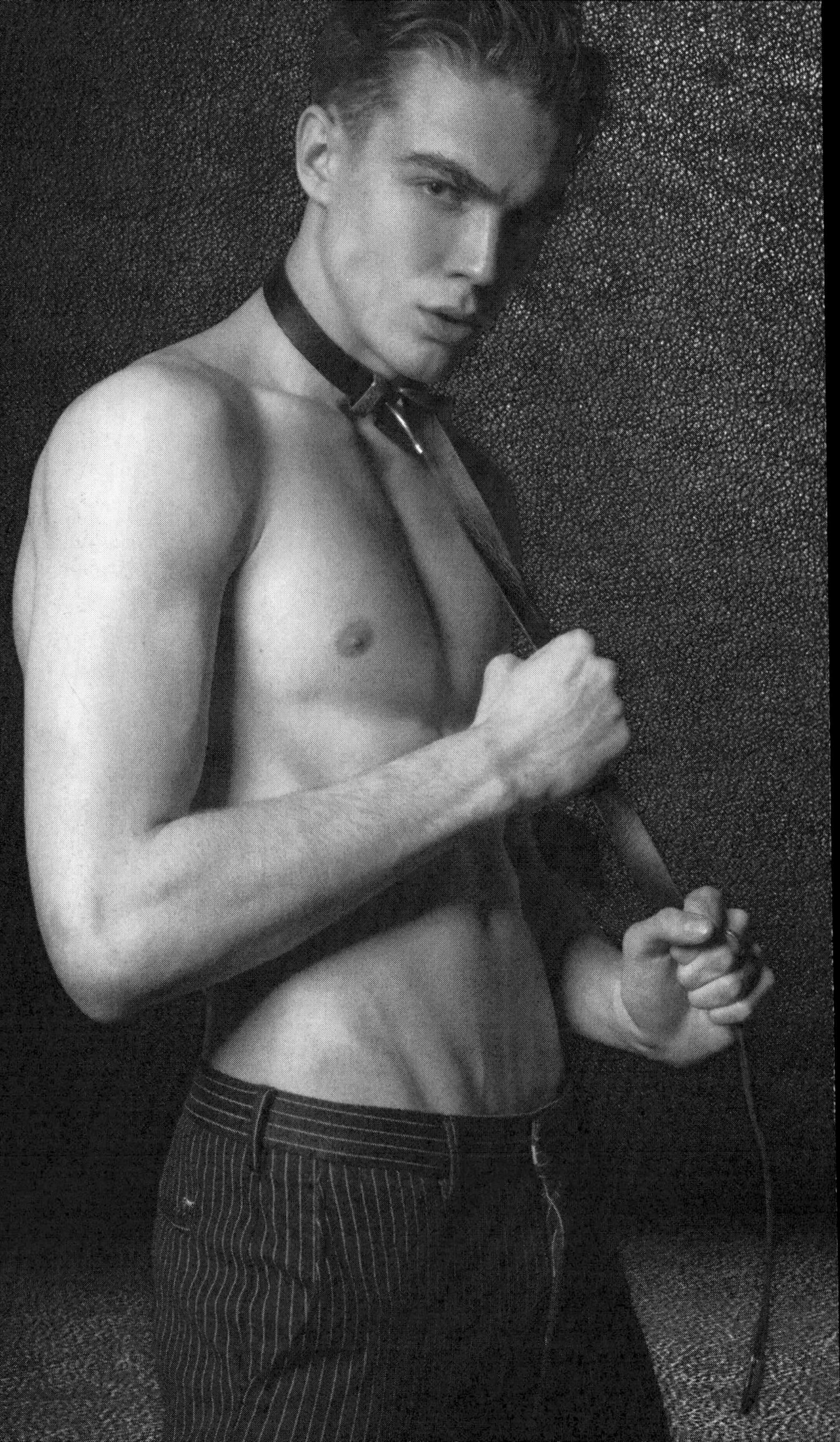

FOUR
LIAM

I went directly to the bathroom and stuck my head under the faucet to rinse the cheese from my hair and face. I ran my hands through it several times before standing and checking to make sure I'd gotten it all. I'd just grabbed some paper towels to dry it when Andy and Max walked in.

"Man, what a bitch," Max said, holding out a black T-shirt.

"Thanks," I mumbled, taking the shirt and pulling it on.

"Well, you didn't want to wear that shirt anyway. Now you don't have to," Andy said, shrugging as he leaned against the sink and crossed his arms over his chest.

"I wonder why they selected you to be the rat today," Max thought out loud.

"Probably because I ran into them in the hall and got into it with Lucas."

Both of their eyes widened. "What happened?"

I shrugged as I turned back to the mirror to style my wet hair. "I checked out Asha, and Lucas didn't like that. Oh, and I called her a whore." I didn't know if she *was* a whore, but it felt like something that would piss them off, so I'd said it. Bad idea in retrospect. And quite honestly, I did feel guilty about it, even if she was a bitch. I wasn't the sort of guy to be mean to anyone, especially a female, but fuck.

"Damn, man. You got a death wish?" Andy asked.

My hair looked as presentable as I was going to get it without hair products, so I turned to face them. "I'm just sick of them and their shit. I mean, why do they get to do anything they want around here? They smoke weed in the storage room. You know if any of us did that we'd be dragged to the office by our fucking ears."

Max nodded. "Yeah, but it's just the way the world works. There were a million kids just like you before, and there'll be a million more after you. There's no changing it."

I shook my head. "It's a bunch of shit. I can't wait until I'm out of this place. Let the real world teach them popularity doesn't fucking matter. I bet half of them won't do anything with their lives. They'll end up lying on their parents' couches until they're fifty, living off their parents' dime."

"Hey, did you hear about the assignment Mr. Farris is handing out today?" Andy asked, changing the subject.

Good thing because my temper was flaring. I was bound to do something really stupid if I didn't get sidetracked quickly.

Max and I shook our heads.

"Apparently, it's a group project, and Mr. Farris is determined to bring two groups together. Joey, my friend in band, he was grouped with Heidi." His eyes narrowed.

"Oh, fuck. That's just great," I mumbled. Already I could see my bad luck playing out before my eyes. Sofia, Max, and I all had sociology with Asha and Lucas. I prayed I got teamed up with Sofia or Max, but I knew deep in my bones that I wouldn't be that lucky.

The bell rang, and the sounds of the students filling the hallways outside of the bathroom sounded out. There was endless chatter, laughing, and lockers slamming.

"Guess that means we better get to class and accept our fate," Max said, pushing off the wall he was leaning against.

I gave myself one last look in the mirror then followed them. Andy went one way, and we went the other. Max and I stopped to grab our books from our lockers before trudging toward sociology with Mr. Farris. The classroom used to be an old biology room so there weren't any desks. Instead, there were lab tables with two stools to each one. Max and I always sat together, so we took our spots at our usual table. Moments later, Sofia walked in, and she took the stool closest to me at the neighboring table.

"I heard about lunch," she said quietly.

I only nodded.

"You okay? I understand if you're upset."

"I'm fine. It was cheese not a knife," I pointed out.

She pressed her lips together and looked uncomfortable. "I heard we're going to be teamed up today for an assignment. Maybe we'll get lucky and get one another."

The class grew noisier.

"I hope so," I mumbled, but I knew it wouldn't happen. The whole point was to learn to work with someone you didn't know or like.

The bell rang, and Asha and Lucas walked in with Mr. Farris following behind.

"That's a tardy for you two," he told them, looking at them from above his glasses.

They didn't say a word as they took their places in the back of the class. Mr. Farris was the only teacher in the damn place who didn't mind getting his hands dirty with the elite crew. He went toe to toe with them without batting a lash. But even his reach only went so far.

Mr. Farris strode behind his desk and clapped his hands together. "All right class. Today, as I'm sure you've all heard by now, we're grouping together. I want a three-thousand-word essay *each* on the subject of my choosing. I'm going to pair you up, and from there, you'll spend time together and get to know someone new. I want to know their likes, their dislikes, their hopes, dreams, fears. Get their family and friend dynamic. I want it all. This is sociology. Let's get to know what makes your partner tick. Think of it as a little crash course in psychology as well." He looked us over. "All right, let's get started. After you've been paired, come to the front of the class and stand by your partner. Sofia, you're first, my dear."

Sofia stood up and walked to the front of the class. I watched as she twisted her hands together nervously and worried her bottom lip.

"Sofia, your partner will be Lucas," Farris said, pulling Lucas's name out of the box on his desk.

"Great, I get the fucking nerd," Lucas grumbled quietly.

But Sofia still heard him. Pain crossed her face.

Damnit, Sofia. Keep it together. Don't let them see your weakness.

Lucas got up and sauntered to the head of the class and stood next to Sofia. Sofia offered me a sad smile.

"Max and Lilly," Mr. Farris ordered.

Max let out a sigh as he took his place next to Lilly, a quiet girl who kept to herself.

"James and Emily," Mr. Farris pointed at the two, then motioned for them to move to the front.

He kept counting off people into pairs until there were only two of us left. "I guess that leaves you two, Asha and Liam. Now, move seats and sit by your new partner. This assignment will be due before we head into homecoming. Every day from now on, you'll sit together. You'll talk, interview each other, get to know one another. Bridge the gap, people!" He clapped his hands. "Get started!"

With that, everyone moved to their new seats. I grabbed my books and headed to the back of the room, taking the seat Lucas had vacated.

He came to get his books and sent me a dirty look. "Better keep your eyes on the paper and your hands on your pencil, dickwad." He turned to face Asha. "Let me know if he bothers you, babe." He gave her a quick kiss on the cheek before moving away.

"You smell like vomit," she muttered, making a dramatic scene of waving her hand in front of her face. Her long, bejeweled, pink nails flashed beneath the fluorescent lights.

"It's probably the fermented cheese," I threw back as I opened my notebook to start making notes, but I noticed she didn't move to do anything. She was too busy picking at the skin around her manicured nail.

"Sorry about your *suit*," she said, using air quotes as her brows arched.

"Do you even know what this assignment is?" I asked, ignoring her jab.

Her blue eyes cut to me, and she scoffed. "Of course, I do. I'm not stupid."

"What is it then?"

"Who really cares? You're going to do all the work anyway." She blew a strand of blonde hair out of her face, rolling her brilliant blue eyes.

I shook my head. "You're such a fucking bitch. If I do all the work, you're not going to have an assignment to turn in because guess what? You can't turn in an assignment about yourself, you narcissistic hag."

Her brows pulled together, and her lips parted.

I plowed on before she could snap back at me. "The assignment is we have to get to know one another and write a report. You know, what makes us who we are, what our lives are like, family dynamics... that kind of shit."

She pursed her lips and narrowed her eyes at the last thing I listed. "I don't see how my life is any of your business."

"Trust me, princess, I don't want to know any more about you than I have to. I'm not happy about this either."

She snorted. "Yeah, right. You were dreaming of getting me alone. Weren't you?" She leaned forward, giving me a peek down her shirt.

I looked. I couldn't help it. A perfect set of breasts and deep cleavage greeted my eyes. My dick pulsed, and I shifted to sit forward.

"The only way I'd dream of getting you alone is if I could sew that mouth of yours shut." I started moving my pencil across the page, writing down the assignment and the due date, but I noticed her still staring at me. "Take a picture. It'll last longer."

"And what would I do with a picture of you?"

"I don't know. Use it as bait to summon one of your demons, you heartless witch." Her mouth dropped open in surprise, but she quickly righted her face.

"Be careful, you little nobody," she hissed back "I'll ruin everything you touch, including the nerd you keep tucked in your back pocket."

I glanced over at Sofia sitting with Lucas. She looked like she was going to puke as Lucas rolled his eyes at her.

"You leave Sofia alone. If you even think about bothering her, I'll—"

"What? Be the little bitch you are and cry with her?" Asha laughed and tossed her hair over her shoulder. "Spare me."

"I'm serious," I growled. "Leave her out of your shit. Your beef is with me. Not her."

"Whatever." She rolled her eyes at me. "In case you forgot, *I* run this place, and I'll do what I want, *when* I want. The sooner you learn that the better off you'll be."

Tired of the back and forth, I let out a sigh and shook my head. "What's your full name and birthday?"

Her eyes rolled. She straightened her back and crossed her arms, refusing to speak.

I took a deep breath, growing impatient.

"Why don't we play a game?" she suggested.

I ran my hand through my hair. "I'll bite. What kind of game would you like to play, princess?"

She smiled. "Instead of asking questions and getting answers, let's make assumptions and confirm if they're right or wrong."

Seemed like another way for her to insult me but whatever. At least we'd be doing something other than arguing. "Fine. I'll go first.

Your full name is Asha Bitch-Face Blake, and your birthday is on Halloween?"

Her eyebrow raised. "My birthday *is* on Halloween. How'd you know?" she asked, a frown marring her pretty face. She didn't seem to give a damn I'd just insulted her.

I shrugged. "Figured someone as evil as you would have to be born on Satan's day."

She rolled her eyes again and sneered at me. "My middle name is Morgan, not Bitch-Face. My turn to guess." She placed her index finger on her chin and thought. "You're a nerd who jerks off to porn because no one wants to touch your virgin dick. You sit at home playing video games and taking pictures of sunsets. You probably hide in the girls' locker room with your camera, your tiny dick in hand, hoping for some action. When you aren't here, you're probably crying in your room, wondering why no one likes you. Wondering why you're invisible to those who matter." She sent me an evil grin, thinking she'd gotten the best of me.

I took a deep breath to cool the rage bubbling in my stomach before I spoke. "Well, princess, if I'm invisible to those who matter, *who the fuck are you,* Asha Blake? You *seek* me out, don't you?"

A muscle feathered along her delicate jaw as she glared at me. I let out a soft laugh.

"OK. We'll play your way then, but I gotta correct you on the size of my cock. We both know it's not tiny." Her cheeks reddened, and I plowed on. "You're a rich bitch who wouldn't know a hard day if it came up and bit you in your fake tits. You're vapid and fake in every sense of the word. You have no self-control. You're over-indulgent, and mark my words, your little boyfriend is going to be fucking your frenemy before homecoming. How does that sum things up?"

Her jaw cocked with anger as her eyes moved from me to Lucas to Tiffany then back, settling on me. "Let's get one thing straight. My tits aren't fake. You have no idea what you're talking about with anything you said. You think my boyfriend is going to fuck her because you don't know what real friends are. Your group of *friends* was chosen for you before you even arrived at this school. Your social status determined that." She gave me a look that suggested I was shit she'd stepped in with her overpriced designer heel and she couldn't get rid of the smell.

Fuck, she was a nightmare.

"Tell Farris you want a new partner. I'm not going to work with you. I can't fucking stand you. You're a piece of trash with a pretty face and a fancy purse."

She kicked me in the shin as hard as she could. I let out a hiss of pain and rubbed my leg as Mr. Farris approached.

"Everything OK over here?" Mr. Farris asked, staring down at us as I straightened in my seat.

"It's great, Mr. Farris. Thanks so much for letting me get to know Liam. I'm sure we'll be great friends," she simpered, giving Mr. Farris a sweet smile.

I scowled at her.

He smiled back. "I knew it was a good idea pairing you two together. Perhaps Mr. Hastings can utilize his photography skills for this project."

Mr. Farris walked away before he could hear me mutter, "She'd break the camera."

"Only over your face." She smiled brightly at me.

The bell rang, and she wasted no time grabbing her books and darting toward the door where Lucas and Tiffany already were. She froze when Tiffany slipped her arm around Lucas.

I smirked as I walked up behind her. "That's gotta hurt," I whispered with a chuckle in her ear as I moved past her. "Pretty sure I'm more spot on about you than you are about me." I shifted past Lucas and Tiffany, now aware that Asha had her sights set on them, and headed down the hall, hearing the screaming and shouting behind me.

I hated the assignment we were given. I fucking hated Asha. But what I hated most of all was how I didn't hate Asha as much as I would've liked. She got under my skin and infected it. She was like an itchy rash that wouldn't go away. Even when she wasn't near, I was still thinking about her and the things she said, wondering if she was right. And what sucked most of all was the assignment wouldn't be over for a few weeks. Two months of sitting with her, meeting with her after school, having to talk to her, understand her. There was no becoming friends with her. She was pure evil. A grade-A bitch who didn't worry about what people thought of her, or at least, she played it that way. I hoped and prayed my words settled in her brain the way hers settled in mine. I hoped they became a seed of doubt that would grow and drive her fucking crazy. Most of all, I hoped I was right. I hoped Lucas was fucking her friend. I hoped she'd have the pleasure of walking in on them. I hoped her fucking heart broke and shattered so I could piss in the dust left behind. I'd pay money to see Asha Blake cry.

Somewhere in my vision of her crying, things changed. She wasn't standing in the school hallway with tears pooling in her eyes anymore. Suddenly, we were in a dimly lit room with her on her knees before me, my dick in her mouth as big, fat tears trickled down her cheeks, their trails dirty with smeared mascara. The thought alone made my dick twitch with excitement as I took my seat in my next class.

I had issues. They stemmed from the torment inflicted by the blonde haired, blue-eyed bully I just couldn't stop thinking about.

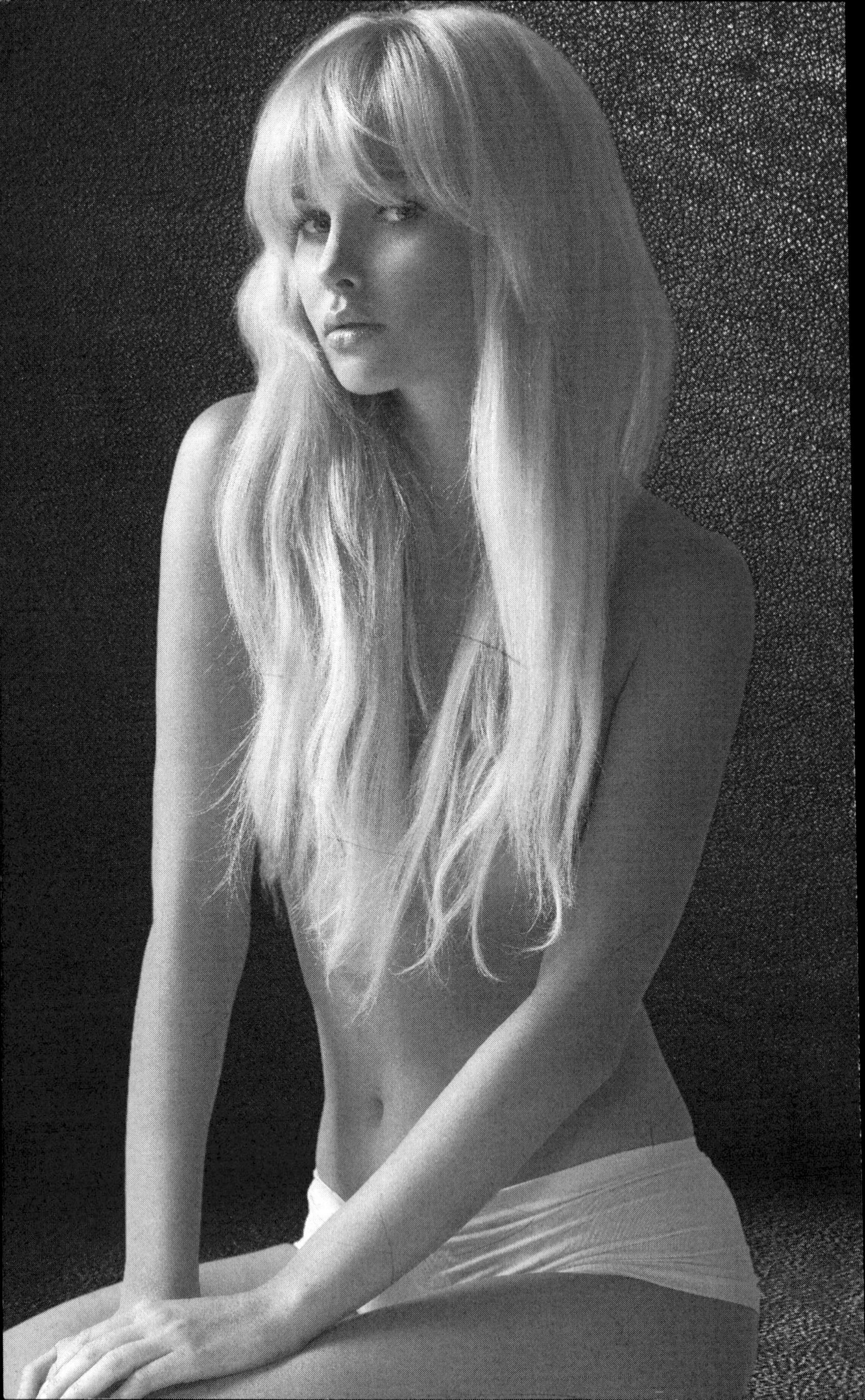

FIVE
ASHA

"What the hell is this?" I asked when I marched up to Lucas and Tiffany.

She quickly yanked her arm away, her green eyes wide with alarm. "What? Nothing. We're just goofing off. How'd your little project go?" She tried changing the subject.

I narrowed my eyes at her. "Screw the project. Why is your hand on my boyfriend?"

Lucas stepped between us. "Chill, Asha. It was nothing." His hands landed on my shoulders as he tried directing me away from her.

I turned for a moment, allowing the action before my anger got the better of me.

"*Chill?* You're telling me to chill? I'm pretty sure if some guy's hands were on me, you wouldn't be *chill*."

He rolled his eyes.

I turned to face Tiffany. "Keep your hands to yourself or you'll be dining with the likes of her." I jutted my chin toward Sofia.

Sofia quickly grabbed her books and took off, looking embarrassed and upset.

Mr. Farris came over. "All right, enough is enough. Drop this and get to your next class before you're late." He shooed us along, his eyes lingering on me for a moment longer than they should have.

Lucas wrapped his arm around my lower back, his hand resting on my hip as he steered me out of class and into the hall. He walked us a few feet away before turning and pushing my back into the lockers.

"What the fuck was that?" he asked, resting his hand against the metal above my head as he leaned into me.

I shrugged. "She's a whore and needs to keep her whore hands to herself."

He snickered as his left hand moved up to cup my chin and direct my eyes to his. "You're sexy when you're jealous," he said, planting his lips on mine.

His tongue danced along with my own as he pressed his body against me. I felt him grow hard, but I was still ice cold and angry. I didn't know why I was suddenly so determined to keep Lucas for myself. I didn't love him. Hell, I didn't even like him half the time.

What hurt was that Liam was right.

Of course, he was. Lucas and Tiffany were probably already fucking behind my back. So why did I want to keep him?

I placed my hand against his chest and pushed him back a step. I was over this. Dealing with the petty drama turned my guts. I had more important things to concern myself with. But in the back of my head, all I could ask myself was, *are all guys the same*. God knew I didn't have a shortage of disappointment from them in my life.

"I gotta get to class. If I fail, my stepdad will kill me," I told him, shoving him away from me.

He didn't say anything as he stared wordlessly at me leaving. That was a first. Usually, he'd track me down and demand whatever he wanted. It only made me believe more that he didn't care as much as he pretended.

The rest of the day passed unusually slow. After the last bell, I grabbed my books and started for the parking lot. I tossed my stuff into the passenger seat of my BMW and rounded the hood to climb behind the wheel. That was when I heard my name being shouted.

I paused and glanced around, finding Liam as he jogged toward me. My heart jumped in my chest at the sight of him in his tight, black t-shirt, ripped jeans, and black Chucks. His dark hair was a perfect mess, his green eyes bright. He came to a sudden stop and gave me the dashing smile he gave to everyone. His woodsy cologne wafted toward me. I inhaled but cut myself off quickly, hoping he didn't notice my moment of weirdness.

"Asha, we need to get together this weekend to get started on our assignment."

I scoffed and rolled my eyes. "We have plenty of time, nerd. There's no need to start it this weekend." I opened the door and climbed behind the wheel.

When the car purred to life, he took a hesitant step back, and I wasted no time in getting the hell out of there.

When I got home, I locked myself into my room and got to work on my homework. Lying on my bed as music filled my ears, I finished my calculus, American History, and pretend stock market assignment for econ. Then I wrote my English Lit paper. When everything was done, I dug around in my desk drawer and pulled out the joint I'd been holding onto. I stepped out onto my balcony and put the joint between my lips. I brought the lighter to the end and inhaled a long drag.

The smoke filled my lungs, and my stress began to evaporate. Using my phone, I looked over Liam's Facebook page to try to gather clues about him for this assignment. I didn't want to spend any more time with him than I had to. If I could gather enough hints as to who he really was, it was less time I had to spend looking at his sexy face and listening to his smart mouth.

From his page, I learned his favorite band was Highly Suspect— at least the guy had good taste in music—and he spent a lot of his free time with a camera in his hand. He posted pictures of sunsets, trees, the beach, and butterflies. I looked over his liked pages and found most of them to revolve around photography or art. Honestly, the guy didn't seem half bad. I'd never taken the time before to explore the reason he was at Acadia. I guessed he was an art scholarship winner. He even had photos up of things he'd drawn. They were so strikingly realistic, I had to pause to check. Of course, he had to be completely gorgeous and talented. *Lucky jerk.*

In addition to photos of his work, he also had images of him and his friends. It looked like they liked to play video games, go to concerts, and hang out at Mondo's—a hole in the wall place none of us rich kids would dream of stepping foot.

My phone started blowing up with messages from our group chat, and I blew all of them off as I gathered more and more information about Liam Hastings. The longer I looked at his page, the more I wanted to know him. The *real* him, not the version of him he put on his public profile. I moved over to Instagram where he only posted the pictures he'd taken and then over to Twitter to find the things he'd posted. I read over his tweets to find most of them were re-tweets for a good cause, family in need…raise money for… and save the planet. Liam was a really good person. It only made me feel worse about myself. I put the phone down, the sickness back.

Around seven, I left my bedroom to find some dinner. The house was quiet. When I walked into the kitchen, I found a note on the counter from Mom.

Asha,

Gone to the Bennet's charity ball. Won't be home until late. I had Gordon fix you a salad. It's in the fridge. -Mom.

Rolling my eyes, I shook my head and picked up the piece of paper. I wadded it up and tossed it into the trash. I shuffled around the island and opened the fridge. The light inside lit up the kitchen as I pulled out the Tupperware container of salad. I grabbed the fat free ranch and moved everything back to the island where I removed the lid from the bowl and poured some dressing on. Grabbing a fork out of the drawer, I took everything to the table to eat alone, in the dark.

I didn't know if Gio went with my mom or not, but I didn't want to give away my location by doing something stupid like turning on a light. I was a prisoner in my own house. I had to hide in order to survive. That meant staying out of sight. If I reminded him of my presence, there was no telling what he'd make me do.

I ate my salad quickly and went to put everything into the dishwasher. My plan was to return to my room where I could shower and go to bed. But all that changed when I was rounding the staircase.

The front door opened, and Gio walked in. His bloodshot eyes landed on me, and I saw the evilness in them. My blood ran cold.

He smiled. "Asha, just the girl I need. Come with me to my office." He swayed his way from the entryway to his office, leaving the door open for me to follow. He had to be drunk or high. Maybe both.

I walked inside and waited by the door as he poured a drink and loosened his tie. When he turned around and found me, he looked surprised. "Shut the door."

With a sigh, I shut the door but didn't move.

He took off his jacket and sat behind his desk. "Come here," he demanded.

I ground my teeth together and balled my hands into fists at my side, but I pushed myself forward, knowing I'd pay the price if I didn't listen. When I made my way across the floor to his desk, he motioned for me to come around.

"On your knees," he demanded.

My brows pulled together in confusion. It had been a long time since Gio wanted anything from me, and he'd never wanted *that* from me, or at least he never acted like he did. He simply threw me to the wolves at his club whenever he deemed me good enough to be eaten.

"I said on your knees!"

I quickly dropped to the floor before him.

"Your mother thought she'd stay at the party and flirt with younger men instead of taking care of her husband," he said, unbuttoning his pants and lowering the zipper. "So now I guess it's your job."

He pulled out his dick. It was big, hard, and angry looking. He peered down at me with one lifted brow.

"You want me to suck your dick?" I choked out, pissed, annoyed, surprised. Disgusted.

He nodded once. "That's what happens when your whore of a mother doesn't listen. *You* get punished. When you don't listen, she gets killed. Now, do what you're fucking told."

I shook my head. "No."

Faster than I could process, he grabbed the back of my neck and pulled my head into his lap. His dick was pressed to the side of my face, but I refused to put it in my mouth.

He grabbed a handful of my hair and yanked my head back. Taking himself in his left hand, he guided it to my mouth. The tip started to drip, and he spread the wetness across my lips.

"Suck it, you whore." His fingers tightened in my hair, making me cry out from the pain of my hair being torn from my scalp.

"Fuck you," I snarled at him.

His left hand released his dick, and he drew back, landing a solid hit to my jaw. My vision started to fade around the edges, everything growing blurry, either from the tears or the threat of losing consciousness.

"You can either suck my dick, or I'll beat you until you can't fight me anymore. Then I'll just fuck your little pussy that's making me so much money. And we both know I won't wear a condom. Imagine the betrayal your mother will feel when I get you knocked up. Because I will. I'll take away your birth control. I'll let the men at the club fuck you raw. I'll throw a party where we fuck you until you bleed from all your tiny, tight holes. Does that sound like fun?"

Tears dripped from my eyes as I opened my mouth and let him guide himself into me. My heart felt like it was being squeezed as I moved up and down on his length, sucking, swirling, and gagging.

"That's right," he breathed out. "Good girl. Fuck, you have the mouth of an angel. Faster," he ordered.

I worked his length faster, gagging at the thought of having him in my mouth. I wanted to bite. I wanted to rip his dick off and leave him bloody on the floor, but I knew if I did there'd be nothing to stop him from killing me. I wanted to die, but not by his hands. If and when I died, I wanted it to be my way. Or by the hands of the creeps in his circle because then he'd have to explain why I was found in some seedy underground club. Of course, knowing him, he'd probably just dump my body somewhere.

Both of his hands fisted in my hair as he dragged my lips up and down his length, jabbing at the back of my throat. He finally let out a roar, and his seed filled my mouth, sour and salty and completely revolting. I gagged when the liquid started seeping down my throat, but he wouldn't let me pull away. I could choke on it or swallow it willingly.

When he finished, he pushed me back until I fell on my ass.

"You know I like a little fight, don't you, bitch?" His hands went to work on putting himself back in place. "Get the fuck out of here. You're a dirty little whore, sucking cock for freedom. *Pathetic.* You're just a disgusting piece of trash, aren't you, my little slut?" His dark eyes flashed at me, daring me to come back at him with something.

I didn't have it in me though. So, I quickly pushed myself up and ran from his office, up the stairs, and to my bedroom where I locked the door. Sobs broke free from my mouth as I ran to the connected bathroom. I fell to my knees in front of the toilet and shoved my fingers down my throat, puking everything up. I couldn't bear the thought of having any part of him in me.

When there wasn't anything left to get rid of, I stood and moved to the sink to brush my teeth. A faint outline of a bruise was already forming on my jaw. *Just great.* I had to worry about covering that up. Sighing, I dropped my toothbrush and turned on the shower. I felt dirty. Used. I climbed in and started scrubbing my body until my skin was raw.

Then I fell to the bottom and wrapped my arms around my knees. Tears were still blurring my vision as I reached for the razor. I watched the water bead up and roll off the sharp blade. Taking it in my right hand, I moved it to the inside of my left bicep. I pressed the sharp corner into my skin and dragged the blade across. Bright red blood rolled down my arm and dripped off my elbow into the tub where it washed down the drain. My body was suddenly filled with energy and tingles as endorphins flooded my system.

I'd started cutting myself the night my virginity was stolen. It was the only way I could release the hate, the rage. It felt like my blood had been poisoned, and the only way to get the toxin out was to bleed it out, a little at a time. I'd been cutting myself for almost two years. But I still felt tainted. They weren't big, noticeable cuts. I made them small and in places I could explain them away. Or I hid them as much as I could.

Once my high wore off, I climbed out of the shower and wrapped a towel around my arm while I dressed. On autopilot, I opened the bathroom mirror and found the bottle of sleeping pills I'd stolen from my mom. I poured out two and threw them into my mouth. I just needed an escape, sleep, the darkness to hide away in.

I threw myself into bed and pulled the blankets and pillows around me. When my eyes closed, all I saw were flashes of Gio and his office. The way his face contorted with anger. The way he smelled. Tasted. How he moaned out his release as he shot it deep into my throat. My jaw throbbed. I felt the blinding pain. Then, nothing. Darkness.

Finally.

The darkness wasn't as black as it usually was though. There was a small sliver of light. The sliver appeared to get closer and closer. The closer it got, the more shape it took on. It wasn't a speck. It wasn't even a circle. It was a face. A man's face, with green eyes, dark hair, a sharp jaw covered in stubble, and high cheekbones. It was Liam.

Why was Liam in the darkness? He was a good person. He wasn't trash like me. But then he offered me his hand, and I took it. The moment we touched, I felt warmth and the darkness turned to light. He pulled me up and held me close. He leaned in and kissed me. It was a kiss like I'd never experienced before. It wasn't like the way the men kissed me in the club. It wasn't even the way Lucas kissed me.

It was different. It was soft and strong and full of need, yearning, emotion. Our kiss lit a fire in my stomach, and tingles took over my body. Every inch of my skin felt alive. It was a sensation I'd never felt before. Something I'd never had the chance to feel before. Everything I'd ever had to offer had been stolen from me. But that image of Liam gave it all back, and I didn't even understand it.

All I knew was I was desperate to stay asleep, to keep the warmth Liam in the dream gave me, because my reality was a cold, dark hell.

And freedom?

The only escape was death. Mine or Gio's.

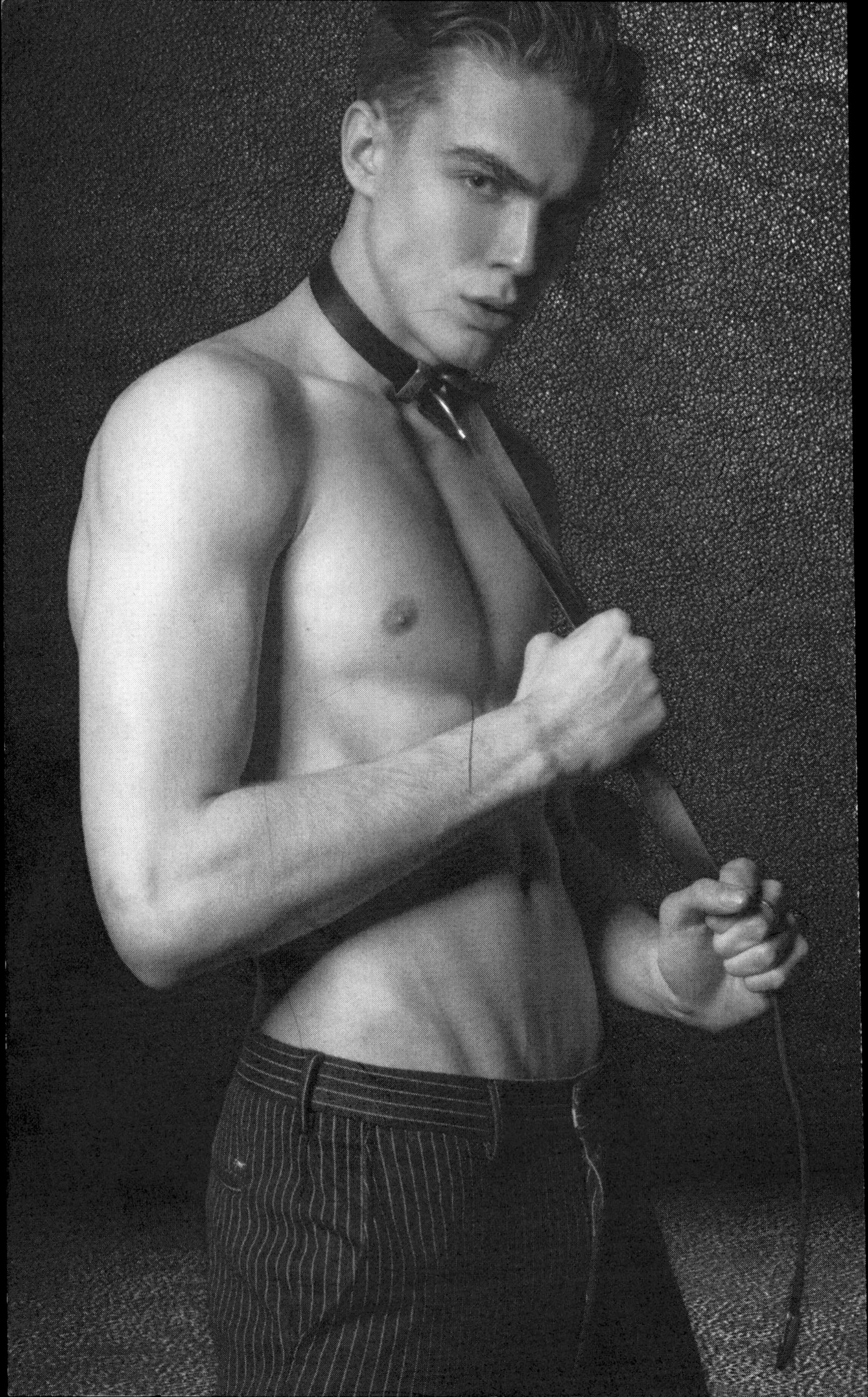

SIX
LIAM

I tried getting ahold of Asha all weekend. I emailed her school account. I messaged her through Facebook and Instagram. But everything went unanswered. I didn't have her phone number, so I couldn't call or text.

When Monday rolled around, I didn't have anything done on my paper. I'd hoped to hammer out some details in class, but to my surprise, she didn't even bother coming to school at all.

I was getting tired of being ignored. It wasn't just her ass on the line, and I knew I couldn't bat my lashes, donate some money, and get an A like she could. My presence at school was based on my work. Which meant I had to do every assignment and get decent grades. After class, I cornered Tiffany in the hallway.

"What do you want, loser?" she asked, wrinkling her nose at me like just having to breathe the same air as me was revolting.

"Asha is my partner, and I need to get this work done. She's not here and not returning my emails. Will you give me her number so I can call her and get started on this project before I fall behind, fail, and get kicked out of school?"

"What? No. I'm not giving you her number." She forced me to

take a step back when she stood up straight, no longer leaning against the lockers outside of class.

I knew if I wanted anything from Tiffany, I'd have to give her something she wanted in return. That or blackmail her. But I didn't have anything she wanted. And I didn't have anything to blackmail her with either, but that wasn't going to stop me from saying I did.

"It'd be a shame if Asha just so happened to get her hands on those pictures I took of you and Lucas."

Her eyes popped up and locked on mine. They were wide, filled with fear. "What pictures?"

I shrugged and ran my hand through my hair, acting nonchalant. "I might be a nobody around here, but I see more than people think. You and Lucas think you're being sneaky, hanging out behind Asha's back. But I've seen it with my own two eyes, and I've got the pictures to prove it."

Tiffany ground her teeth together and dug a pen out of her bag. She yanked my hand in her direction. "If you tell Asha I gave you her number, I'll rip your balls off, little boy. Destroy those pictures and never speak to me again," she said, writing the number across the back of my hand. When she was finished, she rushed down the hall.

I guess that information didn't come as a surprise. She only confirmed what I thought. Nausea washed over me. Only days before I'd hoped for something like this. It seemed like a real dick move now considering I'd been right.

Of course, what the hell was I going to do with the information? Keep it? Tell Asha? The voice of reason lulled my confusion.

You've got nothing, Hastings. Keep your mouth shut and know your place.

Maybe it would be an entirely different story if I did have photos. Maybe I should get some. Have an ace up my sleeve in case I needed it. In this academy, you just never knew. I tabled those thoughts for the moment. I had more important things to worry about.

As I headed to my next class, I transferred the number from my hand to my phone and saved it before wiping the ink from my skin. Out in the hallway before entering class, I sent her a text.

ME: Asha, it's Liam. I need to get started on this assignment. Quit being a bitch and make a plan with me to get to work. This isn't just your ass on the line.

I sent it, tucked the phone into my pocket, and went into class.

Class had just begun when my phone vibrated in my pocket. I leaned back in my chair and removed my cell, hiding it under my desk to read the screen.

ASHA: Pick me up after school. We'll go to your place.

She wanted me to pick her up? She wants to go to my place? I expected more of a fight. And why hadn't she come to school anyway?

She obviously wasn't sick if she was asking to come to my place. Or maybe she was sick and hoping to spread it. Yeah, that sounded more like her.

Either way, I needed to get started on the assignment, so as soon as school was over, I drove over to the big mansion she called a house. Iron gates welcomed me. They were left open, allowing me to drive up the brick pathway. Both sides of the driveway were lined with perfectly trimmed trees. When I got to the end, the whole property opened up. A big fountain sat in the center of the drive. The house was massive, made of brick, stone, and pillars. The bushes and shrubs circling the house were perfectly manicured as well. I wished I knew how much those people wasted on gardening alone.

I parked directly in front of the house and killed the engine. I opened my door, but before I even got one foot on the ground, the passenger door opened, and Asha slid onto the seat.

"Oh, ugh," I mumbled, thrown off guard by her sudden appearance.

"What?" she asked with wide eyes. "Drive, loser."

I shut my door and turned the key. "I don't need to come in and meet your parents or anything?"

She scoffed and pushed a lock of blonde hair behind her ear. The faint outline of a bruise marred her jaw. It looked like she'd desperately tried to cover it with makeup. "Ha, no. Nobody is even home anyway. Just go."

I shifted into gear and started back down the drive. The car was silent as she sat at my side. The air felt charged and thick—awkward but also completely relaxed. During the drive, I learned that the hair on the back of my neck didn't stand on end with her like it did with the rest of her crew. Maybe I hadn't judged her correctly. Maybe she wasn't just some mean queen bee who ordered others around. Maybe she was just this scared, timid, little girl who used her friends as a front to protect herself. The thought made me chuckle.

Her eyes cut in my direction. "What's so funny?" she asked with the arch of one brow.

I shrugged. "Just taking some mental notes, that's all."

"About me?"

"Well, this assignment *is* about you...so, yeah."

She nodded once as she pressed her lips tightly together. "Well, I'm taking notes on you too. Want to know what I have so far?"

"Nope."

"Your car is a piece of shit," she stated, ignoring my objection. "You drive slower than old people fuck, and it smells like a boys locker room in here with the scent of old McDonald's mixed in."

I smiled. "Is that all?" I asked, wondering if she forgot to eat her bowl of *instant bitch* for breakfast. What she'd said weren't her typical below the belt insults. They were more off-the-cuff like she didn't know what else to say.

"You want more?" she asked around a smile. "I can keep going," she offered.

"Why don't we wait until we have a pen and paper at hand to take notes?"

She rolled her eyes and crossed her arms over her chest. We rode in silence until we'd almost made it to my house.

"Why is this stupid assignment so important to you anyway?"

I glanced her way before turning onto my street. "Why is this assignment important to me? *Every* assignment is important to me, Asha. I'm at that school on a scholarship. If I fail, I get kicked out. Nobody can buy my way through like they can yours."

She snorted. "How can someone be so smart and so dumb at the same time? You think my father would buy me anything? The most that man would buy me is a plane ticket to another country and that'd only be because he wanted me out of his hair. Oh, and you could bet it would only be one way." She shook her head. "He wouldn't want me coming back. Hell, he doesn't even try now when I need him. . ." Her voice faltered, and she pressed her lips closed.

I pulled up to the curb and shifted into park. "Is that true?" I asked, almost feeling bad for her, but she didn't answer.

Instead, she changed the subject. "This your place?" She nodded toward my house.

"Yep, that's it in all its glory," I joked, wondering if I should push the subject she seemed eager to skirt around.

So she had major daddy issues.

She offered up a smile as she looked at the house. "I like it."

It was just a typical two-story house. There wasn't anything special about it.

I snorted. "Yeah right."

"I'm serious. It looks..."

"Small?"

She shrugged. "I was going to say quaint."

I laughed. "That's just a polite way to say small. I'm surprised you can appreciate any house that doesn't have iron gates or gargoyles outside of it."

She rolled her eyes. "I hate my house. Everyone looks at it and thinks it must be great to live there, have all that money, be important. But what they don't know is everyone who lives in my house hates each other. After my mom married Gio, she changed. My mom hates everything so it seems. She's withdrawn and spends most of her time at spas or drunk on expensive wine. There's no love in our house. No warm family meals. There's nobody to welcome me home. It's big, dark, cold, and lonely."

My mouth dropped open. I wasn't expecting her to be that honest. Apparently, she didn't mean to do it either because her eyes instantly went cold, and her face tightened back up. It was like her whole body tensed the moment she realized she'd let her guard down.

She grabbed her bag off the floor and said, "Let's go get this shit over with." She opened the door and climbed out, leaving me to chase after her.

My parents weren't home yet, and I knew neither of them would be until seven. That gave us around three hours to get our work done. I unlocked the door and pushed it open, letting her walk in ahead of me.

"My room is this way," I said, heading toward the stairs.

"What? No tour?" she asked, ignoring me and sauntering into the living room.

I let out a long breath and turned to follow her. In the living room, I leaned against the doorway as she moved around the room, surveying our family photos and running her hand over the back of the couch. "Is this your brother and sister?"

I walked over to her side and peered at the picture in her hand. It was from last year. The picture was of the three of us, sitting in front of the Christmas tree.

"Yeah," I said. "That's my middle brother Levi and my older sister Lisa. He's in college at State, and Lisa just got married and is expecting her first baby."

"Nice. Liam, Levi, and Lisa. Your mom must love the letter L, huh?"

"Yeah well, her name is Linda, and my dad's is Lonny. I guess she figured she'd keep the theme going."

Asha put the picture down and moved to pick up the one of our entire family. I watched her as she examined it. It was easy to see the longing in her eyes. She didn't have a close family. She was basically alone in the world, wishing she had the one thing most people had.

And it didn't have anything to do with money, big houses, or expensive cars. It was simple. *Love.* A family. Someone who always had her back.

"What's your family like?" I asked softly.

She set the frame down and turned to face me. "They're nothing like this," she answered before turning and striding into the kitchen. She dragged her fingers along the kitchen island before brushing them against the vase of wildflowers my mother had placed in the center. "My mom isn't all bad, but she seems to care more about money now than me. She used to read to me before bed when I was little. When she was still married to my real dad, we'd have girl nights where we'd eat popcorn, watch movies together, and put on makeup. Everything changed after the divorce though. She has to have the most expensive handbags, shoes, clothes. She spends entire weeks at the spa, getting her nails and hair done, having these treatments done to preserve her youth. I sometimes think she does it to avoid reality. Like when she's gone, she doesn't have to face our life." She blew out a breath before continuing, "My stepdad, Gio Valetti, he's just a dick. All he cares about is his business. He doesn't care who he hurts or has to stomp on to make his money." She opened the fridge and pulled out an off-brand soda. "Then there's me. The girl who doesn't belong anywhere." She leaned down on the island with her forearms, holding her soda in both hands as she gazed up at me.

"Giovanni Valetti is your stepdad?" I asked, blinking at her. "He's a huge mob boss—"

"He wishes," she muttered. "My real dad, Nicolai Reznikov, is bigger. They're rivals. That's what this entire mess is about. My mom left my dad for him after she found my dad cheated on her. It's been hell ever since."

I swallowed, not even sure how to follow up with that information.

"And so that's it. That's my home life. I really don't belong anywhere."

She was letting her guard down again, and I wondered why the sudden change in front of me. Not that I could complain about it. I needed the information for the project. But for reasons I really didn't want to explore in the moment, my heart went out to the blue-eyed beauty in her tight jeans and pink cashmere top.

"You fit in everywhere you want to fit in, Asha. Come on, let's go up to my room."

I headed for the stairs, and she followed me up and into the third door on the left. I took a seat at my desk and flipped open my notebook. She slowly made herself at home, first walking around my room, looking over everything. She checked out my old little league trophies, the pictures on the walls of me and my old public-school friends, my book collection, and all the photos on the walls I'd taken. Finally, she flopped down on the bed. She set her soda on the bedside table and took a deep breath as her eyes fluttered closed.

A bolt of lightning traveled through my body at the sight of her so relaxed on my bed. She had one hand under her head while the other rested on her flat stomach. When she shifted, her shirt moved up the slightest bit, giving me a peek at her belly button. Her long lashes fanned out across her cheeks, and her hair was a mess of waves covering my pillow. I hoped her scent stayed in my bed for me to enjoy later. Again, I pushed the crazy idea away.

"All right, where do you want to start?" I asked, trying to pull my mind away from her on my bed.

Her blue eyes popped open and landed on mine. "Really?"

"Really what?" I asked, trying to take control of my body, which was coming alive in ways it shouldn't.

"You have me at your house, on your bed, and your parents are gone. Yet all you want to do is the assignment?"

I swallowed the excess saliva pooling in my mouth. "What else would I want to do, Asha? We're not exactly on friendly terms."

She sat up and shrugged. "I'm not friendly with a lot of people, but they still want me. Are you saying you don't?" She tilted her head to the side as she searched my eyes for the truth.

"You need more than a hot body and a pretty face for me to want you." Not entirely the truth, but not a lie either.

She intrigued me, and for that, I desired the knowledge that having her would provide, if only to sate the wild curiosity growing in my guts.

She nodded. "Like what?"

I took a deep breath as I rested my elbows on my knees. "Like a nice personality. A girl needs to be friendly, giving, kind, caring."

"So...like Sofia," she said, standing up and stepping in my direction. Her nearness made me sit up straight.

"Sofia and I are just friends."

"You mean, the two of you have never done anything?" She took another step.

I swallowed hard and shrugged. "We've made out a couple of times after getting wasted, but that's it. And I wish we hadn't done that."

"Why?" Another step.

"I think it confused her," I confessed, plowing on with my overshare. "She keeps waiting around for the day we'll get together, and I have no interest in her like that. At least nothing past the moment."

"So you're not banging the geek. You're not intending to bang me. So, who are you fucking?" One final step put her directly in front of me.

She placed her hands on my shoulders, and I looked up at her, meeting her blue eyes. My pulse roared in my ears.

"You say you don't want me, Liam, but I'm *very* good at reading body language. You want me. I know you do." She sat on my lap, straddling me.

Out of panic, I clenched my fists at my sides, afraid of touching her. My wildest dreams were playing out before me, and I was sitting like a fucking idiot with my hands at my side.

"I can feel how excited you are," she whispered as she rocked her hips against me.

My hands flew to her waist, stilling her as I squeezed.

This might be a game. Stop it before you get your ass beat by her crew.

"I'm a guy, Asha. I can watch *The Little Mermaid* and get the same reaction, so don't for a minute think my dick has any say when it comes to you."

I eased her back until she was no longer straddling me. She flopped back down onto my bed in a pout, her arms crossed over her chest.

"You done fucking around? Can we get to work now?" My dick continued to thicken in my jeans, protesting and calling me a fucking idiot for turning her down. I drew in a deep breath to calm myself before offering her a forced smile.

She rolled her eyes. "Excuse me if I think my life is my business."

I laughed and shook my head. I needed to focus. Burying myself between Asha's legs was off the table. "If you were willing to sleep with me to get out of telling me about yourself, your life has to be pretty fucked up. Trust me, I don't want to know about you anymore than you want to tell me. So let's just be adults about this and get it done. Okay?" I picked up my pencil. "So birthday is on Halloween, huh?"

She nodded as she stared out the window behind me.

"You're a little hellcat. Think that's what I'll call you from now on." I glanced her way, and the corners of her mouth turned upward. "Where were you born?"

"Here in Chicago."

"Why don't you give me some back story on your parents? How did they meet, fall in love?"

She pushed herself up higher on the bed, resting her back against the headboard and stretching her legs the length of the mattress. "My dad was at a strip club, conducting some business, when my mom offered him a lap dance. He accepted, and they went back to the VIP room. She danced for him, and he fell in love. He paid for the dance, tipped her graciously, and then asked her out. She said no, that they weren't allowed to date the customers. But he kept coming back every night until he wore her down. They finally went out, where he wowed her with an expensive meal, his expensive car, and probably the size of his dick. It was a match made in heaven. My mom only wanted a life. A family. Financial security. My dad wanted a young beauty on his arm to flaunt around all his parties. Win, win."

I watched her tell the story with my mouth hanging open. My hand didn't budge to write any of it down. This was a high school project. I couldn't exactly write about strip clubs and random hook-ups.

"How long after they got together did they have you?" I asked, knowing it wouldn't go into the paper either, but I suddenly needed to know more.

She had a faraway look in her eyes. "They dated for about a year before he proposed. They got married exactly eighteen months after meeting, and then I came nine months later. They were together until a few years ago. That's when my mom met my stepdad at one of my dad's functions. He wasn't supposed to be there. He and my dad being mortal enemies and all." She let out a soft, sad laugh. "But he crashed the party to piss Dad off. My mom took one look at him, and it was over for all of us."

"So, you hate your stepdad and don't have a great relationship with your mom, so why not live with your dad?"

"I wanted to, but my mom won custody after my stepdad got his lawyers involved. Then my dad quit trying to reach out to me. I assume he thinks I *chose* my stepdad over him. It's not the case. I'd never pick him." Her voice cracked before she hauled in a deep breath and continued, "Or maybe Dad just doesn't want me. It's not like he tries. He probably thinks I'm a gold digger like my mom turned out to be." She shrugged. "I'll be eighteen soon enough though. Then none of them can stop me from doing what I want."

"And what do you want?" I asked, leaning forward, enthralled by her story.

She swung her legs over the edge of the bed and bent toward me.

"Leave. Run away. Go find myself. Live the life I've always dreamed, a life where I can be free."

"How's that any different from how you live now?"

She rolled her eyes. "I'm not free. I'm trapped in that big mansion everyone assumes is so great. I'm told what to do and how to do it. And when I don't listen, it doesn't go over very well."

"Is that how you got that bruise on your jaw?"

Her gaze pulled from mine and landed on the floor between us. Her mouth opened and closed, but no words came out. Finally, her eyes found mine again. "Let's just say that living at that house isn't for the weak."

"Who hit you, Asha? Your mom?" I asked gently, watching her face closely for any changes. "No, your stepdad."

Something flashed in her blue orbs, and I knew I was right. Her stepdad had hit her across the face, leaving a bruise on her jaw she'd attempted to cover with makeup. *What had he asked her to do that she refused?*

"It *was* your stepdad, wasn't it?"

Throughout the conversation, we'd been drifting closer and closer to one another. There was only an inch left between us as we looked into one another's eyes.

"Trust me, Liam. You don't want to know anything about me," she whispered.

"Oh, I think I do," I replied, reaching for her and taking her hand in mine.

I expected her to pull away, but she didn't. In fact, she actually gave my fingers a gentle squeeze. Her blue eyes were wide. Her plump, pink lips parted.

I didn't know what made me do it. Temporary insanity maybe? I'd definitely gone absolutely insane. But damn, it felt good to touch her like that without the worry of someone kicking my ass. At least right then. If she ran back and told Lucas I'd touched her, even just holding her hand for a second, I'd be a dead man because Lucas was a pussy and wouldn't fight me alone.

In that instant, we weren't enemies. We were strangers having a moment maybe we both needed.

Someone started pounding on the front door.

"Liam, open up!" Max shouted, his voice carrying through my open bedroom window, causing me to release her hand.

The easygoing look she was just wearing disappeared, replaced with her queen bee coldness.

Well, whatever moment we'd had was gone. *Damn.*

"I'll be right back."

"Get rid of them," she ordered in a breathy whisper.

My cock jumped at her soft command. I left the room without responding. I took the stairs two at a time until I was at the front door. I yanked it open, finding Max, Andy, and Sofia.

"What took so long?' Max asked, pushing me back as he strode in.

Andy and Sofia followed.

Wordlessly, I closed the door and turned to address them. Max came walking out of the kitchen with a soda.

"I can't hang out right now, guys. Asha is up in my room. We're finally starting our assignment."

Max's eyes bugged out of his skull. "No shit? She's in your room?" he asked with excitement.

I nodded.

"I gotta see this. Come on, guys," he said, rushing up the stairs, completely disregarding what I'd just told him.

Andy chased after him, and Sofia just gaped at me with an expression I didn't understand. *Was she hurt that Asha was in my room? Was she mad?*

"We're just working on our assignment, Sofia," I told her.

"If she'd show up to class, you could do it then instead of having to take her to your bedroom, Liam." She turned and marched up the steps.

Yeah, but I couldn't get to know her in school. This Asha was different. This Asha...well, maybe this Asha I might actually start to like.

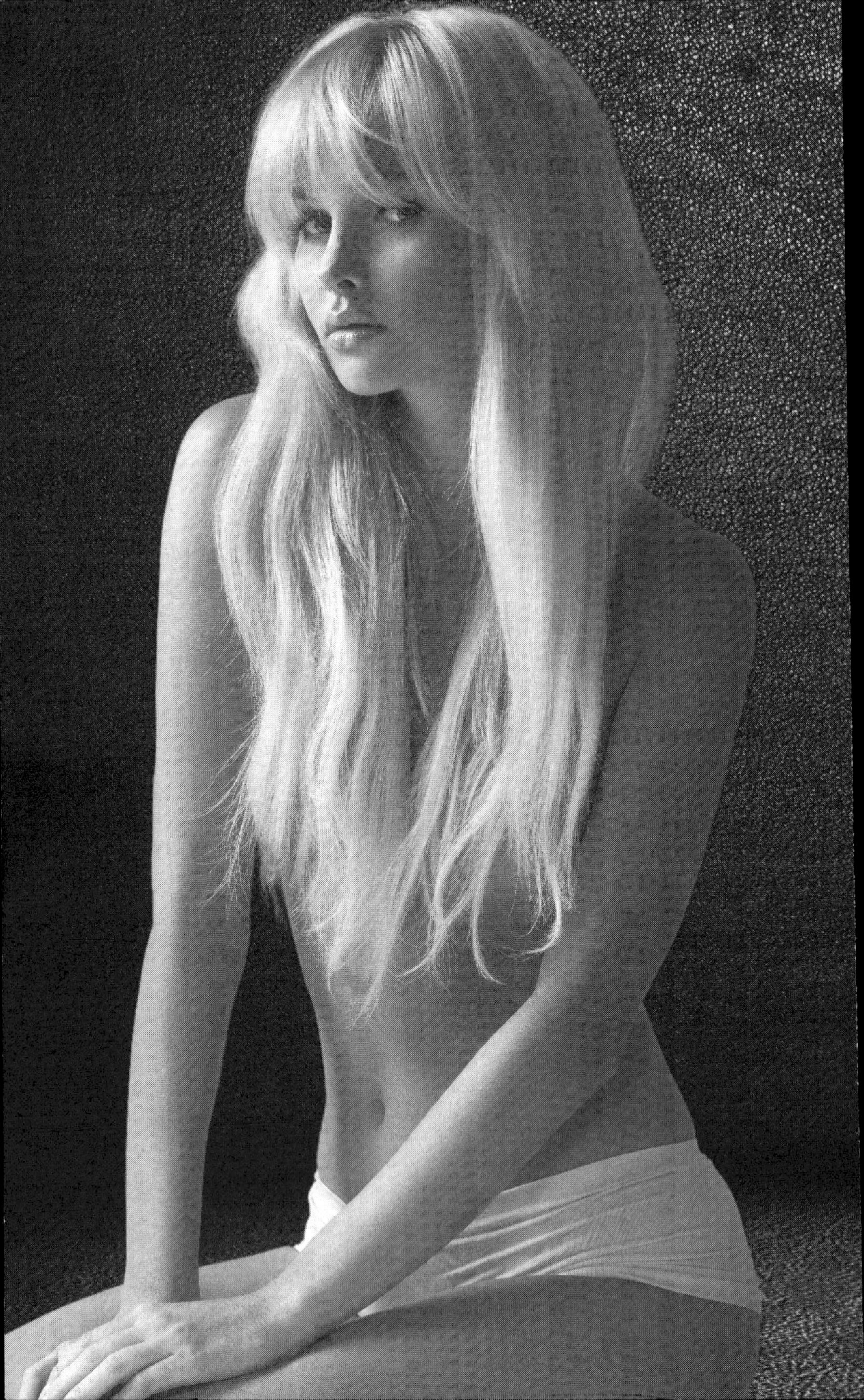

SEVEN
ASHA

I was lying on Liam's bed when his friends came strolling in. The nerdy one came to a complete stop when he saw me. His mouth dropped open as he took me in.

"Like what you see?" I called out, sitting up.

The guy, Max, I was pretty sure his name was, snapped his mouth closed and turned to stare at the other two walking in. Sofia's eyes found me, and they narrowed as lines formed between them. She was pissed I was on Liam's bed, that we'd been here alone. I could see the questions written all over her face. *What were you two up to in here all alone?*

I wanted to laugh but was able to hold it back. Instead, I thought of something more fun to do. Flirt with Liam and see how she reacted.

If I was being honest, Liam's earlier actions had ignited something inside me I didn't want to let go. I'd never had anyone act like they gave a shit before. I treated him like garbage, and he still was kind to me when he saw the cracks in my armor. Rather than finish me off, he sat and listened. Sure, maybe it was just for the assignment, but he didn't have to hold my hand or treat me as good as he was. It made me question everything I thought I knew.

Liam came in and quickly glanced at all of us gawking at one another before taking his seat at his desk again.

"Liam, how are we supposed to work with your friends here?" I asked him, batting my lashes.

"Good question," he said, staring pointedly at them.

Max shrugged. "Oh, don't get all butt hurt. We won't be here long. We just thought we'd come see what you were up to. You rushed out of school before any of us could even talk to you. You haven't answered our texts. Why the silence?"

Liam's eyes grew in size. "Because I had to pick Asha up. If she's willing to work on this assignment, then I'm on her time. I cannot fail this."

"Oh, so she's top priority now? What are we?" Sofia asked.

"You're a loser, just like you've always been," I told her, like the answer was the simplest in the world.

She let out a long huff before holding up her middle finger and moving to sit on the window seat. I smirked at her.

"Enough, guys," Liam told us. "I'm not trading you guys in for her. She's not here because she wants to be," he said, shooting me a look. "She's here because we have work to do. Now if you guys want to stay and hang out, fine. But do it quietly so the two of us can actually get some work done." He stood up and grabbed a folded-up chair that was slid between the wall and his dresser. He unfolded it and placed it beside his before gesturing toward me.

I smiled at Sofia as I got up from the bed and took the chair next to Liam. The two guys turned on the TV and started playing Xbox, but Sofia stayed in her place, watching us.

As Liam asked me questions about growing up, I leaned toward him, placed my hand on his thigh and flirted every chance I got. If he noticed, he didn't say anything. But Sofia did, and she kept getting more and more bitter. At first, she refused to even look our way, opting to stare out the window instead. Then I heard her scoff and mumble something to herself. It was clear that I was getting under her skin by flirting with Liam and knowing that made me smile a little more.

"Do you have any place that's a secret? Like somewhere you go when you just need to be alone and think?" Liam leaned in to speak to me softly.

My heart fluttered at his nearness. I nodded, swallowing. As much as I hated to admit it, I liked the feeling he created in me. "There's this place on my property. I guess it used to be staff housing, but it's way back and is all grown over. You wouldn't know it was even there just by looking. I like to go there sometimes. It's quiet and dark. There's a fireplace and a couch. It's like a frozen piece of time. All the furniture is still there."

"It sounds really cool," Liam murmured.

My eyes darted to his lips as they turned up into a small smile.

I wondered what it would feel like to kiss him. To kiss just a normal guy. Someone who wasn't paying for me and probably didn't want anything in return but my time.

I grinned in return, hoping to calm myself. "I'll have to take you sometime."

His expression indicated his surprise. "Yeah? I'd love to take pictures of it."

I toyed with my hair. "You should take pictures of me sometime. I'd like to be under your lens." I don't even know why I said it. I was being a flirty bitch, sure, but there was truth to my words. I *wanted* him to hang my photo on his walls and post me online. I wanted someone to care enough to make me a part of their life, however small a part that was, even just some stupid image online.

"Oh, my God! Tell me you're not falling for this, Liam," Sofia said, stealing the attention of everyone in the room.

I wasn't quiet when I'd spoken. My plan was for her hear me, at least in the beginning.

Liam glanced from me to Sofia. "What?" he asked, holding his palm upward.

"You know she's only flirting with you to piss me off. It's so obvious." Sofia rolled her eyes.

Liam balked. "Sofia, you're being crazy."

Sofia's anger melted and turned to sadness before our very eyes. She crossed her arms over her chest and got up, rushing for the door.

"Fuck," Liam mumbled, standing and chasing after her.

The two guys left looked from one another to me.

I lifted my brow. "What's the deal with those two? Are they messing around or something?" My guts twisted at the possible answer I'd get. Liam had said they weren't, and I'd believed him. But why chase her?

The geeky one, Max, shrugged. "She likes him. He likes her too, but only when he's fucked up and she's the only one around. They've messed around a couple times, but that's it. I think Sofia is hoping for more, while Liam is..." He shrugged. "Actually, I have no idea what Liam is doing anymore. Not since you came into the picture."

I laughed, butterflies flapping in my guts at his words. "Oh, I'm not in the picture."

"Then what was going on in here? Don't tell us it was *studying*," Andy said.

I waved my hand, dismissing his question. "It was nothing. I was just trying to distract Liam from this stupid project. Even that didn't work." I shook my head, remembering how I'd tried and failed to seduce him. "Why am I even explaining myself to you? It's not like what you think matters."

I turned back to the notebook Liam had been writing in. I began to read through his notes. His handwriting was perfect—smooth, clear, and easy to read. I was surprised he hadn't written with as much hate as I'd flung at him. Instead of writing *gets beaten by stepdad*, he wrote *not close with family*. Instead of writing *her mom was a whore*, he wrote *mom is free-spirited*.

I'd been scared of gearing him up with ammo to fire at me later, but it was clear he wasn't looking for ammo. *Why was he being so nice?*

And why did I feel so comfortable opening up to him? I told him about things I didn't even tell my best friends or boyfriend. Lucas didn't know about my little hiding spot, but Liam did. And I'd offered to show him? To let him take pictures?

Liam worked for the school paper with his friends. Anything I provided him would be ammo if he chose to shoot. I swallowed as I considered the possibility he wasn't genuine, only wanting to dig information out of me. That was what reporters did. But his words...

I bit my lip and scanned the notebook again. There was nothing there to suggest he was being malicious.

Yet, Asha. He was only getting started.

Liam strode back into the bedroom with Sofia behind him. He took his spot next to me, and she went back to her place at the window. I wondered what he'd said to get her to come back. Maybe it hadn't taken much. Maybe she was that much in love with him, or maybe he was just that good at getting what he wanted. Either way, I planned on finding out and didn't even know why.

Sofia didn't speak again as we worked, and I did everything I could think of to get under her skin. When we decided to call it quits for the day, I turned to find her eyes on her phone and her earbuds in place. No wonder she'd kept quiet. She couldn't hear us.

When Liam and I stood, everyone's eyes followed us. "I'm going to take Asha home. You guys going to hang here while I'm gone?"

They all nodded, and then he led me out of the house and back to his car. I climbed into the passenger seat while he sat behind the wheel.

"Thank you for finally starting this project with me."

I rolled my eyes, feigning being cool. "No problem. It wasn't as bad as I thought it'd be," I confessed.

"Are you saying you actually *enjoyed* spending time with me?" He raised a brow at me.

I laughed, letting go for a moment. "I guess I am."

Silence filled the car around us, so I plunged on, "It's just that...I don't know. I feel like I can be myself around you. You're not like my friends. All they care about is money, partying, and judging people. You're different. It feels easier with you."

"I can't believe you're not the royal bitch I thought you were." He laughed out. "Tentative friends?"

Friends? Could we be friends? Could my crowd at school deal with that? I guessed they could deal with anything I made them.

"Tentative friends," I agreed with a smile, an idea taking shape in my mind. One I'd have to seriously think through before I blurted it out to him.

I hadn't realized we'd already made it to my house when Liam turned into my driveway and stopped the car. I turned in my seat to look at him. He was watching me with a smile playing on his lips. Something formed in my stomach—something I'd never felt before. Most men looked at me and wondered what I could do for them. Lucas looked at me expecting me to play some slut who'd bend over anytime he wanted. But Liam, he didn't look at me in either way. He gazed at me in awe. It was like he thought I was perfect, innocent, good.

How wrong he was.

"When do you want to do this again?"

He shrugged. "I'm free tomorrow after school."

I smirked at the thought of getting to see him again tomorrow. "How about, after school, you come over here, and I'll show you my hideout? You can take some pictures. I'll wear something nice."

His brows lifted, and the corners of his mouth curved up slightly, but he held back a full smile. "OK, great. See you tomorrow."

I climbed out and waved as he drove away. When he was gone, I had no choice but to go inside. My mom's heels clicked off the floor in the kitchen., I followed the sound. I grabbed a water out of the fridge while she poured a cup of tea.

"Hey, Mom."

She cast me a cursory glance. "How was school?" she slurred.

"I didn't go," I told her.

"Huh, well, don't make that a habit. Miss too much and you won't graduate." She tapped the spoon against her cup before lifting the mug and taking a sip.

"Where's Gio?" I asked cautiously.

"He's out of town for a couple of days. Some kind of business meeting." She took her cup of tea out to the garden, leaving me alone.

I rolled my eyes. She didn't even know I'd skipped school? She didn't notice the bruise on my jaw?

Just as well I guessed. Then I'd just have to lie to her. No way could I tell her the truth. A part of me wondered if she already knew about the things Gio made me do. I mean, what mother didn't question when her husband took her daughter out at ten at night and didn't bring her back until the next morning? Money must have meant more to her than I did. It only made me hate her and then hate myself for trying to protect her.

But she was my mother. I remembered a time when she wasn't like this. When she'd read me stories in bed and tuck me in. When she'd make special pancakes with chocolate chips in them on Sundays while the house staff was off duty. *That* was the woman I wanted to protect. I wanted her back so much it hurt.

Silently, I went up to my room and started my assignment, engrossing myself in all things Liam.

I made a list. Family who loves him. Incredible photographer. Kind. Compassionate. Donates money to save animals. Scholarship kid. More than just a pretty face and incredible talent. Pure. Untainted. Beautiful.

I closed my notebook and let out a sigh, wondering what Liam was doing. Quickly, I shoved the thought out of my head. It was absurd to think about him. My mind and feelings were all over the damn place. I needed to get a grip.

Around eight, Lucas called and begged to come over. I told him no, but it didn't stop him from climbing onto my second-floor balcony and helping himself into my room. I'd just walked out of the bathroom from my shower, wearing nothing but my robe. When he saw the easy access, he jumped at the opportunity.

"I missed you at school today," he said, sauntering up to me with his hands held out. They latched onto my hips and pulled me against his chest where his lips found mine.

I couldn't help but notice the difference between his touch and Liam's. Liam's was soft, gentle. Lucas's was forceful and commanding. And sure, Liam only held my hand, but I bet any other touch would've been gentle. He'd never push me. Force me.

I kissed Lucas for a moment, hoping it would be all he wanted. But like every other time, his hands pushed my clothing out of the way to get to what he really wanted.

I shoved him back before he could get my robe open. "Lucas, stop," I told him.

He let out a long, drawn out breath before running his hands through his hair. "Fuck, Asha. Why are you even dating me?"

I ignored his question and went to sit at my vanity.

"Do you know how many girls would love to be in your position? Hell, do you know how many of the girls you call *friends* would love to be in your position?"

I snorted as I dragged a brush through my locks, my hands shaking. "If that's what you want, Lucas, then go for it."

He scoffed. "I don't *want* them. I want you, but you act like I'm the last fucking thing you want. I mean, you pull away every time I try to touch you!"

"Maybe that's because every time you touch me, you're trying for sex! You never just hold my hand or brush my hair from my face. You don't *touch*, Lucas. You grab. You squeeze, and I'm a human being. I'm not just some piece of meat put here for your pleasure."

He shook his head. "Whatever, Asha. But you need to figure out what it is you want. You want me, this is me. If you don't want this, then you don't want me." With that, he turned and climbed out the window.

I tossed the brush onto my vanity and got up to lock all the doors. Nobody was coming in for the rest of the night. I changed into some pajamas, put my earbuds in my ears, and played music that would take me out of this world. As I scrolled through Facebook, I got a text from Liam.

LIAM: Want to work on our assignment some more?
Excitement coursed through me.
ME: Sure. What's your favorite color?
I rolled my eyes at my stupid question, but for some reason, I wanted his distraction. In fact, I craved it.
LIAM: Blue. What's yours?
ME: Black.
LIAM: Black? Black isn't a color. It's the lack of color.
ME: Wrong. Black is a mixture of all the colors. Plus, I'm pretty sure it's the color of my soul by now.
LIAM: I don't think you're as bad as you think. I think it's a front to keep yourself protected. Tell me I'm wrong.
ME: You're wrong.
LIAM: *laughing emoji*
I plunged on, asking the question that had been burning in the back of my mind all evening.
ME: What did you say to Sofia today to get her to come back in the room?
There was a long pause.
LIAM: Why?
ME: *shrugging emoji* Just curious.
LIAM: ugggggh...I just told her that she and I would hang out later.
ME: And did you?
LIAM: Yes, after I took you home. I got back. The guys took off, but Sofia stuck around.

I was hit with a ping of jealously. *How could someone like me be jealous of someone like her?* She was a nobody, and I was the fucking queen of the school.

LIAM: Does that make you mad?

I shook out of my daze.

ME: What? No! Why would that make me mad?

LIAM: It just seemed like you were bending over backward to make her jealous today.

I stared down at the phone. I honestly thought he hadn't noticed what I was doing because he didn't act one way or another about it.

ME: Goodnight, Liam.

I shut off my phone and dropped it onto the mattress beside me. My eyes closed, and behind my lids I felt his warm hand on mine. I listened to his voice in my head.

I bit my lip as my fingers traveled to the edge of my waistband, Liam's face in my mind, No one had ever touched me to make me feel good. And it was just a fucking hand. I couldn't fathom how I'd react if he touched me for real. The thought made me pant.

It's Liam Hastings. He's like the rest of them. He doesn't give a shit about you.

My waistband snapped back in place as I moved my hand away from the apex of my thighs. I was a complete psycho, touching myself over the memory of someone being nice to me. I made myself sick.

How could someone like me like someone like him? Sure, he was hot, had loads of hard muscles. Plus he seemed to be a nice guy when we were alone, but he was nobody, a loser, the bottom of the pyramid.

I repeated those thoughts over and over with one ugly, niggling one in the back of my mind I couldn't silence.

He's better than you. You're the loser. The trash. He's better in every sense of the word.

Sleep tugged me under, but I woke frequently, and each time it took forever to go back to sleep. I finally gave up on the idea altogether and decided to get ready for school at five in the morning.

I turned on the light and sat at my vanity, carefully using makeup to cover the bruise on my jaw. I lined my eyes darker than usual. I painted my lips with bright, red lipstick and let my blonde hair hang straight.

With September nearing an end, the weather was getting cooler, but I didn't take that into consideration as I slipped on a pair of stockings and a jean skirt. I slid my feet into my black Doc Marten's and left them unlaced before tugging on a black shirt and my leather jacket.

I grabbed my purse and headed downstairs. I stopped in the kitchen and poured a cup of coffee before rushing toward my car. I didn't know if my mom was home, but I didn't want to bump into anyone, including the housekeeper. My mom would've said something snarky about the way I'd done my makeup. And any employees would've just told on me, the loyal assholes.

It was too early to go to school, so I found myself driving around aimlessly. I was thinking about Liam and wondering how today's meeting would go when I noticed I was driving down his street. I glanced at his house as I drove by, but there didn't appear to be any movement inside. I decided to hit up a drive-through with the hopes I could get my head on straight because if I was falling the way I thought I was, it was really going to hurt.

And a girl like me had to protect herself.

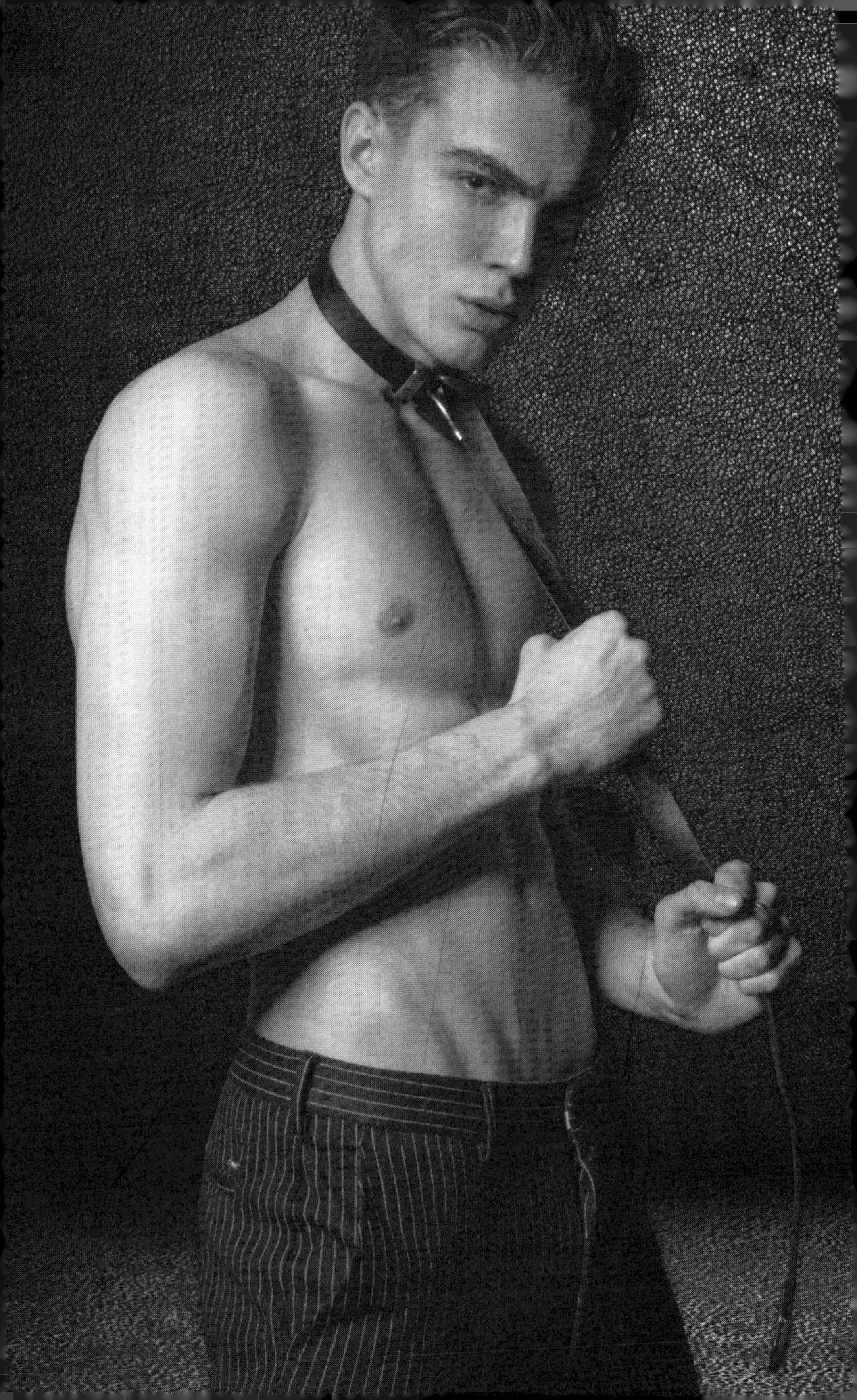

EIGHT
LIAM

In the morning, I woke with excitement, eager to see what the day could bring for me and Asha. It felt as if I'd gained some ground with her the day before, like we'd crossed the line from enemies to friends. I wondered how it would play out at school, in front of her crew and mine. As I lay in bed, I was consumed with thoughts of her, reliving our time together yesterday.

I imagined the way she straddled me earlier in the day, how good she felt pressed against me, how hot her center felt against mine. Even now, I could still feel the weight of her hand on my thigh, and I envisioned it inching its way up. I became rock hard at the memory.

The next thing I knew, I had my hand down my boxers as I worked myself over, picturing her hand stroking me instead of mine. As my release started to build, I thought about what it would be like to have her mouth against mine, how she'd taste, how soft her lips would be. I pictured there being nothing between us and envisioned how I'd pull her hips downward as I slid into her, the sounds I could force out of her. My release bubbled over the edge and wracked my body with waves of pleasure I'd never felt so strongly before.

After showering quickly, I shaved the light scruff from my face. Then I styled my hair, giving it the messy look I always aimed for. Dressing in a pair of loose-fitting jeans and a black t-shirt, I grabbed my shit and made my way downstairs. Mom was in the kitchen, and Dad was rushing toward the door, late as usual.

"I expect the yard to be mowed by the time I get home, young man," he said, pointing at me as he flew past the stairs.

"Yes, sir," I mumbled, offering up a salute like a cherry on top. When I entered the kitchen, Mom set a cup of coffee on the island in front of me.

She smiled and leaned in to kiss my cheek. "What's my boy up to today?" she asked as she pulled two waffles out of the toaster.

I hauled out a barstool and sat down, sipping my coffee and then pouring syrup over my waffles. "School. I have to photograph the cheerleaders and football team today for the yearbook. Then I guess mowing the lawn on top of doing the mounds of homework I'll have."

"Don't worry about the lawn. I'll pay the lawn care company in town to squeeze it in."

"But Dad said—"

"Don't worry about your father. What he doesn't know won't hurt him. It'll be like how every time he buys me jewelry, I return it for store credit until I have enough saved up to get what I really want." She giggled and shrugged.

I laughed and rolled my eyes. "You seriously do that?"

She moved her head from side to side. "Guess you'll never know... and neither will your father. Now, eat up before you're late." She grabbed her coffee and turned toward the laundry room.

I scarfed down my waffles and finished my cup of coffee before grabbing my keys off the counter and heading for the door with my backpack. "Bye, Mom," I called out.

"Love you," she said, just as I was pulling the door closed behind me.

I practically jogged to my car and jumped behind the wheel. I tossed my bag into the passenger seat and twisted the key to make the car roar to life. Excitement pumped through my body, making my heart hammer away and my breathing pick up. I couldn't wait to see what the day brought.

A few minutes later, I pulled into the parking lot. Everything looked the same even though I expected it all to look different for some reason. The sky was blue. The grass was green. And the parking lot was crowded with kids hanging out around their cars. I parked in the last row and shut off the engine. I took a deep breath to prepare me for whatever came my way and climbed out, throwing my bag over my shoulder as I made my way across the concrete.

Max, Andy, Sofia, and the rest of the scholarship kids were hanging at the bench in front of the building the way they always did.

I came to a stop next to them. "Hey."

"Hi," Sofia said, using her overly sweet voice.

"What's up?" Andy asked.

Max looked me up and down. "Where's your partner?"

I rolled my eyes. "No idea." I shrugged. "You still acting pissy because I wouldn't give you all the juicy gossip you wanted?"

He laughed. "Nah, I'm just fucking with you. I started *Riverdale* like you suggested. More than enough drama for me."

"Hey, I like that show," Sofia said, hitting him in the ribs with her elbow.

"Ow," he mumbled, rubbing the spot, causing us all to laugh.

The bell rang, and everyone started moving toward the building to get to their first class. I stopped at my locker to gather my books for the morning. I got a quick glimpse of Asha as she sashayed down the hall. My eyes had a mind of their own as they traced up her long, bare legs under her skirt. Her blonde hair was straight, and her eyes were lined in black. Everyone was whispering about her new look, but I thought she looked better than ever.

I couldn't get her face out of my mind all morning. Since we didn't have any early classes together, I had to settle for quick glimpses as she walked past. At lunch, I sat with my group under the big tree in the quad and watched as she sat with her friends. They talked, laughed, and stuck to themselves.

Asha didn't glance in my direction. None of them did, and I found that unusual. Nobody got up to start shit, and I wondered if maybe she'd talked with them about laying off me now that we were friends. I didn't know anything for sure, but I planned to ask her in class.

When I got to class, I sat at our table and waited for her to enter. Slowly, the class filled up, but she never came in. Mr. Ferris marched into class and shut the door behind him. He placed his things on his desk before turning and addressing the class.

"All right, everyone. You know the drill by now. Get to work."

I raised my hand, and he motioned for me to speak. "My partner isn't here. What should I do?"

Mr. Ferris shrugged. "Do what you can on your own or use the period to study another subject. Up to you."

He turned to answer another question and left me feeling irritated. I pulled out my phone and immediately sent her a text.

ME: Where are you?

I tucked the phone into my pocket and waited for her response as I started writing my paper with the notes I'd already taken. The hour passed slowly, and I never got a response out of her. I tried again.

ME: Everything okay?

I put my cell back in my pocket as I headed to my next class. After the last bell had rung for the day, I put my books away and made my way out to the football field to start snapping the pictures I needed. I was supposed to take photos of every player on the team and then a couple of the whole team together.

"Hey, bitch, still drying up pussies?" Lucas called out.

I scowled and clicked a picture of his shit-eating grin.

"What's wrong? Got a dick in your mouth?"

Grinding my teeth together to keep from talking was no longer working. "No, just been having a hard time washing the taste of

Asha's pussy from my mouth. Gave me bad breath." It was a nasty, low blow. I regretted bringing her name up the moment the words left my mouth. Call me crazy, but remorse flooded me at having used her like that.

Lucas took a dangerous step toward me, his lip curled up into a sneer.

"Easy, man." Jude stepped in front of him and pushed him back. "You know damn well Asha doesn't spread her legs for you, so why the hell would she do it for him?"

Well, that was news.

"It's cool. You know our boy is only playing, right, William?" Hudson asked, grinning at me.

"It's Liam," I grunted, going back to taking a few shots of a couple guys on the field who were tossing the ball back and forth.

"Really? It's not short for William?"

"No."

"Guess the only thing short on you is your dick then." Hudson let out a burst of laughter.

Lucas and Jude joined in, making me shake my head.

Luckily, Coach called everyone over for the group photo. I wasn't sure how much longer I could put up with their shit before I lashed out.

Annoyed, I moved on to the cheerleaders. Most of them posed and smiled, wanting to take the best pictures possible. But Asha and the rest of her elite friends had other things in mind. They didn't give a shit about their pictures. Instead, they did nothing but focus on me and how they could fuck up the decent day I had going.

"Ugh, it's you. Couldn't they have sent someone who isn't so repulsive? I mean, how am I supposed to smile at that?" Tiffany asked loudly enough for everyone to hear.

They all started giggling.

I did my best to ignore them as I took the other girls' pictures.

"I mean, look at him. He shouldn't even be allowed on the field.

His bad luck is going to taint the field and make us lose the game this weekend!" Heidi exclaimed.

I peeked over at Asha, waiting to see what she was going to do. *Would she stick up for me after the time we'd spent together, or would she join in with her friend for a game of bash the loser?*

Asha smirked and rolled her eyes. "Come on, girls. If anything, he's just going to suck up all the bad mojo and help us win." She looked at me. "I mean, that's what you do, right? Suck?"

Her crew giggled.

"Really?" I asked, my anger at her taking over as I wondered how we could be so hot and cold.

She changed back and forth so quickly it nearly gave me whiplash.

She just shrugged one shoulder, her long, blonde ponytail falling over it. "Well, it's what you do, right? You and Max and Andy. You all take turns sucking one another off?"

A group of cheerleaders heard, and they gasped, waiting for my response. I'd be damned if I let her show me up like that. I turned to face her and gave her a cocky smile. "Just because I turned you down yesterday doesn't make me gay."

That only made them gasp again as their eyes stretched wide.

Asha took a step toward me. She straightened her back, squared her shoulders, and raised her chin. "Yeah right. Like I'd make a move on you." A shaky laugh fell from her lips. "You're so into guys you don't even know when a girl is trying to sleep with you. You can't even score with that loser girl you hang out with. But I guess the thought of any vagina getting close to you is enough to make that small dick of yours go limp."

"Small?" I asked with a raise of my brow. "I think you know my dick isn't small, hellcat."

Her nostrils flared, and her chest puffed out as she put one hand on her jutted-out hip.

"Liam—"

"What's going on over here?" Lucas stepped between us, glaring only at me and cutting Asha off short.

I was sure nothing good was going to come out of her mouth anyway, so it didn't matter.

"Loser boy here got mouthy. Told everyone I tried to fuck him yesterday, and he turned me down," Asha told him.

Lucas's eyes flew wide in amazement. "Is that right? You're telling people my girlfriend tried to fuck you? Look at you and look at me. You really think she'd cheat on me with your loser ass?" He raised his hands and pushed me.

I stumbled but didn't fall.

"Don't fucking touch me," I told him quietly as I tried to hold back my anger. I didn't want to get into a fight. Not in the middle of the football team. Not only could I get expelled from school, but I'd also end up with my ass kicked since Jude and Hudson were coming up behind Lucas, ready to jump in on the fun.

"Don't let him talk to you like that," Asha said, knocking my camera from my hand.

It fell to the ground, and the lens broke on impact. Rage surged through my entire body and made me grind my teeth. A bout of pain shot through my jaw.

"Oh, loser boy here isn't getting off that easily," Lucas said, drawing his fist back and sending it flying toward my nose.

It happened too fast for me to see it coming. The next thing I knew, blackness took over as another pain shot through my face. I fell backward from getting sucker punched. My head snapped and hit the ground with a thud, which made pain race along my spine.

Jude stepped up and sent a kick to my ribs. I called out as more pain took over.

Lucas bent over me and pointed his finger in my face. "You better watch your back and keep my girlfriend's name out of your mouth. Or next time, you won't be able to get up and run away." He stood up and reached for Asha.

I glanced over at her in time to see her stomp on my camera, further breaking it to pieces.

She took his hand and shot me a smile before they all strutted away together.

After they left the field, I got up and gathered the pieces of my broken camera. Fury bubbled throughout my whole body as I made my way back inside to my locker. I grabbed my bag before slamming the door shut and heading for the exit. Not only was I pissed, but I was confused too.

How in the fuck could she change so quickly? And what had happened to make her go from flirting and friendly to picking a fight and breaking my camera? She knew how important my camera was to me. She knew how much it cost and how long I had saved up for it, because I'd told her in my bedroom when we were working on the project.

~

THE REST of the week passed quickly as I avoided Asha every chance I got. I even managed to get Mr. York to excuse me from my sixth-hour class to work on the yearbook so I didn't have to sit next to her or talk to her. I managed to get the remaining photos I needed with my old camera. I prayed I'd be able to hide in the shadows at Friday night's game since I still needed live shots during a game before I could mark football off my list.

~

FRIDAY NIGHT, Andy, Max, and Sofia met me at the field just in case I needed backup. As soon as the ball was kicked off, I snapped a few pictures and then retreated to the darkened corner of the field to hang out with them. They were passing around a flask full of vodka and chasing it with a blue slushy they'd picked up at the food stand. After the week I'd had, I tossed back several shots rather quickly and enjoyed the buzz I got. It was the first time all week I was able to relax. My tense muscles loosened, and everything felt easy instead of forced.

When the game wrapped up, we made our way to the parking lot. We hung around my car while the parking lot emptied, and then Andy pulled out a joint.

He grinned as he held it out in front of his face. "Who wants to get high?" he asked, putting it between his lips and lighting it.

The orange-red glow of the cherry lit up his face as he sucked in a drag. Coughing, he passed it to me. I took it and inhaled the smoke, holding it as long as I could before coughing it out and passing the joint. We took turns taking hits as we sent it around the circle. When it was gone, nobody was in any kind of hurry to leave. The four of us stayed by my car, listening to music, talking, and just fucking around.

"I'm hungry." Max rubbed his stomach for emphasis, wincing as it gave a loud grumble.

Andy laughed. "I could eat. You guys in?" He looked over at us.

Sofia shot me a quick look before clearing her throat. "Nah, could you just take me home, Liam?"

"Sure." I cocked my head at her, trying to get a read on what she was really saying. It was unlike her to turn down food with the guys.

Max and Andy lumbered off in search of food. As soon as Sofia and I were alone, the air around us changed—just like it usually did whenever we found ourselves alone and high.

Sofia was sitting on the hood of my car, and I climbed up next to her.

She bumped her shoulder with mine. "Are you okay?"

I turned my head slowly to her, confused. "Why wouldn't I be?"

She shrugged. "You've had a rough week. I just wanted to let you know you can talk to me."

I lay back, resting my upper body on the windshield. I gazed up at the dark sky and all the brightly lit stars. "It's been rough, but I'll be fine. I won't give them the satisfaction of breaking me."

Sofia leaned, mirroring my position. "You're too strong to be broken, especially by a group of rich assholes. They don't know how easy they have it, and for that reason alone, we'll always be stronger than them."

My head rolled so I could look at her. There was a darkness in her eyes. Her tongue came out, wetting her lips and making them glisten. Right then, something changed.

I'd spent the week with ugly words tumbling in my head. I wasn't some fucking piece of shit. I certainly wasn't a virgin. *So what if I gave in?* That was what would make me cool. It was what I was supposed to do.

Asha.

The thought of *her* sent anger coursing through my body. *Fuck her and her crew.*

I leaned in and closed the space between me and Sofia, pressing my lips to hers. *Fuck it all.* Sofia instantly kissed me back, her tongue pushing its way into my mouth. Her hands wrapped around my neck, and she pulled me until I rolled over and settled between her parted legs. My hand ran up her smooth leg, feeling the coolness of her bare skin under her skirt.

My lips fell from hers, trailing hot kisses down her neck to the exposed area of her chest then farther down her body. My hands pushed their way up her skirt until they found her panties. I hooked my fingers around them and yanked them down her legs. I worked her skirt up her legs until she was exposed to me. Under her clothing, I found her to be completely bare, and when I trailed my finger between her folds, I found her pink center glistening with need for me.

I moved my mouth to her heat and dragged my tongue against her clit. Her hips jumped upward, and a moan slipped past her lips. Her fingers laced into my hair, yanking my head closer. As my mouth worked her over, I slid my fingers inside her. Sofia's moans of pleasure filled my ears and made me rock hard. I didn't stop with my torture until her moans had quieted and her body went limp. When I pulled away and glanced up, it was to see Sofia in blissed out glory. Regret slammed into me harder than Lucas's fist had.

Fuck. What have I done?

No wonder she wouldn't let go of this idea of us being together. I always got fucked up and shattered any space I'd had managed to put between us.

Maybe Asha was right. Maybe I really just was a piece of shit loser.

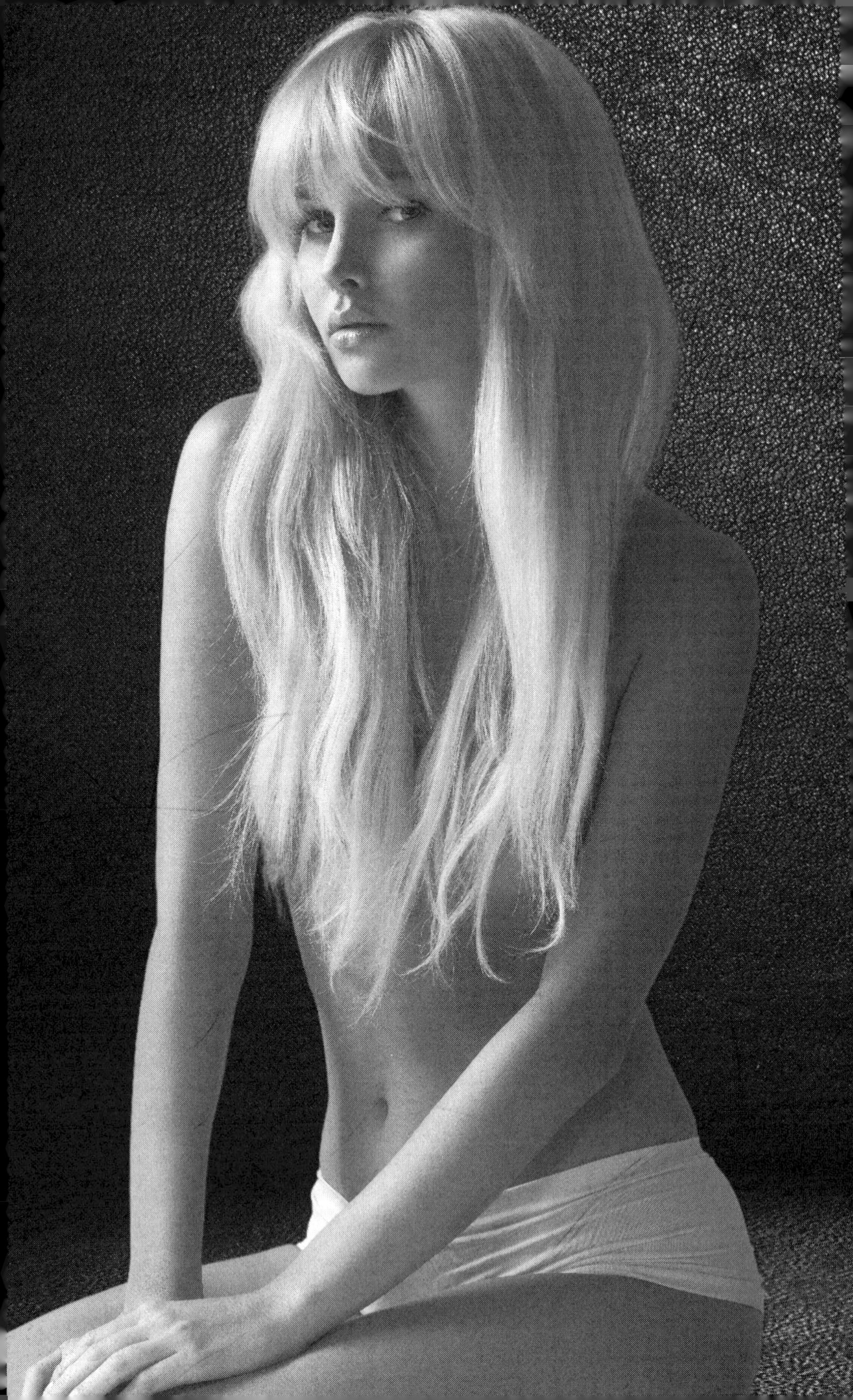

NINE
ASHA

My weeklong reprieve from Gio ended the Saturday after the game. When he stuck his head into my room, he tossed down a duffle bag and told me to get ready. I knew what I had to get ready for. I immediately went out on my balcony and smoked an entire joint for myself. In a daze, I got ready. I didn't even remember leaving the house or driving to the club. The next thing I knew, I was crawling across the stage, letting men pour shots down my throat.

I was long gone by the time my song ended, but somehow I still had control over my body. I was able to get up and exit the stage. Gio waited by the changing room with his arms crossed over his chest. I came to a stop as I peered up at him.

"How fucked up are you right now?" he asked, looking down at me.

I couldn't form words, so I shrugged.

My response made him smile. "Good. You're going to need it," he said, nodding toward a man standing in the darkened hallway which led to the private room.

A sigh escaped me as I shuffled down the hall. My legs were heavy, and my ankles wobbled as I moved in my killer heels. I was like Bambi taking his first steps. I swayed to the right and then to the left, grazing each side of the corridor as I went.

The guard opened the door for me, and I walked inside. The man followed me into the room wordlessly and landed a firm smack to my ass. The force nearly made me fall. I stumbled but managed to catch myself.

"Take off your clothes and lie on the bed," he ordered as he shut the door.

I removed my G-string and flopped back on the bed. The softness welcomed me, and I instantly wanted to melt into the mattress. The man sat in the chair by the foot of the bed, watching me as he removed his jacket and tie and then unbuttoned his shirt.

"Touch yourself," he barked, unfastening his pants.

With a sigh, I slid my hand down my stomach to the junction between my legs. I spread my folds for him to see as I dipped my finger inside. He pulled out his dick and slowly started pumping.

His teasing didn't last long before he stood. "Get on your knees," he ordered.

I did as I was told, and he guided his dick to my lips. This time, I'd effectively numbed everything inside of me. So, I felt no rage or hate as I took him into my mouth. His hands tangled in my hair, and he worked me back and forth along his length. The closer he got to release, the harder he yanked my hair. My eyes watered from the pain, and my lungs cried out from lack of enough oxygen. He jammed himself down my throat, blocking my air supply momentarily before pulling out and doing it again. Right before he came, he removed himself from my mouth. I jumped when his come shot out, landing on my face and chest.

"Thanks, whore," he said, turning his back to me while he righted his clothing. He grabbed his jacket and exited the room, leaving me alone.

I pushed myself to my feet and went to the bathroom to clean up the mess. It felt like I wasn't even in control of my actions anymore. Every move I made was purely robotic. Once my face and chest were clean, I went back to the bed and curled myself up in a ball as dizziness took over.

Sleep pulled at me, and I was eager to let it take me.

All week, I hadn't been able to get Liam off my mind. I knew I'd messed up with him. I was an awful human, and for that, I hated myself even more. The look on his face when his camera broke was frozen in my mind. My heart had jackknifed in my chest, and I immediately regretted what I'd done. He'd told me how long it took him to save for that camera. He was avoiding me now. I sniffled and squeezed my eyes tighter.

Gio knew where I was, and I knew it was only a matter of time before he sent someone else after me. If I was going to sleep and escape the hell I was in, I needed to do it fast. I reached under the mattress where I'd stashed some of Gio's magic pills earlier in the night and swallowed another down.

I woke later, but I was too out of it to put much together. All I got were flashes of a man moving behind me. I could hear his grunts and moans. I could feel him pushing his way inside of me, but the amount of drugs and alcohol in my system wouldn't allow me to do anything but drift back to sleep.

That happened several times during night. I'd wake and find myself in one position or another. I had no idea what had happened to me or how many men had been inside me while I was out, and to be honest, I preferred it that way. *If I didn't have the memory of it happening, was it even real?*

∼

I DIDN'T REMEMBER GOING HOME, but the next morning, I woke up in my bed. I was tired, sore, and sick, but I was home. The night was over. I'd survived another night with Gio at his club. That was all that mattered. Plenty of girls there never got to say that.

I slept off and on all day Sunday, not getting out of bed until nearly two in the afternoon. I took a long, hot shower. Then I had the maid bring food to my room to ease my upset stomach. After the shower, food, and some Tylenol, I almost felt human again and decided to text Liam to see if he wanted to pick back up on our assignment. It was worth a shot.

ME: Hey. It's Asha. Want to work on our paper?
LIAM: Fuck off.

I guessed he had every right to be pissed at me. I did break his camera and cause him to get his ass beaten.

God, what was wrong with me? Why would I do something like that?

Because I was a rotten, horrible person. I'd just agreed to be his friend, and what did I do? I took the trust I'd earned and made him regret ever giving it to me in the first place.

Truth be told, I was afraid of being his friend. I didn't have any real friends. Real friends meant real feelings. It meant giving someone power over me. And I had to protect myself at all costs. With nothing else to do, I took a couple sleeping pills and killed the rest of the day and night.

Monday rolled around, and I didn't know what to expect. For so long, Liam had been watching me around school. It was like he was waiting for the moment when the popular kid reached out to the loner so the two of them could join forces.

But ever since I broke his camera, he was different. He no longer watched me, waited for me. In fact, he refused to look at me at all. Instead of going to him, I decided to wait it out. He was a nice guy, so how long could the silent treatment really last?

I waited all week. He never looked my way and never talked to me. Even in the class we had together. The week before, he'd managed to get out of class, leaving me alone every day. This week, instead of working on our assignment, he sat at my side, writing his paper. I didn't talk to him, and he didn't talk to me.

The following week was the same, and shit was getting annoying. I thought I was stronger than him, but the fact he wouldn't look at me or talk to me was killing me. His indifference was even starting to make its way into my drug-induced sleep each night.

I had a recurring dream of sitting in class with him by my side. Nothing I said or did got his attention. In the dream, I climbed up on top of the table and yelled his name. Nothing. He didn't flinch or glance away from his paper. I took the paper from under his arm, but he just started at the table, like the paper was still there. I even stripped naked. He didn't budge.

The dreams only made things clearer. I had to apologize. But apologizing wasn't something I specialized in. I didn't know how to go about it. I had no idea how to make him forgive me. And on top of it all, I definitely didn't want my friends or anyone else at school to know I'd uttered those words. I was supposed to be a hard ass, not some girl who came crying and apologizing.

What would make Liam forgive me without actually saying the words?

I had it. At least, an idea anyway.

Liam was a nice guy, and even I knew he didn't deserve the shit he got around school. Maybe if I could get my friends to welcome him to the group it would fix things. He wouldn't have to deal with being bullied anymore, and he'd be so thankful he'd forgive me. It was worth a shot.

The bell for lunch rang, and I followed my group to our usual table. Chatter started, and I zoned out, focusing on Liam and the way he talked and laughed with his friends as he sat across the quad from me. He used to look in my direction, but now he was like a stone, refusing to let his eyes move my way.

"I have a problem," I stated, getting the attention of everyone sitting around me.

"What?" Tiff asked as she picked at her fries.

"I pissed Liam off by breaking his camera, and now he refuses to talk to me. Getting this project done requires that we talk."

She shrugged. "Just flunk it, and buy your way out like we always do," she suggested.

I blew a piece of fallen hair from my face. "I can't. If my stepdad has to bail me out one more time, I'm afraid he'll ship me off to some prep school across the world or something. I have to make Liam forgive me, and I need all your help."

They all gave me a questioning look.

"OK so I was trying to think of a way to get him to forgive me, and I think I figured it out. He has a hard time here at school, right? He's always getting picked on and bullied. So I thought if maybe we brought him into our circle, things would be better for him. Then he'd be so thankful he'd let this little fight go and forgive me. That way I can get this assignment done, not be shipped off, and we can kick him out as soon as I get an A on my paper. What do you guys think?" I rushed on with the last part.

Lucas thought it over as everyone watched him. All I really needed was his approval. Everyone else would fall in line.

"Yeah, OK," he agreed.

"Really?" I asked, not expecting it to be so simple.

He nodded with a smile in place. "Yeah, I mean it'll suck having to wait a few weeks before we can fuck with him. But it'll be even more fun when he thinks we're his friends and then suddenly turn on him." Lucas laughed. "Actually, I'm kind of disappointed we didn't think to do this sooner."

I forced a smile while everyone else joked about it. The rest of the lunch hour was spent with everyone chattering about how much fun it would be to lure Liam in only to fuck him over later. I ignored all of them. I wasn't sure that was how I wanted things to end with us. Liam was a nice guy. But I figured I could always convince my group to not to go through turning on him later. All that mattered at the moment was they were going let him in our circle and he'd talk to me again.

When sixth hour rolled around, we all went to class. I took my seat and waited for Liam. He was one of the last people to walk in. Silently, he sat beside me and got to work. I took a deep breath to prepare myself.

"How long is this silent treatment going to go on?" I asked softly.

He only shrugged and didn't bother turning my way.

"Liam, I'm sorry for being a bitch, OK?" I whispered the words, not wanting anyone else to overhear, but it was enough to get him to look at me.

He lifted one brow. "Did you just apologize for busting my camera and causing me to get my ass kicked?"

I rolled my eyes. "You got punched once. That's far from getting your ass beat," I pointed out.

"No, you don't get to downplay it. I got shoved, punched in the face, knocked on my ass, and kicked in the ribs. I got my ass beat, and for what? Because you were too afraid to go against your friend when *she* decided to be a bitch? I mean, what happened to the friendship we'd agreed to?"

I took a deep breath. "I don't do friendships, Liam. You of all people should know that. I have a group I hang with. None of them are my friends and none of them consider me their friend. At least, that's how I see it."

He shook his head, irritated with me.

"Look, we don't have to be friends to get this assignment done, right? And you need this grade just as much as I do, remember? You really want to let this fight get you kicked out of school?"

He appeared deep in thought for a moment. He gritted his teeth, and his angular jaw flexed. "Fine, we'll work on the assignment and get it out of the way, but I'm not going to be happy about it, and I won't make the mistake of trusting you again. Deal?"

I gave him a shaky smile. "Deal." I grabbed my notebook and pencil, ready to get some work done.

For the rest of the hour, we did nothing but work. He asked me questions and wrote down my answers, and I did the same to him. When the bell rang, everyone stood and started gathering their things to go to their next class.

"Liam?" I asked.

"Hmm?" he mumbled, still saying as little as possible but at least he was talking.

"Do you want to get together tonight to get some more of this work done?"

He shrugged. "I'll text you and let you know if I'm free or not." He got up and strode out without another word.

I went to my next class slowly and found myself hoping he'd get ahold of me.

I wanted to get him alone again. I didn't know why, but when Liam and I were alone, it felt different. I felt like a different person. I wasn't the queen bee hanging with the loser. We were just Asha and Liam.

There were no prying eyes. No judgements. Nothing but the two of us. He had a way of quieting the negative voice in my head, and I craved the peace. Plus, if we managed to get together, I planned to invite him into the group. I didn't understand all the reasons why I wanted him there, I only knew that I did. I wanted more time with him.

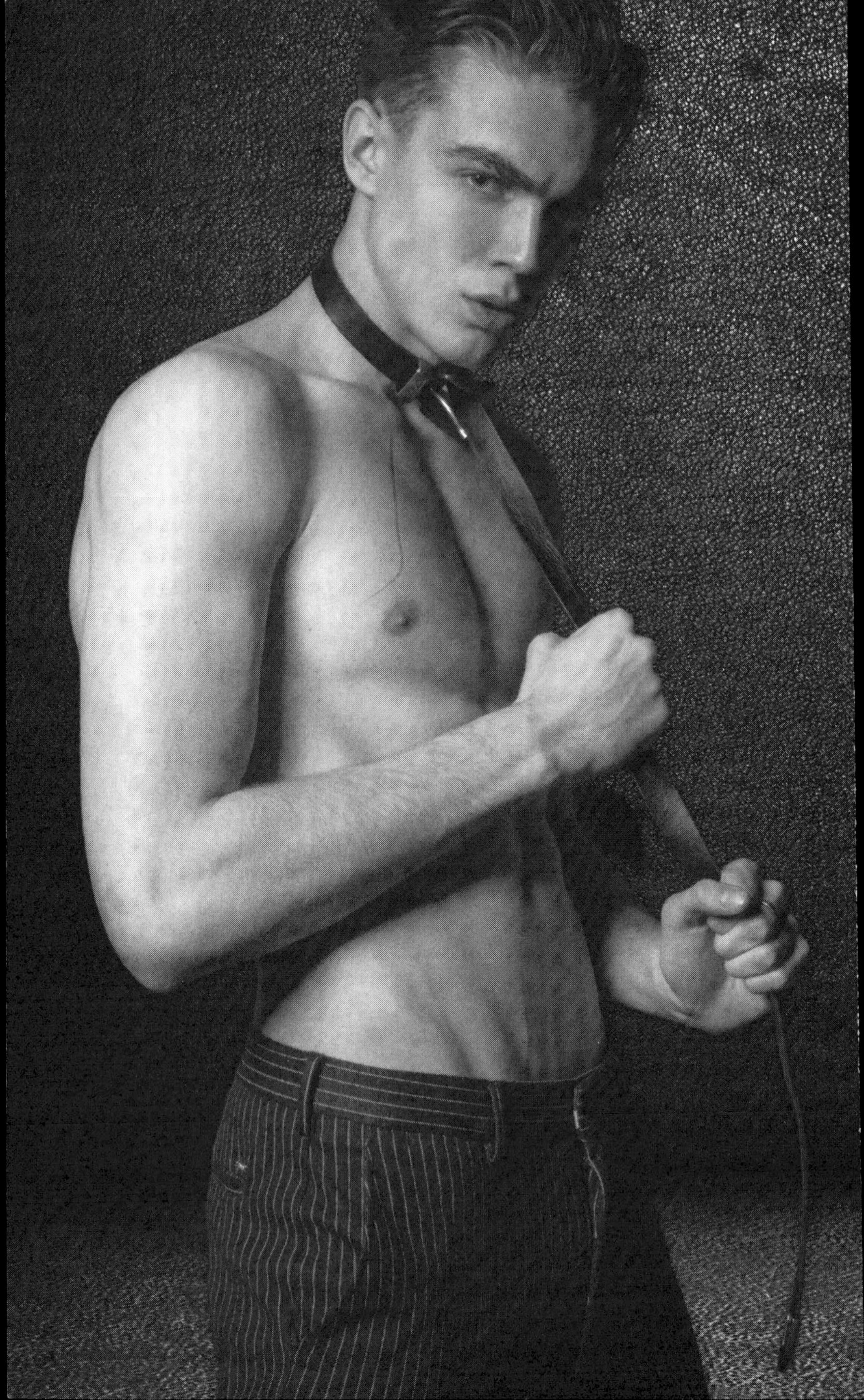

TEN
LIAM

When I left the class I had with Asha, I moved in the direction of my locker to exchange my books for my next class. I was all up in my head, unsure how I felt or how I *should* feel regarding Asha.

I was pissed beyond belief, but she also made it hard to stay mad at her. *Why was I considering letting it all go after sitting next to her for one hour?*

I paused when I rounded the corner and found Sofia leaning against my locker. She'd left before class ended to run an errand for our teacher. I ground my teeth and pushed forward. When she saw me heading her way, a big smile spread across her face as she shifted to allow me access to my locker.

"What's up, Sofia?" I asked, paying more attention to my lock as I spun in the combination.

Out of the corner of my eye, I saw her shrug.

"I was just wondering if you wanted to hang out after school today. We haven't hung out much since...you know, the game." Her voice was quiet, and I knew it was because I filled her with uncertainty.

I'd almost had her convinced there wasn't anything between us. But all that was blown to shit the moment I sucked her clit into my mouth. *What the fuck was wrong with me?*

"I don't think so. I've got too much shit going on," I said as I tossed books into my locker. "I gotta try fixing my fucking camera. Plus I still have a lot of work to do with Asha. And my dad is on my ass to mow the lawn again. My life just fucking sucks right now."

"Oh," was all she said with a slight tip of her head.

I could hear the hurt in her voice, and I knew I was the one who put it there. Unable to bear seeing the pain in her eyes, I kept my head down as I dug out my next hour books.

"Sofia, I know you're probably confused. I mean, I say I don't want anything to happen between us, but then I go and fuck it up." A heavy sigh left my lips as I shook my head clear. "For your own good, don't let me touch you again, OK? We're *just* friends. That's all we'll ever be. Save yourself the heartache." I slammed my locker shut and turned in the opposite direction, not wanting to see whatever expression she wore on her face.

The rest of the day dragged by. I felt every minute, every second, that ticked by. I couldn't focus on my teachers or the lessons they were trying to teach. Worry over hurting Sofia competed with thoughts of Asha for space in my head. I hated Asha, and yet, I didn't hate her nearly as much as I wanted to. I didn't know what it was about her I couldn't resist.

Why was she different than every other girl I'd ever met? Sure, she was hot, but she made my life hell time and time again. Even after she busted the camera I'd spent years saving for, all I wanted to do was throw her down and bury myself so deeply inside her that she wouldn't be able to walk right for a week.

I hated her, but I wanted her. I had no idea what that said about me.

When school finally ended, I made a mad dash for my car, not wanting to run into Asha, Sofia, or anyone else. I had to get out of there. I needed time to think and space to breathe clearly. I drove straight home and went directly to my room to try and piece my camera back together. It had been lying on my desk, busted for weeks. I'd been too angry to even try and fuck with it. Every time I'd caught a glimpse of it out of the corner of my eye, it just made the rage double, made the acid in my stomach bubble.

Now, I took a seat at my desk and tried to fit the pieces back together. A few of them clicked into place, but others were completely shattered and needed to be replaced. I fucked around with the stupid ass thing for an hour before my anger got the best of me, and I sent it flying toward the wall. It hit hard, broke into even more pieces, and fell to the floor.

I stood from my chair and took the stairs two at a time. In the kitchen, I yanked open the door to the fridge. I needed something, but I didn't know what. As I was examining the selection in the fridge, my phone vibrated in my pocket. I slammed the fridge shut and pulled the phone from my pocket.

ASHA: Want to come over?

I let out a long breath. Being close to her, seeing her, was the last fucking thing I wanted to do. But she was right. I needed more details for my paper, and the only way I was going to get them was by keeping my head down and getting to work, even if it killed me.

ME: Fine.

I grabbed a soda out of the fridge to take with me and gathered my things before heading to the car. I'd just climbed behind the wheel when my phone chimed again. I started the car and looked at the screen.

ASHA: Meet me at the end of the block. Don't pull into the drive.

I rolled my eyes. *What the fuck? She wanted me to come over, but she didn't want anyone to know I was there?* Typical Asha. Use anyone she could to get what she wanted, but she didn't want anyone to know she was hanging out with the loser. My thoughts only made my bad mood worse.

I dropped my cell onto the passenger seat without replying and shifted into drive. I made the drive over to Asha's and parked at the end of the block like she'd asked. I snatched up my bag and climbed out of the car. I rounded the vehicle and stepped up onto the sidewalk. Asha slipped out from a row of trees, lining the edge of her property.

My brows pulled together in confusion. "What are you doing?"

"Shh, follow me," she said, stepping back through the branches.

Shaking my head, I muttered under my breath and did as she asked. The far side of the brick wall which surrounded her house ran through the tree line. She led me over to a tree at the edge and started climbing it.

"Seriously, what the fuck are you doing?"

"My stepdad is home," she said, not bothering to glance down at me as she climbed the branches. "If he sees you, I'll be in major trouble. He's...protective. I figured I'd bring you back to my little, secret spot." She moved from the tree branch to the top of the brick wall. "Come on. It's safe. I've been doing this for years."

With a sigh and a roll of my eyes, I started climbing the tree until I could make my way onto the brick wall. The wall was only about six foot high, so jumping down wasn't bad.

"How do we get back over?" I asked as she led me farther onto the property.

"There's another tree down there on this side." She crossed her arms over her chest and kept her head down as she led the way. It felt like we walked for miles, but my watch said we'd only gone half a mile. I guessed the bouts of silence and awkward conversation between us made the time drag. Eventually, though, the trees gave way. In the center of them, an old, brick two-story house sat perfectly untouched.

The house had seen better days. I could envision how it must have looked when it was new. But time was cruel, and the weather was relentless. The shingles were missing on parts of the roof. A few shutters had fallen off the ground floor windows. The landscaping that had once lined the front of the house was all dead and dried up.

Asha paused, allowing me to peer up at the building she called her secret hideout. "So, what do you think?"

I shrugged, not wanting to appear like I was enjoying my time with her. "It's a house," I mumbled.

She frowned as she spun away and headed for the front door. She picked up an old flowerpot and snatched up a key to unlock the door. The knob turned easily, and the door opened inward. She stepped inside the dark house, which was lit only by the light shining through the open windows.

I followed her in and closed the door behind us. The foyer of the house was grander than the one in my home. It made my stomach tighten when I thought about how this was the house for staff members. If the house for the staff was this grand, I longed to see the beauty of the main house. My gaze darted about taking in everything. The railing on the staircase was dusty, but the wood was dark in color and still managed to have a shine to it. The staircase curved along the right wall. A modest-sized chandelier hung in the center.

Asha dipped into the room on the left. I followed and found her bending down in front of a fireplace, lighting a fire. There was a couch in front of it, covered with a dusty, white sheet. Asha got the fire going and jerked back the sheet, giving us a place to sit down. She motioned for me to join her.

I pushed myself forward. My backpack slid down my arm as I sat, dropping onto the floor at my feet. For several moments, I watched the flames dance, wanting to keep my attention off Asha in any way I could.

From the little I had peeked at her, she seemed different than she had at school earlier. Her face was wiped clean of makeup, making her blue eyes appear bigger and more innocent. Her blonde hair wasn't curled to perfection like it always was. Instead, it was piled into a messy bun on top of her head with tendrils sweeping down on either side of her face. Her black clothing was gone and had been replaced by a simple pair of skinny jeans and a hooded sweatshirt. Even dressed down, she was the most beautiful girl I'd ever seen.

My body tingled with the need to reach out and touch her, but it only made the hate in my gut bubble out of control. Fuck, I hated her, but not nearly as much as I hated myself for wanting her. The thought was on repeat in my head.

"Look, I really am sorry, Liam," she said, causing my gaze to dash from the fire over to her.

Her blue eyes seemed to tear up, and my hand itched to cup her cheek. I longed to tell her everything would be OK and she didn't need to cry. I managed to hold back, though. I was tired of showing her kindness when all she showed me was malice.

"I hate that I'm such a bitch sometimes. It's just my go-to, you know?"

I didn't move or speak. I felt if I did, it would be like giving her permission to act that way.

"To show you how sorry I am, I got you a present." She reached to the side of the couch and plucked up a box. It was wrapped in plain white paper with a white bow which glistened and sparkled when the sun hit it.

She held it out, her smile wobbling like she was nervous.

I shook my head. "I don't need presents, Asha."

She rolled her eyes and scoffed. "You don't want to open it? Fine. I'll open it." She placed the box on her lap, slipped off the bow, and then tore off the paper. Beneath the wrapping was a box containing a new camera. A damn good camera—better than the one I'd saved up for. I couldn't even imagine how much it must have cost.

The corners of my mouth turned up slightly as excitement pumped through me, but I quickly righted my face when I realized I couldn't accept it. "I can't accept that, Asha."

Her mouth dropped open. "What? Why?"

"Because you can't just buy your way out of this. Money means nothing to you, which means this apology means nothing to you. Whenever you have a problem, you throw money at it. That's not how the world works."

She took a deep breath. "My apology was real, Liam. The camera isn't part of it. The camera is because I broke yours, and replacing it is the right thing to do. You break it, you buy kind of thing." She offered the box again.

I couldn't stop myself from surveying the package, and my hands wanted to reach for it.

"Ugh, just take the damn thing already. I know you want to." She pushed it into my hands and let go of it, so I had no choice but to catch it or let it fall.

It would serve her right after she broke mine if it hit the floor, but it would've done no good. Money meant nothing to her.

I leaned back and studied the box, reading over all the camera's updated features. Asha watched like a proud parent on Christmas morning.

"It's too much," I thought out loud.

"It's nothing, Liam. Would you feel better if I told you I didn't pay full price for it?" She lifted one eyebrow.

I cocked my head to the side. "God, you didn't steal it, did you?" I set the box on the floor and stood, pacing.

She giggled softly. "No." She rolled her eyes and shook her head. "It was on sale. Just, please, accept my gift."

"You don't *owe* me anything, Asha," I told her, marching back and forth.

She sat watching me. "I kind of do. I broke yours."

I dipped down, grabbing my backpack as I spun for the door.

"Where are you going?" she asked, following me with her eyes.

"I'm leaving."

She jumped from the couch and dashed in front of me, blocking my way. "Why are you leaving?"

I dragged my fingers through my hair and let out a long breath. "Because," I breathed out. "This whole thing is...weird. You're giving me shit and apologizing. I don't know what's happening. Are you having a stroke or something?"

She leaned back against the door, preventing me from exiting. "God, why do you make it so hard to be nice to you?"

I shrugged. "I'm a firm believer in people don't change. So whatever *this* is, is just another game to you."

Her eyes stretched wide as she shook her head. "I know my word doesn't mean anything to you. And at this point, I don't blame you for not believing me. But I swear, Liam, I *am* sorry. I bought you the camera to replace the one I destroyed. If you don't believe me, just wait and see. Let my actions show you what my words can't."

I ground my teeth together and shook my head once, already annoyed with what I was about to say. "Fine, but the first time you fuck me over, I'm out. And next time, I will be getting even."

"Deal," she said around a bright smile. "Can we get to work now?"

With a sigh, I nodded and turned back for the couch.

We took our seats and pulled out our notebooks to take notes.

"Other than taking photos, what else do you do in your spare time?" she asked, peeking up at me from beneath her lashes.

I shrugged. "Play video games, hang out with friends, the usual I guess."

She nodded as she scribbled down my response. "How do you want to spend your life? What do you want to do after college?"

"I'd love it if I could make a living with my photography, but I know I won't make much money as far as art goes. So maybe I'll have my own studio. Or it would be really cool if I could get a job with a magazine where I could travel and take pictures of rarely seen places."

"That would be cool," she said as she jotted my answer.

When she was done writing, she lifted her head and our gazes locked. It felt as if something was being exchanged. There was a connection between us that wasn't there moments before.

"What are you most afraid of, Asha?" The soft question tumbled out of my mouth before I could stop it.

She bit her bottom lip as she thought it over. "I'm afraid of water, like deep water. It scares me so much I won't even go swimming."

A crooked smile formed on its own. "So what, while everyone is swimming at the beach you just sit on the sand, looking pretty?"

The corners of her mouth tilted upward, and her cheeks turned a light shade of pink. "You think I'm pretty?" she asked softly. It was almost like she was amazed I'd think that.

I scoffed. "I think you're beautiful, Asha. But you're kind of a bitch and need to do something about that." My smirk stretched across my face.

She threw her head back and laughed. "I'll work on it," she agreed.

We asked each other questions back and forth until the sun started to fall from the sky. The room grew dark, only lit by the small fire left in the fireplace. Since it was too dark to see to write, we called it a night and started putting our things away.

"Hey, you want to hang out with me and my crew sometime?"

I dropped my notebook into my bag and froze as I gaped at her. "You want *me* to hang out with your friends?" I wanted to make sure I'd heard her right.

She nodded her head, causing her messy bun to bounce with the action as she twisted her fingers together.

"How would that work? Your friends hate me."

"I already talked to them. They're down with the idea."

"But they *hate* me," I pointed out again.

She rolled her eyes. "They don't hate you. They just liked giving you shit. You made it really easy." She winked.

"So what? They want me to hang out with them to make it *easier* for them to give me shit?"

She laughed. "No. I just told them how cool you actually are now that I'm getting to know you and how I thought you'd make a great addition to the group."

I shook my head as I zipped up my bag, thinking it over. I knew it had to be another trick. After all the shit they'd given me, there was no way they wanted to be my friend.

But being in their inner circle would help me to gather some dirt on them for when they fucked me over. And I could get the proof I needed that Lucas was cheating on Asha behind her back too. Then when the time came and they fucked me over, I'd have all the ammo I needed.

"Seriously, it'll be fun. Come on." Asha batted her long, dark lashes at me and offered up a flirty smile.

"All right," I finally agreed, not having high hopes for a happy ending.

She squealed and clapped her hands together in excitement. Then the two of us left the house and started our stroll back to the brick wall circling her property. On the way out, we talked about how joining her crew would work. She promised I'd sit with them at lunch, walk the halls with them, basically rule the school. And most importantly, I wouldn't be harassed by them daily.

"But first we need to go shopping. How about tomorrow?"

"Why?"

"To get you some new clothes, silly."

"I don't understand why I need to go shopping. I don't have the money for a whole new wardrobe."

She scoffed and rolled her eyes. "You can't rule the school wearing discount jeans and store brand sneakers, Liam. And it's on me. No worries."

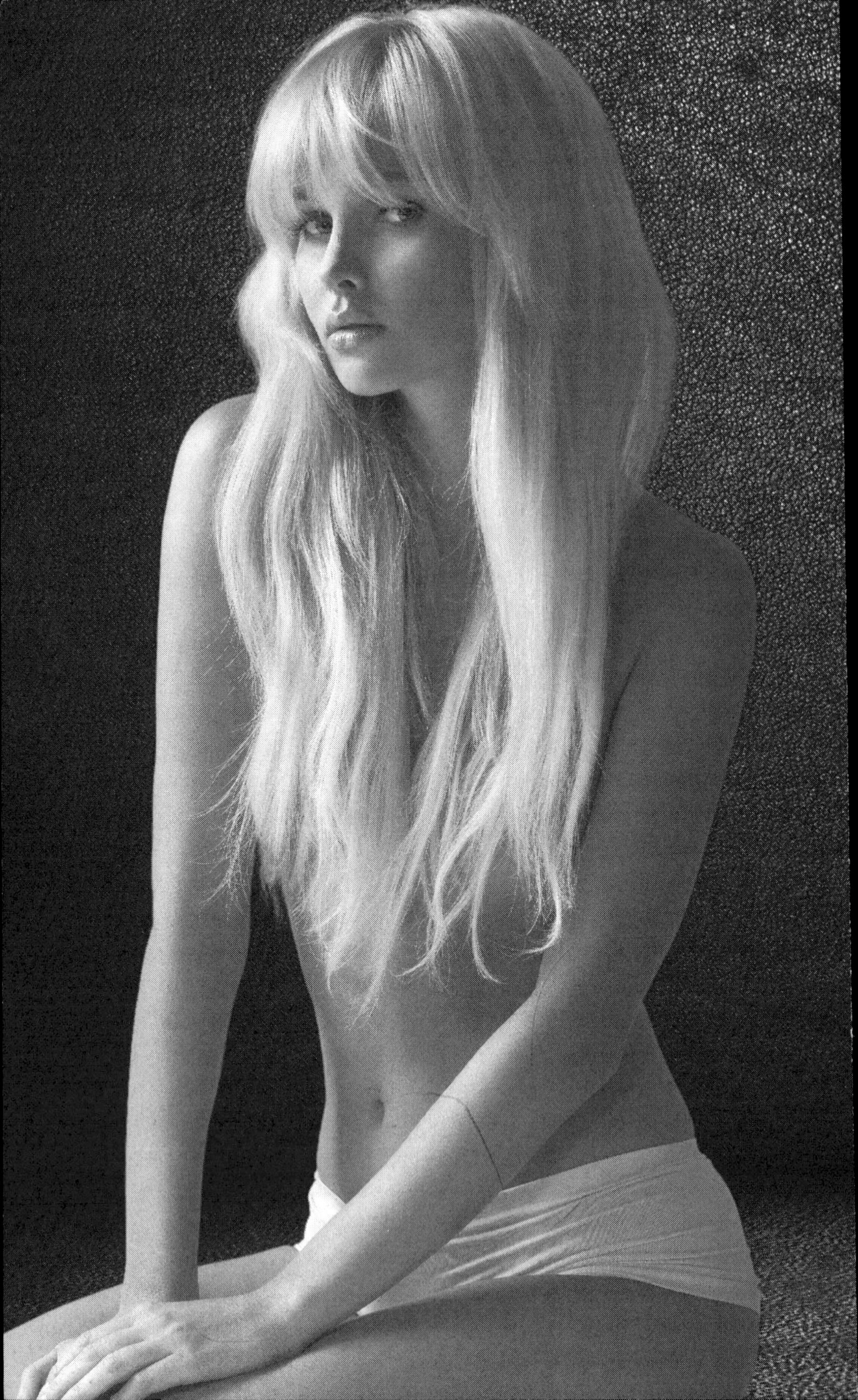

ELEVEN
ASHA

I pulled up outside of Liam's house at ten on the dot. I honked the horn twice. Moments later, he ambled out, rubbing his eyes. Even tired he looked better than anyone should be allowed to. His dark hair was messy but sexy. His green eyes were lit by the sun, and it made them sparkle. As he reached for the door handle, his jaw flexed, and it made my stomach tighten.

Ugh, why was he so sexy?

The door opened, and he slid into the passenger seat. "It's a little early to be out of the house on a Saturday," he said with his brows drawn together like he was annoyed.

"What are you saying? I'm not good enough to wake up early for?" I gave him a teasing smile.

He let out a soft laugh and rolled his eyes. "Back to the dramatics, huh?"

I shrugged one shoulder. "It comes naturally."

"Are we going to go, or are we just going to sit in my driveway all day?"

"Actually, I was thinking you could drive."

"Oh, all right. I'll have to run in and get my keys." He reached for the handle.

"No, I meant, you could drive my car."

His eyes doubled in size. "You want me to drive this? A BMW? An i8?"

I wanted to laugh, but I held it back. "It's just a car, Liam. I promise there's no seat eject button."

His smile widened. "It'd be pretty cool if it did though."

The two of us switched places, and I watched the expressions change on his face as he took it all in.

"Money can't buy you happiness, but I think it'd be a lot easier to be happy from behind the wheel of an i8," he said as he drove us through town.

It was really not. When life was bad enough, no amount of money, no fancy sports car, or designer clothes could make a person happier. I knew from experience. I tried buying my way into happiness. It never worked. I'd even considered paying a hitman to take Gio out. It would've been one form of buying happiness. Problem was all the hitmen I knew worked for him, and they didn't want to roll over on the guy who paid the bills.

Snapping back to the present, I pushed the negative thoughts away and instead focused on how happy Liam looked as he sped through town. We made it to the mall in record time. He stomped on the brake and threw it into park, then looked over at me with a smug grin.

"Anyone ever tell you that you're not in the Indie 500?"

He chuckled. "No, but I've never driven a car this nice before. It's probably for the best that I'm poor. If I could afford a car like this, I'd be dead already."

I laughed and shook my head. "Let's go Mario Andretti." I opened my door and climbed out.

As I rounded the car, Liam removed himself from the seat and hit the lock button on the key fob. As we walked toward the entrance, he gave the car a longing look.

I laughed. "You only like me for my car, don't you?"

He chuckled. "Who said I liked you at all?"

I held up my middle finger, but a smile spread across my face.

Once we entered the mall, I led him from store to store. I managed to buy him a pair of new shoes, a black leather jacket, and a bottle of cologne without argument. It wasn't until I suggested a watch that he started to fight.

"I don't know, Asha. I think it's too much. All of this is too much," he said as he peered down at the new Apple Watch on his wrist.

"It's not. You said it yourself. Money means nothing to me. Just let me buy the damn watch, Liam."

He shook his head. "Did you see the price tag on this thing?"

I laughed and rolled my eyes. "Of course, it's not going to be $29.99, Liam. It looks good on you. Get it," I urged. "You can get texts and calls right to your watch. It's so much easier."

He removed the watch and handed it back to the salesmen. "So, should I wrap it up?"

"No," Liam said.

"Yes," I told the man. I grabbed Liam's arm and led him over to the register.

"Asha, I don't need all of this."

"Liam, you don't realize how much money gets stuffed into my account each month. I could buy you a hundred Apple watches, and I'd still have more than you've ever seen. It's nothing. Stop fighting. You're taking all the fun out of this."

He sighed and shook his head, relenting. "Fine. But we're going to dinner, and I'm buying," he insisted.

"Deal," I agreed.

I swiped my card and paid for the watch. The man handed over the bag, and I dragged Liam out by his elbow, heading for the next store. Liam turned into my own personal Ken doll. I dressed him in outfit after outfit. In the end, he gave up fighting me and just let me do what I wanted. He ended up with ten new pairs of designer jeans, twelve shirts, and a new belt to match his coat.

He tried most of it on, but tired long before I did. By the end, he just let me throw things into the basket that I thought would look good on him.

"You know, if I have to hang with *your* friends, you have to hang with mine sometimes too."

My nose wrinkled. "That wasn't part of the deal."

He rolled his eyes. "Why don't you get some things for yourself? You know, clothes that don't have some dude's name splashed all over them. I know the perfect place." He grabbed my arm and hauled me through the mall until he came to an abrupt stop in front of TJ Maxx.

"Here?" I asked, pointing up at the sign hanging in the storefront.

He nodded, a big smile in place. "Yep. This is where us *poor* people shop," he said around a laugh before grabbing my arm and pulling me into the store. He led me through racks and racks of clothes, grabbing things he liked and throwing them over his arm while his free hand dug through more racks.

"This place is a wreck. How does anyone even find anything in here? Not once have we even been approached by a worker. Why can't I give them my size and let them find things for me?"

He laughed. "This isn't that kind of store." He shoved a pile of clothes to my chest. "Here, try these on. And don't forget to come out and model them for me." He wagged his brows, and my cheeks burned.

I wanted nothing to do with those clothes, but for some reason, I wanted to model the clothes for him. I wanted his eyes on me.

I took the items into the dressing room and tried them on, making sure I came out to show him each thing he'd picked out. Each time I strutted out, I'd spin in a circle and let him see me from all angles. Every smile on his lips made my stomach tighten. Every smirk had my blood boiling.

When I sashayed out in a two-piece bikini and he said, "Fuuu-uck," I almost dropped to my knees to suck him off right there in the middle of the store. And *that* was the sort of thing I'd never given away freely.

I paid for the things he'd chosen for me. As we walked out, I said, "Why did I get a bikini. You know I'm never going to use it."

He shrugged. "I didn't say you had to swim. But anything you look that hot in, needs to be in your closet. Time for dinner." He grabbed my hand and led me back to the car.

A little while later, I was pleasantly surprised when he pulled into a parking lot at a local Chinese restaurant. I looked forward to spending more time with him, in the quiet of a restaurant where we'd be in close proximity.

The two of us were seated in a private corner where we both ordered soup and our dinners. He sipped at his Coke, and I stirred up my sweet tea as I tried to think of something to talk about.

Finally, I spoke up. "Are you nervous about hanging out with my crew on Monday?"

He shrugged. "Not nervous, but I'm not exactly looking forward to it either," he said, leaning back and getting comfy in the booth.

"Why not?"

He bit his bottom lip. "I'm kind of worried about what my real friends will think, you know? I just don't want them to think I'm trading them in or anything."

I nodded. "What do you think Sofia is going to have to say about it? She really seems to like you. Do you like her?"

He shook his head, and his dark hair fell into his eyes. "I like Sofia as a friend. But the lines have been blurred between us. I've fucked up too many times with her. I don't want to hurt her, but it's all I seem to do."

I shrugged one shoulder. "You're a great guy, Liam. I can't blame her for having a crush on you."

His eyes moved up and locked on mine. He wet his lips, and it looked like he was going to say something, but his words were cut off when our waiter appeared and placed our food on the table before us. The moment was lost, but my body tingled with excitement that the feeling was there to begin with.

With the food to distract us, conversation moved to something easier. We talked, laughed, and teased one another as we ate. When we finished, he paid the check, and the two of us loaded back up in my car. He drove at a much slower pace on the way back to his house. A part of me wondered if he was wanting to spend as much time with me as possible. We'd been together all day, but even that wasn't long enough for me. Without the pressures of school or friends, I got to see a whole new side of Liam. He was cute, funny, sweet, and an all-around good person. I wished I could be more like him. I wished a guy like him would rescue me and take me away from the life I was forced to live. I even wished a guy like him could love me, see me as more than just trash to be used and tossed to the side. But I knew what I was. And because of that, I wasn't holding my breath for a happily ever after.

By the time I walked in the front door of my house, I was on cloud nine. I hadn't been happy in a long time. A day with Liam had me almost ecstatic. That was until I tried to go up the stairs and heard my name being called from deep within Gio's office.

I froze when he bellowed my name. I quickly looked around and listened hard, but I heard no signs of my mom being home. Her car hadn't been in the garage either, but I'd been too happy to notice much else. I was lost in thoughts of Liam as I walked in a daze to the house.

With a deep breath, I turned and moved to the open doorway of Gio's office. He sat behind his desk. Another man I didn't recognize was across from him.

"Come in and shut the door," Gio ordered as he lit a cigar, heavy smoke circling around him like the devil himself.

"I...I didn't realize you were home early. Where's Mom?" I asked, trying to play the innocent card. But really, I knew what the meeting was about. The last time I'd seen Gio, I'd been blown out of my mind. I couldn't even remember the night. I didn't know how I'd gotten home. I guessed it had to have been him who brought me home and put me to bed.

"Your mother is gone for the evening. We have some business to discuss," Gio said, puffing out a cloud of thick, gray smoke. He stood up and strode up to me slowly, his shoes scraping off the floor with each step. "You broke the rules, didn't you?"

"Wh-what rules?' I stammered as nerves got to me.

"What rules?" he laughed out.

Faster than I could process, he swung his hand up and smacked me across the face. The sound echoed throughout the room.

Tears burned my eyes as I cradled my cheek, hoping to ease the tingling burn.

"You were so goddamn fucked out of your skull the other night you couldn't even stay awake to do your job. Want to know how many men had their way with you?" He cocked a smirk.

I didn't want to know. I prayed he wouldn't tell me, but he knew the number would make me sick in the worst way. It was another form of torture.

"Four," he told me. "They fucked you while you were blitzed out of your fucking head."

My stomach knotted with the threat of vomit.

Gio pointed his finger in my face. "You will *not* let yourself get out of hand in that way again, you hear me?"

I nodded, but it did no good.

"You work for *me*." He pointed at his chest. "You don't even want to know how much money I lost because you couldn't stay conscious enough to choke on a fucking dick. I sold you for half price just to make up for it." He shrugged. "But now, it's time for me to make my money back." He turned to the man who was sitting in front of his desk. "Leonard?"

The man stood and approached me as Gio retreated back to his leather chair. Gio took a seat as the man grabbed me by the back of my neck. It felt like my neck was caught in a vice as the man squeezed and dragged me over to the desk with him. Quickly, he slammed my head down on the wooden surface. Pain shot through my skull. His hands were rough and fast as he ripped my leggings down my legs.

I retreated into my head, disappearing from the moment. *Liam's smiling face. His laughter. The way butterflies made my insides tickle.*

It's OK, Asha. Breathe. Just keep breathing. This is nothing. You'll see Liam tomorrow. You'll smile. This doesn't mean a damn thing. It's not real. It's not real. It's NOT REAL.

I was thrown to the floor, snapping me out of my thoughts. My legs were numb from being bent over the desk for so long. I could no longer support my weight. But when I hit, I immediately got up and ran from the room, trying to yank my ruined leggings up as I went.

I dashed up the stairs and to my bedroom where I slammed and locked the door. Tears flooded my eyes and ran down my overheated cheeks. I was breathless as I stumbled to the shower. With trembling fingers, I turned the hot water on full blast. It scalded as it cascaded over my tired, sore, broken, and abused body. The water burned between my legs where my flesh felt ripped and torn. I sank to the shower floor and cried until I made myself sick.

As the water ran cold, I crawled out of the tub, across the floor, and over to the toilet where I emptied everything inside. When there was nothing left, I shut the lid and flushed it away. I pushed my back against the wall and held my shaking body as more tears streaked down my cheeks. My gaze landed on the vanity. I knew what I needed.

I opened the drawer and brought out the razor. I pressed it against my flesh and dragged it across, slashing the skin. A tiny line. Blood made its way to the surface. It ran down my arm and dripped onto the floor. The surge I was so addicted to pumped through my body. I was finally able to breathe. My whole life was painful to the point it felt like I was barely breathing most days. But when I cut myself, it was like someone was puffing a breath of fresh air into my lungs. I inhaled deeply and then exhaled with a sigh.

Eventually, the pleasure of the pain wore off, like it always did, and I found myself in bed, hiding away from the world. My pillow was wet with tears, and I wondered how I had any water left in my system to cry. I didn't know what else to do. I'd had such a good day with Liam. I'd almost felt normal until I walked back into this house. Liam was the only person who could take it all away. So, I picked up the phone and called him.

"Hello?" he answered with a yawn.

"Hey," I said quietly into the phone.

"Asha? What's wrong? You sound upset." He immediately perked up, concern laced in his voice.

"I got into a fight with my stepdad. It was a bad one," I said, not wanting to give away too many details. I never wanted Liam to find out about what I did, what my life really was like. I knew if he did, he'd never be able to look at me the same.

"That sucks. What was the fight about?"

"I don't really want to talk about it."

"Then why'd you call?"

I shrugged, even though he couldn't see me. "You made me happy today. You took all the bad shit away without even realizing it. I guess I was hoping just talking to you would do the same thing now."

There was a long pause. "Do you have a TV in your room?"

"Yeah," I said, sniffling and confused.

"Turn on Netflix."

"What?"

"Turn on Netflix."

I sighed but did as he asked. "OK."

"Now, pick your favorite movie, and we'll watch it together, drown out the rest of the world."

I smiled, and just like that, everything else was gone.

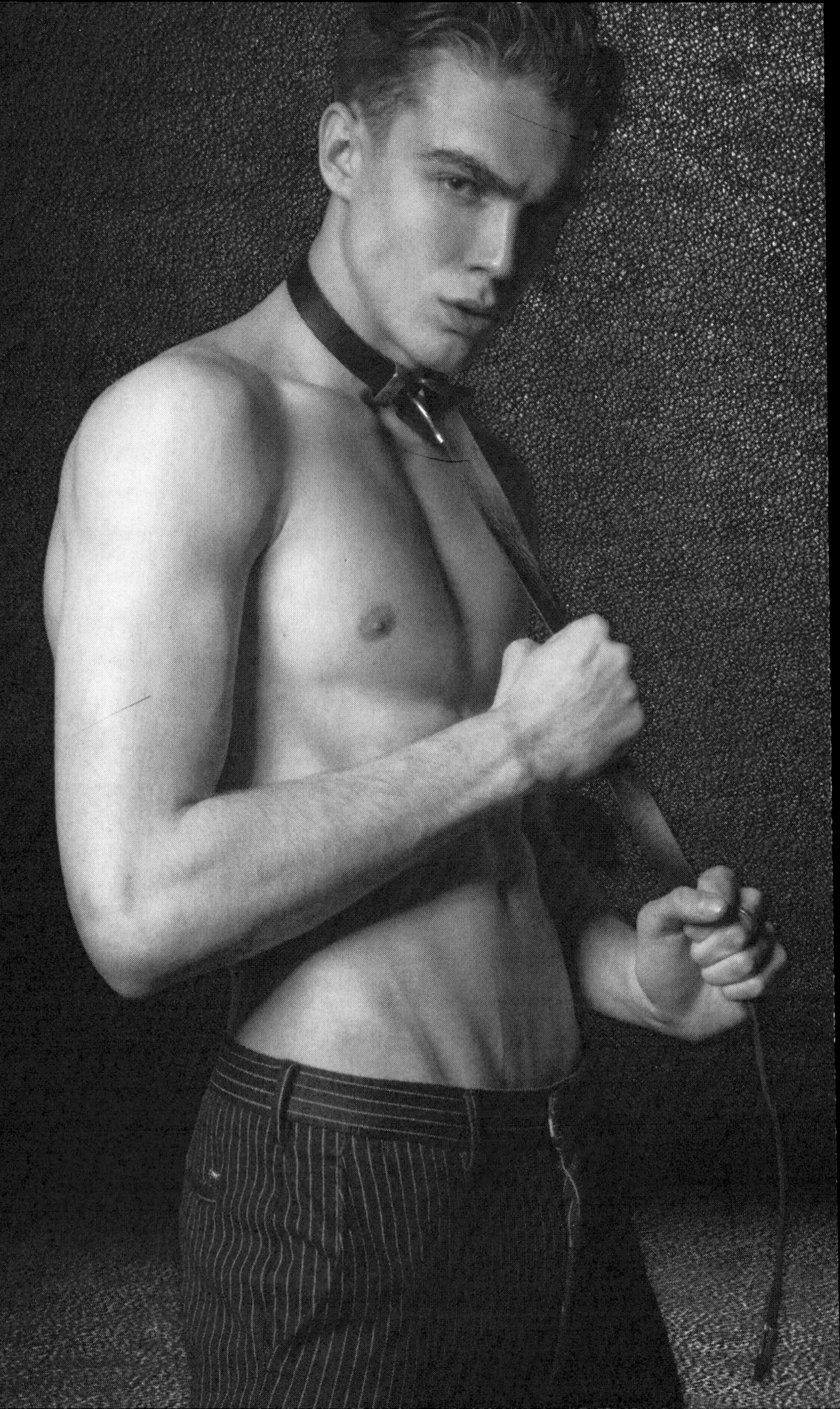

TWELVE
LIAM

My alarm clock blared away in my ears, waking me far before I was ready. Actually, nothing could've made me ready for the day I had ahead of me. Today was the day I was to join the ranks of the elite, rule the halls with them, make everyone jealous as I sat at their table, laughing and carrying on like nothing in the world was out of place. But there would be something out of place. *Me.*

With a groan, I silenced the alarm and pushed myself out of bed. I trudged to the bathroom and showered. The only reason I wasn't in a full-fledged panic attack was because I forced myself to shove everything from my mind. I focused on each task at hand—washing up, brushing my teeth, fixing my hair. Then came time to dress. I looked at all the clothes Asha had purchased for me and didn't know where to start. I tried to remember what she paired with what, but I couldn't remember. It was all a blur. That whole day was like a roller coaster, and all I remembered about it was being happy, seeing her laugh, and noticing how beautiful she was when the light caught her eyes a certain way.

With a sigh, I shook my head and grabbed at random. I ended up in a pair of light-colored jeans with more holes in them than my old jeans had. They hugged my hips but were loose enough around my legs that they weren't terribly uncomfortable. I put on the belt and shoes, then focused on a shirt. I landed on the green button-down Asha had really seemed to like. She mentioned how the shirt made my eyes shine brighter and hugged my biceps. I crammed my feet into the new Doc Marten boots and then shrugged on the black, leather moto jacket that matched everything.

I checked myself out in the full-length mirror and nearly froze. I looked nothing like myself. I didn't appear laid back like usual. I seemed...like them. Like an asshole douchebag nobody could stand.

Shaking my head, I turned and headed for the door. With nothing left to do but grab some breakfast and drive to school, the issue I'd been avoiding thinking about couldn't be ignored any longer. *Them. The elite.*

I couldn't imagine they'd be warm, friendly, and welcoming. I knew I could deal with them, if I had to. What worried me more was wondering which version of Asha I'd get that day. She was always so hot and cold. One minute, she broke my camera and called me a loser. The next she bought me an even more expensive camera and invited me to hang out with her friends. I wondered if she'd be the cold Asha who tormented me or if she'd be the warm Asha I got to see when we were shopping.

Unable to delay leaving any longer, I made my way to the car, setting my bag and new camera into the passenger side seat. With a deep breath, I shifted into reverse and backed out of the drive. I went as slowly as I possibly could without holding up traffic, but eventually I made it and had to face the crowd.

I parked by the elite instead of by my friends. My old Honda looked stupid next to their shiny BMWs and Audis. It stood out like a sore thumb. I dragged my backpack onto one shoulder and hung my camera around my neck. As I made my way to the front yard of the school, everyone I passed stopped, stared, and whispered or just straight up pointed. *Everyone.*

My group of friends sat on the stone bench in front of the school.

I shot them a small smile as I passed, heading for Asha's group. I hadn't told them what I was doing.

Asha was on a bench with Lucas, his arm around her shoulders. Everyone else huddled around them. I came to a stop beside Jude.

Asha glanced up. The moment she saw it was me, her eyes lit up, and a smile formed. "Hey, look at you," she said, standing up and walking around me in a circle in her tight, pink sundress and high heels.

"Yeah, I would've never guessed he used to be a loser. He's pretty hot," Tiffany said.

"I'd do him," Heidi added.

Asha didn't let either of them bother her. She continued her loop around me until she came to a stop directly in front of me. "Looking good. What do you think?"

I shrugged. "'Snot so bad, I guess." I was trying to play it cool but felt anything but.

"Good," she said.

The bell rang, cutting through the moment.

"Let's go. You get to walk with us today." She looped her arm through mine and practically dragged me past my friends, who were staring, and into the school.

The looks on their faces ranged from amazement to confusion to anger. Sofia looked angrier than anyone else though. Her brows pulled together. Her eyes narrowed into slits as they followed me. Her back was straight, arms crossed over her chest. I was so distracted by my friends that I didn't have much time to notice anything about Asha or her crew.

Once the eight o'clock bell rang, we had fifteen minutes to gather our things and get to class before the tardy bell sounded. That was fifteen minutes I had to spend with my new friends, and I had no idea what the fuck to say to them.

"Where did you get the clothes?" Marcie asked, pushing her auburn curls behind her shoulder as she sized me up. "You didn't have this the whole time, right? I mean, if you did, you would've worn it before now."

I glanced to Asha. She gave me a slight headshake. She didn't want her friends to know she'd taken me shopping and bought me all this shit.

So I shrugged. "I had some of it. I bought some a few days ago. It's just clothes. What's the big deal?"

"Oh, and you brought your camera," Heidi said, beaming. "Take my picture." She placed her hand on her hip and jutted it out. In the same instant, her lips puckered and her free hand came up to give me the peace sign.

I wanted to laugh at how ridiculous it was, but I just uncapped the lens and took a picture.

"Oh, me next," Tiffany said, pushing Heidi out of the way and stealing her spot in the hall. She turned to her side and peered at me over her shoulder, offering up a seductive expression.

I snapped the picture, but before anyone else could jump in Asha said, "Enough losers. Liam has better things to do than to take pictures of your ugly faces all day."

Tiffany gasped. "I don't have an ugly face, do I, Liam?"

I felt put on the spot and didn't know what to say. I didn't want it to seem like I was taking sides, so I said, "Your face is fine to me."

It seemed good enough because she smiled. "See?" she told Asha. Tiffany's gaze flashed back to me. "You should see what I can do with this mouth though. It makes the whole picture a lot better...if you know what I mean."

Asha rolled her eyes and shook her head but didn't say anything. Lucas was still standing at her side, silently sizing me up.

Tiffany, happy she'd gotten the best of Asha, looped her arm through mine. "Walk me to class, Liam?" She didn't give me time to answer. She just pulled me down the hallway, leading me away from the others.

"You know, you *are* pretty cute. You got a girlfriend? Please tell me that weird girl you hang out with isn't your girlfriend."

"No, no girlfriend," I told her, sounding as bored as I possibly could, hoping she'd get the hint.

"Good. Well, I'm single, you know?" She offered up a flirty smile as she batted her long lashes at me.

"That's...good to know."

She slowed outside the science lab and shifted in front of me. She took one big step toward me. Her chest pressed against mine. "I don't know if you've heard, but I'm pretty easy." She smiled and arched a brow. "Take me out, and I guarantee you'll go home a new man." Her hand pressed the fabric over my heart.

I looked from her eyes to her hand then back. "I think the man I am is good enough."

I took her hand by one finger and lifted it off me before dropping it. It smacked off her thigh as I pushed past her and walked away.

The rest of my morning went by smoothly since I didn't have any classes with the rest of them. But when it was lunch time, I knew I had to put my game face back on. Even though I didn't want to, I knew I needed to be friendly to get them to trust me and share their secrets with me. That way, when they fucked me over, and I was sure they would, I'd have something on them to fuck them over with too. It was the silver lining to the whole damn plan. I may go down, but I wasn't going alone. I'd take each one of those mother fuckers with me.

I went to Asha's locker—the same spot they always gathered—to wait for the rest of the crew. Lucas had Asha's back pressed against her locker, and they were talking quietly. Jealousy ate at me, burning its way from my stomach up to my throat from seeing his hands on her. *Why in the hell did she let him touch her? Why didn't she pick someone like me?*

I hid my emotions well enough that Tiffany felt the need to pick back up where she'd left off earlier. Her arm snaked around mine, and she pulled me to her side. "Hello, my name is *All Yours,* and I'll be your guide," she said with a flirty smile that made my stomach hurt worse than it already did.

I thought I caught a flare of jealousy in Asha's eyes from over

Lucas's shoulder, but when I tried to doublecheck, the look was wiped away.

As a group, we went to the cafeteria and got lunch, which consisted of ham and cheese sandwiches, carrot sticks, a cup of fruit, and a graham-cracker cookie that was in the shape of a fish. We took our trays out to the quad where they sat at their usual table. I sank down at the far end. Of course, Tiffany was right by my side. Asha was across the table from me diagonally. Jude was right in front of me. In the space between him and Asha, I could see my friends, watching with wonder and anger in their eyes.

I turned my attention to the people sitting with me. The whole group was full of endless chatter. They all seemed to have their own conversations going. Looking over at their table from my usual seat, I'd always thought they were having one big group discussion. But that wasn't the case. I wondered if they were playing nice for my sake or if it was how their lunches usually went. Everyone at the table was talking. Everyone but me and Asha. She looked up, and her blue eyes locked with mine.

"What's up with you? I've never seen you this quiet before." My voice was low as I addressed her.

She shrugged one shoulder. "Just stepdad drama."

Tiffany bumped my shoulder with hers. "It's always stepdad stuff with her. If you get bummed staring at her frown, just look my way. In fact, where is that camera of yours? Let's get some group shots!" She quickly stood up, and the girls followed—all of them but Asha. They did a typical cheerleading pose, where they all bent their knees and rested their hands on top as they lined up. I snapped a few pictures. Then I got one of Asha as she picked at her food. She looked beautiful, deep in thought as the sun shone down on her and lit up her blonde hair.

The girls in the group were giggling and having a blast with me as their photographer. They kept repositioning.

"The lighting sucks here. Too many shadows," I lied, tired of taking their pictures. I sat back in my seat.

"Aw," Tiffany pouted.

"Looks like the girls have a new toy," Jude said.

Lucas laughed.

"Hey, how did you get into photography anyway?" Jude ran his hand through his dark hair.

I shrugged as I replaced the cap on the lens and tucked the camera away. "I don't know. It's always been a hobby, I guess."

"Yeah, I mean, we know nothing about you, man. You got a girlfriend, or do you like to stay single and play the field?" Jude pressed.

Hudson piped up, "Yeah, you make any pussies wet lately or you need some lessons?" He laughed.

Tiffany leaned into me. "I'll volunteer," she whispered, loudly enough the whole table could hear.

My gaze shot to Asha's, and I saw her give Tiffany a look.

I smiled, happy she seemed to be as jealous as I was.

"Gross, Tiffany. Have some class," Asha spat out.

Tiffany smiled sweetly. "You're just jealous, Asha. You always get whatever you want. But not this time. I'm staking my claim on Liam. Plus, you've got Lucas, right?" she asked, cocking her head to the side, waiting for Asha's answer.

Asha pressed her lips together and lifted her brows. "I do have Lucas, Tiffany. And no matter how many guys you fuck or how often you give it away, you'll never have him. We all know you want everything that's mine. You want my boyfriend. I made friends with Liam, so now you want him too. Get your own fucking life and stop trying to steal mine."

The bell rang, indicating lunch was over. The conversation got dropped as everyone headed for the doors into the school. The group kind of scattered from there, everyone dumping their trash and going their separate ways to their next class. But Asha, Lucas, and I had sixth hour together. Asha and I started toward our lockers, but Lucas was nowhere to be seen. Asha paused at my locker while I grabbed my books.

"You sure you're OK? You're too quiet."

She nodded. "I'm fine, Liam."

"You want to hang out after school today? We could work on our papers or just..." I shrugged. "Hang out and escape everything."

That made a smile form. "Sure, I'd love to. Same as before? My secret spot?"

"Sure," I agreed, slamming my locker closed as we strolled down the hallway and stopped at her locker.

I waited while she got what she needed, and then we walked to class together. I couldn't help but notice the looks I got from everyone in the hallway because I was with Asha. I knew the whispers were about me. They probably wondered how I'd managed to go from scholarship kid to the elite. Fuck, I wished I knew the answer, but even I couldn't figure it out.

The afternoon was pretty uneventful other than the continuous stares and whispers. When the bell rang, I was more than ready to get out of there. I made it to my car before anyone had even pushed out the school doors, and I was out of the parking lot before anyone noticed I was gone.

Driving away was the first time I'd been able to breathe all day. It was like I'd started holding my breath when I drove into the parking lot earlier and was just now letting that breath out. I was almost dizzy as the anxiety from being everyone's main focus fizzled away. I went home and found the house was empty like normal. I grabbed some cold pizza as a snack and went up to my room to do my homework. At around five, I left before anyone got home. I was supposed to meet Asha at six, and I wanted to talk with my friends beforehand to explain everything.

I knew since they weren't at my place, they'd be at Andy's. Sofia wasn't allowed to have boys in her room. Her mom made everyone sit in the living room with their shoes off to not ruin her precious, white carpet. And we couldn't even watch what we wanted. Nothing rated R. Boring. Max's place was cool, but his uncle lived with them. He had a serious case of man-child syndrome. He was in his late thirties and still acted like he was seventeen. We couldn't hang there without having to deal with him. So, to Andy's I went.

Andy's mom and dad had split up when he was nine, so we only had one parent to worry about there. And Mrs. Winchester wouldn't be home until after seven. I pulled into the driveway and killed the engine. I strode up to the door and didn't bother knocking. The three of them were in the living room, watching TV, when I went in.

"Hey," I said, flopping down on the love seat next to Sofia.

The guys sat on either end of the couch directly in front of the TV.

Sofia frowned at me but didn't open her mouth. She didn't need to because Andy and Max were already hurling questions my way. I held up a finger to silence them and started walking them through the whole story.

"So you and Asha *aren't* fucking behind Lucas's back?" Max asked the moment I finished.

"What? No, man," I breathed out.

"Why do you think she invited you into the group though?" Andy asked.

I shrugged. "No idea. Best guess, she actually felt bad about getting my ass kicked and breaking my camera."

"This is Asha we're talking about. She doesn't *have* feelings," Max pointed out.

I moved my head from side to side. "I thought the same thing, but this project has really brought us together. She's opened up, and I almost kind of understand why she is the way she is. She's really not bad when you get to know her."

"Well, shit," Andy muttered. "I think if I were you, I'd definitely hit that Tiffany bitch up. She sounds easy, and I've heard some freaky shit about her." He blushed just saying the words.

Sofia let out a long, annoyed huff as she shook her head.

I glanced over at her. "What Sofia? I know you have something to say."

"All guys are the fucking same," she said more to herself.

"What?" Andy asked.

"What's that supposed to mean?" I asked at the same time.

"All you need is some pretty girl with big boobs to show you a little attention and your common sense flies straight the fuck out of your head!" She sat up straight. "This is the elite we're talking about. They don't *invite* outsiders into their group. They don't play nice. If they brought you in, it's for a reason, and you're falling right in her fucking trap, you dumb ass!"

I rolled my eyes. "Look, I'm not stupid. I know there's a pretty good chance they're all going to fuck me over as some epic prank or whatever. But that's also why I'm doing this. I'm on the inside now," I said, gazing at each one of them. "I can finally get the dirt we need to bring their asses down. To pay them back for all the shit they've done to us. Don't you see?"

Sofia shook her head and stormed out of the living room. Nobody moved or spoke until the bathroom door slammed shut.

"So, what kind of dirt do you think you can get?" Andy asked.

I shrugged. "I don't know. I mean, I've only been with them a day. I bet Tiffany is fucking Lucas behind Asha's back, but I don't have proof yet. But if that's happening, you know there's more. Something good. Maybe even something illegal to get their asses kicked out of school once and for all."

"I don't know, man. They've been caught before, and nothing has happened," Max said.

"Right, but this time I'll have proof. And if the headmaster doesn't want to see it, we'll go higher. Get enough people involved so the school will do anything to shut it down. Even if it means kicking out the scum who fund the place."

∼

"IT'S WARMER IN HERE TODAY," I said as I entered Asha's empty staff house.

"Yeah, I've been out here a while. Avoiding my stepdad, you know?" Asha flopped down on the couch next to me.

I nodded as I crossed my ankle over my knee. "I just left Andy's. He, Max, and Sofia were hanging out. Figured I needed to explain my sudden absence."

"How'd they take it?"

"Max and Andy are cool." I shrugged.

"And Sofia?"

"Not so cool." I shook my head to clear the confusing thoughts. "Things with Sofia are weird as fuck."

"She likes you." Asha leaned her head back against the couch and peeked at me from beneath her long lashes.

I nodded. "I know, and that's all my fault."

"How so?"

"I know I kind of explained it before, but I want you to understand exactly how it is with her. We'd all go out and party together. I'd get fucked up and flirt with her. Kiss her, touch her..." I left out the rest. "And she thought it meant something to me when it clearly didn't. I've hurt her a lot. She thinks this is just one of your games. That you and your crew are just setting me up to fuck me over later."

"Sounds like she's just trying to keep you for herself." Asha smiled around the words.

I shot her a smirk but didn't respond.

"Lucas and I are going through something too."

"Yeah? What?"

She shrugged. "I don't know. I just feel like something is changing with us."

"He's a dick and treats you like shit. Why do you put up with him?"

One side of her mouth turned up. "He knows who I am, mostly. I don't deserve anything better."

My brows pulled together. "Why would you think that?" I asked, reaching over and taking her hand in mine. I couldn't help myself.

Her eyes moved from mine to our hands and back. "You don't

know everything about me yet, Liam... And I hope you never do. You'd never be able to look at me the same way again."

"I do know you, Asha. Actually, I probably know you better than any of those people you call friends, definitely better than *he* does. And you know what? I wouldn't treat you like that. I'd give you everything, *anything* if you were mine."

There was a long-drawn-out silence, and my heart raced, unsure of what the hell I was doing. I didn't mean to touch her or to say the things I did. All I knew was I needed to get out of there before I fucked up more.

But I couldn't get my feet or my brain to work, so I did something stupid.

I leaned in and gently pressed my lips to hers.

A spark. A flame. A raging fucking fire swept over me as she came to life beneath my kiss. Her hands moved to cradle my face as she parted her lips to allow me entrance.

I took what was offered and slid my tongue inside her mouth, brushing it against hers in a sweet dance that tasted like a delicious mistake and a beautiful nightmare, all topped with cherry lip gloss.

I deepened our kiss. My hands drifted to her waist to bring her closer to me. She came easily, her fingers raking through my hair. I squeezed her waist. She whimpered softly into my mouth. It shot straight to my hard cock.

We had to stop before we both lost control. Breathlessly, I broke the kiss off and ran my knuckles along her jaw.

"I should go," I murmured, dropping my hand from her soft skin.

The distance between us was too much, and I almost went back for a second round, but I willed myself to stay in my lane. It took everything I had to get up and walk to the door.

"Wait," she called out just as breathless, following me.

I stopped and turned to face her.

"Why are you leaving?" she asked softly.

I could see an innocence in her eyes that usually wasn't there. A pang shot through my heart.

"It feels like things are changing between us, and I don't know what to do about that. It's confusing. I know I need to remember who you want everyone to *think* you are and forget the side you show only me." I reached out and cupped her cheek as I crinkled my brows. "But if I had to pick, I'd pick this *you*. The person you are when nobody is around or watching. *This* is who you are, Asha. Not the lost girl who rules the halls at school." With that, I leaned forward and placed a soft kiss to her cheek.

She sucked in a breath, but she didn't say anything. Neither did I. I just turned around and left before things got out of hand.

The hike back to the car went by faster than last time. My legs pushed me forward quickly while my mind raced about what had just happened.

Why didn't she jerk her hand away? Why didn't she smack me when I kissed her?

If I was having confusing feelings about her, maybe she was having them about me too. A guy could only hope, but I needed to remember my place. Fancy clothes didn't mean I was worth more. You could put a dress on a pig, and it would still be a pig.

But fuck me for being a pig in a fancy dress.

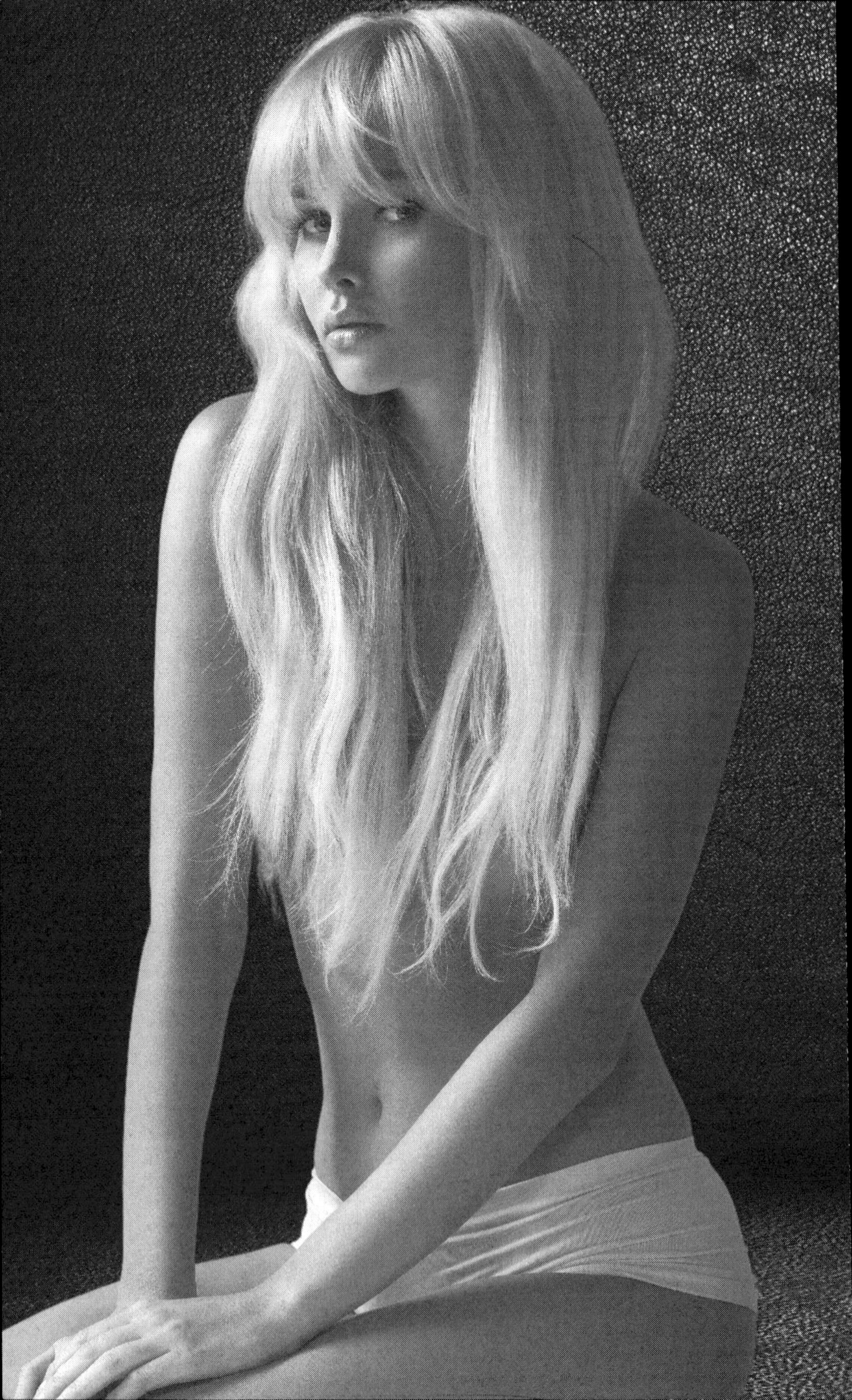

THIRTEEN
ASHA

My lips tingled. Mindlessly, my hand flew up to cover the spot he'd kissed. I was frozen, staring at the door he'd just ran through, the taste of him on my lips. It was as if my feet had been planted in the floor. My heart raced while my breath was heavy with happiness and confusion. It was the best kiss I'd ever had. In the past, all of the kisses I'd received were from boys who wanted something from me or men at the club *took* something from me. None of them were soft, caring. None of them were Liam.

In a daze, I wandered back to the house. The sun had set, and the sky was dark, but I didn't notice anything as I went inside, still completely wrapped up in Liam and his kiss. I wondered what had gotten into him. *Why did he kiss me?* It had nothing to do with Lucas. If it had, Liam never would've laid a hand on me to begin with.

"Good, you're here. Let's go," Gio said, sauntering out of his office, snapping me from my thoughts.

"Go where?"

He frowned. "The club, where do you think?"

"I have to finish my homework. It's a school night." Panic rose in my chest.

He shrugged. "Who gives a shit? It's not like you *need* an education for what life has in store for you. One of my girls is out dead. I need you to fill in." He grabbed my wrist and directed me to the door.

I didn't fight. There was no point. I could go and do what I had to, or I could get the shit beat out of me and still go anyway.

～

THINGS at the club were in full swing when we arrived. I glanced over the faces as we walked in and noticed several people I'd never seen before. Gio shoved a bag into my arms and shooed me toward the dressing room.

"Do something with that face. The boys like it when you girls are dolled up."

I spun away from him, heading to the changing room. Inside, the room was dead. No other dancers were in there. They were already on stage, in the crowd, or giving private dances. I was all alone. I needed some time to get everything right in my brain anyway.

I wasn't afraid. Not anymore. I was filled with hatred though. I hated myself for ever being born. I despised my mother for leaving my father to be with Gio. And I loathed Gio the most. I hated myself and everything about my life.

For the first time, a new thought crossed my mind. *Why not just kill yourself and get it over with? It'd be easy enough. Instead of cutting to release the pain inside your head, just cut a little deeper. Let it all go. Put an end to the misery.* The option sounded too good to be true.

Filling my lungs with air, I closed my eyes and shook off the idea. As good as killing myself sounded, it also meant nothing would get better. I knew I wasn't put on Earth to suffer. I was there for a reason. One day, I would escape. One day, my life would be mine. One day, I'd be happy.

As I put on my makeup, I considered all the ways I knew my life would change one day. I decided to go extra heavy, contouring my cheeks to give my face a sharper angle. I darkened my eyes and made my lips hot pink. My outfit for the night was a black G-string covered by a tiny, red and black checkered skirt. It was so short my ass hung out the bottom. The top was a loose-fitting, black shirt that was cut short so the bottom swell of each breast was visible. I slid my feet into my high heels and looked myself over. I despised the reflection in the mirror. She was the bad one, the one who was trash. Since I was living two different lives, I decided to be two different people. The seventeen-year-old schoolgirl was Asha. She had a popular boyfriend but liked someone else. She had a messy teen life, but a decent one. Asha had a large group of friends, and her life was *almost* perfect.

The girl in the mirror, she didn't have a name. She answered to whatever *they* called her. She was dirty, a whore, trash. Putting on the outfit flipped my switch from Asha to the nameless, broken girl. I had to learn to keep them separate.

The door opened, and a dancer sashayed in. "Careful out there. They're kind of restless tonight. One of those mother fuckers bit me!" She yanked her top down to show me the teeth marks on her breast.

My eyes widened as I took in her already bruised skin. I took a deep breath and forced myself forward. I yanked the door open just as my music started. Purposefully, I made my way to the stage, and the crowd cheered. They ate up the flirty smile I gave them. They started tossing dollar bills on the stage before I'd even taken anything off. I didn't bother to pick any of it up though. It was pointless. At the end of the night, all the money would be collected and given to Gio. What he did with it from there, I didn't know. But I never saw a dime of it.

I wrapped my hand around the pole and swung around it. The fast action caused my hair to blow around me. I twirled down the polished metal and onto my knees, where I crawled across the stage to a group of older men in crisp suits. One of them leaned forward, cheered, and flashed me a hundred-dollar bill. I stopped in front of him and removed my shirt. With that, he held out the bill, and I opened my mouth, closing my teeth around it.

Dirty. Just like me.

I got back up to my feet to work the pole some more. After a few spins, some splits, and a little giggling, I reached beneath my skirt and pulled my panties down nice and slow. I twirled them around my finger before letting them fly into the crowd. They cheered and tossed more money. The stage was practically covered now. I slid through dollar bills—fives, twenties, and the random hundred.

I slithered to the end of the stage and sat on my ass with my legs stretched in front of me. The regulars knew what I was teasing, so they gathered around, yelling and cheering. Money rained down on me. Slowly, I eased one foot back toward my body, bending my leg at the knee. More money fell. Then, as leisurely as possible, I repeated the move with my other leg, giving them the view they wanted so badly.

There I was, on stage, topless, with my legs spread wide open, and all anyone did was cheer and throw money. Nobody wanted to save me. They didn't wonder how old I was or what I was doing on this stage. All they saw was a piece of meat they wanted to have their sick twisted way with.

As the bills fell around me, someone grazed the inside of my leg. I quickly snapped my legs closed, knowing I couldn't allow them to touch me on stage. Gio said if I did, they'd have no reason to pay more in order to go in the back with me. I planted my foot on the man's chest and pushed him back. He stumbled, and his hand fell from my skin. The song ended, and I exited the stage, hurrying down to the floor, making a beeline for the bar.

I was only a few feet from the liquor I craved when Gio stepped in front of me.

"Didn't learn your lesson last time?"

A sigh left my lips. I'd been hoping I could sneak a shot or two.

"Your first client is waiting for you in room one. Get to work. You have a line forming." He stood in place, watching as I pivoted and headed toward the private room.

When I entered, the man was already there, sitting in a lounge chair, completely naked. His body was old and wrinkly, pale, and covered in thick, black hair. Just looking at him made me want to vomit.

I swallowed down my nausea and said, "What would you like?"

He motioned for me to come over. Dread curdled in my gut as I shuffled across the floor to stand in front of him. He gave me a kind smile as he grabbed ahold of my wrist. His hand was soft against my skin. At least, if nothing else, he was gentle.

Well, I thought he was.

I was wrong.

He yanked my arm so hard I was sure he'd pulled it from the socket. I cried out. and he laughed as he pushed me onto the floor. He dropped to his knees and wrapped his fingers around my throat, squeezing.

"I'm not the kind of man who likes blowjobs or romantic screws. If I wanted that, I'd get it from my wife."

"Then what do you want?" I wheezed, trying to pry his fingers off my throat.

An evil gleam filled his eyes. "I want you to fight me."

Panic filled me as I tried to shove his hand away. My nails dug into his skin. He drew his free hand back then sent it flying toward my face. Tears filled my eyes at the contact.

"Don't leave any marks for my wife to find, you little bitch," he spat out the words as he guided himself into me.

For once, I was allowed to fight, but in my world it didn't mean I'd win.

∼

THE REST of the night passed in a blur. All I could think about was that guy and how I knew Gio was responsible for the abuse I'd suffered. Gio's anger was getting worse and worse with me. He never touched me himself, except the one time he made me go down on him. He liked to jackoff while watching other men fuck me, but now he found someone to play out a rape fantasy on me?

Was Gio preparing me for something more? Like the day he'd demand to be inside of me.

Finally at two in the morning, Gio pushed me into the changing room and demanded I change into my street clothes. When I came out, he ordered me into the car. Silently, he drove me home. I was expecting some kind of speech about needing to do better, but he didn't utter one word, which confused me even more. It was like his lack of talking was almost praise for how well I'd done tonight. *What the fuck was wrong with me?*

Inside, I climbed up to my room, showered, and went straight to bed.

I woke the next morning ready to put the night before behind me, reminding myself I was a different person. I was Asha again, not the nameless girl from the club. I shoved the blankets back and shuffled to the bathroom. I relieved my bladder and then started brushing my teeth.

That was when I noticed the dark blue and purple bruises around my neck. I froze as I took them in. *This can't be right.* Somehow, during the night, nameless girl merged with me. Even though *I* wasn't the one who'd acted out the rape fantasy, I was the one marked and bruised.

My toothbrush clattered to the counter. Dazed, I got right back in bed, knowing there was no way I could go to school with something like that so visible.

Around eight, I got a text.

LIAM: Where are you?

ME: Not coming.

LIAM: Why? What am I supposed to do with your friends?

ME: Hang out, make friends. You'll be fine.

LIAM: I don't have you here as a buffer.

ME: Then hang with your friends. I have to go.

My heart ached as I recalled his kiss. His touch. I just wanted to fall into his arms and be held by someone who gave a damn. But I knew I couldn't. No one could ever know about nameless girl, not even Liam.

~

ON DAY TWO, he texted me.

LIAM: You're avoiding me.

When I didn't answer his text, he finally called until I picked up. My throat was so tight with the threat of tears that I didn't greet him, this seemingly perfect boy. Lucas had only sent me one text during my absence, saying he hoped I felt better, but he didn't ask what was wrong or if I needed anything.

"You don't need to talk. I'd rather you just listen anyway," Liam's deep voice greeted me softly.

A tear slid down my cheek as I gripped the phone tight.

"I'm sorry if I made you feel like you needed to avoid me because of the kiss or anything else I may have done. I don't regret doing it though. I wanted it. I know you have Lucas, and I'm not much in comparison as far as status and money go. But I'm still here for you. For anything. I feel like you need me right now." He huffed out a breath before continuing, "And I want to be there for you, but I don't know how. So, just know when you're ready for a friend, I'm here. Be safe, hellcat."

The phone clicked, going silent on my end. I let out a shaky breath, a sob tearing through me.

Why me? Why this life? I closed my eyes, willing myself to sleep through the agony of never getting what I wanted.

By Thursday, the bruises had finally faded enough to cover with makeup and a turtleneck sweater. I dressed and went to school, planning a story of a spa trip with my mom if anyone asked why I hadn't been at school.

I wanted to see Liam. I kept replaying his words in my head. *I don't regret doing it. I wanted it.* His words were exactly what I felt. It made me realize how far under my skin he'd burrowed. I'd gotten used to seeing him every day, talking, and hanging out. I hadn't seen him since our kiss. Somehow, I needed him more than anything I'd ever needed in my entire life.

I was a few minutes late for school. When I arrived, everyone was already heading inside. I wasn't bothered by the lack of messing around before the bell. I just wanted to go in and get shit over with. I marched in and went straight to my locker. Andy, Max, Liam, and Sofia were across the hall at her locker. Liam was laughing at something. When he noticed me, he wiped the smile away. He pushed off her locker and crossed the hall to me. He leaned against the neighboring locker and looked me in the eye as I stilled in his presence. It made every hair stand on end.

"Hey, you're back."

"Yep, I'm back," I responded, my voice void of any kind of emotion.

Dragging him down into my spiral of self-pity and hatred was stupid. He was too kind. Too pure. Too sweet. He needed a girl who could smile *with* him. I wasn't her. I-I couldn't do this to him. Or myself.

"Were you sick?" His brows furrowed together.

"No." I cleared my throat and forced a smirk onto my face. "My mom took me to a spa. She does random shit all the time. She didn't want to go alone. What did I miss here?" I grabbed my books and closed the locker.

He narrowed his gaze. He wasn't buying my shit. "Nothing, really."

My eyes drifted down his body. I loved the way he looked in that black, leather moto jacket. He wore a white t-shirt and a pair of name-brand jeans. He looked hot as hell, especially when his jaw flexed as he studied me.

"Are you OK? You seem off," he finally said.

"Oh, yeah. Just struggling to get back into the swing of things, you know?"

He nodded, and his Adam's apple bobbed in his throat. "Right, well better get to class." He pushed off the locker. "See ya at lunch."

In some kind of dreamy state, I watched him walk away. I jumped when Sofia bumped into me.

"Watch it, skank," I spat in her direction.

Her eyes narrowed on me as she took a deep breath. "Don't fuck with Liam. We both know you don't want anything to do with him. This is all just some fucked up game of yours. He's a good guy. He doesn't deserve whatever shit you and your friends have planned for him."

My off mood vanished as royal bitch kicked in. "I'll do anything I fucking want to, and there's nothing you can do about it."

Her gaze fell to the floor between us. "Just...don't hurt him, OK?"

I sneered. "Oh, I'll take good care of Liam. Don't you worry about that." My phone chimed in my pocket, and I pulled it out.

LIAM: What's your favorite flower?

I smiled when I read the text and showed her the screen. "See there. He wouldn't want to buy me flowers if I was mean to him, now would he?"

I waited for her answer, but one didn't come.

"Liam is well taken care of. In fact, he's probably never been taken care of so well before. Certainly not by you." I stepped forward and rammed my shoulder into hers as I passed.

I smiled to myself, happy I'd gotten the best of her and made her jealous. *But why did I do it?* I'd decided I couldn't have him, so why would I deny him any sort of happiness he could maybe have with someone else? I pushed the thoughts away and answered him.

ME: I like sunflowers.

LIAM: If you could be any animal, what animal would it be and why?

I slid into the seat of my first hour class and replied.

ME: A bird, so I could fly away.

I smiled sadly down at my answer. I daydreamed of the day I'd be able to run, but I got pulled out of it when my phone vibrated in my hand again.

LIAM: Why not a fish so you could learn to swim?

I grinned at his answer.

ME: Ha-ha. Funny.

LIAM: I thought so.

The texts stopped once the tardy bell rang. I put my phone away to pay attention. School was a great way to keep my mind off the girl who had no name.

Lunch rolled around, and as usual, my group met in the hallway, got our lunches, and went to our table. Liam sat across from me. While everyone else talked, we worked more on our assignment.

"Favorite season?" Liam asked.

"Fall. Crunchy leaves, cool weather, Halloween. My eighteenth birthday," I answered with a wistful tone to my voice. *Eighteen. The magical year.*

"Favorite holiday?"

"Ummm, Halloween," I shrugged. "The one time a year when I get to be whoever I want."

"And who do you want to be, hellcat?" He lifted his dark brows at me, pencil poised over his notebook.

The bell rang, ending lunch before I could answer, which was just as well, because the answer dancing on the tip of my tongue was one I shouldn't say.

Yours. I want to be yours.

The two of us made our way toward our sixth hour class.

"What's a secret you've never told anyone?" He reached for me as Jude jostled past us, sending me tottering into Liam.

I exhaled as his warm hand steadied me at my lower back. It dropped away sooner than I wanted.

I forced my mind back on his question as we navigated the halls. I wanted to tell him about Gio, but the words wouldn't come out. So, instead, I went with, "I don't love Lucas."

Liam frowned and shot me a look that said more than his words ever could. He cared. He wanted to know more. He looked. . . hopeful. Thoughtful. My heart cracked a bit more as I once again screamed *NO* in my head. Not Liam. I refused to take him down with me.

The remaining class periods passed, and school came to an end. I still wasn't feeling particularly chatty, so I ducked out the moment the bell rang. I spent the evening in my room, doing homework and talking with Liam through text.

My phone chimed beside me, and I dropped my pencil to read the message. To my surprise, it wasn't a message but a picture of Liam. He was lying in his bed with his shirt off, his muscles hard and toned. I bit my bottom lip as I stared at the picture.

LIAM: Send me a pic of you.

I snapped a picture of me on my bed. I was sprawled on my stomach with my schoolwork spread before me. The mattress pressed my breasts together, making them look even larger.

LIAM: * heart-eyed emoji*

My heart sped up. I wished more than anything I was in his bed. Then he could hold me and make all the pain go away. *If just talking to him made everything fall away, what would happen if he actually held me, touched me? If I gave in and confessed how I was starting to feel, what would he say?*

LIAM: Time for Netflix?

I quickly changed into some pajamas and crawled beneath the blankets.

ME: Time for Netflix.

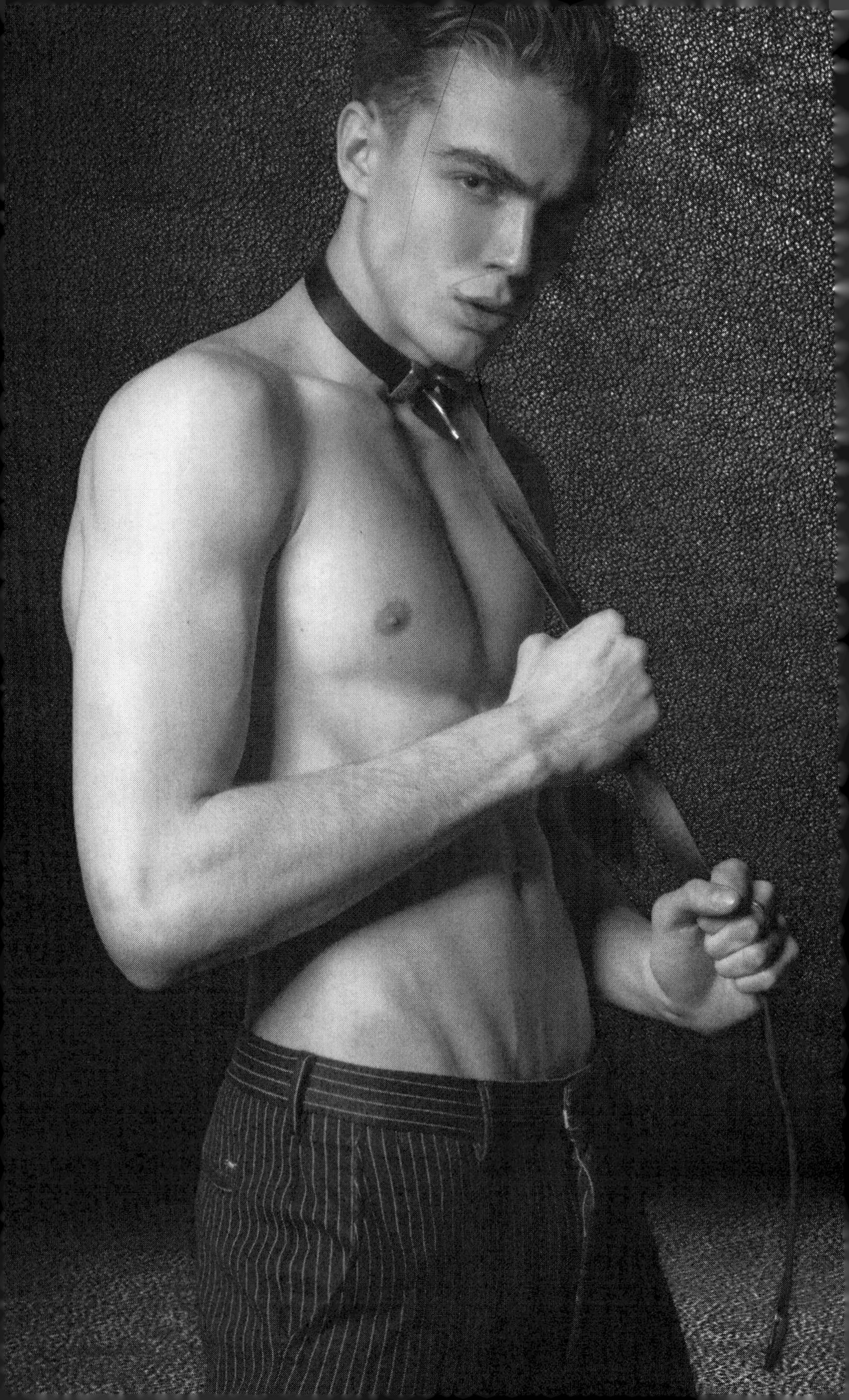

FOURTEEN
LIAM

I lay in bed, watching some stupid, girlie movie on Netflix Thursday night with my phone stuck to my ear. Every once in a while, Asha said something to let me know she was still there or she'd laugh at what we were watching.

When the movie was half over, several minutes passed in silence, so I assumed she'd fallen asleep. I was just about to hang up the phone when she mumbled something incoherent. It was enough to keep me hanging on and listening for more.

"No, Gio," she grumbled.

My ears perked up to listen for other sounds in the room. *Was someone trying to mess with her?*

There were no other noises that would lead me to believe someone else was in there with her. The muffled noise of the movie played in the background. It was about two seconds faster than my own TV.

"No club. No club," she cried weakly.

"Asha?" I said into the phone, hoping to pull her out of whatever nightmare she was having. *What the hell kind of nightmare was set in a club?* "Hellcat?"

"Don't touch me," she muttered, sounding angry.

"Asha?" I said louder.

She let out a sigh at the same time the blankets ruffled against the speaker. Then my phone beeped, indicating the call was dropped. I shook my head as I set my phone onto the bedside table. I shut off the TV and settled against my pillow. But when my eyes closed, I was lost in thoughts of her.

I wondered about her sleep talking and the dream she'd been having. *What kind of dream would have her stepfather, a club, and an unwanted person touching her?*

The mention of her stepfather was probably just from all the fights they'd had lately. And the club could mean anything. And a lot of girls got unwanted attention in clubs from drunk guys.

But why didn't she want to go to the club to begin with?

For days, I'd been worried about her being mad at me for the kiss, but she'd seemed indifferent about it. I knew she was with Lucas, but it still hurt to see him pawing her at school. The guy didn't speak much to me. Not that I gave a shit, but Asha didn't look happy with him. Her smile never reached her eyes. Not like it did for me. She didn't rake her fingers along his scalp or mold her body to his. She said she didn't love him.

So why be with him?

It was probably just clique politics. I'd asked her what her secret was, already knowing the answer. And it wasn't what she'd confessed. It wasn't a secret to me that her feelings for Lucas weren't real.

Me. I was her secret. No one would ever know we'd had a moment together with our lips and bodies molded to one another's.

Grunting in frustration, I pounded my pillow, exhausted. *When had my life become so damn complicated?* I'd only been trying to survive Acadia before. Now, I was trying to survive Asha.

Sleep took me easily enough. Before I knew it, my alarm blared in my ears, waking me for school. After going through my morning routine, I ambled downstairs. My dad had already left for the day, but

Mom was making breakfast. I plopped down at the island, and she handed over a cup of coffee.

I took a sip. "Thanks."

"You look handsome today. Is that jacket new?" She turned her attention back to the stove.

"Yeah, I got it last weekend."

She glanced over her shoulder at me. "It looks expensive." She set a plate of bacon and eggs in front of me as she dragged her other hand over my shoulder. "Is that real leather? How did you afford this?"

I shrugged. "It's not real. Just a good knockoff I found at one of those street fairs."

She rolled her eyes. "I told you to stop going to those things. Half that crap is stolen. Haven't you seen the documentary?"

I chuckled into my coffee and shook my head.

"It was really interesting. At least the one about the black-market makeup was. You can't imagine the stuff they try to pass off as makeup. A lot of people have gotten sick."

"Well, this is a jacket, Mom. Not makeup."

"It could be the same. Who knows how it was stored or what could be on it?"

I rolled my eyes. "I promise, if I start getting a weird rash or something, I'll take it off." I scooped some eggs into my mouth and snatched a piece of bacon off the plate as I stood. "Gotta get to school," I said, heading for the door.

She followed me down the hallway. "I ran into Sofia at the supermarket yesterday. She said the two of you had a fight and haven't really been speaking?"

"It's fine, Mom. Leave it alone."

She leaned against the wall and crossed her arms. "She's a good girl, Liam. Don't hurt her."

"Don't plan on it, Mom." I yanked the door open and strode out, shutting it before she could say anything else.

I arrived at school earlier than normal thanks to my mom probing too much and chasing me out of the house. So I sat in my car, waiting for the parking lot to fill up. As I played with my phone, I remembered the picture Asha had sent me. Thumbing to our message thread, I stared at it for the hundredth time. She was beautiful in the picture. Her long, blonde hair fell over one shoulder. Her blue eyes were lit up with the light of the phone flashing in them. She was on her stomach, and the position pressed her breasts together, giving me a nice shot of cleavage. Staring at the picture had my body coming alive in ways it didn't need to in the school parking lot. Instead of swiping it away, I decided to save it as the background on my home screen because apparently, I needed to punish myself a bit more.

When I put my phone aside, I found I'd been staring at her longer than I'd thought. The parking lot was full, and kids were hanging in the front yard. Some of them were already making their way into the building. I tucked my phone away, grabbed my bag, and climbed out. I sauntered up the sidewalk and found the elite group fucking around at their usual bench in front of the school. A glance to my right, revealed Andy, Max, and Sofia. I offered them a smile before turning left, heading for Asha and her friends.

"There you are. I was starting to wonder if you were going to get out of your car," Tiffany said, flipping her long, red hair over her shoulder as she clutched my arm and tugged me to her side. She kept her fingers around my forearm as she rested her head against my bicep.

"Lost track of time," I muttered, my eyes finding Asha.

She seemed lost in thought as she sat next to Lucas, her gaze on the sidewalk in front of her. I wanted to ask her about the dream, but I knew now wasn't the time.

"Guys, I forgot to tell you. My parents are gone this weekend. You know what that means, right?" Hudson said, staring at each and every one of us.

"What?" I finally asked when nobody else did.

Hudson smiled as his gaze met mine. "Party tonight after the game!"

The group started talking up a storm—everyone but Asha and

me. Worry or nerves clouded her features, and I was too busy watching her to actually think about anything else.

Tiffany turned to face me. "Liam, will you be my date for the party?"

The guys started hooting and cheering.

"Trust me, man. You want Tiff as your date," Hudson said, smacking me on the chest as he stepped by me to head into school.

I turned back to Tiff. "I don't know if I'll be able to make it."

"Oh, come on," she pouted, pressing her tits against my chest as she batted her lashes at me.

"I..." I started to reject her again, but then I saw the way Asha leaned into Lucas as he wound his arm around her waist.

She didn't pull away when he kissed her. A tiny flash of jealousy flared in her eyes as she pulled away from Lucas and glanced at me.

"All right, fine," I agreed, causing Tiffany to bounce and giggle.

The bell rang, and everyone started making their way inside. Lucas's arm draped around Asha as they walked in together, so I knew I wouldn't be able to talk her yet. Tiffany's arm was laced through mine anyway. Talking to Asha would have to wait until later. We parted ways in the hallway.

I grabbed my books and went to my first class. My phone vibrated inside my pocket.

ASHA: You don't have to go to the party if you don't want to. It's always a disaster.

ME: I already told Tiffany I would. Can't back out now. Plus, I'll always take an opportunity to hang out with you.

I went to tuck my cell away, but it vibrated again.

ASHA: I'll be stuck with Lucas, so don't bother going if I'm the only reason you're going.

It almost sounded like she didn't want me to go to the party. *Was she jealous Tiffany asked me?* I didn't know, but I wanted to find out.

ME: Nah, it's part of the whole experience. I've

never been to an elite party before. Can't turn it down now that I've officially been invited.

My teacher came into the room, so I had no choice but to put my phone away.

∼

"WE GOING TO THE GAME TONIGHT?" Andy asked as he strolled into my living room and plopped down onto the sofa.

"We always go to the game," Max said.

"Yeah, but we always go to the game so Liam isn't there alone. Since he's hanging with the elite now, we don't really have to go anymore," Andy corrected.

"Of course, we're going. What the hell else would we do?" Max shot back.

Andy turned to Sofia who was sitting in the lounge chair with her arms crossed over her chest, looking bored and angry. "You want to go to the game?" he asked her.

She shrugged.

Annoyed with her lack of response, he looked at me. "Are *you* going?"

I nodded. "I've gotta take more pictures for the yearbook. Still need some candid shots of the game."

"Then it's settled. We'll go, hang out while Liam does his thing, then we'll all go grab a bite to eat, and party it up."

Sofia's eyes dashed to me, probably recalling the last time we'd gotten fucked up together.

But I didn't want to remember. "I can't. I'm going to the elite party after."

Andy shot up, his eyes wide with excitement. "You got invited to their party?" he asked like he couldn't believe it.

"Well, yeah. I hang with them now so...it makes sense."

Sofia let out a puff of air, catching our attention. "None of this makes sense," she muttered.

"What's that?" I asked, leaning forward and resting my elbows on my knees as I stared at her.

"I said none of this makes sense. I mean, since when does the elite bring a scholarship kid into their group? And out of all of us, why *you*? You know they're up to something. And when all this shit blows up in your face, don't come crying to me because I'm done waiting around for you."

I shook my head at her outburst. "Sofia, I thought we'd settled this. I know they're up to something behind my back, but I'm up to something behind theirs too. But all of that shit has nothing to do with why you're mad at me. Yeah, I went down on you on the hood of my car. Big fucking deal. It doesn't mean I'm yours now. We're nothing but friends. We agreed! So just... *stop*." I stood and started toward the door.

Behind me, Max and Andy were having a field day with the information I'd just laid on them. They knew Sofia and I would sometimes get fucked up and make out, but they had no idea how far it had gone.

Sofia muttered, "Whatever."

Annoyed, I shook my head. "I'm going to get cleaned up for the game and afterparty." Without another word, I marched upstairs.

I was angry with Sofia, but I tried to push it from my mind as I showered. It wasn't her fault I'd treated her so shitty. I hated myself for it, but what else could I do? I couldn't change the past. I had no interest in Sofia, and she knew that before we did anything. We'd agreed before we'd even kissed. I thought she'd gone along with it for the same reason I had. It wasn't my fault she'd been secretly holding back her feelings for me. *But it was my fault I'd risked our friendship.*

Around seven, I left for the football game. A little later, with my camera in hand, I strode through the gate. Andy and Max were waiting for me.

"Hey, what's up, guys?"

Andy shrugged. "Just hanging out. You ready to go in?"

I nodded. "Yeah, where's Sofia?"

Max chuckled. "After the two of you got into it today, she got up and stormed out. We haven't heard from her since. When Andy tried calling to see if she wanted us to pick her up, she didn't answer."

Great, I gotta fix this.

Sighing, we went into the game.

As the game kicked off, I moved around the sidelines, snapping pictures while Max and Andy followed behind me, chatting amongst themselves. I clicked several shots from ground level. Then I climbed the bleachers to get some shots from higher ground. At the top, I trained my camera on the cheerleaders. I captured their big pyramid stunt. When they tossed Asha into the air, I fast shot to get several images. While she was flying upward, she wore a look of pure happiness on her face, like she was finally free. When they caught her, a wide smile tipped her lips.

Looking back, I probably snapped a hundred pictures of Asha alone and only fifty of the game. Max and Andy sat by my side, chatting about TV shows, video games, and girls they thought were hot while snacking on popcorn and sucking down slurpies. I pretty much ignored them, keeping my eyes on Asha.

When the game ended, I said goodbye to the guys and went to meet up with the crew. They huddled on the sidelines.

"There's my hot date," Tiffany said, pulling me to her side.

A nervous laugh slipped out as I decided to play along. I eased my arm around her, letting my hand rest on her hip.

Asha's eyes flinched when she saw that. The carefree expression she'd been wearing disappeared. "Come on, Tiff. Let's go get ready for the party." She grabbed Tiffany and pushed her along in front of her. As Asha passed by me, she mumbled, "See you at the party, Liam."

I didn't want to show up super early to the party. That was something only the losers did. So, I went to a local gas station and filled my car with gas. A man stood out front, holding a change cup.

"I'll give you twenty if you go in and buy a bottle of tequila," I offered.

He surveyed me. "How old are you?"

"Twenty-one. I just don't have my ID on me," I lied.

He shrugged. "Good enough for me. Give me the money for the booze."

I handed him some cash and waited outside. A few moments later, he was back. He handed over the alcohol, and I gave him twenty bucks as promised. "Thanks, man."

"Thank you." He took his money and booked it out of there, having made his cash for the day.

I climbed back into my car and started in the direction of the party after hitting up the drive thru. I knew I didn't need to get hammered on an empty stomach. On the drive over, I ate my double cheeseburger. It was gone by the time I made it to Hudson's house.

There were several cars in the driveway and along the street, but it didn't look too busy yet. I grabbed the bottle of tequila from the passenger seat and sauntered to the door. I got nervous, wondering if I was supposed to knock or just go inside. Hudson and I weren't exactly on friendly enough terms to lead me to believe I should just walk in, but it was a party after all.

Weighing my options, I turned the knob and entered. His house was almost as big as Asha's, all stone and pillars. The entryway was empty, but people were talking in the next room over. I followed the sounds of their voices. When I strode into the kitchen, Tiffany practically jumped on me.

"Oh goodie! Tequila, my fav!" Tiffany said, taking the bottle from me and moving to the island.

Asha peered at me, her face lighting up. My eyes seemed to have a mind of their own as they roamed her body. She was clad in a short, pink tube dress. She was all legs. Thin, tiny straps rested on her shoulders. Her tits looked so big in the tight dress I was surprised the fragile looking straps hadn't snapped. She wore a sexy pair of high heels that gave her long legs a nice shape. I couldn't help but imagine how they'd feel wrapped around me.

"Let's get this party started!" Tiffany shouted.

Everyone gathered around the island to take a shot of tequila.

We tossed them back and slammed the glasses onto the marble countertop.

"Now, let's really get it started," Hudson said, holding up a joint. He placed it between his lips and lit it, taking a long drag. It got passed around.

I wasn't new to smoking pot, so I took a few hits before passing it along.

"Look at the party animal," Tiffany said, strutting over to me. "I have a great idea." She spun around and poured another shot of tequila. When she pivoted back, she had a shot in one hand and a lime wedge between her tits. "Lick my neck," she demanded.

"What?" I asked, making sure I'd heard her right.

"Lick my neck," she ordered again.

I laughed and glanced around at the guys. They nodded in encouragement. So, I leaned forward and licked her neck. Once I lifted my head, she tossed some salt onto the wet spot.

"Body shot," she said with a giggle.

"What order am I supposed to do this in?" I asked, motioning between the three.

"First you lick," she said, giving me a seductive look. "Then you sip." Her eyes dropped to the shot glass in her hand. "Then *you suck*."

The guys whooped and hollered.

I shrugged and stepped toward her. I licked the salt from her neck, swallowed down the shot, then bit the lime between her tits. When I removed the lime from my mouth, everyone cheered. Everyone but Asha.

I hated that I felt like such a big shot. There I was partying it up with the elite. I was smoking weed with them, throwing back shots, and they kept egging me on. Asha didn't appear pleased, but she'd made her wants clear. It wasn't looking good for me.

Maybe I was bitter, and that was why I decided to let go a little bit with Tiffany. I didn't want to ponder it, so I didn't.

Fuck it.

After that, the party was in full swing. The house filled up quickly, and things got loud. Music pulsed through the house so I had to yell to be heard. Tiffany was hammered and easily distracted. So anytime I didn't want her hanging on me, I pointed her in a new direction and she'd stumble off. Asha on the other hand seemed happy and a little drunk as she sashayed up to me in the living room.

I was leaning against the doorway with a cup of beer in my hand. She stopped when she was inches from me. Her blue eyes locked on mine, and she had a smirk on her lips.

"Do you like my dress, Liam?"

I wet my suddenly dry lips and nodded.

"You should see what's under it," she whispered, leaning in just enough I could see down the front.

Her tits were pressed together, making my mouth water.

Earlier, Hudson mentioned she and Lucas were fighting in his laundry room.

Was she using me?

God, she was two different people—one when she was with the elite and another when she was with me. I never knew which one was being genuine.

"There you are," Tiffany said, strolling up and wrapping her arm around mine again.

Asha quickly straightened up but didn't bother backing away.

Tiffany squinted at her. "Where's Lucas?"

Asha shrugged. "Who cares? I'm doing what I want, and he's doing what he wants."

Tiffany laughed. "You mean he's doing *who* he wants."

Asha rolled her eyes and marched away, probably to find Lucas.

"Dance with me," Tiffany whined, draping her arms around my neck.

She was having a blast grinding on me, but I tried to distract myself from the way she was making my body come alive with the constant friction. I searched for Asha in the swarm of bodies. When I finally spotted her, she and Lucas were in a heated argument near the keg.

I needed to divert my thoughts so I asked, "Which guy in the group do you have a crush on?"

She smiled. "You, silly."

I rolled my eyes. "I meant before me. Who did you like?"

She shrugged as her hips moved against mine. "None of them, all of them. I just like sucking dick."

That made my eyebrows shoot up. "The guys in the group?" I questioned.

She nodded with a wicked smile on her face. "I'm thirsty. Let's do a shot.

Tiffany dragged me back to the kitchen where everyone else was—Lucas and Asha included. Tiff poured another round of shots. Asha and Lucas's argument must have ended, but Asha looked sullen. Like always, I couldn't keep my gaze off her. Her back was against Lucas's chest. His hands were on her hips while his mouth kissed and sucked her neck.

But Asha's eyes were on mine, her expression unreadable. I didn't understand what she was trying to tell me. *Was she trying to make me jealous? Did she need my help?*

Confused, annoyed, and pissed off, I swallowed down another shot. Each time I tossed one back, Tiff poured another. My stomach rolled from the liquor, but I refused to give in to the urge to puke. I was elite, and the elite didn't puss out. The elite started the party. and they ended it. I had a name to live up to.

Lucas jerked Asha's hips back, pressing her ass against his crotch. Her eye contact broke from mine when he spun her around. My stomach turned when I saw the way he grabbed at her ass and hips while shoving his tongue down her throat. As fucked as I was, I knew I'd need a lot more if I had to watch him treat her like that all night.

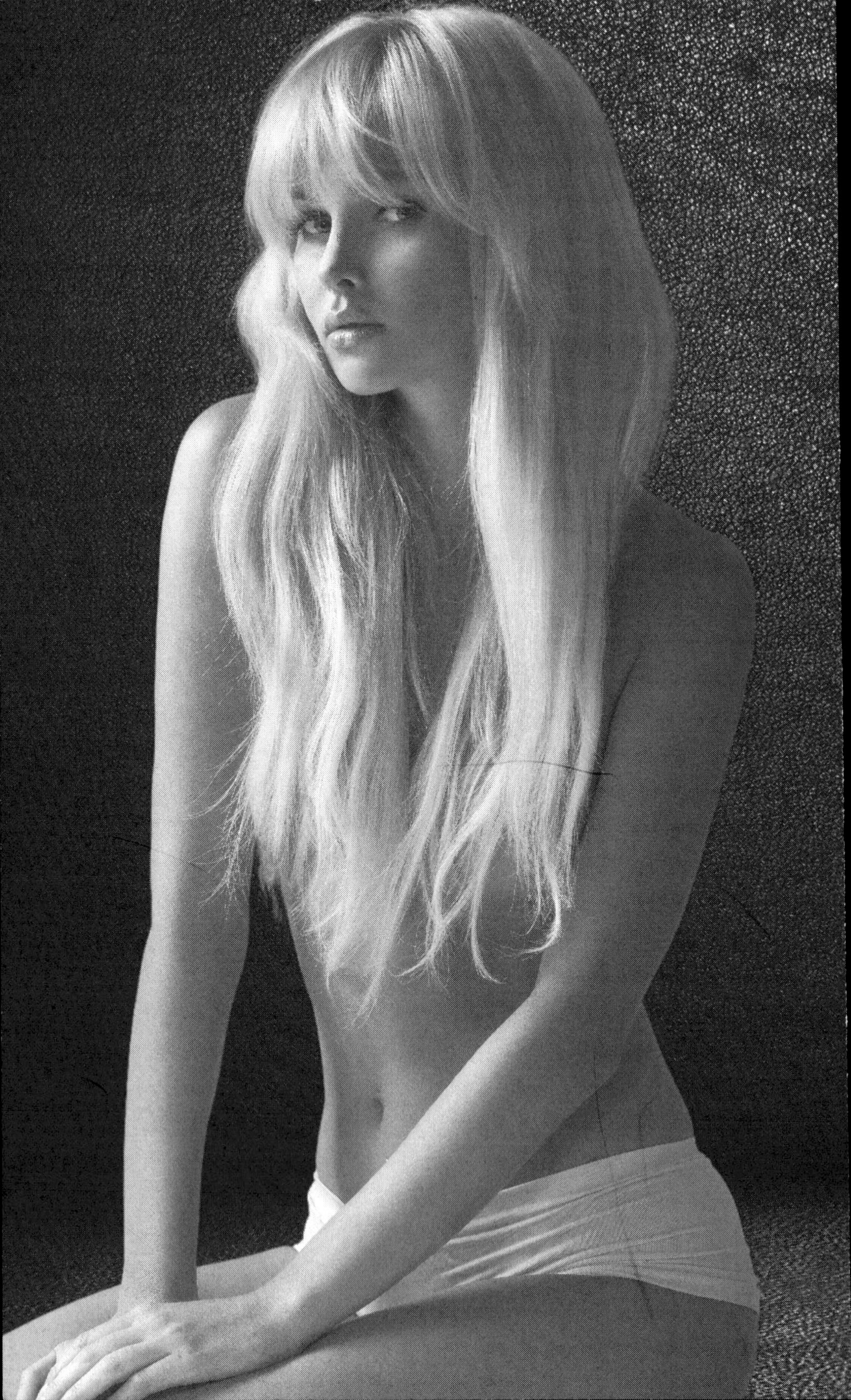

FIFTEEN
ASHA

Internally, I rolled my eyes as Lucas's hold on me tightened. My terrible night just kept getting worse. I'd been in a bad since the game ended...

A smile played across my lips as I walked off the field with the rest of the squad. My heart was still soaring from the flying sensation I got from doing the stunts earlier—the only moments each week where I felt truly free. When I glanced up and saw Liam approaching, that same freefalling feeling grabbed my heart.

And then Tiffany latched onto him like a leech. It infuriated me she thought she could claim him. I was the one who'd brought him into our group. I'd been pissed with her ever since she'd asked him to be her date. And the fact that he hadn't declined ... I sucked in a deep breath, trying to quiet my fury.

I tuned out the chatter around me. More than I hated Tiffany at the moment, I hated how Liam seemed to be into whatever stunt she was pulling. He didn't push her away. He hadn't rejected her. Why did he keep playing along? Did he really like her?

I thought he liked me.

Without much thought, I somehow found myself pushing Tiffany in front of me toward the locker room.

"What's with you and Liam?' I asked, pulling my skirt down.

She shrugged with a smile in place. "I don't know. He's cute. And he's a guy I haven't been with yet. You know those are few and far between." She giggled.

I rolled my eyes as I tugged my cheer top over my head. "He's a good guy, Tiffany. Don't fuck with him."

She scoffed. "I'm not going to fuck with him. I'm going to fuck him," she said matter-of-factly. "And I think the party tonight is the perfect time to do it. Don't you? I mean, you don't have a problem with that, right? You do have Lucas after all."

She'd put me on the spot. She knew I wouldn't admit to her that I had feelings for Liam, and I sure as shit wasn't going to admit it in a crowded locker room where the whole team could overhear me.

I slipped my dress over my head and slammed my locker shut. "You and Liam can do whatever you want. I'm just saying he's good. He's not like us. Don't ruin him." I snatched up my bag and headed for the door.

My mind was a million miles away as I drove to the party. Before everyone else arrived, I threw back a shot and smoked a joint. I just prayed it'd be enough to get me through the shitshow.

Lucas refused to let me out of his sight. All night, he'd kept me at his side and always had his arm around me or his hand on me in some way. But his eyes were on every other girl at the party when he thought I wasn't looking. Mentioning it earlier had only caused an argument, so I eventually just gave in and tolerated his divided attention.

To hell with it.

Besides, I enjoyed the way Liam looked when he noticed Lucas touching me. Liam looked angry, pissed off, and jealous.

But after a while, he surrendered to the drugs and booze in his system, so he didn't seem to notice me as much. When he and Tiffany disappeared into another room, I could no longer see them.

My heart thundered with anxiety. *What if she didn't wait, and she took him up to one of the bedrooms? If Liam slept with Tiffany, would change the way I felt about him?*

You don't feel anything. He's off limits.

I tried to ease myself out of Lucas's hold so I could go check on Liam and Tiff. But Lucas always got more handsy when his mind was altered with alcohol or drugs. He was bad enough sober, but fucked up, I had a fight on my hands. Tonight was no exception. Not that he was the only one acting like a sex-starved being. The parties the elite put on were always filled with people fucking. It was like they spiked the keg with Molly. By the end of the night, I wouldn't be able to turn a corner without bumping into someone fucking.

Even though Lucas kept a firm hand on my hip, he gave me no attention as he talked with Hudson, Jude, and some other guys from school. I was nothing more than arm candy to him. I waited until he was in deep discussion with them before trying to step away again. The moment his hand fell back to his side, he grabbed my arm and tugged me back.

"Where are you going?"

"To the bathroom," I lied.

He released me and went back to chatting with the guys. I wandered around the house, looking for Tiffany and Liam. Liam was hanging with some people in the corner of the living room. I didn't want to bother him, so I continued searching for Tiffany. When I didn't find her, I decided to go to the bathroom. The door was closed and locked. I leaned against the wall, waiting my turn.

When the door opened, Tiffany sauntered out. "Oh, hey. I didn't think Lucas was going to let you off your leash."

I rolled my eyes. "I'm not on a leash. I do whatever the fuck I want."

She giggled. "Yeah, sure," she mumbled, pushing past me.

With the bathroom empty, I shuffled inside and peered in the mirror. I didn't recognize the person staring back at me. She wasn't the broken, nameless girl from the club. She wasn't Asha, queen bitch who ruled the school. This girl looked sad and confused. I let out a long breath and shook my head at myself. *How many people was I going to keep finding when I looked in the mirror? And how did everyone else only see one?*

Someone knocked on the door, and I pulled it open, more than happy to not examine myself further. Lucas pushed his way inside.

"What are you doing?" I asked as he turned his back to me and locked the door.

He spun around with a smirk as his hands found my hips. "I just thought we could use a little alone time." He tugged me against his chest, and his lips found mine. His tongue slid into my mouth, and I had no choice but to kiss him back. Pushing him away would've done no good. He would've only gotten pissed off and become more forceful. I had to be more skilled when it came to breaking away.

I allowed him to kiss me and even did a pretty convincing job of pretending I wanted it. I laced my fingers through his hair and tugged at the roots. It made his lips and tongue more forceful, like I was egging him on.

When I playfully nipped his lip, he let out a growl and picked me up by the hips, setting me on the edge of the counter. He stepped between my legs, and his hands roamed my body. There weren't any tingles where he touched. I didn't feel hot either. If anything, I felt ice cold. I prayed someone would knock on the door, but knew I'd never get that lucky.

Finally, after feeling like I'd given him enough time, I slowed the kiss and gently pushed him back. "Let's get back out there," I said with a fake smile.

He shook his head. "I'm having more fun in here." His mouth was back on mine.

"Me too, but if we do this now, what are we going to do later?" I surveyed his face as he thought up an answer. "Let's enjoy the party a little longer. Tease ourselves."

Someone finally knocked on the door, and it was enough of a

distraction I was able to slide off the counter and open the door. Two very drunk girls came stumbling in.

"Oh, sorry," one of them said.

I ignored her as I took Lucas's hand and led him back to his friends in the kitchen. I grabbed another beer and leaned against the counter to sip it while keeping an eye on Tiffany and Liam in the living room. They weren't touching, but they were close. Their lips were moving, so I knew they were talking. *What were they were talking about? Was he asking her all the same questions he asked me? Was he busy worming his way into her heart like he already had mine?*

I watched as she laughed, throwing her head back dramatically. *Fucking bitch.* She knew what game we were playing, and she was playing well. I couldn't help but think that while I'd been playing checkers, she'd been playing chess. Somehow she knew I was developing feelings for Liam. And from the moment I'd suggested bringing him into the group, she'd had a plan. She was going to use Liam to get to Lucas. She'd always wanted Lucas. I didn't doubt what Liam said our first day together about the two of them hooking up behind my back. It wouldn't have surprised me in the least. I was sure if I gave Lucas what he wanted from me—sex—that the moment it was over, he'd dump me and start dating Tiffany. He only wanted me for one thing.

I had tossed back a couple more shots. When I noticed Liam's gaze on me, I sent him a flirty smile. It made his grin widen. When Tiffany saw the exchange, her eyes cut to me, and she pulled him away, someplace where I couldn't see them. This party was lasting way too long. I only wanted one thing—to get out of there. Well, two I guessed. I wanted Liam to leave with me before he could find out the secret meaning of the party to begin with.

Liam was too decent to be at an elite party. He was too nice to hang out with people like us. He was far too good to be fucked over by someone like Tiffany. And if he was too good for Tiffany, then he was too good for someone like me. I needed to let go of my feelings for Liam because things could never work out with us. But more than that, I had to get him out of the party before things went too far. I didn't want him changed by us or the things we did. And the longer he was a part of our group, the more he was going to change. Liam was going down, and he didn't even know it. It made me feel like shit knowing I was the reason he'd sink to begin with.

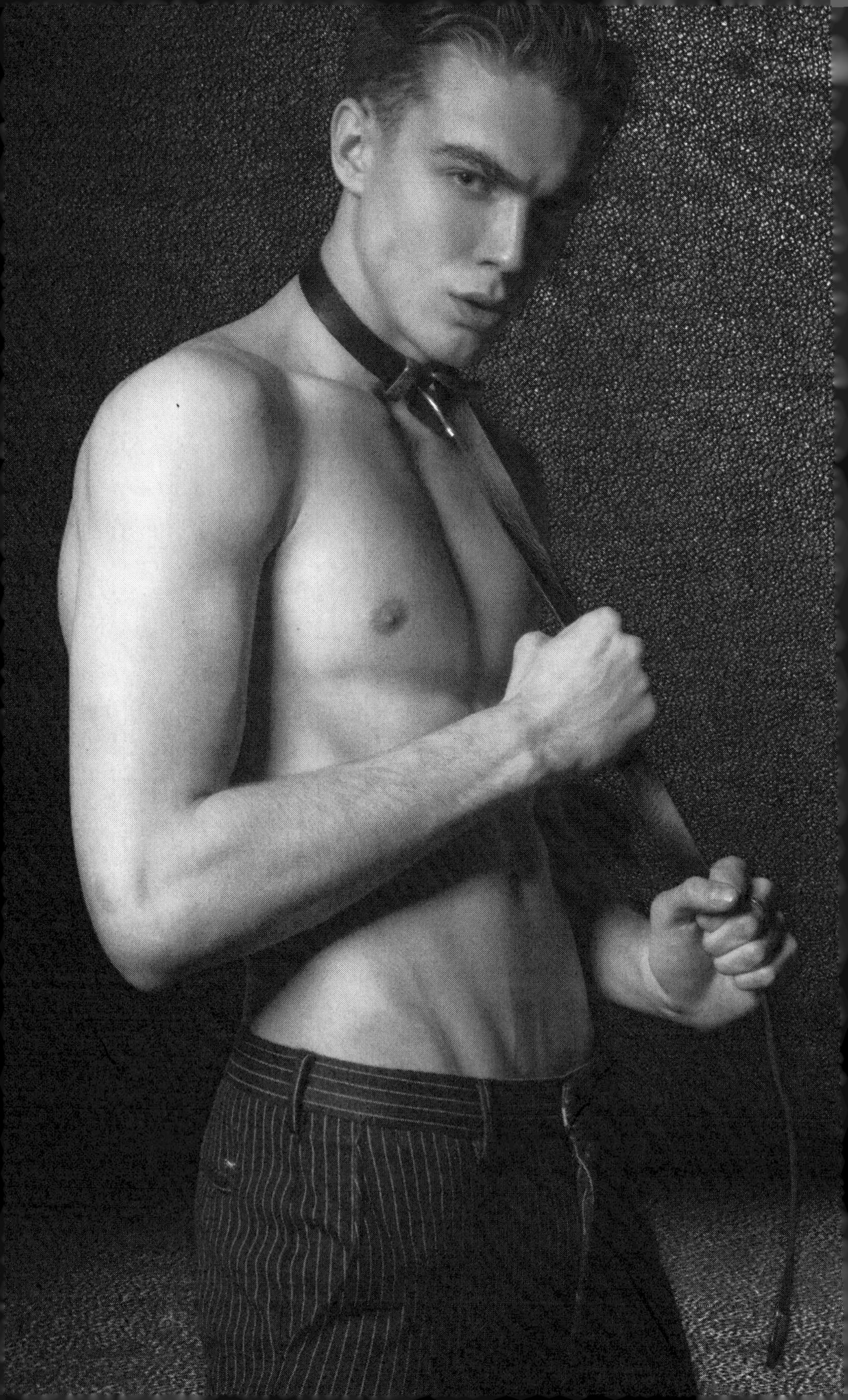

SIXTEEN
LIAM

I tossed more and more alcohol down my throat while someone lit another joint. My head was spinning, but I was still standing. That was all that mattered. I was so drunk I couldn't see straight. The next thing I knew the elite were huddled up, passing something out. Moments later, Tiffany was back in front of me, pushing her chest against mine.

"I have something for you," she whispered.

"Yeah, what's that?" I slurred.

"Open your mouth," she continued, her lips only slightly touching mine.

When I did, she dropped something onto my tongue.

"Swallow it, and I swear, you'll have the time of your life." Her green eyes were wide with excitement.

"What is it?" It felt like a pill.

"Molly," she said, showing me her pill and making a show of putting it on her tongue. She swallowed and opened her mouth for me to see that it was gone.

If she could do it, I could do it. I swallowed and showed her my empty mouth. Her grin widened, and she leaned in, pressing her mouth to mine.

She pulled away abruptly and went walking through the house.

It seemed the whole group had dispersed into different areas. Hudson and Lucas were by the bar, talking to a couple girls.

Asha walked over to me. "You want to get out of here?"

My back straightened. "Are you offering to leave with me?" I asked, confused.

She shrugged as she peeked up at me from beneath her lashes.

Before I could say more, Tiffany was back. She took my hand in hers while shooting Asha a look. Hudson and Lucas both came back into the room.

"All right, boys and girls. It's time to move this party into the VIP room," Hudson said with a wide smile while rubbing his hands together.

Asha glanced over at me. "You should probably go." There was a seriousness on her face that wasn't there moments before.

It felt like she was trying to get rid of me. But I was bound and determined to find out what the VIP room was. If for no other reason than to have some dirt on them if I needed it.

"I think I'll stick around," I told her. "I'm having a good time."

Tiffany smirked, happy with my answer. "See, Asha. He's having fun with *me*. Shouldn't you go join Lucas?"

Asha pressed her lips together and turned so fast her long hair smacked me in the face. I watched as she stepped up to Lucas's side. He pulled her in close as a door in the kitchen opened. They walked through and starting going down some steps.

There were quite a few people between Asha and Lucas and Tiffany and me, but slowly, everyone in line descended down the dark steps. By the time I got to the bottom, the room opened up. It was a finished basement with four different couches, a bar, a pool table, and a round table that looked to be used for poker games. The overhead lights were off, replaced by a flashing, strobe light and a multicolored disco ball. It was like a fucking dance party, but nobody was dancing. And only the elite were down there with a handful of people they deemed good enough.

Tiffany led me over to a couch, and the two of us sat down. When I looked up, I found we were sitting directly across from Asha and Lucas. He wore a wide smile and had shrugged out of his button up shirt, leaving him in a t-shirt.

What the hell was going on?

Hudson plopped down on Tiffany's other side and held up a remote. Hitting the button, loud music started playing. It was like a cue. He dumped some white powder onto the glass coffee table, arranging a line before snorting it up. Tiffany followed, doing another line while Jude and Lucas did one each. My gaze locked on Asha. She wasn't looking at me. Her eyes were focused on her lap.

"Liam, you're up," Hudson said, flopping down beside me on the couch.

"I'm, uh, good, man. I've had way too much already."

I thought he might fight me on it, but he shrugged and turned the music up louder with his remote before settling back in his seat, a dazed expression on his face. Lucas was back next to Asha on the couch, and Tiffany was on my other side.

Once the music grew louder, couples everywhere started making out.

Hudson peered over at me with a smirk. "Watch and learn, young one." He grabbed ahold of Tiffany from over me and dragged her across my lap and onto his lap.

She giggled but allowed him to manhandle her. She ran her hands through his hair, and he pulled her mouth to his for a kiss. I was frozen and so confused. She'd been on me all night, and now, she was just going to start making out with him right in front of me?

Across from me, Lucas and Asha were kissing. His hand was on her knee. Beside them was Jude, who was making out with Marcie while Heidi gave him head. It felt like my eyes bugged out of my skull. I was at a sex party. The elite were all fucking around and trading the girls back and forth.

Stunned, I glanced back at Hudson and Tiffany. She was grinding on him while they kissed. Against my will, I turned my attention back to Asha and Lucas. His hand was slowly creeping up her thigh as they made out. Her eyes opened and locked with mine. Immediately, she closed them back and ran her fingers through his hair, pulling him closer.

Anger surged through me, burning its way up my chest like acid. She'd been flirting with me most of the night. *But now she suddenly wanted Lucas?* He had his hands all over her—her legs, her breasts, up her dress.

Hudson smacked my arm, getting my attention. "You want some of this?"

I was fucked out of my mind and wasn't even sure any of it was real. *Was he serious? He was going to* share *her with me?* Tiffany peered at me with a smile and a hopeful look in her eye.

"Sure," I mumbled, needing something to kill the anger swimming through my veins.

Tiffany shifted over to straddle me. Her lips pressed to mine, and her tongue slid into my mouth. She laced her fingers through my hair and tugged it as her hips moved back and forth.

Even though I didn't even want Tiffany, my body came alive under her. Every sensation felt stronger than it ever had before. In that second, there wasn't anything I wanted more than to get off. My dick was painfully hard and in serious need of attention. After all I had to drink, I didn't even know how my dick was still working. Probably had something to do with the pill Tiffany had given me, but I didn't know for sure. I'd never done Molly before.

"Take her shirt off, man," Hudson urged, nudging my arm.

Tiffany broke off our kiss and sat back with a grin, watching me to see if I'd actually do it. I reached for the hem of her shirt and yanked it up over her head, dropping it onto the floor. She started grinding on me again. Hudson reached behind her and unsnapped her bra. Her big tits dropped out the bottom, and she dragged the straps off her arms.

My eyes zeroed in on her breasts as they bounced in front of me.

"You think you can make her pussy wet, or do you need some help?" Hudson leaned over and asked, his hand high on my thigh.

I glanced at Asha. Her eyes were closed, and Lucas's face was buried in her neck. It seemed almost like she was trying to pretend she was somewhere else. But she was there. And it was happening.

"I think I can manage," I said, slipping my hand up to cup Tiff's breast. I squeezed her nipple between my thumb and forefinger. Her head fell back, and she let out a soft moan.

"Can I help anyway? Looks like a lot of fun," Hudson murmured, his hand traveling higher on my thigh.

I shook my head, trying to clear it, before I nodded at him and blinked, my focus tilting and hazy.

Pretend she's Asha. It'll be easier that way. Or leave. Just fucking leave.

No. I need to stay.

Fuck. Where am I again?

"Do whatever you want, man." I leaned forward and sucked Tiff's nipple into my mouth, flicking my tongue across it again and again.

"She's not wearing panties. Tell me how wet she is," Hudson whispered as his hand shifted to the button on my pants.

I let my hand drop from her chest and land on her thigh. Slowly, I moved it upward, under her skirt. He was right. When I got to the junction between her legs, there was no cotton stopping me. I found her bare and dripping wet.

I gripped her hip with my left hand and lifted her up enough for Hudson to slide two fingers inside her. Her nails dug into my shoulders as she let out a gasp.

"She's wet," Hudson grunted.

I nodded and blinked, trying to focus on Asha.

"Stick a finger in her ass. She loves that." Hudson slid his fingers out of her before leaning into me and running his lips along my jaw.

I blinked rapidly, trying to orient myself as Tiff giggled. Someone's hand reached into my pants and rubbed my stiff cock. I sucked in a sharp breath, almost positive it was Hudson on my junk.

What the fuck am I doing?

I shifted, needing air.

"Easy," Hudson murmured into my ear.

Then I was certain it was his hand on my cock as he stroked me up and down.

"Just let go. It'll be fun," he husked out.

My heart thudded hard as Tiff sucked against the skin of my neck.

"Damn, man, that's a big cock," Hudson grunted.

I squeezed my eyes closed. *This wasn't going to work for me. I had to get out of here.*

I tried to shift again, but both Tiffany and Hudson had moved to the floor, between my legs. I chanced a glance down and found them kissing. Tiffany's hand was wrapped around my cock with Hudson's hand as they slowly pumped me. Like a magnet, my gaze lifted. Asha was staring at me. My heart ached as she untangled herself from Lucas and got to her feet, her eyes darting from my face to Tiffany and Hudson stroking me.

Without a word, she turned on her heel and left the room. Lucas swore and followed after her.

Hudson took his hand off my cock to undo his pants.

"I-I need to go," I rasped as Tiffany slowed her stroking of my dick.

Hudson's tongue was buried in her mouth. I took the opportunity to stuff my dick back in my pants and stagger to my feet. Asha was the only thing on my mind. If I went out there and got my ass kicked by Lucas for going after her, so be it.

I managed to get up the stairs a moment later and started searching around the house for her. My head was spinning, but I forced myself to focus on the prize.

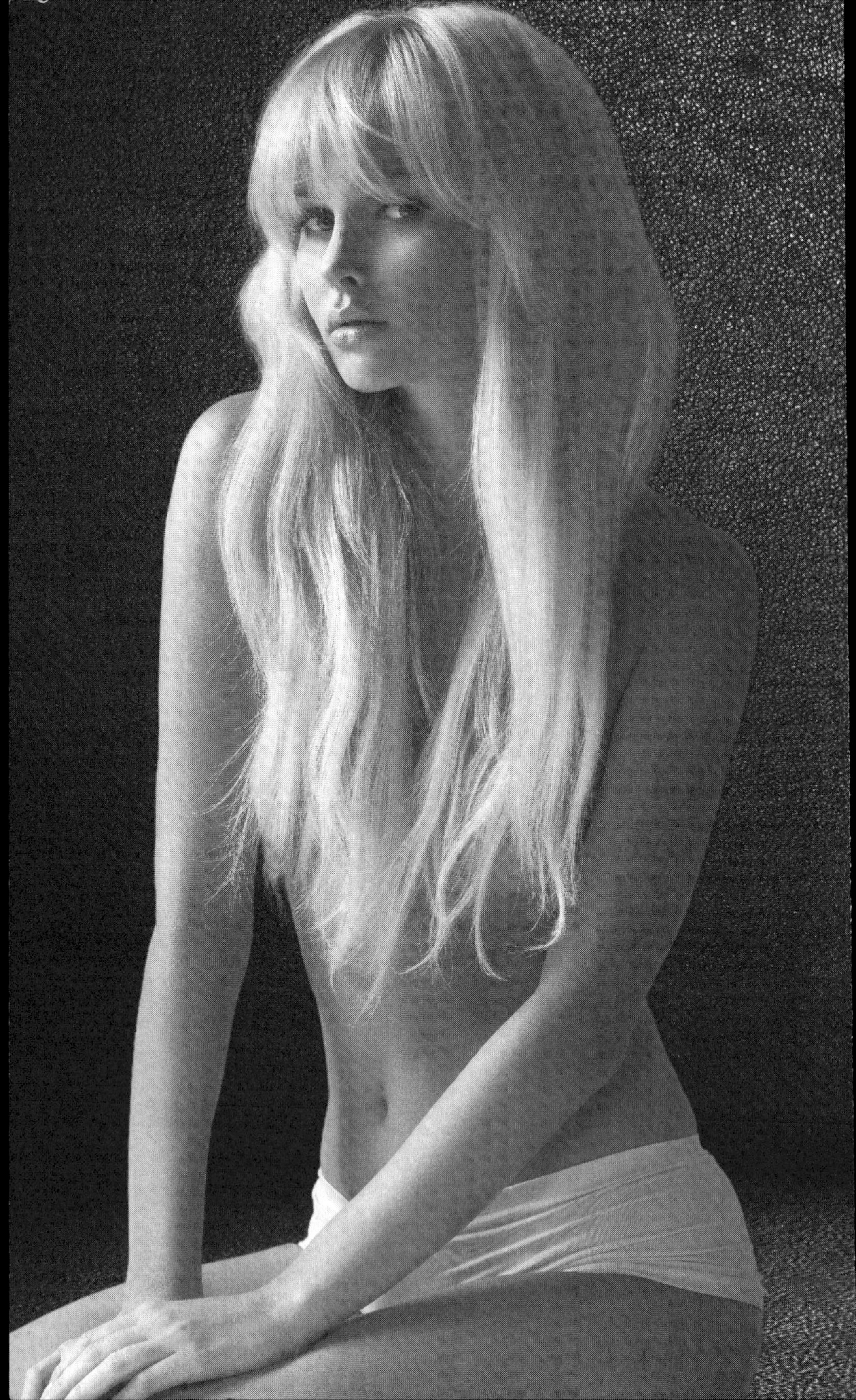

SEVENTEEN
ASHA

"What the hell?" Lucas asked the moment he caught up to me outside the bathroom.

"I just don't feel good. I-I need to be alone," I told him as I tried to close the door on him.

He wasn't having it. He moved into the bathroom with me. I turned away, but he gripped my biceps and spun me around to face him. Staring into my eyes, he pushed my back against the door.

"You were feeling just fine five seconds ago. What's wrong?" His hands cupped my cheeks.

I shook my head, not wanting to give him the chance to read me. "I don't know. My stomach is doing flips. Maybe I've had too much to drink."

He frowned. "I've watched you all night. You barely had anything to drink, and you didn't drop any Molly either."

I shrugged. "Then maybe it was something I ate. All I know is if I don't get out of here soon, I'm going to be puking in the bushes and you'll be holding my hair. Now, do you want to do that or would you like to let me go so you can go back in and enjoy the party?"

"Asha, you don't think I pay attention, but I do. I know I'm a piece of shit in a lot of ways, but I do care about you. I *know* your tells. You're lying. What's going on?"

I swallowed before the words came tumbling out of my mouth. "I think we should break up."

He blanched and released me. "What?"

I licked my lips. "I know you and Tiff—"

"I didn't fuck her, Asha. W-We kissed in my car after Jude's party a few weeks ago. The one you couldn't go to. I was upset because I felt like you were blowing me off. It's no excuse, I know. I fucked up. I *know* I did. I told her it wasn't like that for us. Me and her. She was upset about it but agreed. That's it. I *swear* to you."

"I find that hard to believe. You *always* push me for sex—"

"I'm an asshole. I don't mean to disregard your feelings, Asha. I really don't. I care about you. I just think you're beautiful, and I have a hard time controlling myself around you. Again, not an excuse, I know..."

"Lucas, please. I need this. My head's a mess."

"You've been my girlfriend for almost two years," he said softly, taking my hand.

"Maybe you'd enjoy a little freedom to get perspective. Maybe we both would?" I breathed out, my heart hurting.

What the hell was I even doing? Lucas was my normal. He was the one who the smiling girl in the mirror kissed. He played the part next to her. But I wasn't the smiling Asha. That girl was a fake. I wanted to *feel*.

And I'd felt *something* when I'd watched Liam with Tiffany on his lap and Hudson trying to feel him up. I'd felt a million feelings I'd never experienced so strongly before. And even if Lucas could be a dick, he still deserved to be happy too.

"Asha..." He scrubbed his hand over his face and blew out a breath. "Fine. If this will make you happy, then fine. I'm not going to tell anyone though in case you change your mind. Just.... take your time. I'm here."

I was floored by how calm and sweet he appeared to be. It was completely unlike the Lucas I knew.

I nodded as he reached for the doorknob. "Are you going home?"

"I think so," I whispered, my body feeling weak.

"Text me when you get there, so I know you made it safely."

"I will," I murmured as he opened the door and cast me a final look before leaving.

The moment he was gone, I burst into tears. *What had I done? I wanted that, right? I needed it, didn't I?*

My heart ached as I thought about Liam in the VIP room probably getting his dick sucked by Hudson and Tiffany. He was wasted. I knew he was. I had to rescue him.

My heart skipped as a knock vibrated the door, and Liam's voice called out to me.

He came for me?

It took me a moment to gather my wits before I pulled open the door to find him bleary-eyed and staring at me, his hair a wild mess. He pushed into the room, the door clicking and locking behind him.

I said the only words I could. "I...we broke up."

"Good." He closed the space between us as my pulse thundered in my ears.

"Why?" I stared at him in confusion.

"Now we can do this." He brought me into his arms, and his lips crashed against mine.

He was the flame to my wick, and I ignited, melting against him as his tongue slid along mine.

It was fate. Destiny. If only for one night because maybe that was all I could ever give him or myself. I wanted it, whatever *it* was. No regrets. None where it concerned Liam Hastings. But first ...

"What about Tiffany? And Hudson?" I managed to say against his lips as we slowed the kiss to a halt.

"I'm *here*, not out there," he said softly, tilting my chin up so I had to look at him. "If I'm going to be locked in a room kissing and touching someone, I want it to be *you*."

I stared at him in utter disbelief. "Even if it won't last? Even if it's just for the night?" My eyes watered as I peered up at him.

"Yes." He kissed me gently. "But I'm a little wasted, so I may be a bit sloppy if that's OK."

I bit my bottom lip and nodded. "O-OK."

His lips met mine again as he lifted me in the air. My legs wrapped around his midsection. Liam set me on the marble countertop, our lips never parting. He pushed the strap of my dress down, exposing the top of my breast. His cock was hard as I ground against it. My soft gasps and whimpers were muffled by his mouth. I was desperate for him to touch me. It was a strange new sensation. He made me feel out of control. Excited. Hopeful.

Reverently, his hands moved beneath my tiny dress, skimming along the thin strap of my thong on my hip. His finger followed the edge, feeling the heat between my legs as he pushed aside my thong.

"I want to touch you, hellcat. I want to taste you," he rasped.

I moaned softly, spreading my legs to make room for him. Gently, he ran his fingers along my wet folds. I gasped and bucked against his touch as he rubbed my clit. My nails dug into his back as he slid his finger down and breached the entrance to my tight heat.

"L-Liam," I breathed out, kissing him, peppering his name on his lips as I shook beneath his touch.

"I want to make you come, hellcat. Fuck, you don't know how much."

"Please," I rasped, grinding my hips against his finger.

He slid another in me as he claimed my mouth again. When he hooked his fingers to rub a spot inside me, I lost control of my movements.

My breast slipped out of my dress, making Liam groan. He immediately moved down and sucked my nipple into his mouth. The sensation of his mouth on my sensitive flesh made me ride his hand harder. My breathing grew hot and heavy as he sucked harder, like he was trying to mark me. Little did he know he already had.

As he slowed the tempo of his fingers, I let out a soft cry of protest. He pressed a kiss to my lips and rested his hand against the center of my chest. I blinked at him in confusion as he slowly pushed me down onto the counter.

He gradually moved down my body, kissing the breast that was out before easing the top of my dress down so he could lavish the other one. He sucked and kissed along both, alternating from left to right. I relaxed against the cool marble as he shifted my dress up. I closed my eyes as his soft touch moved down my body.

Could I do this? Was it real? My pulse thundered in my ears. I wanted this so much it hurt. "Can I..." he asked, locking his gaze on mine from between my legs.

I nodded wordlessly. That was all it took for him to lick up my slit. He rolled his tongue over my quivering bundle, making my back arch up off the counter as I panted heavily beneath his onslaught. He slid his fingers back inside me, one at a time, slowly. His mouth stayed fastened to my clit, licking and sucking, until I was a trembling mess desperate for release.

It didn't take long. My breathing picked up, and my fingers twisted in his hair as I held him against my center. Uninhibited, I ground myself against his mouth. With one final suck and flick of his tongue against my clit, I let out a moan. I savored the moment—the first time I'd ever actually enjoyed someone touching me. I basked in it. The way his touch erased a multitude of previous unwanted hands on me. The growl of satisfaction that rumbled against my wet flesh. The look of hunger and adoration mixed in his eyes.

When I came back to Earth, he slid his fingers out and tenderly swiped his tongue all over my folds and up my slit. Then he pressed a series of kisses along my heat before he rose to his feet. I sat up, my face flushed as I brought my dress up to cover my breasts.

"What about you?" My gaze darted to the impressive tent he was sporting then back up at him.

"I'm OK." He took my face in his hands, holding me like I was the most precious thing he'd ever touched. "I wanted you to feel good. That's all that matters to me."

"But—"

He pressed a finger to my lips. "No. It was about you tonight, hellcat. Just you."

I breathed out and fell into his arms, my fingers twisting in his shirt as he held me. He pressed a kiss to the top of my head. I wished we could stay like this forever. But it had to end because someone pounded on the door.

"We should go," he said softly, not moving an inch.

"I don't want to," I mumbled against his chest.

He held me and ignored the pounding on the door. Once the door opened, things would have to go back to how they were before. Right? Maybe not? Fuck, I hoped...

∼

IT SEEMED like things moved in fast forward after Liam and I broke apart. He called Andy and Max to come get him. We left the bathroom separately so as to not draw attention to ourselves. When I got home, I parked in the garage and slipped in the back door, wanting to avoid Gio if he was in his office. Instead of using the staircase in the entry way, I took the back one that only the staff used. I managed to get to my room without being detected. I let out a sigh of relief the moment I closed my bedroom door and locked it.

I dropped my purse on my vanity and went to the bathroom. I realized I'd left my cheer bag in the car, but I wasn't going back down. Not after I'd made it safely to my room. I turned on the shower and stripped down in front of the mirror. My face was covered in makeup, and my hair was a mess from Liam's fingers. I smiled at the memory as I touched my lips. God, that boy could kiss.

And suck. And lick. And make me feel so good.

I spun and stepped into the shower. The hot water was soothing to my tense, sore muscles. I rolled my head from side to side, trying to relax. I dipped my head back and let the water cascade over my hair. Behind my closed lids, all I could see was Tiffany on Liam's lap. I imagined her moans as she ground herself against him. I pictured Hudson stroking him. My eyes popped open, and I found I was still in my bathroom, not the basement.

Liam had been mine. Not theirs. He came to me. He wanted *me*.

After washing my hair and shaving my legs, I wasn't ready to climb out of the shower just yet. So I sat in the bottom of the tub and let the hot water rain down on me as I spaced out, dreaming of a better life, a life where I was a normal girl. A normal girl would have a normal boyfriend, someone good, like Liam.

I let the fantasy carry me away. I could see Liam and myself walking the halls of school hand in hand—and nobody paid us any attention. I envisioned him taking me out on dates, dinner and a movie, or maybe a school football game where he sat with me instead of running off to hang with the guys. I imagined us making out in his car. My fantasy was so vivid, I could feel his soft lips against mine, and his hands touching me with care and love. In my perfect world, he'd kiss me deeply and trail his hot mouth down my body as I shivered in anticipation of what was to come. His focus was all on me. Even when I wanted to give to him, he'd give to me first.

There in my shower, lost in my fairytale, I imagined the first time I'd give myself to him, how soft and slow he'd be, making sure not to hurt me. It would be a magical moment full of heightened emotions—fear, excitement, and love.

My body came alive as I thought of him touching me the same way he had in the bathroom. How warm his tongue was as he slid it against my heat. As he sought out the bundle of nerves that had me calling out his name. I could still feel his fingers as they moved inside me. The taste of him was still on my tongue.

My eyes popped open, and my body went cold as I reminded myself that I'd never have any of it again. It was one night I'd never forget, but that was it.

I didn't deserve more. I was trash, and Liam was good. I'd never deserve him. The best thing I could do for him would be to let him go and never talk to him again. He needed to get away from me and my friends before we ruined him. Hudson had already tried to take advantage of him in a wasted state. I knew Liam wasn't even close to bi-sexual, but he'd been so messed up down in the basement. Worry coursed through me as I thought about how he'd react when he woke in the morning and remembered what had happened.

Would be mad? Would he even remember it? Would he remember. . .us?

The possibility of him forgetting everything that happened between us in the bathroom hurt, but it would be for the best. I had to let Liam be free.

I wasn't freedom. I was chains and handcuffs and all the nasty things that broke people.

The rest of the weekend passed slowly. I didn't feel like going out, so I just stayed locked in my room all hours of the day and night. The maid brought me breakfast, lunch, and dinner and left it on a tray outside my door. When the coast was clear, I opened my door and pulled the tray inside. Gio came to my room a few times, trying to get to me come out, probably to take me to the club, but I refused to answer him. I could've been dead, and neither him nor my mom would've noticed.

Monday rolled around like it always did, and I pulled myself together to go to school. For the first time since Friday night, I turned my phone on and had a massive flood of texts. All from Liam.

LIAM: Hey. Can we talk?

LIAM: Are you OK? Why aren't you texting me back?

LIAM: Are you mad at me? I'm sorry about everything.

LIAM: Damnit, Asha. Answer me. You're starting to worry me.

LIAM: Is this about the bathroom stuff? Or Tiffany? Hudson? Fuck, hellcat, answer me. Please. I'm dying here. I know you said it was one night but come on. Talk to me.

LIAM: Fine, don't answer me. But you're going to have to see me at some point unless you plan on dropping out of school.

I slipped my phone into my bag and headed for the car. When I got to school, I parked in my usual spot. I peered out the windshield. Everyone in their usual spot by the bench. I considered trying to sneak past them into the building without them noticing, but I figured it'd never work. With a sigh, I grabbed my bag and exited the vehicle, heading for the school.

I could feel the weight of Liam's stare as I sauntered up the sidewalk, but I refused to glance at him. Instead of going to the bench, I strode into the school and straight to my locker. There were a few kids in the hallway, mostly the nerds who didn't use their free time to hang out. Some were sitting in front of their lockers, reading or studying. Others were in small groups, probably discussing the meaning of life or something else just as profound. I ignored them all and opened my locker to get my books for my morning class.

As I was digging around in my locker, the hairs on the back of my neck stood up. My body felt like it was coming alive, every nerve ending tingling. I knew it had to be Liam. Moments later, he leaned against the neighboring locker.

"What's wrong?" he asked in a soft voice.

I shrugged. "Nothing."

"You ignored my texts all weekend."

"I didn't turn my phone on all weekend. I just needed a break from everything."

"Oh," he said, sliding his hands into his pockets. "Is it because of what we did? Or what you saw me do?"

My eyes flashed over to him quickly. I didn't want to look at him. I knew seeing his pain would only hurt me. "I know you're not gay or bi or whatever. You were wasted. I definitely don't think anything bad about it. In fact, if it wasn't Hudson or one of the elite douches, I may have even enjoyed watching."

He let out a soft snort, and a smiled teased the corner of his lips. "Yeah? You liked that?"

Shit. How did we get to this spot so soon?

I swallowed. "Well, yeah. You're beautiful, Liam."

"So are you, hellcat."

We smiled awkwardly at one another.

"Are you sure you're OK?"

I slammed my locker shut, making everyone jump. It was hard to keep my cool around him when all I wanted to do was launch myself into his arms and kiss him until neither of us could breathe.

"I'm fine, Liam. Just under a lot of stress. Shit hasn't gotten any better at home. It's just…" My words fell away. "We're about to run out of time on this project. You wanna meet tonight to work on it some more?"

He nodded. "Yeah, that sounds good, but Asha, about me and you in the bathroom—"

"It was one night, Liam. That's it. That's all it can ever be." The words practically strangled me. "We're still friends, right?"

He nodded tightly, a muscle popping along his jaw.

"All right. See you at lunch." I swiveled and walked away, leaving him staring at my back. I felt his eyes on me until I turned the corner and was no longer in sight.

Finally, I could breathe again. I was supposed to be Asha, queen bitch. I refused to let him see how much I was hurting inside. I needed to avoid him until I was able to push past the pain. I knew I would eventually. It was what I always had to do.

Lunch rolled around, and I made my way out to our table. I was the first to arrive because I didn't bother to go to the cafeteria. My stomach couldn't stand the thought of food. I knew I wouldn't keep it down. I took a seat and sat alone for several minutes before Liam came out, a tray of food in his hands. He sat across from me.

"So, how was the rest of your weekend?" he asked, uncapping a bottle of water and taking a sip.

I shrugged and stared down at my sparkly pink, manicured nails. "Fine. Didn't do anything."

Lucas plopped down next to me and put his arm around my shoulders. He pulled me in and kissed the top of my head. "Feeling better, babe?"

I stared at him in confusion, wondering if he'd forgotten we'd broken up. I glanced at Liam to find him frowning.

"Um, not really."

"You were sick?" Liam asked, snorting.

Before I could answer, Tiffany came out with Marcie and Hudson. They filed in across from me and Lucas.

"Whoo, that was some party huh?" Hudson said. He winked at Liam who refused to look away from me. "I say we do it again this weekend. Who's down?"

"I am," Tiffany said, bumping her shoulder against Liam's. She peeked up at him from beneath her lashes, her lips turning up into a smile. "We can finish what we started."

Liam's back stiffened, and his jaw flexed. He didn't look like he was down for another party.

"Why don't you give everyone a chance to recover first, Hudson?" Marcie asked. "I mean, I still feel like a rotted-out asshole. And look at Asha. She seems only slightly better."

I grinned at her. I couldn't help it. Marcie was the closest thing I had to a real friend. She was blunt, honest, and didn't take shit from anyone. Not even from me. She didn't go around trying to sleep with my boyfriend either. Not that it mattered since Lucas wasn't my boyfriend anymore.

"You're fucking sick, Marcie," Jude said as he eased down next to Lucas.

She just offered up a sweet smile and shrugged. "Didn't hear you saying that Friday night, did I?"

He laughed. "No, and I don't remember you saying a whole lot either actually. I think your mouth was pretty occupied."

Her cheeks flashed pink, and she turned her attention to her lunch.

"My mouth was pretty occupied too, right Liam?" Tiffany whispered, but I was close enough I could still hear.

Liam rolled his eyes and didn't answer, but that didn't stop Tiffany.

She stood and walked around him, moving to his left side where she slid herself into his lap, forcing him to sit back. He stared straight ahead with angry eyes as his jaw flexed with tension. She leaned in and whispered something in his ear. I tried to listen in, but I couldn't.

Whatever she said, Liam didn't like it, or maybe he liked it too much because he shifted her off his lap, stood, and walked away, heading back into the school. Tiffany returned to her spot with a smile.

I wanted to know what she'd said to him. It pissed me off thinking she'd upset him, but I knew I couldn't ask. Everything in me shouted for me to follow him and ask him myself what she'd said, but I stayed still.

Lucas, who'd been absorbed in a totally different conversation until then, pulled me against his side. "We had a pretty good time too, didn't we, babe?" he asked, popping a fry covered in ketchup into his mouth. The smell made my stomach turn.

I forced a tight smile and nodded once. No one knew we'd broken up. Hell, he might not even remember it.

"I'm always down for your parties, Hudson." Lucas tried to tug me in for a kiss, but I leaned back.

He offered me a quick smile and didn't call me out on it.

"Ugh, I started my period this morning." Heidi groaned as she arrived at our table, rubbing her stomach.

"Man, fuck this. Let's go," Lucas cringed and nodded to Jude as he got to his feet. "Asha, check your phone." And with that, he walked away with Jude beside him.

"Wait up," Hudson hollered, chasing after them, leaving us girls at the table.

"Why were you late?" Marcie asked, glancing at Heidi.

"Probably still recovering from the dick that was in her ass Friday," Tiffany said around a smirk.

I rolled my eyes, and a sigh slipped out as Heidi sneered at Tiffany.

Tiffany's eyes cut to me. "What's wrong with you today?"

"I think I caught a bug or something. I haven't felt good all weekend." It was easier to lie.

"That's too bad. I had a great weekend. Liam took me out to dinner Saturday night. Then on Sunday, we just hung out at my place all day. We watched Netflix, cuddled on the couch, and ate a ton of junk food. He's taking me out again tonight too."

I ground my teeth together but refused to say anything. I knew if I responded in anger, it would only push her to keep fucking going. And I refused to give her the power she wanted. Instead, I got up. "I'll see you guys later," I said, striding away.

There was no way Liam took her out. I refused to believe that.

I darted into the bathroom and touched up my makeup to waste some time. When I pulled my phone out, I checked the message Lucas had sent me.

LUCAS: I didn't tell anyone. I think it's best if we don't. We can just pretend we're still together, that way if you decide you do want to be, there won't be rumors or drama over it. Does that sound OK to you?

I swallowed and shot back a reply.

ME: OK.

Stuffing my phone back into my bag, I left the bathroom and stopped at my locker. I figured it was as good a time as any to clean it out. I tossed old notes, homework, and trash into a nearby garbage can before gathering my books and going to my sixth hour class early.

When I walked in, Liam was already in his seat. Initially, I froze when I saw him, but I pushed myself to take my seat. I dropped my books onto the table loudly and sat by his side.

He huffed out a long breath. "Seriously, tell me what your

fucking problem is. You said and you Lucas broke up, but then he was all over you at lunch. Should I expect to get my ass beat after classes because you lied to me and clearly didn't break up with him?"

I kept my eyes facing forward. "I don't have a problem, Liam." That couldn't have been a bigger lie. I had *tons* of problems.

He let out a snort and shook his head.

"We are broken up." My voice was barely above a whisper.

He looked over at me, and he shook his head again.

"We are. He thinks it would be best if I figure out what I want before we announce it. I said OK, but we *aren't* together."

"So you're just testing the waters to see if anyone else wants you first? Nice."

"Liam, it's not like that." I turned to him and shook my head. "I promise, it's not. I'm just confused. That's it."

"Just say what you want, Asha. It's not that fucking hard. At least, act normal, so I don't think I somehow fucked up."

"Did you hang out with Tiffany over the weekend?"

"*The fuck?* No. If I wanted her, I wouldn't have left to go find you. And if Hudson says the same shit, he's lying too. I was home all weekend, mowing lawns and doing family shit. Max and Andy came over Saturday night. We played video games and watched movies. Fuck. Just act normal, Asha."

I crossed my legs and lifted my chin. He wanted me to act normal, so that was what I was going to do. Act like my normal self at school. The queen bitch was back.

"I'm fine, really, but I guess not as fine as Tiffany after Friday night. I really hope you don't fuck her. Girl is on antibiotics every other week if you get my drift."

"What?"

I shrugged. "None of my business, I guess. But if you did, you may want to go and get some tests done, you know, from a *friend* to *friend*."

"So this is about *Tiffany?* Christ, Asha, I already told you—"

"Tiffany is as cheap as they fucking come, Liam. If you want a cheap piece of trash toy, go for it. But it will cost you more in the long run...in medical bills that is. Shit gets expensive."

He shook his head. "I don't know what you think you *know*, but you're wrong. Ask Max and Andy. They were at my place. I'm not a fucking liar, hellcat, and the fact you think I am pisses me off." He shifted closer to me. "Didn't you have fun with me? Sure looked like you fucking did."

My eyes widened. "I know more than you think I know, Liam. And I *did* have fun with you, but at the end of the day, that's all it was—fun for one night. I told you that. You're acting like every other guy who wants me. I don't need to be poked and prodded. I said I was fine and to leave me alone. You're mad about Lucas, but it is what it is, OK?"

Liam stood and grabbed his stuff. "Whatever, Asha. I'm not in the mood for your stupid, fucking games right now." With that, he stormed out and left me alone.

I bowed my head, hating what I'd done. I was a bitch. *Why was I pushing him away when all I wanted was to bring him closer?* None of the shit I'd said was true. I cared about him, damn it. I didn't think he was like the other guys. In fact, he was *nothing* like them. *What the hell was I doing?*

The rest of the day was slow and boring, and my shitty mood didn't help matters any. I ignored everyone, and when the bell rang, I went directly to my car and made the drive home. When I got there, instead of going inside, I shuffled straight back to the staff house where I'd be meeting Liam. I made myself at home and started a fire. Then I paced the floor as I waited. We'd made plans this morning. I was desperate for him to show up. God, I was a mess.

I jumped when the door flew open and slammed shut as Liam stalked his way up to me. His back was straight, his chest puffed out, his jaw hard and flexed with anger. "What the fuck is your problem?" he asked.

I stopped pacing and turned to face him, crossing my arms. My mouth opened, but he cut me off.

"No, no more fucking lies, Asha. There's nobody around to hear us. Nobody around to see you act like a decent human being. Tell me what your fucking problem is or I swear, I'll walk out of here right now, and I'll never talk to you again. This is all bullshit, and I'm over it."

"God, you're so fucking stupid! What do you think my problem is, huh, Liam? It couldn't possibly be that our friendship has been changing. It couldn't be that you listen to me and talk to me and treat me better than anyone ever has. Or that you held my hand and kissed me and made me a priority for once in my pathetic life. I-I'm frustrated because I don't have answers. I'm afraid I'm going to lose you before I even have you. Worried you'll choose Tiffany over me—"

"I'm stupid?" he yelled, pointing at his chest. "You're the fucking stupid one, Asha. Yeah, things are changing between us. And I want you like I've never fucking wanted anyone, but you're *with*—" He made air quotation marks around the word. "—Lucas, and for whatever reason, think that's all you deserve. And yeah, Tiffany tried to suck my dick. It wasn't what I wanted. And ...Hudson, fuck, I guess he gave me a hand job, but I'm not fucking gay or bi or whatever. The party was fun and different. But you know what? The whole time, in my mind, it was *you*. I wanted to fucking come thinking about you since I couldn't *have* you!"

I scoffed and shook my head. "You're just like everyone else. Out fucking with Tiffany and whoever else while still trying to drag me along, even if it's only in your head. If you want Tiffany, or even Hudson, just be a man and fucking admit it. Don't pull me through your bullshit."

Liam moved in a blur. One minute he was standing a good five feet away. Then in the blink of an eye, he was right in front of me, yanking me against his chest. His lips landed on mine. His hands cupped my cheeks, and they weren't soft. They were strong, not allowing me to pull away. I was frozen while his lips moved against mine, but when his tongue demanded entrance, I let go and fell into the kiss, my resolve breaking.

I locked my arms around his neck and hauled him closer. His fingers fell away from my face, dropping to my hips and holding firm. As our kiss deepened, his hands moved around to the small of my back, wandering up and down my back, making goosebumps pop up along my skin. I wasn't sure how long our kiss lasted because time was lost to me. I knew nothing but Liam and the way he was kissing me, making me see stars. Every muscle in my body tensed with anticipation. Each nerve ending vibrated, coming alive because of his touch, his lips.

The kiss slowed until it broke off completely. I was lost, confused, excited as I peered into his darkening green eyes. Like always, he was perfect. *God, I'd destroyed perfect.*

"You need to chill the fuck out and just accept that I have feelings for you. Tiffany is nothing but a liar. I don't want her. I didn't spend any time with her. And Hudson? Never going to happen. I was wasted and had my eyes on you the whole time. I want *you.* You're all I've been able to think about for fucking weeks now. Stop pushing me away. Let me in, hellcat," he pleaded.

I shook my head in disbelief. "You're crazy. I don't deserve anything you have to give me."

He offered up a smile and nodded. "I know I'm crazy for falling for a hellcat like you, but I am." He shrugged. "You can't push me away."

"I don't want to push you away, Liam. I just...don't know what else to do," I whispered.

"Don't think. Just live in the moment." His eyes fluttered closed as he leaned in once more. His lips found mine, and they were much softer this time.

I nodded against him, agreeing to just live in the moment with him. I felt more alive than I ever had before.

He picked me up against him and carried me over to the couch where we settled against one another. He kept his arms wrapped around me, and I rested my head against his shoulder as I watched the flames dance in the fireplace. Hours passed with us doing nothing but touching innocently, talking, and kissing. His hands were always soft and left me wanting more as they ran through my hair, cupped my face, or held my hand—his thumb in constant motion as he swept it back and forth against my skin.

"No one has all the answers, Asha," he said during a comfortable silence. "What's the fun in knowing? Please stop looking for them. The only answer you need is I'm here. You're here. And it's all that fucking matters right now."

"OK."

"Good girl."

The way he said that made tingles rocket through my stomach.

"Hudson's not gay," I said after a moment. "He's more straight than bi, but when he gets wasted, he does like to play."

He scoffed. "I found that out rather quickly."

I giggled softly. "Once, Tiffany and Heidi had a four-way with Hudson and some dude Tiff was dating at the time. Hudson nailed the guy in the ass while Lucas watched."

"Why didn't you watch?"

I shrugged. "I didn't want to watch an orgy."

"Did Lucas join in?"

"I don't know. It was never confirmed, but if he did, that was probably when Tiffany decided she wanted him. Lucas told me they only kissed. I don't know if I should believe him, but he seemed genuine. It's just... I know her. I know him. He's gone almost two years without anything? His character makes that hard for me to believe."

Liam nodded without saying a word. I saw the way he took in everything I was saying, which made me even more comfortable with him. I decided to change the subject. "What are you looking for in a girl, Liam?"

His eyes met mine. "Long, blonde hair. Blue eyes. And when she smiles, it lights up my world. She has to be strong but also soft. She keeps everyone else away, while only letting me in."

I laughed and rolled my eyes. "Did you just describe me?"

He smirked. "I'll never tell," he whispered, moving his lips back to mine.

I couldn't get enough of his kisses, and I knew I never would. "I don't know how well this will work between us," I said against his lips, already worrying about everything that couldn't be changed.

"Just shut up and live in the moment," he mumbled against my mouth, deepening our kiss.

His fingers drifted from my cheek down to my breasts where he squeezed gently. Then his lips moved to my throat. I angled my head for him, relishing in the heat of his lips on my skin.

Slowly, his hand slipped beneath my top, his forefinger and thumb tweaking my nipple, sending a zing of electricity between my legs.

I moaned softly as he shifted himself over me, his lips never leaving my skin as he pushed my top down to reveal my breasts. With a soft sigh, he lavished each stiff peak—sucking, licking, and nibbling as I tangled my fingers in his hair. No one had ever made me feel like *this*. Made me feel good. Had actually cared enough about me to make me feel like this.

When he slowed his ministrations, he stared at me, his hand cradling my ass gently.

"I want to taste you again," he said softly.

My heart thudded unevenly at his soft words, want washing over every facet of my being.

I nodded, swallowing hard.

He didn't need telling twice. He eased his body lower, peppering a hot trail of kisses down my abdomen until he was between my legs. His tongue darted out as he licked his lips in anticipation. The moan made me breathe harder. He pushed my dress up and dragged my panties off gently as he gazed down at me.

"God, you're perfect," he said in a throaty voice. "I'm going to gobble you up, hellcat."

"Please," I whispered, wet and wanting.

"I want to hear you come for me, OK?" He licked up my slit, making me mewl and arch my back. "Can you do that for me?"

"Y-Yes. Please," I begged softly, giving everything over for him to control.

The look on his face made my heart race. He wasted no time burying his face in my heat and lavishing my hot, aching button as I writhed beneath him, moaning and breathing hard.

With a gentle finger, he eased into me, his tongue whirling and swirling against the aching bundle of nerves. When he inserted a second finger, I ground myself against them, fucking his fingers just as much as they were fucking me.

When the hot sweep of impending pleasure crashed over me, I cried out, coming hard and fast in his mouth and all over his hand. I trembled as he continued eating me, devouring every last bit of pleasure in my body until he wrung me dry and I lay there panting and shaking.

He sat up on his end of the couch, his mouth and chin glistening with my release, and licked his lips.

"I love the way you taste," he admitted softly. "I may never fill of it."

Heat rose in my cheeks as I leaned up, my dress around my midsection and my body exposed to him. His chest heaved as I shifted to my knees before him and stared up into his eyes, my fingers fumbling on his zipper.

"You don't have to," he murmured, resting his hand over mine.

"I-I want to," I said, swallowing. And I *did* want to. For the first time ever, it was something I wanted.

His lips parted, and wordlessly, he let his hand fall away.

I undid his pants, and he lifted up so I could pull them down, releasing his very impressive length.

Damn, I wasn't sure I'd be able to suck the entire length, but I was eager to try.

A pearl of excitement blossomed at the end of his dick. My

tongue darted out and licked the droplet away. He groaned softly, his lips still parted and his eyes hooded as he watched me.

It made me feel empowered and in total control, something I'd never been before. Eagerly, I sucked him into my mouth, relishing in his soft moans and his fingers in my hair. It took everything I had to fit him into my mouth, but I sucked his length in as far as I could, his engorged cock hitting the back of my throat. Enthusiastically, I continued sucking and licking, loving how his fingers felt in my hair as he guided my pace to what he liked.

When he thickened against my tongue, I knew his release was coming, so I braced myself and sucked harder. Within moments, he groaned out my name as he came hard in my mouth. I swallowed everything he gave me and sucked him dry until his body went lax and he was staring at me with a dazed smile on his face.

I climbed onto his lap, and he immediately dragged me against him, both of us still practically naked.

"You're incredible," he breathed out. "The best."

I swallowed and bit my bottom lip. "Was I the first one to. . ."

"You were the *best* one." He pressed a gentle kiss to my lips.

"Promise?"

"Swear it, hellcat." He kissed me again, his warm arms around me, holding me against his hot hard body. We stayed in one another's arms for hours, whispering, touching, kissing, making promises I prayed we could keep because I meant them.

I wanted him. I never wanted to let him go. *Ever.*

When it came time for him to go, he kissed me again, a long slow one that left a tingling on my lips. Watching him walk away, I was kinda sad our time together was over, but when I got back to my room and took out my phone to put my pajamas on, I found a text from him.

LIAM: I already miss you.
ME: I miss you too.
LIAM: Don't overthink now that I'm gone. Promise?
ME: Promise.

LIAM: Good. You're more than I even imagined. Being with you is like tasting heaven.

My cheeks warmed with his words.

ME: Netflix?

Moments later, my phone rang, and I answered it. The rest of the night was spent on the phone, both of us watching the same thing on Netflix until we fell asleep together.

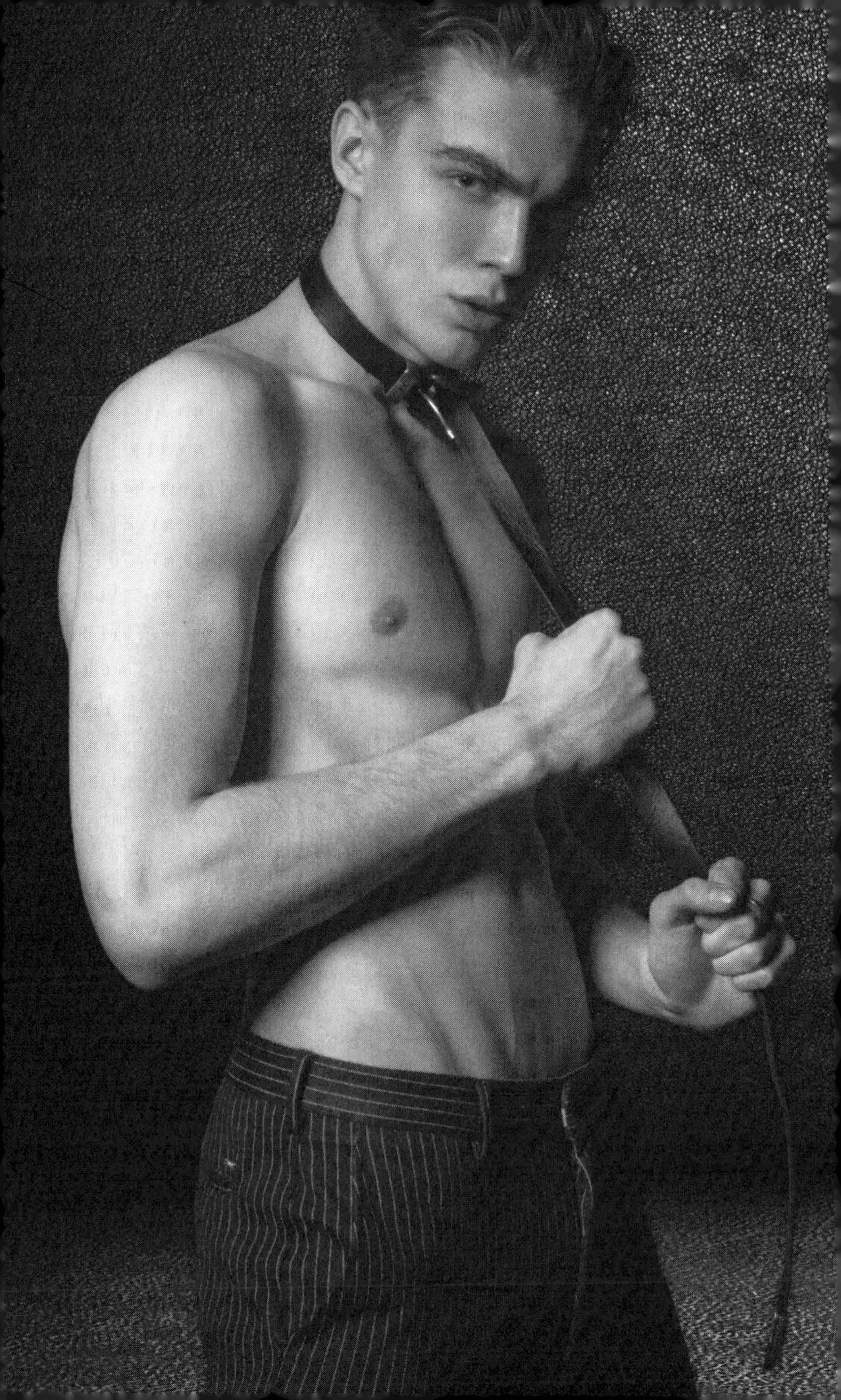

EIGHTEEN
LIAM

After finally getting to confess my true feelings to Asha, I was riding the best high ever. My whole body felt energized, charged, almost tingly. I stayed on the phone with her for a long time, until she fell asleep and started mumbling. After hanging up, I was too wound up to sleep, so I got up and grabbed a snack from the kitchen. As I ate my dry cereal, I started cleaning my room. Then the thoughts started.

The memories of her mouth on mine, of her sucking my cock. She'd made me feel so fucking good. She was the best I'd ever had, and that wasn't a lie. I could still taste her. Even now, I wanted more of her. I'd eat her sweet pussy again if she were here. My cock ached in my pants like her lush lips hadn't sucked me to completion a few hours ago. *Fuck, what was she doing to me?*

I closed and locked my bedroom door before lying on my bed and using my phone to pull up the photo of her in her bed. I stared at her cleavage, her eyes, her lips as I took my cock in hand and stroked. It wasn't long before my load shot onto my stomach as I moaned softly, desperate to bury myself in her tight heat.

I lay breathless and not even close to sated after cleaning myself off. As I tried to fall asleep, my mind moved to darker places.

Sofia was going to be pissed when she found out about me and Asha. *What if Sofia is right? What if Asha and the group are just trying to pull off some epic trick? What if this is part of it? Asha making me think that she has feelings for me. Getting me to fall in love with her and then just yanking the rug out from under me in front of the whole school.*

I'd told Sofia I was doing my own little recon to take down the group if something like that happened. Maybe it was time to start putting everything together. Just in case. If I didn't need it, great. If I did, I'd have it ready and waiting.

Sighing, I got back up and sat down at my computer and started typing everything up. I spilled all I knew so far. Everything about Hudson with his bi tendencies. Everything I'd witnessed in the VIP room with the snorting of coke and taking Molly. The couples openly having sex in front of others. The way some even joined in to create an orgy. I wrote about Tiffany and the four-way Asha had described. I chronicled the use of alcohol and drugs among the members of the elite. I also added in my suspicions about Tiffany and Lucas going at it behind Asha's back. How they'd definitely kissed based on Lucas's confession. I just needed to get everything down so nothing would be lost over time. I stayed up until almost two, writing down every last detail before calling it a night and falling back into bed.

The next morning, I overslept, which left me rushing for school. By the time I whipped into the parking lot, the morning bell had already rung. I rushed inside to find everyone still moving about the hallway.

I went directly to my locker and grabbed what I needed for my morning classes. I checked my watch and found I had about three minutes to get to class before I'd be tardy. As I hurried, I caught a glimpse out of the corner of my eye of Asha and Lucas. He had her up against the wall of lockers, and they were talking softly.

I knew I had no claim to Asha. I doubted anyone ever would

considering how guarded she was, but it still hurt that she was keeping up the charade of still being with Lucas.

I shook my head to try and clear the image, but it was already burned into my memory. I made it to class with only seconds to spare. As I fell into my seat, I thought more about the situation Asha and I were in. I didn't expect her to announce her break up with Lucas over the intercom, but I guessed I wasn't prepared to see her with him like that either. When they were together, she always pushed him away. So why wasn't she now?

Did she just want a convenient excuse to keep me her dirty little secret? If she never broke it off with Lucas completely, would I still be interested? Would I allow myself to be hidden away? Did being with her in public mean that much, or would just being with her be enough?

Deep down, I just wanted her any fucking way I could get her. Nothing else mattered.

Lunch finally rolled around, and I was starved thanks to my rush to school. I grabbed a burger, some fries, a piece of cherry crumble, and a bottle of water before going to our usual table. Eagerly I started stuffing my face, and more than half my food was gone before anyone else sat down with theirs. Asha sat across from me as usual. She offered me a small smile. I winked in response, then glanced around the table to make sure nobody had seen our exchange. They hadn't. Lucas was too busy having a conversation about football with Jude while dipping his fries into a mound of ketchup. Hudson was whispering something in Marcie's ear. And Tiffany and Heidi were in middle of discussing a dress Katy Perry was recently photographed in.

I was nearly done with my lunch when Tiffany bumped my shoulder with hers. She leaned in and grinned. "I was thinking, if you're free tonight, Liam, maybe you could come by my place. We could do our homework together. My parents will be gone."

I let out a long breath. It was time to get Tiffany off my back.

"Look, I had a great time with you at the party, but... I'm just not interested."

Her smile fell, and everyone around the table started laughing, even Lucas who was running his fingers through Asha's curls while whispering something in her ear.

Tiffany's back got ramrod straight. "You seemed pretty interested when your dick was in my hand."

I let out a chuckle and reminded myself to be as ruthless as the rest of them were. "It's hard not to be interested when someone is stroking my dick. But sorry, that's all it was." I got up, tossed my trash, and sauntered into the building, eager to get away from Lucas touching Asha.

I ducked into the first empty room I found and waited just inside the door. Moments later, Asha sashayed into the building. Quickly, I reached out into the hall, grabbed her by the waist, hauling her into the classroom with me. In one swift move, I had her backed against the wall. My lips found hers, and she didn't push me away. Instead, her arms wrapped around my neck as she deepened the kiss, our tongues thrashing wildly against one another's.

Breathless, she eased back, staring up at me intently. "I'm sorry about Lucas. I swear, I'll fix it."

I shook my head. "I don't care," I lied. But I trusted her to handle things the way she thought she needed to. I nibbled her lower lip. "I know you're mine. That's all that matters."

She pulled my mouth back to hers. While we kissed, my hands toured her body—moving from her hips to her back, down her sides, then up to cup her cheeks. It was like neither of us could get enough of the other. When I finally slid my fingers deep into her tight heat beneath her skirt, she moaned my name against my lips, her body trembling against me as I worked her over until she came all over my fingers in a flurry of gasps and tremors.

The rest of our lunch hour was spent hiding from everyone else while we kissed, touched, and talked as much as possible.

We managed to put some space between us moments before the

bell rang, ending lunch. We made our way out of the dark classroom before we could get caught. I went to my locker and she went to hers. Then we met back up in our sixth hour class. When everyone got to work on their assignments, I placed my hand on Asha's thigh under the table.

"Ummm, what's your favorite..." She giggled.

"My favorite what?"

"I don't know. I can't think straight when you're touching me." Her hand landed on mine. She eased my hand down her thigh to her knee instead. "OK, what's your favorite dessert?"

"Hmmm," I say, running my hand back up her thigh. "*You.*"

Her face reddened, sending all my blood straight to my cock. I'd never seen her blush like that.

"Really?"

I leaned in and whispered in her ear, "You have the *sweetest, most delicious* center, hellcat."

"Liam," she breathed out.

"Yeah?" I gave her a coy smile as I leaned back, enjoying that the flush I'd created on her had traveled to her chest and painted her cleavage red.

"I can't put *that* in my paper."

I smirked at her and sat back in my seat. "Cheesecake."

She licked her lips and cocked her head. "Why?"

"It's sweet but also tangy. It's rich, flavorful. It's good whether it's plain or dressed up with chocolate, strawberries, or caramel. It's all round the perfect dessert, aside from you. Mm, maybe I should combine the two." I lifted my brows at her, and she shook her head, a genuine smile on her face.

"You sound really passionate about your desserts."

"You can apply that to other aspects of my life too." I winked at her, making her cheeks turn red again.

She tucked her blonde hair behind one ear and got busy jotting down my answer. I couldn't help but stare at her. She was stunning with her soft skin, long blonde hair, blue eyes, and perfectly full lips. Those lips were soft too, so talented when it came to kissing. Her tongue darted out, swiping along her lips as she continued to write. And all I could think about was them wrapped around my dick. The thought made my cock instantly get hard. I tried to will it away by tearing my gaze from her and getting to work on writing my paper.

I couldn't wait until the day when she was mine in every way possible, but I also knew it didn't matter if I couldn't call her mine to other people. I knew who she belonged to, and so did she.

I was getting more and more caught up in Asha, and it made it hard to keep myself in check. I wasn't supposed to be falling for her. I was supposed to keep her at arms' length in case Sofia's suspicions were true. My brain knew it could all be a lie, a trick, but I didn't care. It felt real.

To me, what we had was very real.

I looked up from my paper and found Sofia watching us. Her brows were pulled together, and her lips were pressed into a tight line, the corners angled downward. She didn't look pleased to see Asha and me getting along so well. I stared back at her, and after a moment, she got back to work.

I was more annoyed with Sofia than ever before. I had a sinking feeling she was going to ruin everything for me. All because she was pissed at me. I knew I'd fucked up when it came to Sofia, but there wasn't anything I could do about it. Since the last time I was honest about my feelings, I hadn't gone back on my word. I hadn't touched her, kissed her, or done anything else to make her think I'd changed my mind. *What else could I do?*

When the day ended, I drove over to Andy's and found the three of them in the living room. Max and Andy were on the floor, playing a video game while Sofia was on the couch, doing homework.

"Hey, man. Grab a controller. You can play against me after I beat his ass," Andy said, not taking his eyes off the screen.

"No thanks. I just wanted to drop by for a sec. Thought you guys would be interested to know that Asha and I are kinda working on being together." I announced it proudly. I hadn't planned on telling anyone, but I wanted to scream it from the rooftops.

Sofia gasped, and her head popped up. "What does that even mean? Lucas was all over her today at lunch. We saw from our place under the tree."

"Yeah, he's having trouble letting go, but Asha is my girl. We'll work it out," I said, a wide smile stretching across my face.

Andy and Max excitedly tossed their game controllers to the side as they moved to the couch for more details.

"How the fuck did that happen?" Andy asked.

Max nodded along with his question. "And how good is she in bed?"

"What are you doing? Sharing her with Lucas? Gross," Sofia said, shaking her head. "But of course you would do that. Sex is just a sick game to *you elite*, right?"

My anger toward Sofia skyrocketed. "Sofia, can I talk to you privately?" I headed for the front door. I stepped outside and spun around just as she closed the door behind her.

"That's it, Sofia. I've had enough of this shit. I mean, we're supposed to be friends, right?"

She crossed her arms over her chest and nodded.

"Well, friends are supposed to support one another. Not get angry when one of them finally finds happiness."

She rolled her eyes. "You're happy now, but what about when this all blows up in your face? And you know it will."

I shook my head. "Sofia, I'm happy. And I want you to be happy. I've told you time and time again that you and I will never be what you hope for. You need to let go of the idea that I'll come around eventually. What we had between us is never going to happen again. Move on. Make yourself happy." When she didn't say a word, I sighed and jogged to my car parked against the curb.

It was still pretty early in the afternoon, so I went to Asha's and parked in the usual spot. I climbed the brick wall surrounding the property and made the hike back to the staff house. Smoke billowed up out of the chimney, so I wasn't surprised to find Asha when I strolled in. She was sitting on the floor, doing her homework. She jumped when she heard me enter. But when her head jerked and her eyes met mine, her fear fell away.

"I didn't know you were coming."

"I wasn't sure if you'd be here."

I held out my hand, and she took it. I pulled her up and into my arms, where her chest pressed against mine. Our lips met, and it felt like I'd found heaven for the second time that day.

I walked her backward and lay her on the couch, covering her body with mine. I wasn't going to push for sex. I knew it was way too early in our relationship for it, but I wanted to spend as much time as possible kissing her, feeling her body against mine. As my weight pressed her into the cushions, she conformed to me perfectly. Her fingers laced through my hair, and she urged me closer, deepening our kiss.

Her hands on me made every nerve ending come to life and vibrate with excitement. Soon every inch of my body was dying to be inside her. Panting, I ended our kiss and sat up, removing myself from her.

"What's wrong?" she asked, popping up beside me.

"Nothing is wrong. Everything is great...*too* great," I said, glancing down at my lap.

She giggled. "Did you see the looks Sofia was giving us today? Think it's safe to say she hates me."

"Sofia isn't happy that I'm spending all my time with you. She wants things to be how they used to be. She doesn't realize that even if they were, I still wouldn't want to be with her like *that*. I need to give her time and space, let this crush she has fade away."

"Oh, Liam. I don't think that crush will ever go away."

"You don't?"

She shook her head.

"Why not?"

"I think you're a tough one to get over." She grinned at me, and that was all it took to have my mouth back against hers.

～

ASHA and I spent the afternoon in one another's arms, safe from the world. I wasn't sure who was keeping who safe, but it was heaven. When the sun started to set, I made my way home to get my homework done and eat dinner. Before I went inside, I fired off a quick text to Asha, knowing it would make her smile.

Mom had made ribs, pasta salad, baked beans, and dinner rolls. I had my fill while listening to my dad bitch about how the yard needed mowing again and how I should do a better job keeping up with it. When he finished, he left Mom and me at the table while he found a game to watch in the living room.

I helped Mom clear the table before excusing myself to my room to work on homework. I finished my English assignment and my calculus, before moving onto my paper about Asha. I picked up my phone and texted her.

LIAM: Want to work on our assignment?

I waited, but no reply ever came. Figuring she was busy, I wrote what I could and retired to bed for the evening, resuming the movie Asha and I had started the night before, waiting to hear from her.

But she never texted me back.

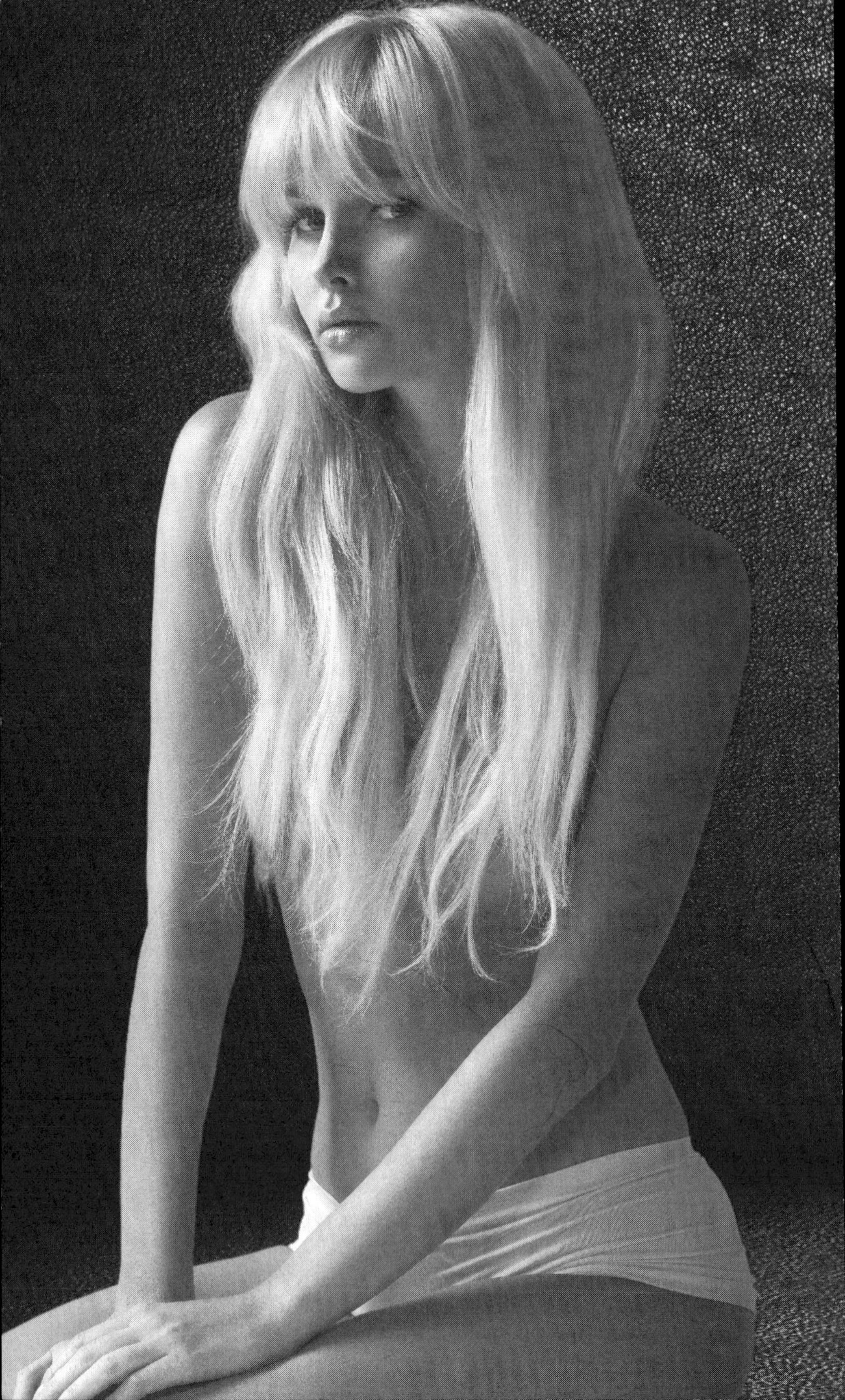

NINETEEN
ASHA

I'd had the best day with Liam. I felt more strongly about him than I'd ever felt about anyone. He wasn't like Lucas who only used me to try and get lucky. He wasn't like my friends who used me for popularity. He wasn't using me for anything. If he wanted sex, he could've gotten it from Sofia. If he wanted popularity, he had it before he even kissed me. He wanted *me*, and he didn't care about what having me could do for him.

I wandered back to the house almost in a daze as I thought about the perfect day we'd spent together. My phone vibrated, and I pulled it out.

LIAM: You're perfect as you are, Asha. Don't let anyone change you. Not Lucas. Not your stepdad. Not anyone. The Asha you truly are belongs on my arm, not anywhere near them.

I beamed as I read it over and over, but my smile fell when I walked into my room and glanced up, finding Gio inside.

"There you are. Let's go." He grabbed me by the bicep as he rushed us down the stairs.

"Where are we going so fast?"

"The club. I have a very important client coming this evening, and he only wants my best girl. That's you, sweetheart." He opened the back door on his SUV and shoved me inside. I fell onto the floor. By the time I was able to sit up, he was already climbing behind the wheel and locking the doors. I tried the handle anyway.

"No, Gio. I can't. Not today. Please, not today." I'd had the best day ever with Liam. I didn't want to lose it. I didn't want it to end.

"Got a hot date or something? Just tell him to come to the club. He can fuck you and not even have to worry about taking you to dinner," he joked as he drove us toward the club.

I leaned back in the seat with my arms crossed over my chest my eyes filled with tears. I wondered if Liam would've sent me the same text if he knew about this side of my life. He thought I was perfect. *Ha, I was lower than low. I was trash.* As we got closer, I shifted in my head from Asha to the girl with no name. It was a scary place to be, but it was the only way I'd found to protect myself. Becoming two people made it easier, but did it matter when Asha was just as bad as the girl with no name? Asha was a bitch who'd ruined too many lives of innocent kids at school. She took them down just for a laugh. Maybe I could be *three* people. The girl with no name, Asha: the queen bitch, and Liam's girl. I didn't know anymore. But being three people sounded hard and was probably an impossible feat anyway. I'd only been trying to be two people, and even that wasn't working very well. I still suffered from her nightmares, still had to heal from her bruises. And all that would be too hard to hide to be the girl Liam deserved.

The vehicle came to a sudden stop, and my stomach dropped with impending doom. There was no telling what I'd be forced to do in there. "Who's this guy?" I asked as Gio put the car in park and shut off the ignition.

"That's not for you to worry about. Just know he's very important to my business, and I want him treated properly. Do whatever he asks. I don't care if he wants to watch you eat shit, you do it." He opened the door and stepped out.

I waited as he walked around the vehicle. The door opened, and the next thing I knew, Gio was reaching in for me. I smacked his hands away as I pressed my back to the opposite door. It earned me a smack across the face before he yanked me out by my hair.

My cheek stung, and my eyes watered as he dragged me across the parking lot and into the building. He led me through the legal club upstairs, then down into the basement where his illegal club operated. The music from up top was loud techno, but the music from the lower level was deep, dark, and sounded like hell. The two sounds met on the staircase and mixed together. I tried dragging my feet as we approached the door, but Gio only tightened his hand on my bicep as he pushed me through it.

He didn't look around when we entered. He just ushered me back to the private room and shoved me through the door. "Stay here and wait." He pointed his finger at me.

Time seemed to stop while I waited. I paced the floor until I could no longer feel my toes. I gave up and threw myself down onto the mattress. I wrapped my arms around myself and daydreamed about Liam. I thought about the way he'd held me as we snuggled on the couch earlier. I imagined how soft his hand always were on my body, how slowly he kissed me. I almost managed to fall asleep and escape altogether, but then the door slammed off the wall. Loud music from the club ushered in a man.

He was big, probably over six foot tall. He was muscular. There'd be no fighting him off. He had greasy skin, dark hair, and even darker eyes. And he wasn't dressed in an expensive suit. No, this guy looked like he'd just stepped out of the gym with his baggy, basketball shorts on and loose-fitting shirt sleeveless shirt.

"Who are you?" I ask, sitting up on the bed.

"My name is Paul O'Keef. I know your father."

I wrapped my arms around my knees. "You know my father?"

He nodded. "I do. He was my partner for a short time. I offered him a deal which he took. It was a brilliant one that would've made the two of us very, very rich. But I should've known better than to trust a criminal. He fucked me over and took all the money for himself, leaving me to run from the police when he set me up."

I swallowed, understanding he wasn't here for pleasure. It was for revenge.

"What are you going to do to me?" I was scared to ask but figured it was better to be prepared.

He offered up an evil smile. "I've paid for the whole night with you, so...any fucking thing I want." He dragged his shirt over his head and tossed it onto the chair by the foot of the bed as he marched toward me. "Stand up. Undress," he ordered.

My eyes filled with tears, but I didn't move.

In a blur, he was next to the mattress. Reaching over, he grabbed me by the hair on the top of my head and lifted me up with one arm. My hair was snapping at the roots, so I quickly put my feet on the bed so it pulled as little as possible. He tossed me across the room, and I fell to the floor.

"We can do this the easy way or the hard way, but either way, we're doing it. Undress."

I sniffled as got to my feet. My hands worked robotically, removing my shirt, unsnapping my bra, unfastening my jeans, and dropping my panties to the floor at my feet.

He smiled sadistically. "Good. Now turn, slowly."

Gradually, I began to spin in a full circle so he could see my body. With us both standing, I only came up to his chest. It was like being beside Liam, except this man wasn't him. This man was evil and angry. I was incredibly afraid of what he was packing in his shorts, especially if it was in proportion to his body. I had no doubt I'd choke on that thing.

"On the bed," he ordered, getting up and giving me room.

I lay on the bed, and he disappeared. He was back moments later, setting a duffle bag onto the foot of the mattress. He unzipped the bag and removed some rope. Silently, I watched as he tied my wrists to the bed frame. Next he shoved a ball gag in my mouth and clamps on my nipples. I was no stranger to sexual fetishes and had endured my own share of weirdos over the years. But the clamps he used weren't designed to bring pleasure. They were meant for pain, and they felt like they were cutting into my skin. A tear slid down my cheek, and a muffled whimper slipped out. When he heard me cry, he yanked on chain connecting the clamps.

"No sounds from you, or I'll only make things more painful. This may be uncomfortable," he said excitedly.

That was my cue to retreat inside the safe space in my mind. So I left the nameless girl lying there helpless on the bed with a sadist who hated my father, and I ducked behind the walls to my hideout. There I snuggled up in front of the fireplace in Liam's arms. It was the only happy, safe place in my life. And there I stayed until I was jerked back to my harsh reality.

Gagging and in agony, I blinked up at the monster towering over me, his dick hanging flaccid against his thigh. He shoved me backward, and I fell to the floor. I was a mess. I had tears running down my cheeks, come on my face, wax and blood on my torso. I winced as I tried to stand. My pussy was on fire. "It burns, doesn't it?" he asked. "It's from the ginger root. *Figging.* I always wanted to try that."

He stood and redressed. "The next time you see your father. You tell him what I did to you. Let him know I'm nowhere near through. I'll be back. And each time this will get worse and worse until I leave you broken and bloody," he said, removing the rope from my wrists and ankles.

I quickly rolled over and spat in his face. It earned me a hard slap across my cheek. My lip busted on impact.

"Fuck you. You think you're getting to my father by using me? He hasn't seen me in years. So tell him your fucking self."

He grabbed my throat and pushed me back against the floor. His fingers squeezed. "If that's the case, I should just go ahead and take you now. Is that what you want?" He managed to wedge himself between my legs.

"No. Please," I managed to croak out as I fought against him.

He reached between us, and I knew he was freeing himself from his shorts. I raked my nails down his face. He let out a loud scream as he jerked away. Blood dripped from the three claw marks I'd left behind.

"You fucking bitch," he said, pulling back his foot and sending it flying toward my stomach. It hit hard, and I had no choice but to coil into a ball and pray that I died soon.

"I'm not paying for this fucking shit," he said, grabbing his bag and rushing out the door.

I couldn't move. I couldn't breathe. I couldn't do anything but hold my abdomen and pray the pain stopped. Little did I know, it was only going to get much, much worse by the end of the night.

∽

I WAS sore and cold as I sat in the backseat of Gio's SUV. My arms were crossed tightly over my chest. My throbbing head lolled against the headrest. I stared unseeing out the window, lost to my thoughts.

Gio was on a rampage—pissed at me for fighting the man who'd tortured me. The man had told Gio I'd scratched him and spat in his face. He'd said I was defiant and I didn't give him anything he asked for. But he hadn't *ask* for anything. He'd just taken. He'd wanted to cause pain, and that was all he'd done.

Gio bitched me up one side and down the other, but I remained strong in my head, not allowing a word of it to enter my thoughts.

Somewhere during the drive, I noticed the city lights were getting farther and farther, not closer. I sat up in a panic.

"Where are we going? Where are you taking me?"

"To learn a lesson," was all Gio had to say.

I knew I was in trouble. I'd clawed the man's face earlier as a means to escape, but I hadn't escaped. I'd only been hurt more. He'd left the room, citing he wasn't going to pay for shit since I'd clawed him.

I sat back and swallowed my fear—watching, waiting, and trying to plan, but I didn't know what to plan for. *Was he selling me? Was he going to kill me, say I ran away since I was such a troubled teen?* I didn't know.

Suddenly, in the middle of nowhere, he jerked the wheel, and we veered off onto the side of the road. We were no longer on pavement. It was a small, dirt road between some bushes I was sure nobody knew existed. I glanced at the GPS on the dash, and it didn't even register a road. Suddenly, he stomped on the brake, and I went flying forward.

Faster than I could process, Gio was out and my door was opening. He grabbed me. I fought against him, but he was pissed so it did no good. He punched me in the jaw, blurring my vision. It stunned me enough that he was able to drag me out. I was dizzy, my head hurting and my ears ringing. I didn't know what was going on. My whole body felt the pain of the entire night as he pushed my back downward. He was bending me over the seat. *Why?*

I tried to stand upright, but he fisted my hair and yanked, making me call out.

"Stop! I'm sorry! Please, stop," I pleaded as he reached around me and unbuttoned my jeans.

Was he going to rape me? My own stepfather? He had made me suck him off before, but he'd never entered me. It was almost like he couldn't do that to my mother. But all that had gone out the window.

"Scream as loud as you fucking want, Asha. Nobody can hear you," he said, shoving my jeans down my legs.

The coldness of the night blew across my body and made me shiver.

"Please, don't. I'm sorry. I'm sorry," I cried out again.

"Maybe next time, you'll fucking listen."

The sound of his zipper filled my ears.

"I'm going to teach you a lesson one way or another, Asha. I *will* break you."

And he pushed forward, my screams echoing in the night.

HE THREW me off in the weeds where I lay as he righted his pants.

"You remember this," he grunted. "You *burn* this night into your fucking memory. The next time I say jump, you'd better drop your pants and fucking jump. I want you sitting on any dick I point out, and I want you smiling while I get paid." He kicked me hard in the ribs before he climbed back in the car and drove off, leaving me in the dust and weeds, vomit covering my face and my body in more pain than I thought was possible.

I couldn't move. I couldn't do anything but cry and hate myself, hate my mother, hate my father, hate Gio for forcing me into this life. I hated that I let things get so bad. I hated that I wasn't brave enough to kill myself. I just lay there—full of anger, hatred, and rage. And pain. So much pain.

As the night grew later, the air became colder and the coyotes began to howl. I stayed there with my pants around my ankles, blood and come drying on my skin. The terrible pain from the events of the night made me cry until I had no tears left.

Fear consumed me. I was certain the coyotes could smell the blood on me, and I knew they could track it. I either had to lay there and let myself get ripped to shreds, or I had to force myself to get up and start walking.

I used every ounce of anger and hate in my body to push to my feet. With trembling hands, I managed to get my jeans in place. I stumbled down the dirt road back to the pavement. It was cold and dark, and I was exhausted and in agony. Every inch of my body hurt. I wasn't sure how I'd managed to get up, let alone keep putting one foot in front of the other. When I tucked my cold fingers into my jacket pocket, they brushed against my cell. Anxiously, I pulled it out and called the only person I could think of.

∽

"WHAT THE HELL, ASHA?" Lucas asked when he found me on the side of the road. He almost looked afraid.

"I got into a fight with Gio. He beat the shit out of me and left me out here." The tears formed again and rushed down my cheeks.

Lucas eased me against his chest. "Shit. You're freezing. Come on. Get in."

He opened the passenger side door and helped me into the car. I winced and cried out as I sat, the injuries only hurting more.

I was grateful it was dark. I didn't want him to see my face. I knew I must have looked awful after the night I'd had. Unable to look him in the eye, I kept my head turned and my gaze on the outside world we drove past. Tears silently tracked down my cheeks as I trembled.

"Are you going to be OK?"

"I'll be fine," I told him, barely loud enough for him to hear.

"Do you need to go to a hospital or something?"

I shook my head. "Just take me home, Lucas." I knew Gio had gone back to the club. It was too early for him to come home.

As we got close to my house, Lucas asked again, "Do I need to call the cops or take you to a doctor?"

I shook my head sadly. Lucas wasn't an idiot. He knew something was up. When I went to get out at my house, he caught my hand.

"Asha, I want to help—"

"No one can help me," I rasped, tugging out of his hold and slamming the door behind me.

Inside, I went straight to my room, where I showered, cried, cut myself, sneaked some of my mom's sleeping pills and a handful of pain pills, and then passed out. I didn't even examine the damage on my body

When I woke the next morning, I stripped my pajamas off and saw my breasts had small blisters from the wax. Red rings littered my flesh from the man's bites. My lip was busted. A big bruise marred my jaw. Small scratches and bruises were scattered all over me. Between my legs was a mess.

Gently, I cleaned myself and grabbed some of my mom's old antibiotics from her medicine cabinet. I took two before bringing the bottle back to my room along with some antibacterial cream in the hopes of keeping an infection at bay.

Liam had been calling and texting, but I couldn't bring myself to answer. I couldn't let him see me in such bad shape. He deserved better, and I knew what I had to do.

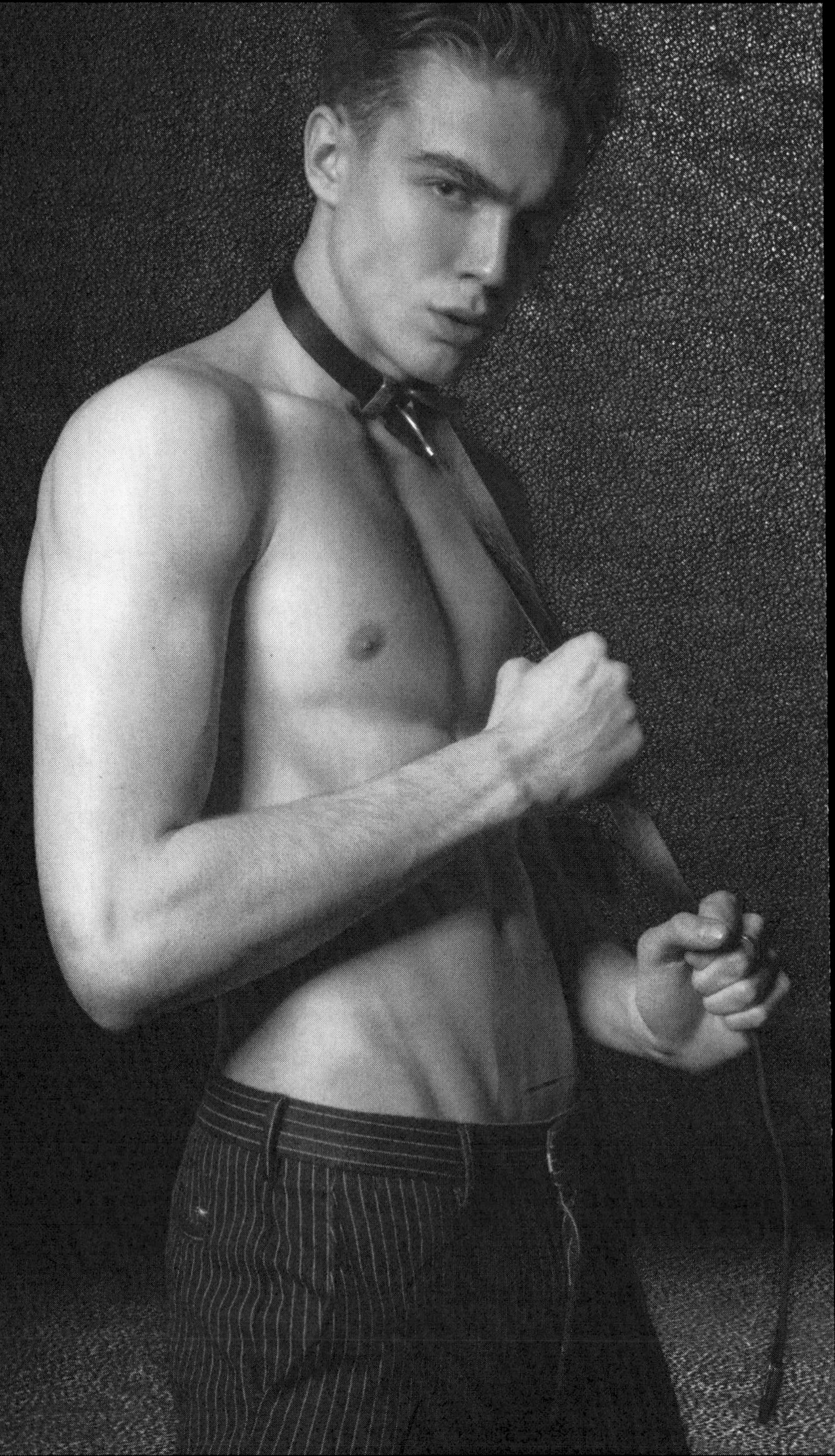

TWENTY
LIAM

It felt like my life had finally fallen into place. I wasn't getting my ass handed to me every day by the elite anymore. I wasn't another face lost in a sea of scholarship kids. And I had Asha. She was mine. When I left her place last night, I felt excited for what a new day would bring.

When I got to school, Asha was nowhere in sight. I shrugged it off as I sat with the elite, listening to them talk shit and fuck around. The bell eventually rang, and we all moved inside for our morning classes. I was surprised at lunch when she still wasn't at school.

"Where's Asha?" I asked Lucas.

He shrugged. "What do you care?"

I rolled my eyes. "Just making conversation. Wasn't trying to be a dick."

He ignored me and went back to his conversation with Jude and Hudson.

On my way to my sixth hour class, I sent her a text.

LIAM: Are you sick today? Do I need to come over after school and take care of you?

I slid my phone into my pocket and went into class.

The rest of the day was a cycle of me texting her and her not answering. I was so confused. I'd thought after last night—her in my arms, her smiles, her laughter, how she'd looked so happy—we'd bridged a gap. Guessed I was wrong.

The time passed like a slow day in hell. All I wanted was to see her, to talk to her, but she wasn't at school and she wouldn't answer her phone.

After school, I tried not to think too much about it. I invited Andy and Max over to hangout.

"What's Sofia been up to?" I asked, wondering if she was still mad at me.

Andy shrugged. "She hasn't been hanging out with us like she used to. You really pissed her off by getting with Asha. Speaking of Asha, where was she today?"

I shook my head, ignoring his question.

"Don't you kind of wonder if things will go back to normal once this assignment is over?" Max asked, grabbing a handful of chips from the bag between him and Andy.

"I wasn't, but now I am," I admitted. I knew Asha had feelings for me, but her going suddenly quiet scared me. Maybe Sofia was right. I guessed it was a good thing I had what I needed in case it all did blow up in my face.

Even though I had the guys over to distract myself from whatever was going on with Asha, it did little to no good, and I found myself checking my phone again and again. I'd sent her over a dozen texts since last night. She hadn't responded to even one of them. It wasn't the first time she'd gone silent on me, but it never lasted long. I told myself to just hang in there.

I was fairly certain I'd see her the following day. Yet, she still didn't make an appearance. As I was leaving school the next day, I noticed a black SUV parked down the row from me. It didn't look familiar, and the windows were so blacked out I couldn't see who was inside. But it gave me the creeps, like someone was about to pop out at any second and throw my ass in the back. I shook off the feeling as I climbed behind the wheel and left the parking lot.

During the drive home, I tried to shake the sensation, but it doubled when I glanced into my rearview mirror and saw the black SUV a few cars behind me. Wanting to put my paranoia to rest, I made a sudden left-handed turn into a gas station. I pulled up to a pump, and the SUV passed by. I filled my tank even though I didn't need gas yet and grabbed a soda before getting back behind the wheel. I breathed a sigh of relief knowing the SUV wasn't following me. But moments after getting back onto the street, I found it behind me again.

This time I was convinced it was in fact following me, so I hit the gas a little harder. After putting some spaced between me and the SUV, I made a series of turns to lose it. I took the back way home. When I pulled into my drive, I followed it around to the back of the house where the car couldn't be seen from the street. I got out and creeped up to the edge of the house, peeking around the corner, but the SUV never passed by.

I felt stupid. *Why would someone be following me anyway?* It probably wasn't even the same vehicle. It was Chicago after all. A lot of black SUVs drove around. I let myself in the back door and locked it behind me.

The following week passed in the same fashion. Asha never came back to school, and she never reached out via text message. I wondered what the sudden change was. I was confused. When we'd last been together, everything had seemed perfect. I couldn't figure out why she'd suddenly ghosted me.

School almost went back to normal with Asha gone. Without her, there wasn't really any point in sitting at the elite table, so I went back to eating under the tree with my friends. They welcomed me back with open arms, even Sofia. Things were like they used to be, except the elite didn't bother picking on me anymore. They actually talked to me when we ran into one another in the hallway.

Andy, Max, and Sofia were all back to hanging out at my house after school, and while everything seemed to go back to its rightful place, something didn't sit well with me. I missed Asha. I missed the sound of her laughter, the softness of her skin against my hand. I missed her soft lips which were always sweet and the secret looks we'd share over lunch. I missed our late-night Netflix binges and talking to her until she fell asleep. I missed the way she tasted, the way she smelled, and her lips on mine.

I couldn't move on or put her behind me. Not without knowing why. All I could do was hang on, and it felt like my grip was slipping a little more each day.

"Dude, I've got the perfect idea for your birthday," Andy said when Sofia left the room to use the bathroom.

"I don't want to celebrate my birthday this year," I told him, still too upset about Asha to think about partying.

Andy always suggested the worst ideas for my birthday. One year he wanted to fly to Vegas and buy me a hooker. Another time, he wanted to throw a party for me and hire a stripper. I didn't even want to hear his idea.

"No, dude. Listen. My cousin told me about this club."

"A club?" Max said, sounding annoyed. "I don't want to go to some overcrowded club with shit music and pay thirty bucks a drink. Let's just bust a keg in the basement and call it a night."

"No," Andy insisted. "It isn't that kind of club. It's an underground, illegal strip club. Like, all the big shots go there—mobsters, drug lords, some bad ass people."

I laughed. "If this place is so secret, how the hell do you even know about it?" I asked.

"My cousin had a meeting there last week."

"What?" I ask, my brows pulling together.

"My cousin, Dave, he used to sell weed. But since it's become legal, he had to move into some heavier drugs to sustain. He got hooked up with a new supplier who brought him to this club to make a deal. Dave said it was fucking badass. He said they have girls who strip on stage, like completely. Not the pasties over their nipples kind of shit we usually see. Then he said they have backrooms where you can get private dances and even buy sex. Come on. Let's check this place out."

"Gross, no way. I'm not paying to stick my dick where a hundred other men have already been. Fuck that."

Andy groaned. "I didn't say you had to buy a whore, man. I just want to check it out, experience it. This is some shit straight out of the movies, man."

"No, and that's my final answer.

~

SATURDAY NIGHT MADE its way around, and to nobody's surprise, Andy got his way. He'd managed to talk Max and me into going to this super-secret club that his drug dealer of a cousin told him about. He gave us the secret password, which I was certain would get him killed if we were caught.

"Are you sure this is even it?" I asked as we got out of the car in front of a busy club.

"Yes, he says it's in the basement. Trust me, boys. I've got this," Andy said, acting big and bad as he strutted toward the entrance.

"We're not staying here all night, man," I told him, pissed even being there to begin with.

I didn't want some girl dancing on me. I could only think of Asha. Two long fucking weeks without her.

Marcie said Asha had to do some family stuff with her parents, but who the hell knew. It seemed weird as hell to me that she wouldn't call or text me but would tell Marcie. It was still driving me crazy that I hadn't seen her or been able to talk to her. I didn't know what had happened or if I'd done something to piss her off or make her upset. As we entered the club, I couldn't think of anything but her.

We flashed our I.D.s at the door and didn't have any trouble getting in which was kind of a letdown. Getting turned away was my last resort for ending this shit. Andy seemed to know where he was going though. Instead of going into the first club, he headed down the hallway to a door.

"Password?" large guy with a goatee who looked like he shot people and ate them for breakfast asked.

"Faraday," Andy said confidently.

The man lifted his brow but nodded us forward.

The door opened inwardly, and he led us down the stairs. At the end of the stairs was another door. He put his hand on the knob and paused. Taking a deep breath, he pushed forward, and the door opened. Before us was a sight like I'd never seen before. There were all the usual aspects of a strip club—a bar with several patrons lined up with drinks, tables and booths, and a stage in the center with chairs lined up around it.

My gaze darted around, taking everything in. The men in the bar didn't look like they'd just walked in off the street though. They were like men you'd see on TV or in the movies. All of them wore nice suits, shiny shoes, and jewelry. Some had big diamonds on their ears or fingers. Some had gold chains. There was a poker game going on at one table. More money was on that table than I'd ever seen before. The men around the stage weren't holding dollar bills. They were holding one-hundred-dollar bills.

Andy tried acting cool as he led us through the club and over to a set of chairs in front of the stage, but I could tell he was anything but cool. He looked nervous and out of place. I was sure we all did. The men there looked nothing like us. In fact, we'd never appeared more like teenage boys than we did in that moment.

"Why are we sitting up front? We don't have hundreds of dollars to throw at these girls," I said, leaning into Andy.

"Chill, we won't stay long."

Max started slapping my shoulder, impatiently.

"Hold on, man," I told him, turning back to Andy. "We're going to get our asses thrown out the moment they notice we don't have any money to spend. And I'd rather not piss off a bunch of..." I leaned in to whisper, "Mobsters."

Max was still smacking the shit out of my shoulder so I turned to him impatiently. "What, man?"

He was staring to his right. He just held up one hand and pointed. My eyes followed his finger. He was pointing at Asha.

Asha was working at the club. Her hair was down, and it was curled perfectly. Her face was painted more than she what she wore to school—dark eyes, red lips, and darkened cheeks, making them appear sharper. She was in a tiny tube top, the bottom of her breasts hanging out. The tiny skirt she wore did nothing to hide her ass cheeks or the thin G-string. She noticed me in the same instant I'd recognized her. I couldn't do anything but stare with my mouth hanging open.

"Is that *Asha?*" Andy asked. "Oh, fuck. It is." He laughed out. "Your girlfriend is a hooker, dude."

"Shut the fuck up," I muttered, getting up and heading in her direction.

I marched up to her slowly and watched as her eyes dashed around like she was looking for an escape, but I didn't give her a chance. I stepped directly in front of her. "Asha, what are you doing here?"

She shook her head slightly. "I'm sorry. I can't do this right now. I have to work." She tried to step away, but I moved with her, blocking her exit.

"Fine. I'll buy a dance. How much?"

She scoffed. "Liam," she breathed out my name.

"*How much?*" I asked through gritted teeth.

"Is there a problem here?" a tall man with dark hair asked as he came over.

"I want to buy a private dance. How much?"

He looked at me, Asha, and then back. "With Asha?"

I nodded.

"How much you got?" he asked, sliding his hands into his pockets.

I froze. I didn't know what to tell him.

"Look kid, I'm guessing you wandered in here on accident and saw a girl you go to school with and have a crush on. Am I right?"

I shrugged.

"All right." He nodded. "You're not our usual customer. Asha usually goes for twenty-five hundred a dance. Now if you want more, it'll cost more. But I can look at you and tell you don't have that kind of dough lying around. You wanna get your rocks off with your high school crush, how much do you have?"

I dug my money from my pocket and quickly counted it. "Fifty-two dollars."

He laughed and was about to walk away.

"Wait, I can get more. Hold on." I rushed over to Max and Andy. "Give me all the cash you have."

Max stood up and gave me all his money.

Andy however said, "What? No. I'm buying my own dance."

"Dude, it's twenty-five hundred dollars just for a dance. None of us can afford that. But I got that guy talked down for me. Please, I need to get Asha alone and figure out what's going on. She's been avoiding me."

Andy scoffed and rolled his eyes. "Fine, but you'd better pay me back." He slapped some cash into my hand.

I went back to where Asha and the man were waiting. I recounted the money. "I have a hundred and fifty."

"Sold," he said, snatching the cash from my hand. "Asha, room one." He gave her a slight push.

She led me to the back. Inside the room, she pressed against my chest, and I fell backward onto an overstuffed, deep purple, velvet couch. In well-practiced moves, she shoved her tiny skirt off her body and kicked it to the side. Moments later, she was on my lap, a leg on either side of my hips.

"Asha, what's going on?" I asked, planting my hands on her bare hips.

"What do you think, Liam? I work here." She swung her hair around and started grinding her center against me.

My dick began to ache, but I tried to ignore it. There were more pressing matters at hand. "Why? And who was that guy out there? Is he your stepdad? Is this what all the fights were about?"

"Shhhhh," she said, her lips dangerously close to mine. "Just enjoy this, Liam. It's what you always wanted, right?" After she pushed down her tube top, she lifted herself up onto her knees and put her naked tits in my face. My eyes fluttered closed when her hard nipple grazed my cheek. I was trying to keep my shit together, but she was making it really damn hard. She wrapped her arms around my neck and slid my face between her tits. I raked in a deep breath.

"Does your stepfather make you do this, Asha?" I whispered against her skin, still trying to stay focused.

She pulled away and got up, moving to dance around the pole in the small room instead. "Stop asking me questions, Liam. Just...*be in the moment with me.*" She spun around the pole then dropped down onto the floor.

On her knees, she crawled back over to me, slowly and seductively. She stopped between my legs. Her palms moved up my calves, over my knees, and across the tops of my thighs. Her fingers eased to the button on my jeans, and then she yanked my pants open. She peered at me from beneath her thick, dark lashes. She reached into my jeans and wrapped her fingers around my aching dick. Then she pulled it out and licked her lips.

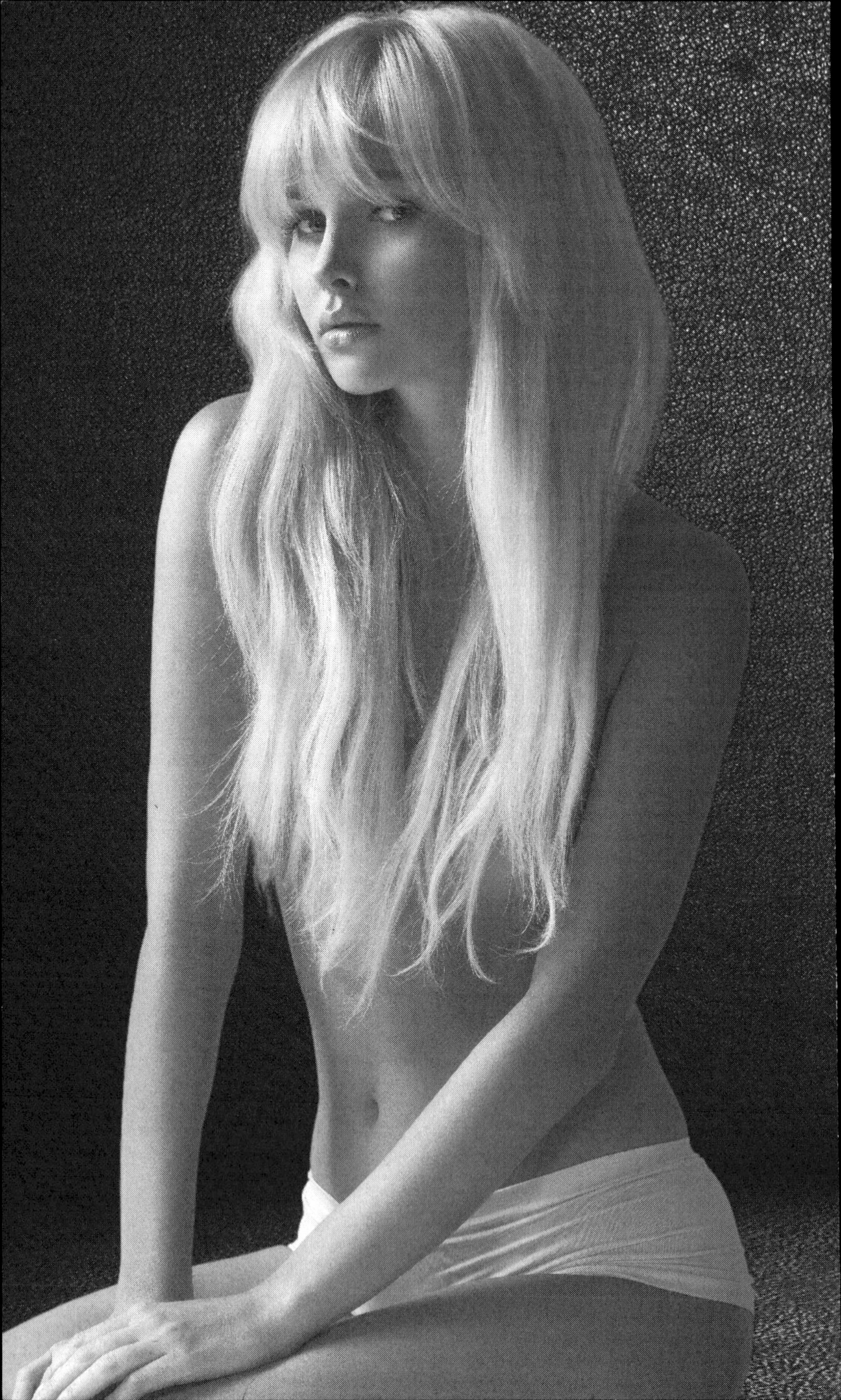

TWENTY-ONE
ASHA

My biggest fear had come to life. Liam knew who I was. *What I was.* I knew he'd never look at me the same again. He wouldn't be able to see the high school girl he'd gotten to know and developed feelings for. All he'd ever see now when he looked at me was a whore, someone who fucked for money, someone he could treat like trash, just like the rest of them.

It didn't matter that when he touched me, I felt it in my soul. It didn't matter I'd never felt a kiss as soft or as strong as his. I knew by tomorrow, his feelings for me would be gone because he would've gotten everything he'd wanted from me.

I gazed longingly at him. It had been too long since I'd laid eyes on him, and I knew that it was my fault. I'd pushed him away. For good reason. He was too good for me in every sense of the word. But our end was finally here in front of us, and it was time I did what I was meant for. Pleasure.

I freed his dick from his pants. Holding him in my hand allowed me to fully see him. He was thick, so thick my fingers couldn't even wrap around his base. His cock was so long. It was hard, and purple veins pulsed beneath his silky skin. A drop of dew was forming on the tip. I longed to taste him again. With my tongue, I wet my lips and lowered my mouth to him. I sucked the moisture off his tip and swallowed it down, hoping to keep a part of him with me always.

"Asha," he choked out. "Stop. I-I just want to talk—"

I moved slow, wanting to build his release up before sending him over the edge. I took him as far back as I could. My eyes watered with the pain of knowing this was the end for us. Tears ran down my cheeks and fell onto his lap as I bobbed up and down his length, sucking and running my tongue across his tip. With each lap, his breathing got heavier.

When I stared up at him from beneath my lashes, his head rested against the back of the couch. His eyes were open though, and they were watching me. When our gazes connected, he bit his lower lip and let out a moaning sound which struck me all the way to my core. I'd never actually wanted sex in this place before. Hell, in general I'd never wanted it at all. I was never given the chance to desire it. Sex had always been taken from me. But I did with Liam. I needed to feel him inside me. I longed to feel his heart pounding with mine. I wanted his touched branded on my body forever. Inside and out.

His hand tangled in my hair. He moaned my name as I came to a decision.

I released his cock from my mouth and quickly straddled his lap, slipping my G-string to the side. He stared up at me, worry in his eyes. *He hurt for me.* I could see his mind running. He was putting the pieces together. I knew it. I couldn't stand that look on him. Liam didn't need to worry about me. I was already a goner.

"Asha, let me get you out of here. Please. You can come stay at my place—" The words faltered on his lips as I slid my heat along his long, hard length.

"Asha, don't do this, OK? Please, talk to me. It shouldn't be like this with us."

I swallowed hard. My bottom lip trembled as I grasped his cock.

"No. Asha, I don't want this. Please. Just talk to me."

I grabbed his arms, pinning them over his head. His brows knit as he shook his head.

"Asha...hellcat. Don't. Please don't do this. I don't want this. Not this way. You know I won't hurt you. I'm letting you decide to walk away with me. Come on, hellcat. Me and you, OK?" he pleaded.

I shut my eyes and slid down onto his length. He gasped, murmuring no as I moved up and down on him.

"Why?" he called out, searching my face as I rode him.

He started to move his arms, but I shook my head at him, desperate for him to let me finish breaking us. He filled me like no one else ever had, his cock almost painful inside me because he was buried so far. But I wanted him deeper. I enjoyed the feeling in my guts as his hard cock poked and prodded my depths.

His bottom lip trembled as his arms went slack. A tear slid out of his eye as I rode him, our gazes locked.

I never dreamed we'd be here doing *this*. It wasn't how I saw giving myself to him when I'd imagined it. Hell, I was *stealing* from him. He'd told me no, and here I was, just as disgusting as the men who'd fucked me. But Liam needed to know. He needed to understand I was trash who took whatever I wanted.

"Is this how it's going to be?" he choked out. "You just want to fuck me and not give me an explanation? I said no!"

I gasped in surprise as he flipped me beneath him on the couch cushions and stared down at me, his dick now completely out of me.

"Is this what you fucking want?" he growled, rage and hurt swimming in his eyes.

I remained silent peering up into his tortured face. He let out a snarl of frustration and thrust back into me, so much anger and agony on his face it made me want to vomit.

"Fine," he grunted, his tears dripping onto my cheeks. "Fucking take it then since it doesn't seem to fucking matter to you. Since *I* don't seem to matter."

I squirmed beneath him, his cock hurting as he fucked me hard, the friction heating my pussy to a boiling point. I clawed and clung to him, sobbing with him as he continued stroking into me with rough movements.

"Is this what you fucking want? Is this who you are?" he demanded as he wrapped his fingers around my throat and squeezed, his voice a choked whisper.

The pulsing of the music from club was quiet in comparison to the sound of our slapping skin and heavy breathing.

"Are you just some girl who fucks random people? You were fucking playing me, weren't you? I was a joke to you, wasn't I?"

My heart broke, but this had to happen. I swallowed and said the words which would be the nail in the coffin of us.

"You were always a fucking joke, Liam. You always will be," I rasped as my orgasm threatened me. No one had ever given me one before except him. Goosebumps rushed along my skin as I erupted around his cock, squeezing him, milking him.

He fucked me harder, breathlessly, painfully, until he let out a low groan and spilled his release deep inside me. He lay on top of me, panting hard, before he pulled out and sat up with his head in his hands.

I stayed where he'd put me, agony coursing through me because all I wanted to do was tell him I'd lied. That it was him I wanted. Confess that I wanted to run as far and as fast as I could with him. I wanted to beg him for help, but I knew it would get him killed.

So I continued to uphold the lies since it was what I was best at.

"I didn't want this for us. I-I said no. *I told you no*," he whispered, his voice cracking. "I wanted to make love to you. I-I didn't want you to just take it like that. I'm sorry. I'm so fucking sorry. I-I shouldn't have done that to you too. *Fuck.*" He yanked his hair angrily before stuffing his dick into his pants and buttoning his jeans. He didn't look at me as he headed for the door. When he got there, he said words that finished breaking my heart.

"I loved you so fucking much, Asha. I really did. I'm sorry for everything."

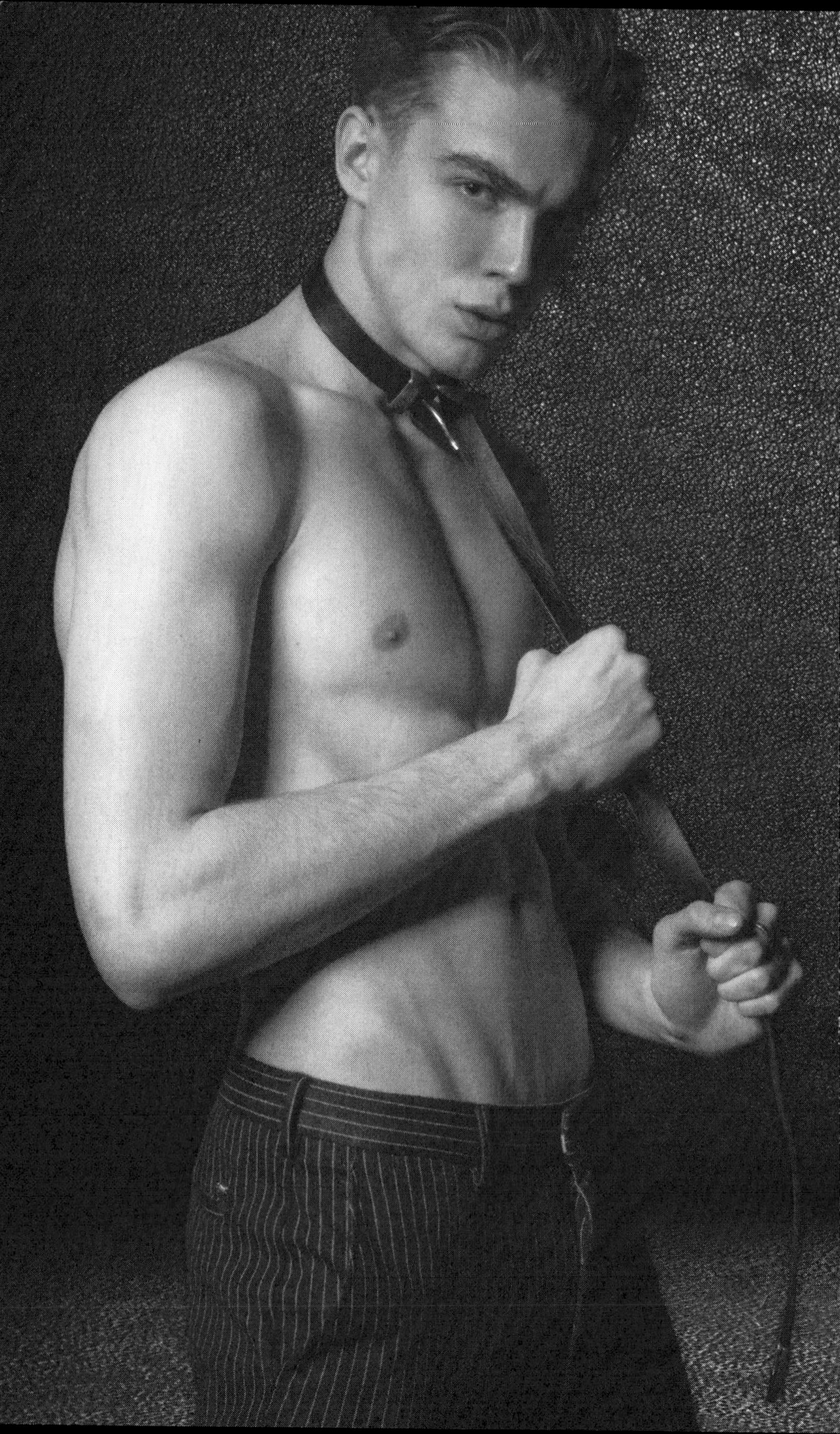

TWENTY-TWO
LIAM

I'd fucked up. I told her no, and she didn't stop. But I was just as bad because I rolled her over and fucked her too.

I couldn't shake her words from my head. I couldn't erase the look on her face as I rammed into her tight heat over and over.

I was a joke.

After I jerked open the door and made my way out of the private room. Andy and Max were by the stage. Max noticed me walk out, and he slapped Andy's arm. Andy was too busy watching the girl on the stage. She was completely naked, her legs spread, letting the club watch while she fingered herself. I wondered if she was being paid to be there or if she was forced into this shit like I knew Asha was. *Was anyone there of their own free will?*

I marched straight past my friends and headed for the door. Anger and loathing pumped through me. I was about to explode. My whole body shook with fury. I was on the verge of tears from not having an outlet for my rage.

I pushed through the door and stomped up the stairs. I was practically running from the club. By the time I rushed through the last door and stepped outside, I was gasping for air.

My head was swimming from lack of oxygen, and my whole body felt heavy, drained. Max and Andy burst through the door and joined me on the sidewalk. My hands pressed flat on the hood of the car as my head bowed in defeat. *Go figure, I'd finally gotten the girl I always wanted only to find out that she fucked for money.*

I didn't really believe that. Deep down I didn't. She wouldn't...

"Whoa, why are you so pissed, man?" Andy asked, looking at me and seeing the anger radiating off my body.

"Was she not as good as you expected?" Max asked.

I spun around to glare at him, but then I saw truth and honesty on his face. He really thought she was here of her own free will. He didn't know she was being abused, raped, and forced into this shit.

I saw it on her face though. As angry as I was, I clung to that. Hellcat was a lot of things, but the girl down in that club wasn't one of them. I fucking knew it.

"Take me home," was all I said as I jerked open the door to the backseat and slid inside.

Max and Andy shared a quizzical look before shrugging and getting in the car.

The ride home was quiet. No radio or talking. I think they were too afraid to speak. The only sounds in the car were the humming of the tires on the road, the roar of the motor in Andy's old Chevy, and the sounds of our breathing.

But I was the only one who could hear the way my heart was about to pound through my chest. My hands stayed drawn up into tight fists the whole way home. Every muscle in my body was hard and tensed, ready for the fight that wouldn't come.

"Hey, does that black SUV look familiar?" Andy asked, glancing back in his rearview mirror.

Black SUV?

I turned and stared out the back window. Several car lengths back and one lane over was the blacked-out SUV I'd seen the day before.

"How long has it been following us?" Max asked.

Andy shrugged and tightened his grip on the wheel. "Since we left the club."

"Fuck! Hammer it. We probably pissed off some mobsters at that club. Lose them, man," Max said, getting anxious and bouncing in his seat.

I didn't move or speak. They didn't need to know the SUV was only after me and it had been. It wasn't anyone from the club coming after us. I didn't know who it was, but I had a feeling I'd eventually find out. Every time I turned around, the SUV had been in my line of sight.

I faced forward. "Get off on this exit," I told Andy.

"What? I can't. I'm going too fast. I'm going to overshoot it."

"Now!" I yelled.

Andy jumped from my anger and the volume of my voice. The jump only made him swerve right onto the exit ramp. He slowed the car, and we made our way to the light. I glanced behind us and saw that the SUV couldn't get into the far lane in time. It passed the exit.

"There. He's off our ass. Now hit the backroads home."

Andy and Max exchanged a confused but scared look, but neither of them argued with me.

When we made it back to my house, I directed them to park in the back instead of up front like usual. They didn't question me, wanting to hide from the SUV as badly as I did. I exited the car and let us into the kitchen through the back door. The only light on inside was the small one above the stove, but it lit up the kitchen enough that we could see.

Max opened the fridge and grabbed one of my dad's beers. He popped the top and started chugging.

"What the hell are you doing?" I asked.

"I don't know what that was or how you stayed so cool, but someone was after us." His eyes were full of panic.

I collapsed onto the barstool at the island. "Nobody is after us," I said, matter-of-factly. "Someone is after *me*," I confessed.

That got their attention, and they both moved to stand by the island.

"I don't know who or why. They followed me from school. I pulled into a gas station, and they kept going. I was able to make it home and into the house without seeing them again. But it seems every time I turn around, I see that blacked-out SUV."

"Is it the same SUV every time though? I know how easy it is to jump to conclusions. It's probably not even the same."

"License plate NCREZ01," I said. I'd memorized it like a bad song I couldn't get out of my head.

"OK," Andy nodded. "Someone is after you, but *why?*"

I shrugged. "Don't know. Don't really care right now."

Andy's brows shot up. "How can you not care?"

"Were you just in that club with me?"

"Asha," Max breathed with a slight nod of his head. "Did you really not know she worked there?"

My fists rested on the island in front of me and I opened them, showing him my palms. "She never mentioned it. All she ever talked about was fighting with her stepdad. He's forcing her to work there. I'd bet money on it. I just..." I ran my fingers through my hair. "I don't know how to get her out of it."

"What did she do? Back in the room, I mean?" Andy asked, his voice slightly shaking.

I scoffed and shook my head, wanting to force the memory out of my head. She'd been hot and tight and had come so hard on my cock. I'd lost control. I knew I'd hurt her because I'd fucked her hard and deep with wild abandon. I'd done it in anger because she hadn't listened and talked to me. I was so pissed when I'd told her no, she hadn't stopped.

I'd always dreamed of seeing Asha beneath me, writhing. But not like that. Not forced. Not either of us hurting.

"She danced for me," I admitted. "Then she..." Tears filled my eyes.

Why didn't I stop her? Why didn't I stop myself? I felt like shit for letting it go on. I only paid so I could get her alone and talk to her to get to the bottom of whatever was going on. I never thought she'd suck me and fuck me, even after I'd told her no. But shit, I also hadn't planned on working my way deep inside of her on my own.

"I-I fucked her," I whispered.

Max and Andy just stared dumbly at me.

Someone banged on the door, and everyone jumped from the noise. "Liam? It's Sofia. You home?"

"Fuck, that scared me," Max said, going to open the front door.

Moments later, Sofia strolled into the kitchen. She took one look at me and worry covered her face. "What's wrong?" she asked, rushing over to stand in front of me. She glanced at the guys. "What's going on?"

Max just shook his head as he finished off his beer. Andy took a deep breath and explained how we'd just found Asha working in an underground strip club. I glared at him as he spilled his guts about what we'd seen. He left out me fucking Asha though.

"I can't fucking believe you idiots," Sofia said, getting loud and even more annoying. "I told you this would happen, Liam. I *told* you."

"What the fuck are you talking about?" I spat out.

"She played you, plain and simple," she said, sitting across the island from me.

My computer was sitting in front of her. She clicked the trackpad and started playing music.

"She didn't *play* me," I argued weakly. *God, I didn't want to believe that.* I was still clinging to the idea she was forced into it.

"Yeah, she did. She knew exactly what she was doing too. She dragged you along. And then she went and stripped and did God only knows what with a bunch of rich men. I guess now we know how she got all her money." Sofia giggled.

"You think she *wants* to be there, doing that?" I asked a little too harshly.

Sofia's eyes darted from the computer screen to mine. "Yeah, I do." Her gaze was wide. "If she didn't, she wouldn't be there."

"She's being forced, Sofia."

She had to be.

Sofia scoffed and tossed her dark hair over her shoulder. "How can someone be forced to strip for money, Liam? Come on. Think about it. If she was forced, wouldn't she try running away or getting help? She was there because she *likes* being the center of attention. She likes money. And she likes being a whore. She played you. In fact, I think now is the perfect time to release this." She turned my computer around so the screen faced me.

I jumped out of my seat so fast the barstool toppled and fell over. I grabbed my laptop and slid it to me, slamming it closed. "What the fuck, Sofia? Why are you going through my shit?"

"The file was left open. Don't you know how to put a password on shit you don't want anyone to see?"

I remembered sitting in the kitchen, eating pizza, and looking at the document before Max and Andy had shown up earlier. I was pissed that Asha was not calling me back. I'd thought about releasing it then, but I'd decided against it. And then Max and Andy had shown up, and I forgot all about it being open.

I grabbed my backpack off the counter behind me and shoved the laptop into the bag. Out of sight, out of mind.

"What did it say, Sofia?" Andy asked.

I narrowed my eyes on her, a silent warning.

"Oh, it was just all the dirt Liam has gathered on the elite since he's been hanging with them. All their dirty little secrets. It needs to be let out, Liam."

"No, I only wrote it so I'd have it if I needed it. Releasing it now would be like calling them out. They haven't done anything to me."

Sofia stood up. "Well their queen bitch did something to you. They stand with her, they fall with her."

Andy had righted my stool. I fell back onto it.

My hands came up to cover my face. "I love her," I choked out. "I can't do that to her."

Andy's brows shot up in surprise. Max's mouth dropped open. And Sofia, I swore I saw fire dancing in her eyes—pure anger, masked by a little pity.

"Please, don't mention any of the shit you saw or heard tonight. *None* of you. I need to talk with Asha. I have to get to the bottom of this. And if you're right, Sofia, *if* Asha did drag me along to fuck with me, if she wants to do those things at the club, then we'll talk about releasing it. OK?" I surveyed them as they thought it over. "Deal?"

Andy nodded.

Max said, "Deal."

And Sofia sat back down as she crossed her arms. "Fine."

Everyone cleared out after that, and I locked up the house before heading upstairs with my backpack to shower. I tossed the bag in my chair and yanked off my shirt as I moved to the bathroom.

The hot water did little to soothe my anger. My muscles were still tense and ready to spring. I couldn't think about anything except Asha—the fear in her eyes when she'd noticed me in the club, and the pain on her face when we'd been alone together. My mind drifted to how fucking hot and tight she was as I stroked inside her.

I shut off the water and climbed out, wrapping a towel around my waist. Back in my room, I got dressed. Grabbing my phone, I sent her a message.

LIAM: I just need five minutes. I have questions.

I waited. I saw the message had been seen and read, but no dancing bubbles followed to tell me she was replying.

A reply never came. I drew back my fist and sent it flying into the wall by my closet door. It plowed straight through the drywall, but it did no good at releasing my anger.

My knuckles were red from hitting the wall, but my rage only doubled. Tears burned my eyes as I fell into bed. Sleep took me easily, but it wasn't restful.

All night long, I saw nothing but Asha—dropping to her knees so easily for me and for everyone else too. In my dreams men touched her and grabbed her. She got pulled into the backroom, where she screamed and cried for help. No help came. I saw her stepdad smack her around until her fight left.

And I woke up covered in sweat when I saw the way he held her down and fucked her while she cried into the pillow.

∼

MONDAY ROLLED AROUND, and I felt like shit. I'd slept like shit the whole weekend. I was still so angry. I wanted to see Asha, but she wasn't in school. She ignored my texts and calls. I drove by her house, but there was never any smoke coming from the staff house chimney out back.

The rest of the week carried on in the same fashion. By Friday, I'd had enough.

It was officially my birthday, but it was the worst birthday I'd ever had. I didn't give a shit about partying with my friends. I didn't care about getting drunk or presents. All I wanted for my birthday was Asha. I wanted her to be mine, for her to be free from whoever was holding her captive. I wanted answers.

After getting ready for school, I sent Asha another message.

LIAM: It's my birthday, and I want to see you. I WILL see you. I'll break down the damn door if I have to. Meet me at our spot after school. If you're not there, I'm coming after you. You know I will. I want to know what's going on because that girl wasn't my hellcat.

She didn't respond, but I hadn't expected her to. I went through school like a zombie. I talked when I was spoken to. I answered questions when I was called on, but I wasn't present. My mind was still back at that club, the last place I'd seen Asha. I knew that was where it would remain until I saw her again.

When the bell rang, I didn't even fuck with going to my locker. I left my eighth hour class and went directly to my car with my books and all. I tossed everything into the passenger seat and sped out of the parking lot at lighting speed. I stopped by my house long enough to get Asha's early birthday present—a stuffed hellhound wearing a witch hat and a voucher I'd made. I stuffed the paper into an envelope and headed for the car.

I made the drive over and parked in my usual spot. Then I scaled the brick wall and hiked back to the staff house. Smoke billowed out of the chimney. When I opened the door, the house was warm from the fire burning in the fireplace. The sounds of sobbing and sniffling filled my ears. When I rounded the couch, I found her, curled in a ball.

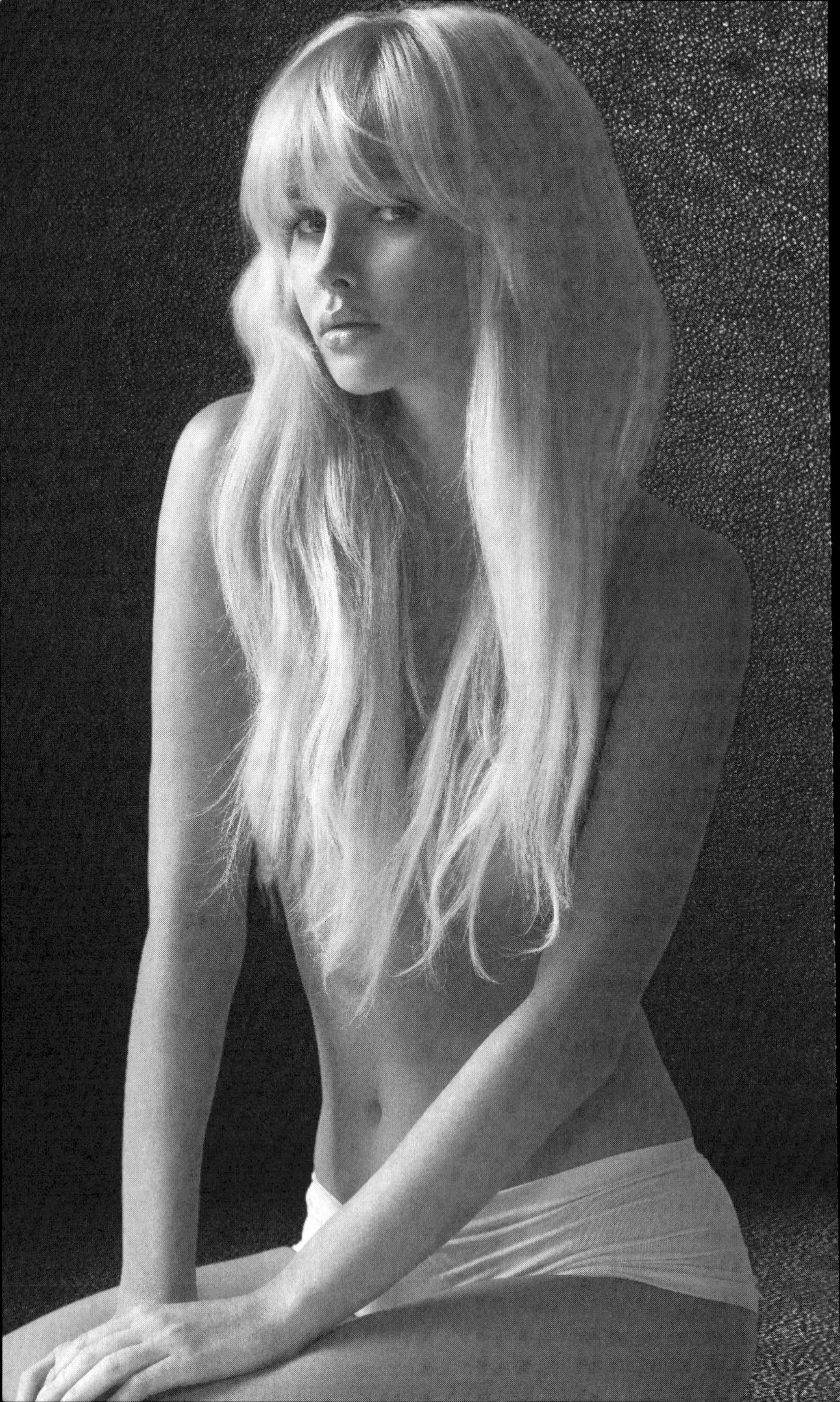

TWENTY-THREE
ASHA

The tears never seemed to stop flowing. My head pounded from the constant crying. My eyes hurt. My whole body hurt. My heart hurt. I wanted it to end. The pain, the torture, my life.

Gio wouldn't do it for me, and I knew it. He'd sell me to be tortured more before he'd do me a favor by ending my life. Since the night before when I'd found Liam at the club, I'd shifted through several ideas of how to get the job done once and for all. I considered overdosing on sleeping pills, but I figured it left too much wiggle room. Someone could find me and call an ambulance. My stomach would get pumped, and I'd wake up, in more trouble.

I thought about going to the roof of the club and throwing myself off. I imagined it would feel like I was finally free, flying for just a moment before it all ended. It would also draw a crowd to the building. Maybe Gio would get busted and locked away for abducting and selling girls. But I also decided against that option because with my luck, I'd end up paralyzed and still have to go through the torture of Gio selling my limp, basically dead body.

I needed something that was a sure thing. I could take my cutting a little too far, but again, I might be found and saved. I needed a gun.

One shot to the head is all it would take, and it would leave little chance of survival.

Someone grabbed me and drew me against them. I fought, not wanting any more hands on me, not wanting to be touched or fucked with. Then Liam's scent surrounded me, and I heard the familiar lull of his heart, so I settled against him.

"Shhh, it's me," he cooed, combing my hair with his fingers as he held me tightly. "I'm here. You're not getting rid of me."

My hands fisted in his shirt, and I held on for dear life as more tears rushed from my eyes. *Why was he here? Didn't he see what I really was? Why did he want anything to do with me after seeing how used and dirty I was? After I'd ignored him telling me no and forced myself on him?*

"I'm here, Asha. I'm not going anywhere," he murmured softly, rocking me, calming me. "Tell me what's going on. Not for the assignment. For me. Let me in. Let me know you. The *real* you," he whispered, never stopping with his swaying. "I know you're hurting. I want to help you."

I turned my head so I could look up at him rather than hide against his chest. I wiped my tears and told him everything. I spilled the whole sordid story of how my mother had left my father for Gio. How Gio hated my father and used me to get back at him. How Gio had sold my virginity to a man twice my age. How he'd watched that man rape me while he sat, jacking off. How my stepfather had abused me by beating me, cussing me out and calling me names. How he'd forced me to do awful things like suck his dick. I sobbed as I told him how it had all led to Gio finally raping me and leaving me with no ride in the middle of the night. I told Liam about being forced to work in the club and the things I'd done there. The stripping, the drugs, getting so high I couldn't stay conscious. I spared no details of how Gio had sold my body for rape while I was passed out. Liam stayed silent as I told him about having to suck guys off, letting them have their way with me, their sick fantasies I had to go along with. I told Liam *all of it,* and by the time I was finished, I felt lighter. I'd never told anyone everything before.

Fury painted his features as he'd listened. His brows pulled together, and two wrinkles formed between his green eyes. His jaw flexed, relaxed, and flexed again and again. I'd felt the way his whole body had tightened, how he'd almost squeeze me when he got angry. But he'd stayed quiet and listened.

To my surprise, he didn't get up and break shit. He didn't yell or scream at me. He just listened and held me like a thick, warm blanket thrown over my world, keeping me safe. I felt secure in his arms. I was like a different person when we were together.

"How can I help you, Asha? I want to help. I want you out of this shit."

I shook my head as a few hot tears slid down my cheeks again. "You can't, Liam. Don't you understand. If I run away, Gio will find me. He has unlimited resources. He'll just drag me back, and everything will be worse. I'll be punished severely for running."

"There has to be a way."

A menacing laugh escaped my chest. "There's not. The only way out of this is death. Either I have to die or he does."

There was a silent minute when I thought I'd finally convinced him there was no happy ending for me, but then he said, "OK, I'll do it."

My head popped up off his chest. "Do what?"

"I'll kill Gio."

Another laugh slipped out. "Don't be stupid. Bigger and badder men have tried and failed. He's the devil. There's no killing him. And I won't let you try. He'd kill you, Liam. I can keep doing this shit as long as I have to, but not if you're dead. I'd never be able to let that go."

He glanced down, and our eyes met. Slowly, he moved his lips to mine, and I savored having his lips on mine. I never thought I'd get to feel them again. I thought once he knew the truth about me, he'd see me like everyone else saw me—dirty, used, a whore. I was certain when he left the club night, it would be the end of us. I just knew he'd hate me for fucking him after he'd told me no. But here he was, being nice to me, fighting for me, kissing me. *Loving* me.

As our kiss increased in urgency, my body started to come alive. Every nerve ending felt like it had been set on fire. Each hair on my body stood on end as goosebumps prickled my flesh. I wanted Liam. I didn't know what would happen in the future, but I knew there was a chance I might never see him again. He couldn't fight and win me. He had no choice but to let me go. I needed just one last good memory.

I eased back and cupped his jaw. "Liam, I do need something from you."

"Name it," he breathed out.

"I need you to take the memories away. I need to replace all of them with one good one. I-I want it to be like it should've been between us."

Acknowledgment flashed in his green eyes and moments later, his lips were devouring mine. His tongue danced with my own. I wrapped my arms around his neck, pulling him closer as he lowered me onto the couch. When his body covered mine, his weight felt perfect pressing against me.

As his hands toured my body, they were soft and slow, switching from a firm grab to a soft caress. Liam kissed his way across my cheek and down my jaw to my ear and neck. His mouth moved lower while his hands worked my shirt up my stomach. When my shirt got in the way, he stopped kissing me. He pulled back, and his eyes found mine before he lifted my shirt over my head.

Instantly, his mouth was back on me, kissing the swell of my breasts as one hand slipped behind me and unclasped my bra. Torturously slow, he nibbled and sucked along my breasts, pushing the cups of the bra away with his lips as his fingers eased the garment from my body.

When he sucked my nipple into his mouth, I arched up off the couch cushions and a whimper left my lips. As he suckled my flesh, his tongue flicked against my nipple, making my hips rock against his hardness which was pressed against my center. Then he kissed lower, down my stomach to the top of my jeans. I was going to explode. I rushed to shove them out of his way, but he caught my wrists in his hands.

"Don't rush things, Asha. Stay here, in this moment, with me," he whispered, his gaze slipping from mine so he could resume his sweet, sweet torture. Gentle fingers unbuttoned and unzipped my jeans. His lips traversed from my belly button to my hip bone.

He sat back on his knees as he tugged the denim down my legs and off my feet. As he leaned over me, his eyes took me in, and even I, a girl who was used to being watched, felt my body heat from his stare.

The tips of his fingers slid into my panties, and he dragged them down slowly and teasingly. His jaw flexed, and his Adam's apple bobbed in his throat as he licked his lips and lowered his mouth to me. He ran his tongue between my folds. When he brushed against my clit, my hips jerked upward.

"Is this OK?" he asked in a hushed whisper as he held my hips down.

I nodded.

"Good," he said, moving his mouth back to my clit.

He sucked my sensitive nub into his mouth and flicked his tongue against it again and again. A fire burned in my belly like someone had thrown gasoline on it. It blazed hotter, burning out of control and consuming everything it came in contact with.

My moans grew louder, and my hands fisted the couch cushions.

"Like this?" he whispered pausing before grinding his tongue against my clit.

"Yes," I said in a breathy gasp as he slid a finger inside me.

He curled his finger upward and hit the magic spot, wringing a moan from me. My whole body tightened as an orgasm racked my body. Not a spot was left untouched by the electricity crackling through me. My toes burned and tingled. It climbed up my legs, taking over every muscle. I couldn't move. I couldn't breathe. All I could do was hold on tight as I rode out every last earth-shattering wave of pleasure he gave me.

When my release ended, I was finally able to suck in a breath. My chest heaved, and my muscles slowly thawed, allowing me to feel them again. Liam crawled up my body, shedding his shirt along the way. A smirk lifted his lips.

"That was the sexiest fucking thing I've ever seen."

His mouth smashed against mine, and I could taste myself on him. I liked it. I liked knowing I was the flavor left on his tongue. Not anyone else. Just me.

My nails dug into his back as I deepened our kiss, wanting more, *needing* more. I heard the sound of his belt clanking as he worked to remove it. It was like each of my senses was heightened. Every place he touched me burned and tingled with excitement. My ears were tuned to only him. The soft sound of him lowering his zipper filled my ears.

Then he shifted and pushed his jeans down with one hand. Freed from the denim, his thick cock pressed against my stomach.

My legs tightened around his hips as he used one hand to guide himself into me. His silky, soft tip pushed against my opening. As slowly as humanly fucking possible, he shifted forward, sliding into me with ease. There was no pain. No burning sensation. It didn't feel like I was being ripped in two. It felt good. Suddenly, I understood why people liked sex, *consensual* sex anyway.

As he kissed me, one hand cupped my jaw while the other held firm at my hip. He kept thrusting forward, claiming me. When I thought he had to be all the way in, he pushed in more.

Liam Hastings was easily one of the biggest guys I'd ever been with. It felt like I was stretching around him, like my insides were moving out of the way to make more room to accommodate him. Finally, his hipbones rested against me, and I knew I had all of him.

He let out a relieved moan into my mouth. Knowing I was the reason he was making that sexy as fuck noise made my stomach tighten with the threat of another orgasm. I didn't want it yet though. I wanted to push it off, hold out just a little longer. I never wanted my time with him to end.

His fingers held my hip in place as he slowly removed himself from me. He slid back until only the tip remained before pushing back in harder and faster than before.

"Fuck, Asha. You're perfect," he whispered against my lips. "So fucking sexy and beautiful, warm and fucking tight as hell. Fuck, I want to come already." He rocked against me again, and I let out a whimper.

"Liam," I moaned his name.

His dick twitched inside of me. "Say it again." He pushed harder.

"Liam," I called out, my release building inside of me. "Don't stop. Don't stop, Liam," I begged as my orgasm rose to its highest peak. Then everything shattered, raining down on me hot and heavy.

Liam raked his fingers tenderly through my hair, his eyes on me as our bodies fused. I'd never seen anyone look at me the way Liam Hastings did. And I never wanted anyone but him to.

His hips became wilder, moving faster and harder each time. His strokes were less precise as he groaned against my lips and dug his fingertips into my hip. "Fuck. You feel too good."

In and out. Over and over. Each thrust of his hips brought on so many waves of pleasure, making me come hard again, milking his thickness. He growled as his hips jerked. He spilled himself inside of me. Each stroke caused a jerk of his hips as he rode out his release. His lips landed on mine, kissing me softly, gently, until we were both weak and breathless.

∽

A WHILE LATER, we were both still naked, lying on the couch. It had grown dark outside, and the flames in the fireplace were starting to dwindle. Liam held me against his chest with his arms wrapped around me, his jacket thrown over our hips, keeping us covered. Our breathing and heart rates had returned to normal, but I knew something inside of me would never be the same.

"You're quiet. Is everything OK?"

I shook my head and swallowed. "I never even *wanted* sex before you. It was always taken from me, so I wasn't given the chance to actually want it. But with you...it feels right."

He gave me a sweet smile. "You didn't even want it with Lucas?"

"I never slept with Lucas. He was my shield. He kept the other guys away. Nothing more."

Liam tightened his hold on me and kissed the top of my head.

"Liam?"

"Yeah?"

"About the club... About me not listening when you told me no—"

"Shh, hellcat. It's OK. I *wanted* to be inside you. I just never expected it like *that*. I'm OK. I promise I am. Besides, I had my way with you too."

I nodded and snuggled against him. I was silent for a moment before I spoke again. "Stay here with me," I begged softly, not even meaning to say it out loud.

"Here? Tonight?"

I swallowed. "I packed for the entire weekend. Gio is out of town, and my mom is probably drunk off her ass and sleeping it off."

"OK," he agreed. "We'll stay here, making this moment last a little longer."

I kissed his chest, and he tangled his fingers into my hair, holding me closer.

Eventually, we had to pull apart. The fire needed to be stoked, and we were both growing cold. We got dressed. While Liam added wood to the fire, I went into the kitchen and made us something to eat. The electricity and water weren't turned on in the house, which was why Gio didn't house any of the staff here. I'd packed enough bottled water to last through the weekend and even snagged a bottle of wine. I'd brought peanut butter, jelly, bread, and chips.

With a smile on my lips, I made us sandwiches and chips and took it all into the living room along with the open bottle of wine. Liam was back on the couch, and the fire was blazing, lighting up the room.

I set both our plates down. "Hope you like peanut butter and jelly."

"Love it," he said, picking up a chip and popping it into his mouth. "I have a birthday present for you." He reached around and picked something up off the floor by the couch.

"For me? But it's *your* birthday."

"Well, early birthday present for you then," he corrected, handing over a stuffed animal of a black cat and an envelope.

I looked at the black cat and laughed.

"Get it, hellcat?"

I snickered. "And she's a real witch," I pointed out, playing with the witch's hat on her head.

He smirked as I set the cat down and opened the envelope. Inside was a piece of paper. It reminded me of when I was little and I made my parents coupons for stupid things like free hugs. But this one wasn't for a hug. It was a promise. A promise to rescue me, take me away.

My eyes teared as I looked down at the paper.

Nothing in this world will keep me from you. I swear to you I'll save you and keep you forever, safe in my arms. Love, Liam

"I'm serious too, Asha. I won't sleep until you're free, living the life you deserve."

I turned and threw my arms around him, squeezing him as I cried happy tears. I had no idea how it all happened, but Liam had not only become a friend, but he'd also become someone I couldn't live without.

WE ATE our dinner of peanut butter and jelly sandwiches with chips then moved onto drinking the wine. We shifted from the couch to the floor near the fireplace. As night drew in around us, the temperature dropped in the house, so we cuddled up under the blanket, directly in front of the fire.

Somehow, the ugly days before were completely erased by the bottle of wine, and we found ourselves talking, laughing, joking, and playing. Everything felt easy. I tried to picture my life always being this happy. I loved how Liam found any excuse to touch me, like finding a fuzz ball in my hair and grazing my cheek as he got it out or drawing shapes for me to guess in my palm with his thumb while holding my hand. When he lay down and I curled into his side, I wrote small messages on his chest with my fingertip while he tried to guess what I'd written.

The drunker we got, the dirtier the messages got.

"I want that big... *duck?*" Liam guessed.

I grinned as I sat up and straddled him. "Close, but nope." I ground my center against his crotch, and his head popped up.

I lifted one brow, smirked, and nodded my head.

He immediately leaned up. His right hand moved to the back of my head, pulling me close for a kiss. I rose onto my knees so I could pull his pants back down. Moments later, I slid down his length. The different position made him feel bigger. Slowly, I eased down on him. His hands gripped my hips, guiding me lower and lower over every inch. A couple of times I was certain that I couldn't take anymore of him, but then he lifted me up a little, and I slid back down lower.

Before Liam, I'd never been on top. I loved the power it gave me. I got to choose the speed. I got to pick the direction. It let me figure out what I liked. I found I enjoyed grinding against him because it moved him inside of me and applied pressure to my clit.

Riding Liam, I found a part of myself I never knew existed. A part of me that liked sex when I was giving it freely. I rode out the waves of my release as Liam watched me in awe. When my body slowed, he rolled us over and pounded into me until I screamed his name like it was my saving grace.

The rest of the weekend passed in the same fashion. Neither of us left our little hideout for long. We had the food we needed, and when nature called, he went outside and I either went outside too or ran back to the main house since it was safe enough with Gio gone. Each time I went in, I checked on my mom and found her sleeping or drinking, which wasn't out of the norm.

Liam and I ate junk food, drank too much stolen alcohol, and made love more times than I could keep track of. When Sunday rolled around, hiding out was no longer an option. The real world awaited us. I didn't know when Gio would come home and start looking for me. I definitely didn't want him to catch me having sex for free, and I didn't want to find out what he'd do to Liam for taking me for free. So Liam and I packed our things and headed for the door. He stopped before opening it and turned to me.

"I meant what I said here, Asha. I won't stop until I've saved you. I don't know how I'm going to do it, but I promise you, I will. I love you." He yanked me in for a kiss.

I was frozen. *He loved me?* He'd said it before, but that moment had been surreal. But this? Nobody had ever loved me. Those happy tears stung my eyes again, and I kissed him back, mumbling how much I loved him too.

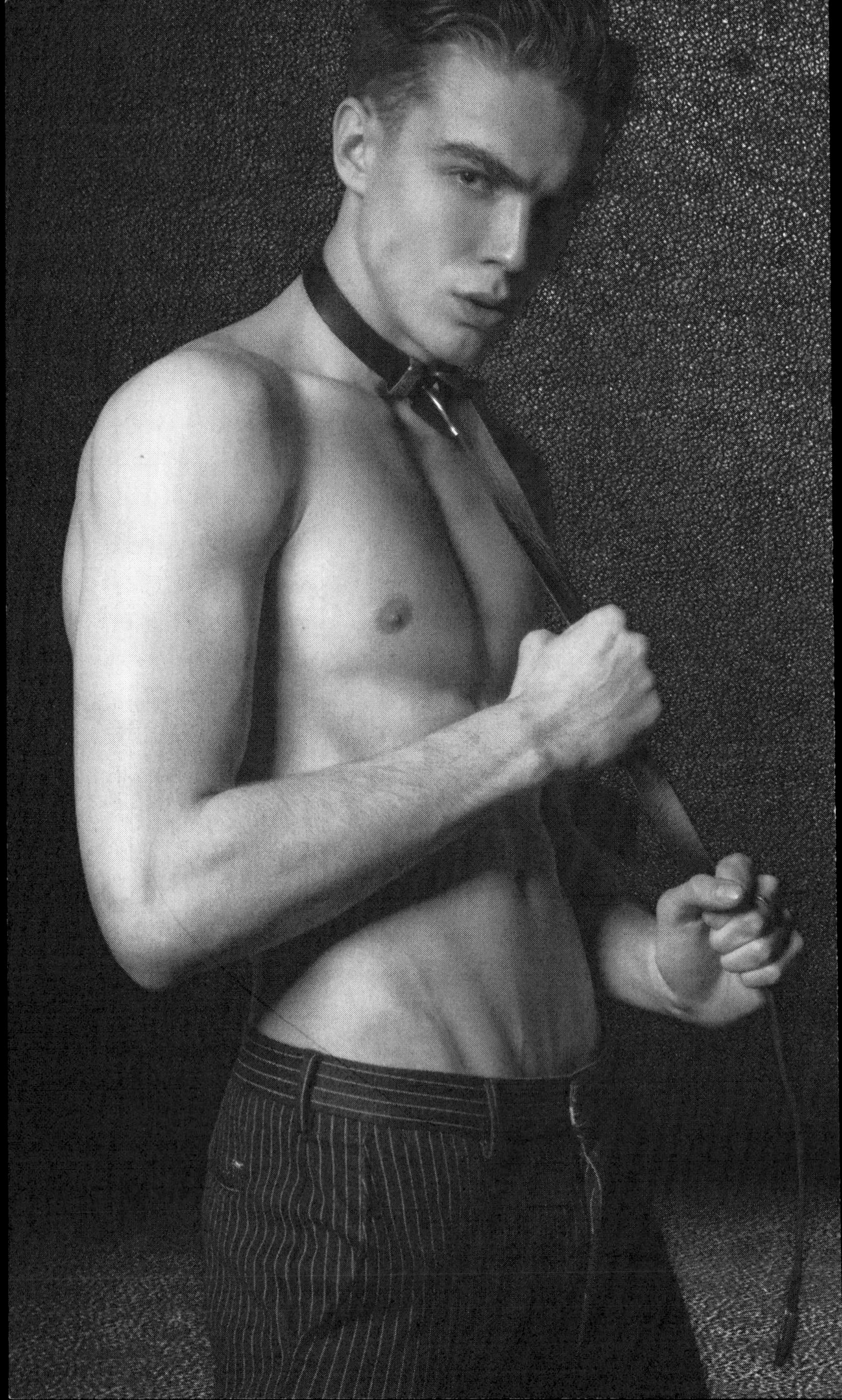

TWENTY-FOUR
LIAM

The sun hadn't even come up yet when I stopped in front of Asha's house. I'd just thrown the car in park when she ran from the gate and jumped in, wearing a big smile. Her blonde hair blew around her, and her blue eyes shone, stealing the air from my lungs.

"Happy birthday, hellcat," I told her, leaning in for a kiss.

"Thank you," she said.

I shifted back into drive and hit the gas.

"It's a little too early to go to school, don't you think?"

"We're not going to school right now."

"Where we going?" The corners of her mouth were trying to lift, but she managed to keep her smile put away.

"I thought we could...I don't know, just have a little quiet time to ourselves before we get to school and have all that noise surrounding us."

She didn't reply as I took a few turns, leading us out of town. A little while later, I put the car in park in a secluded, little spot. A small lake shimmered in front of us, and nothing but trees surrounding us.

"What is this place?"

"My family used to own a cabin out here. I fished in this lake all the time while I was growing up. But my family sold it years ago to have money for mine and my siblings' college funds."

"It's beautiful out here," she said as the sun just started to peek over the tops of the trees in the distance.

"Quiet too," I pointed out.

She glanced over at me, and our gazes locked. The air between us charged and bounced like it was full of life. It seemed to draw us closer, and before I knew it, we were meeting in the middle, kissing. Her hands raked through my hair while I cupped her cheeks, not allowing her to pull away. The intensity of our kiss assured me she didn't want to stop.

My hands drifted to her hips, and I lifted her up to straddle me. She didn't break our kiss. When she was seated on my lap, her arms tightened around my neck, holding me close. It gave me this sense of empowerment, knowing I was the one she trusted when everyone else had only hurt her. I felt like I was on the top of the world, like I had it all. But I knew being on top, there was no place to go but down. I was so scared of losing everything that I wanted to block out the rest of the world and never let anyone come between us.

My hands explored her body, moving from her hips up her back, under her skirt. She finally removed her mouth from mine and pushed her straps off her shoulders.

"Here?" I asked.

She cocked a smile. "It's as good of place as any. I can't wait until the end of the day to feel you moving inside me." She pressed a soft kiss to my lips. "I want you, Liam," she whispered.

I pulled her back in for another long, hard kiss as my body shivered in anticipation. Asha exuded this energy that everyone around her recognized. I had no choice but to absorb it, feel it, let it push me to living in the moment with her.

She was wearing a pretty, blue sundress which made my mouth water. I opened my door and climbed out, keeping her in my arms. I strode to the front of the car and laid her on the hood. She reclined and watched me staring at her as I lifted her skirt and eased her panties off.

My mind instantly flashed back to the night I'd had Sofia in this same position and how badly I'd wished it was Asha. My dick throbbed, finally getting to play out this fantasy.

I moved my mouth to her inner thigh and kissed my way up to her center. The sun was finally over the trees, and it provided enough light to see every detail of her. Using my thumbs, I spread her folds to reveal blushing pink skin which was glistening with need. I closed my mouth around her clit and sucked it into my mouth.

A loud moan escaped her lips as her head popped up. Her fingers moved to fist my hair where she directed on my speed. She tugged harder the moment I found what she needed. Within minutes, she was coming undone. After she shattered and screamed loudly enough to make the birds flee from the trees, I pulled her up.

"Bend over," I ordered as I freed myself from my jeans.

Her legs were wobbly as she stood on her own and bent over the hood. Her big tits pressed against the hood. Her perky ass was bare and right in front of me. If I could've painted that image on my car, I would have.

I grabbed her hips with my left hand and guided myself into her with the other. Slowly, I slid the first couple of inches into her heat. Then I thrust in deeply the rest of the way. Her back arched as she whimpered in approval.

After mere minutes inside her tight body, I was ready to come, but I wanted her falling over the edge with me. So, I reached around her hips and moved my fingers to her clit, applying pressure as I continued to thrust. Her body tightened around mine, and just when I couldn't hold back any longer, she erupted, bringing me over the edge with her.

It took us both several long moments to catch our breath and pull apart. After I removed myself from her, she stood up.

I turned her around and cupped her cheek. "I love you, Asha," I said, moving in for a kiss.

Her hand fisted in my shirt. "I love you too," she replied, just as our lips met.

By the time we loaded back up in the car, we were right on time. We had fifteen minutes until the first bell rang and were only a few minutes away from school. While I drove, Asha fixed her makeup in the mirror, reapplying her lipstick and fixing a smudge of mascara under her eye from her eyes watering when she came on my dick. Just thinking about it made me hard all over again, but I pushed the image away. We were out of time, and there were still so many things between us to take care of before she could really be mine.

Things like her stepfather. I'd promised to take care of him, and I had to keep my word. I kept trying to figure out how in the hell I could do it. He didn't seem like the kind of man who'd take a quiet jog in the morning. Mowing him over with my car on a deserted road would be too easy. I also couldn't see bumping into him alone in a dark alley where I could shoot him. The man I was up against was powerful and calculating. My only hope was if he killed me in the process, at least, I'd get him out of the way too. For Asha.

Plus, as far as the student body was concerned, Asha was still with Lucas.

I finally turned into the parking lot at school. Asha flipped the visor back into place, happy with her appearance. I switched off the engine, and the two of us climbed out. As we walked across the cement, I took her hand in mine. She peeked down at our connected hands and then up at me with a smile, her cheeks turning a light shade of pink.

"Everyone is staring and whispering," she said as we strolled through the crowd toward the school.

"Fuck 'em," I said, smiling, proud of myself for climbing the ranks at school and getting the most beautiful girl there.

As we approached the doors, the rest of the elite were sitting on their usual bench. I didn't even notice the school papers in all of their hands. When Jude looked up and saw me, everything changed.

Jude smacked Lucas across the chest and nodded toward me when Lucas glanced at him. The two of them quickly threw down their papers and rushed at me.

I expected Lucas to give me shit about being with Asha, but I didn't expect him to be so furious. He pushed me hard against the chest. The force was enough that I had no choice but to release her hand as I tried to keep from falling.

"What the fuck, man?" I asked, quickly shoving him back.

Asha jumped between the two of us as Lucas prepared to come back at me. Her hands went up, one on each of our chests. "Hey, stop!" she ordered, looking from him, to me, and back. "What's going on?"

"What's going on?" Lucas asked. He snatched a paper from someone's hand who happened to be walking by and pressed it against my chest.

I took the paper and read the front page. The headline read: **The Dirty Lives of the Rich and Spoiled by Liam Hastings.**

I glared over the article and quickly skimmed it to find it was what I'd written with all their dirty, little secrets. *How the fuck did it get out?*

Sofia.

She'd found the article. She must have emailed it to herself before saying anything. I glanced up and saw the anger painted on her face as she lurked twenty feet away, watching everything unfold.

Asha grabbed the paper from my hands. In horror, I observed as her eyes moved across the words. Fury flashed in her eyes as they narrowed on certain parts. Her face paled, and her mouth dropped open as her gaze moved over to me.

"How could you do this?" she whispered.

I shook my head. "I didn't. I didn't publish that, Asha. You have to believe me." Worry and fear drenched my words.

She had to have heard it, *felt* it.

"I can't believe you'd do something like this, Liam. To my friends, to me!" She shoved the paper into my chest, pushing me back as she did so. "This whole time I've been falling for you, and you've what, been investigating us, gathering dirt? For what, huh? To take us down? It wasn't enough that we brought you in and treated you like one of us? I *trusted* you, Liam. And this is what you do with that trust? While I've been falling for you, it's all been a big lie to you? You just wanted to use me to get to them?"

"*What?* No, Asha. It wasn't like that, OK? Yes, I wrote this, but I didn't *release* it. I was just going to hold on to it."

"For what?" she asked, voice growing louder and her expression growing more and more angry by the moment.

"Just in case I was nothing but a joke to you. I thought all of this —" I waved my arm around to indicate me being part of the elite circle. "—was some epic prank! I thought you were acting like you liked me just to hurt me, and that the moment you gave the signal, your friends would take me down. I wanted to be prepared if that happened." Even explaining it sounded shady as fuck. I regretted ever writing the damn thing.

She shook her head. "I trusted you, and you screwed me over. I thought you were different, Liam, but you're just like the rest of them. We're over." She turned and stalked into school without me. It felt like she'd ripped my heart from my chest and stomped on it.

I was in shock. I was pissed. I'd been on top, and I'd lost everything. All because of Sofia. Sofia could never accept she and I were just friends. She'd always wanted more, and when she'd found out that I was actually getting something I wanted, she couldn't handle it. She'd been against Asha since day one. *But what did she really hope to achieve by releasing the article without my permission?* She had to know I'd be pissed. She had to know that by doing something I told her not to wouldn't bring me to her. I wanted even less to do with her now than I ever did.

"You'd better watch your ass," Lucas snarled, pointing at me before pivoting and trailing after Asha. The whole group shot me dirty looks as they marched into the school, probably going to have a group meeting about to how to fix the mess I'd created.

With the elite gone, I set my sights on Sofia. Andy and Max started my way as I strode for Sofia, but I pushed them away, stomping up to her. The rage was no longer on her face. It had shifted to pure fear as I closed the distance between us.

"Why?" I asked. "Why did you go behind my back and do this?"

She wrapped her arms around her torso, making herself appear smaller as she shrugged. "I'm sorry. I was mad. I was pissed they were treating you so badly and you were just blindly following along with everything they said or did. Asha was using you. You have to see that."

I ground my teeth together so hard a bout of pain shot through my jaw. "I'm fucking done with you, Sofia. You're not a friend—no friend would've done that. I asked you to stand by me, and you agreed to, only to go behind my back and fuck me over? *Fuck you.* I never want to hear your voice again." I marched past her, barely registering the tears filling her eyes. I couldn't have cared less.

I pulled out my phone as I entered the school and sent Asha a text.

LIAM: I'm sorry. Please know I didn't release that. I never would've done that to you, Asha. I love you. Please, meet me. We'll leave together and figure this whole thing out.

She saw the message as soon as I sent it, but no reply came.

At my locker, I drew back my fist, sending it flying into the metal. The locker made a loud noise in protest and dented inward. My knuckles stung, and when I looked down at them, I found blood dripping from one. I wiped it across my jeans as I put in the combination and opened it for my morning books. It felt odd to go about my day as normal when my whole life had blown up, but what choice did I have?

I hung out in the hallway until the tardy bell rang, but Asha nor any other member of the elite made an appearance. With nothing else to do, I headed for class. I walked in late, and the door slammed loudly behind me. Everyone looked up. I had their full attention.

"Please take your seat, Mr. Hastings. I think you've made enough of a spectacle around here today."

I inhaled deeply and pushed forward. When I got to my seat in the back of the class, I fell into it and noticed the way everyone still had their eyes on me instead of the teacher.

He cleared his throat and got most of the focus back. After he started teaching, a guy named Chris leaned over a little.

"Liam, was all that shit true? Do they have wild sex parties where they fuck each other, even the guys? And snort coke too? Do Molly?'

I shook my head and forced my eyes on the blackboard.

The rest of the day passed in the same fashion. In every class, someone pushed for more details that may have been left out of the paper. Asha wouldn't answer any of my calls or texts. By the end of the day, rumors swirled about the elite. People took the things I gave them and twisted them, turning them into shit that wasn't true. There were rumors that Asha was just a cover so Lucas and Hudson could have a secret gay relationship. Jude was suddenly the pimp of the group, telling the girls who to sleep with and when. And Asha was suddenly pregnant with my child and had missed so much school due to morning sickness. They even suggested she'd drop out to abort or finish out her pregnancy just to give our imaginary baby up for adoption. Shit was out of control.

The elite didn't make an appearance at lunch. Their table was left empty which only caused more of a fuss. It seemed the whole group had left after the morning news blew up. The day was long and hard, and I was pissed about having to dodge questions from everyone who wanted more dirt. By the end of the day, I was more than ready to leave. After the last bell, I made a mad dash for my car. I stopped short when I saw Lucas, Hudson, and Jude gathered around it.

I froze as they glared at me. *Fuck.* Hanging my head, I pushed on, closing the distance.

"Look, I swear I didn't publish that shit," I started, but I was silenced when Lucas swung and landed a solid punch to my jaw. My books fell out of my hands, but I refused to fight. "Hit me all you want. Beat the fucking shit out of me. It's not going to change the fact that I didn't do this, Lucas." I held my arms out at my sides.

"Yeah, well someone did, and your name was on it, so..." Lucas said, swinging again, this time hitting me in the stomach.

It caused me to double over. As I fought against the pain, I fell to one knee.

"I told you not to fuck with us," Lucas growled, stalking around me. He drew back his foot, and it connected with my side.

The force of the kick knocked me over onto the pavement. My vision blurred, and pain racked my body. I rolled over onto my back and peered up at the sky. The three of them closed in around me.

"This is what you get for trying to fuck us over," Hudson snarled just before they started kicking the shit out of me.

My stomach churned and felt like it was going to empty. My back ached, my ribs, my chest, my face. I couldn't feel anything but the pain. They continued to kick me over and over. I blacked out several times, only to wake to more kicks. I couldn't do anything but curl myself into a ball to try and protect myself any way I could. I could've fought back. I may have even taken one of them out, but three on one wasn't fair, and the outcome would've been the same. When they finally tired, Lucas grabbed ahold of my jacket and rolled me over onto my back as he hovered over me.

"If you know what's good for you, stay the fuck away from us."

"I didn't publish it," I mumbled through my swollen lips. "I love her," I confessed.

Lucas released me, and my head dropped back against the concrete. The next thing I knew, I was alone. I gave into the pain, letting it pull me under, deep into the darkness.

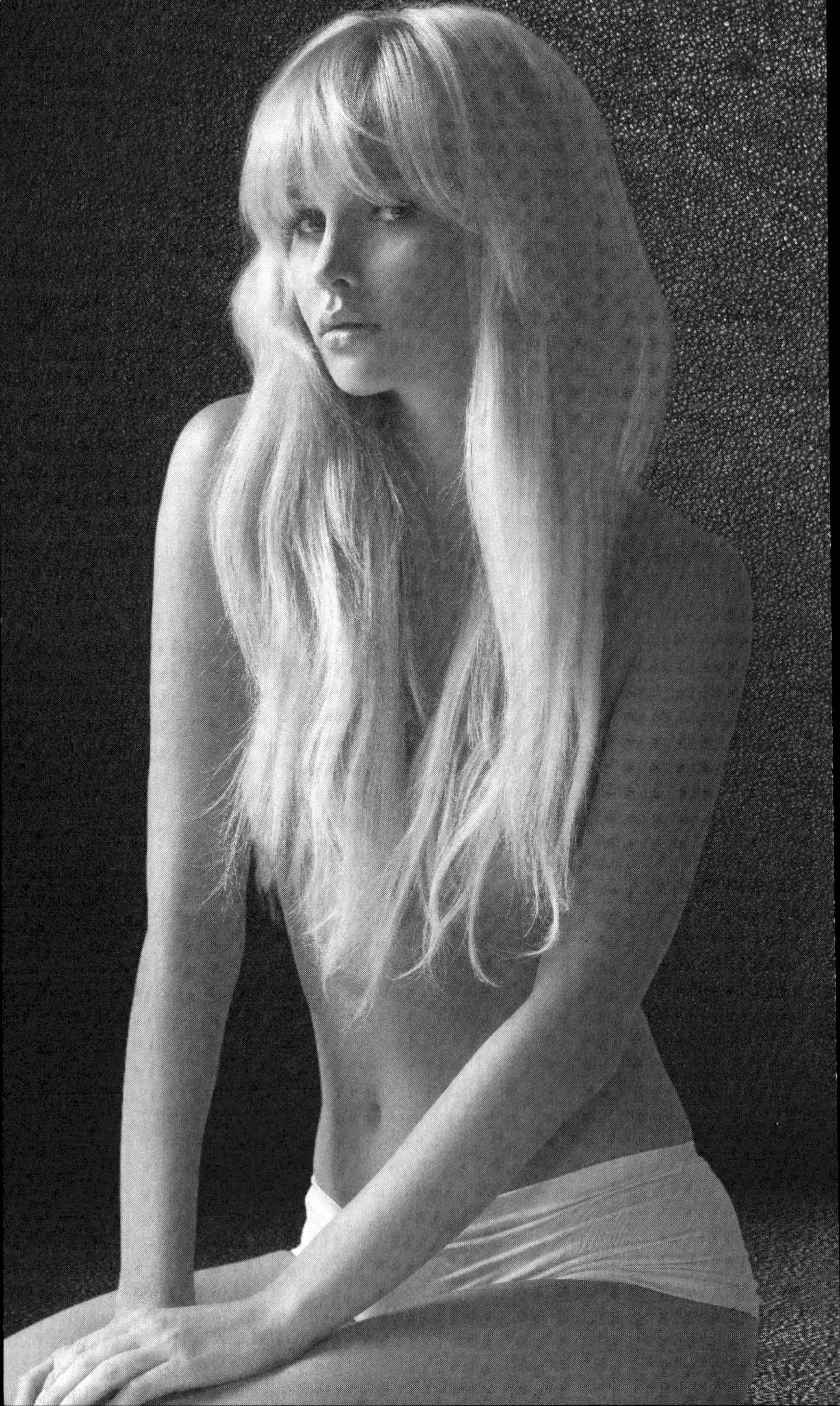

TWENTY-FIVE
ASHA

Part of me felt so guilty because Liam's instincts were right about us. I never expected my feelings for him to change like they had. But more than feeling guilty, I was pissed, so pissed. Even after having all day to think about it, I couldn't let my fury go.

I was furious with Liam for writing all that shit down. I was livid that my friends were stupid enough to open up to him. More than that, I was angry with myself for having doubts. I wanted to believe Liam. But I was convinced it was just my stupid heart talking. The damn thing had been dead so long that when Liam and I were together, it came back to life and felt everything in tenfold stronger. How could I believe him when his betrayal was on paper in black and white?

I just wanted to disappear into my sanctuary at home and pray this whole day was just a nightmare. As I strode across campus to the parking lot after the school day ended, I allowed my mind to drift back to the moment when my birthday went to shit ...

My heart trembled and cracked as I turned my back on Liam and walked away. But I forced my mask of indifference into place as I made my way through the school and directly out the back door to the old greenhouse. It was no longer used, but our group always met there whenever we needed to have a private meeting. Sometimes we'd skip class and hang out there. We'd have a little in school party with booze or weed. It wasn't a place we visited often, only at the worst of times. The building was technically off limits to students. Since it hadn't been used in years, it was no longer considered safe. But we were the elite, and we did what we wanted. So I planned to hide out in our sanctuary all day.

I entered the greenhouse, which was so far back on school property I could barely see the school through its glass walls. Within minutes, everyone else was inside. I hoisted myself up onto an old table and sat while everyone filtered in and made themselves comfortable. Hudson removed a joint from his pocket and lit it. It made its way around the circle, each of us taking a hit.

"Now that we've all had a minute to think, how the fuck do we fix this?" Hudson asked.

"We could beat his fucking ass," Lucas suggested.

Tiffany rolled her eyes and scoffed. "That might make you feel better about your little secret being out, Lucas, but it's not going to fix the problem," she pointed out.

"What secret, Tiffany? I'm not gay!" Lucas said loud enough everyone could hear him.

She smirked. "So letting a dude suck you off isn't gay?"

He squeezed his hands into fists. "I know for a fact you and Heidi messed around. Does that make you gay, Tiffany?" he threw back. "No, it just means we're young and trying to figure shit out." He dragged his hands through his hair as he tried to calm down.

I stood up and threw a dirty look at Lucas. I didn't know when some guy had sucked his dick, and I didn't even care in that moment. "All right, look," I said, getting everyone's attention. "We've all done things we don't want anyone to know about. Throwing it in each other's faces now isn't going to do any good. The point is the shit is out there, and there's nothing we can do about it. We can't go back and change any of it. So what do we do now?" I asked, looking around the group.

None of them answered.

"We fucking own it," I said, sure of myself. "We're the elite. Nobody messes with us. Sure, one guy found out some shit. Who the hell cares? This is what makes us better than the rest of them to begin with. We do things they only dream about doing, and we get away with it." I grinned, and so did the girls.

"Yeah, fuck all of them," Jude said.

"Fine," Lucas grumbled, shaking his head. "But we're still beating the shit out of Liam."

I chewed on my lower lip. Lucas's anger worried me. "Don't hurt him. We're all guilty too. We did plan on humiliating him. He just got the jump on us."

"Whatever, we're going to take care of shit so it doesn't happen again. The last thing we need is people thinking we're going to roll over and take it." Jude glanced at each of us.

Everyone nodded and murmured their agreement, except me.

Lucas cast me a quick look. "It won't be bad. We won't kill him, Asha. He'll just learn not to do shit like that again."

There wasn't a damn thing I could do to stop them, that much was clear. All I could do now was pray Liam was OK, even if I was hurt and angry with him.

"Hey, don't forget, Halloween party at my place tonight," Hudson reminded us. "Naughty costumes encouraged."

The girls started chattering about what they were going to wear while I zoned out.

"Happy birthday," Lucas leaned in and whispered in my ear.

"Thanks." I fiddled with a string on my dress. "Did you really have a guy suck you off?"

He sighed and rubbed his hand across his cheek. "Yeah."

"Are you. . .?"

"Bi?" He laughed softly. "I don't know. Maybe. I know I love *pussy but. . ."* He trailed off and scrubbed his hand over his face again. *"It was good. I know I'd do it again without hesitating."*

I nodded, not even mad. It made sense considering what I knew of him.

"You and Liam. . .?"

I swallowed and nodded.

He gave me a gentle squeeze without saying a word.

None of us went to class all day. We just hung out in the greenhouse, smoking weed and laughing despite the bad situation. If it wasn't for my broken heart, it would've been a good day. In the greenhouse I was able to pretend everything was fine. I didn't have to think about Gio, my life outside of school, or Liam. I was able to let everything go and be with my friends. It was a nice distraction.

When the school day finally did end, the guys headed out first, wanting to catch Liam before he could get away. I waited with the girls a little longer before leaving our hideout. It was time to go home.

Lucas pulled up to the curb and picked me up before I even made it to the parking lot. He drove away quickly while I put my seatbelt on.

"We took care of Liam," he said once school was behind us.

"I hope you didn't cause any permanent damage."

He shrugged. "We left him passed out in the parking lot."

"Lucas, what if he gets run over? What if he dies?" My anxiety rose, and a pain shot through my chest as I pictured him lying unconscious on the ground.

He snorted. "He won't."

"You'd better hope not."

Lucas cast a glance my way. "You know, I think you should believe him."

"Believe him?" I questioned, my brows drawing together.

He nodded. "Yeah, I think he was telling the truth. I don't think he's the one who released the article. If he was, he would've admitted it to get us to stop. He stuck to his word."

"If you believe him, why'd you beat him up?"

"He may not have been the one to release the article, but he is the one who wrote it. He deserved to get his ass kicked. But now, he's paid for his mistake. I don't think he needs you to make him keep paying for it." He paused and peeked over at me. "He said he loves you."

My arms crossed tightly over my chest, trying to hold the pieces of my heart in place. Hope threatened to bloom in the cracks. I thought about Lucas's revelation. I was hard to believe Liam would publish that article after the morning we'd had. Liam was good, kind, soft, sweet. It was hard to imagine he even wrote those horrible things. And writing them and publishing them *were* two different things. Either way, I didn't know how I wanted to handle Liam. I needed time.

The car was silent as Lucas drove until he finally said, "You know, you don't have to go back there. You can come stay with me. My parents love you—they won't mind."

"Thank you, but Gio would just drag me back. He won't let go without a fight."

I was surprised by Lucas's generosity. I figured he would be mad at me. I was the one who originally suggested bringing Liam into our group. I was the reason our secrets had gotten out. Not to mention, I'd broken things off with Lucas to be with Liam, the guy who'd screwed us all over. Maybe Lucas wasn't as bad of a guy as I thought. There was some good in him.

I knew on some level, Lucas and I were a lot alike. He took a lot of shit and beatings from his dad. His father was an upstanding citizen who expected nothing but perfection from his only son. Lucas would never be good enough for his dad's impossibly high standards.

"We should go to the cops. I don't want you going back there, Asha." Lucas shifted in his seat.

I could see how anxious he was getting—more and more the closer we got to my house.

Sadly, I shook my head. "It won't do any good. You have no idea how many cops Gio has in his pocket. They'll rat me out, and Gio will just kill me."

Lucas let out a long breath. "Damnit, there has to be something we can do." He turned down the driveway to my house.

"There's nothing. Trust me, I've been dealing with this shit for years. I've considered every angle, every way. I can't run. I can't tell. I have to handle this on my own."

The car came to a stop outside my house, and I turned to face him.

"Thank you. For everything."

He nodded. "Are you sure you don't want to come back to my place? Just for a little while. You know, to avoid this place as much as possible. W-We can even try to reach your real dad—"

I offered up a smile. "I'll be fine, Lucas. Thanks." I leaned over and pressed a kiss to his cheek. I quickly pulled away and got out before he could stop me.

When I got in the house, it was quiet. I had no idea where my mom or Gio were. Instead of venturing around and looking for trouble, I went straight to my room. I dropped my bag to the floor and fell into bed. I lay on my back, staring up at the white ceiling.

So many emotions coursed through me that it was hard to tell where one ended and another began. I wanted to hate Liam for writing those things about us. I despised he even knew those things, that we'd so openly trusted him with our deepest, darkest secrets. I loathed myself for ever putting the group at risk. Like always, everything I touched turned to shit.

I'd taken a good guy and turned him into someone who listened for dirt, someone who was calculating enough to use every bit of information he could get his hands on and use it against us. Even if he hadn't intended to release it, he never should've written it to begin with. Nothing was ever really private. I would know.

I'd turned him into me. And I really wished I hadn't.

But most of all, what I really felt, down to my very core, was heartbreak. I was in love with Liam, and he'd betrayed me. I hadn't only lost a friend but had lost the only person who'd ever shown me kindness, friendship, love. Tears stung my eyes and overfilled my lids quickly, rushing down my cheeks. My heart hurt so much I felt sick to my stomach. I was exhausted from keeping my walls up. But at the same time, sleep wouldn't come. I tossed and turned and cried, but nothing took my pain away enough to sleep.

I wondered if Lucas was right about Liam, and I wondered if I should call him to talk everything out. Maybe I could even forgive him. But if I did that, it would give him another chance to hurt me, to betray me.

I wasn't sure I could handle it happening again. My phone rang again and again. When it wasn't ringing, it was chiming with texts, messages, and social media notifications. My group of friends and I were the talk of the town, all thanks to Liam and the way I'd carelessly fallen for him.

All I wanted was an escape. I wanted a break, time to recharge. I needed to let myself fall apart, so in the end, I could pull myself back together, better and stronger than I was before. I knew sleep wouldn't find me easily. My head was a blur of never-ending thoughts. I needed quiet.

I opened my social media to see all the tea about me being a stripper. I swallowed the bile creeping up my throat, my stomach roiling. People posted about me giving them lap dances, even though none of the losers could even afford to walk into one of Gio's clubs. Some claimed to have paid me twenty bucks for a blowjob. I ignored everything else they mentioned regarding the elite. My heart hurt as I stared at their ugly lies and bitter truths. I was crumbling under the weight of everything.

This was the final straw.

I stood and went into my bathroom where I found the bottle of sleeping pills I'd taken from Mom. I uncapped it and poured some into my hand. I didn't bother counting them.

What was the worst that could happen? I'd die? Ha, that would've been welcomed. I needed an out. I needed to end everything.

I tossed them in my mouth and filled an empty glass with some water. I took a large gulp and washed the pills down. I had to swallow several times to get the dry pills to stop sticking, but I finally had them all down. I returned to my bedroom and sat on my bed, pulling a notepad out of my bedside table.

Mom,

I'm sorry. Please forgive me for what I've done, but I can't go on living this way. Gio is a monster who forced me to do awful things. Since he came into our lives, I had my virginity sold and stripped away from me by a man I'd never met. I was forced into sex work. Gio has sold me time and time again. I was turned into a stripper, a whore, a drug user. I don't even recognize myself when I look in the mirror anymore. Please forgive me for what I've done. I just need to get out.

I love you, always remember that.

I tore the page from the notebook and left it on the bedside table. Then I started one more.

Liam,

I'm sorry. I love you. Remember that. I'm sorry for all the things I've put you through. I was wrong. I regret all of it. You'll always be my one.

—Hellcat

My vision started to blur, and I gave into the heavenly feelings. All the thoughts stopped. My pain was gone. I was numb as I flopped back and closed my eyes, letting the darkness have me. It was where I belonged anyway.

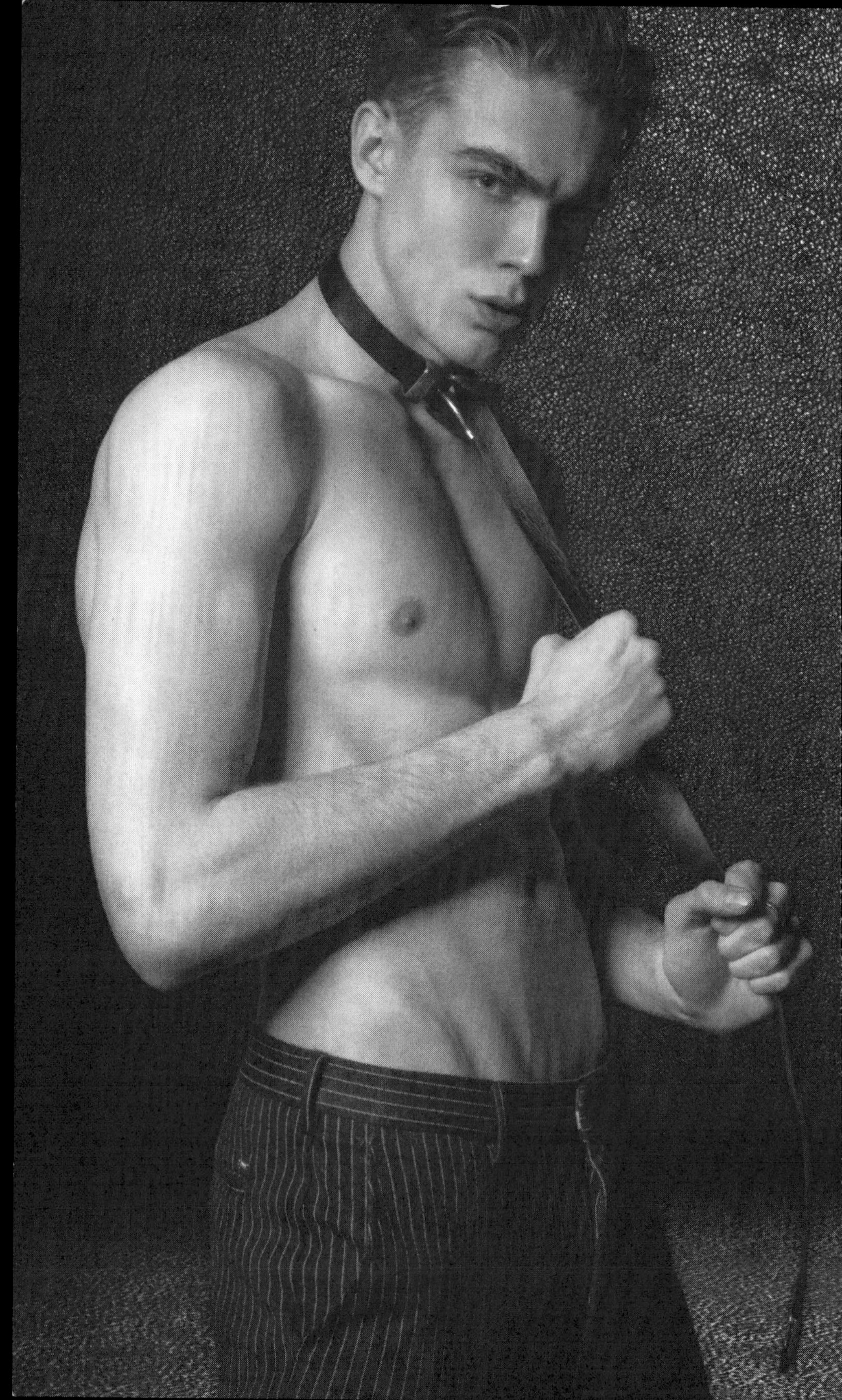

TWENTY-SIX
LIAM

Gingerly I stepped out of the shower and stood in front of the mirror to assess the damages. I wiped the moisture away from the glass and took myself in. A big bruise stained my jaw. A slit decorated my bottom lip which was swollen and bloody. My arms and hands were covered in scratches and bruises. My torso was littered with smaller bruises as well. Both sides were marked with big, dark bruises. When I tried to breathe too deeply, a stabbing pain shot through my ribs. I probably had a few cracked ribs, but none of that mattered. The only pain I felt was from losing Asha, agony she hadn't believed me.

I swallowed four Tylenol and got dressed. If my parents saw the way I looked, they'd freak the fuck out and demand to know who'd beat me up. They'd call the police and probably try suing Lucas's parents. I yanked on a hoodie, a pair of baggy track pants, and my socks. I tugged the hood of the sweatshirt over my head in an attempt to hide from everything—the world and the pain in my heart. All I wanted to do was sleep, escape it all, even if only for a little while.

The ringing of my phone woke me. I had no idea how long I'd

been out. I answered without looking, knowing it couldn't possibly be the only person I wanted to talk to.

"Hello?" I croaked.

"Liam? It's Lucas."

"What the fuck do you want?"

"Have you heard from Asha?"

"No, but I'm sure that's not hard to believe," I said through clenched teeth.

"She isn't answering her phone. I took her home. I'm worried she tried to run and Gio killed her."

"How long has it been since you talked to her?" I asked, sitting up and pushing the hood off my head.

"I haven't heard from her since I dropped her off after school. It's been hours. She isn't answering any of my calls or texts. She said we couldn't go to the cops, but I can't just sit here and not do anything. What if she's in trouble?"

I dragged my hand over my face, trying to wake up a little. I was confused, disoriented. Lucas was talking faster than my brain could process.

"So, what do you want to do?" I finally asked, trying to piece shit together.

"I'm going over there," he said.

"Fine. I'll meet you there."

I hung up and grabbed my keys, leaving my wallet behind because I didn't think I'd need it for the quick drive. I made it to Asha's house within minutes and had just climbed out of the car when Lucas showed up. He threw his car in park and hurried out. We met between the two cars, and he looked at me with a smirk.

"Man, you look like shit."

I scoffed. "Yeah, thanks for that."

"Look, man," he started, but I cut him off.

"Fuck that. Let's go check on Asha."

I led the way to the door and hit the doorbell a few times. We waited, but the door went unanswered.

"Guess nobody is home."

"See if it's open," he urged.

I placed my hand on the handle and pushed down on the latch with my thumb. The door slowly creeped forward. It looked dark inside as I walked in.

"Whoa," I said, taking in the large entryway, all the marble and ivory.

"Come on, you can take in the architecture later," he said, pushing past me and leading the way up the curved staircase.

On the second floor, we rushed down the hallway. He must have known where he was going because he went to a specific door, no opening doors and peeking inside each room. He glanced at me before pushing the door open. The room was dark with the curtains drawn, but the bathroom door was open. The light from within shone across the bed. Lucas flipped on the bedroom light, and I rushed over to the lump on her bed.

Her body was completely covered in blankets. when I reached out to shake her, I found her limp. I yanked the blankets down and rolled her onto her back. Her head lolled to the side. That was when I noticed the vomit.

"Fuck, call 9-1-1," I told Lucas.

He ran over as I shook her. "What's wrong?"

"I think she overdosed," I said as I tried to wake her.

"Fuck, fuck, fuck." He yanked out his phone and called an ambulance.

"Asha, wake up!" I yelled as I lightly slapped her face and shook her body. "Fuck, Asha. Wake up!"

She made a garbled sound, and her eyes rolled beneath her lids, but they didn't open.

"Stay with me, Asha," I pleaded.

Lucas paced back and forth across the floor as he spoke to the 9-1-1 dispatch. His hand fisted in his hair. A look of worry was etched on his face.

I scooped Asha into my arms, moving her to the floor and out of the puddle of vomit on the bed. She was completely limp. Her skin was pale, cool, and covered in a sheen of sweat. I pried her eyelids open, but her eyes were rolled back in her head. I felt for a pulse. It was there but was weak and slow as fuck.

"Fuck, tell them to hurry up," I ordered Lucas.

It felt like the entire world was stuck on pause. Every second felt like a minute, and every minute felt like an hour. Lucas stayed on the phone until the EMTs arrived. I remained next to Asha, shaking her, talking to her, running my hands over her arms and face, trying to get her to respond in any way, but she didn't.

The EMTs rushed in the room and pushed me back. They quickly got to work while I fell back with my back against the edge of her bed. I watched as they got her loaded on a stretcher and hurried from the room.

"Come on. Let's follow her to the hospital, make sure she's going to be OK," Lucas said.

I nodded. "I'm right behind you."

He darted from the room, but I felt heavy, frozen. I couldn't move. My eyes drifted across the floor by her bedside table. There was a notebook. I picked it up to set it on the table. Then I noticed my name on the paper. An apology and a declaration of love. It was a goodbye.

Anger flared inside of me. I used it to propel myself up. I sprinted out the door and back to my car. I climbed behind the wheel and twisted the key. The engine roared to life, and I shifted into gear, ready to drive straight to the hospital. When I glanced at my dashboard, I realized I wouldn't be going anywhere if I didn't stop and get gas. But I'd left my wallet at home. *Fuck.*

I forced myself to calm down. There wasn't anything I could do anyway for Asha right then. I had plenty of time to go back home, grab my wallet, get some gas, and then get to the hospital. I drove back in the direction of my house. I left my car running while I hustled inside. The house was dark and quiet with both my parents gone. I didn't bother turning on any lights. I knew the layout of my house like the back of my hand. Up in my room, I snatched my wallet off the bedside table.

Before turning, I slipped it into my pocket. When I spun around, I bumped into something hard. I bounced back, and the next thing I knew, something hit me over the head. My vision splintered, and darkness surrounded me.

~

I WAS JOSTLED AROUND. My eyes rolled open to see a flash of treetops. My vision blurred again, and my head shifted, but I forced my eyes open in time to see a black SUV. I heard voices around me, but I had no idea what they were saying. Their conversation was muffled like maybe they were wearing something over their heads. I got tossed into the back. The slamming of the doors echoed through my skull. I finally gave into the pain and let it take me away.

Behind my lids, I saw Asha. Her beautiful smile. The way her blue eyes lit up and sparkled. I envisioned her silky hair between my fingers, the heat of her body surrounding me when I sank into her. I imagined her sweet perfume and her soft lips. I didn't know if seeing her meant I was going to heaven or hell, but I didn't care. As long as I was with her, I knew I'd be happy.

Pain was all I could feel, so I was pretty sure I was heading for hell. She was my little hellcat after all. It seemed fitting. My head was killing me, and even in unconsciousness, my ears were ringing. I felt the throb of every bruise Lucas and the guys had left on me. I was dizzy and sick to my stomach, but still my only worry was Asha. I didn't care who had me. All I needed to know was that she was all right.

My eyes opened and rolled. I was lying across the backseat of the SUV. Two men were in the front. Neither spoke as they drove me somewhere. The ringing in my ears was loud. My head screamed in protest from trying to move. I tried to push myself up into a sitting position, but the dizziness came back, and I was out again.

I was done anyway. Asha hated me and was probably dead. I had no friends left. There was nothing left to live for if she died. If these men wanted to kill me, they'd have an easy time because I wasn't going to fight them.

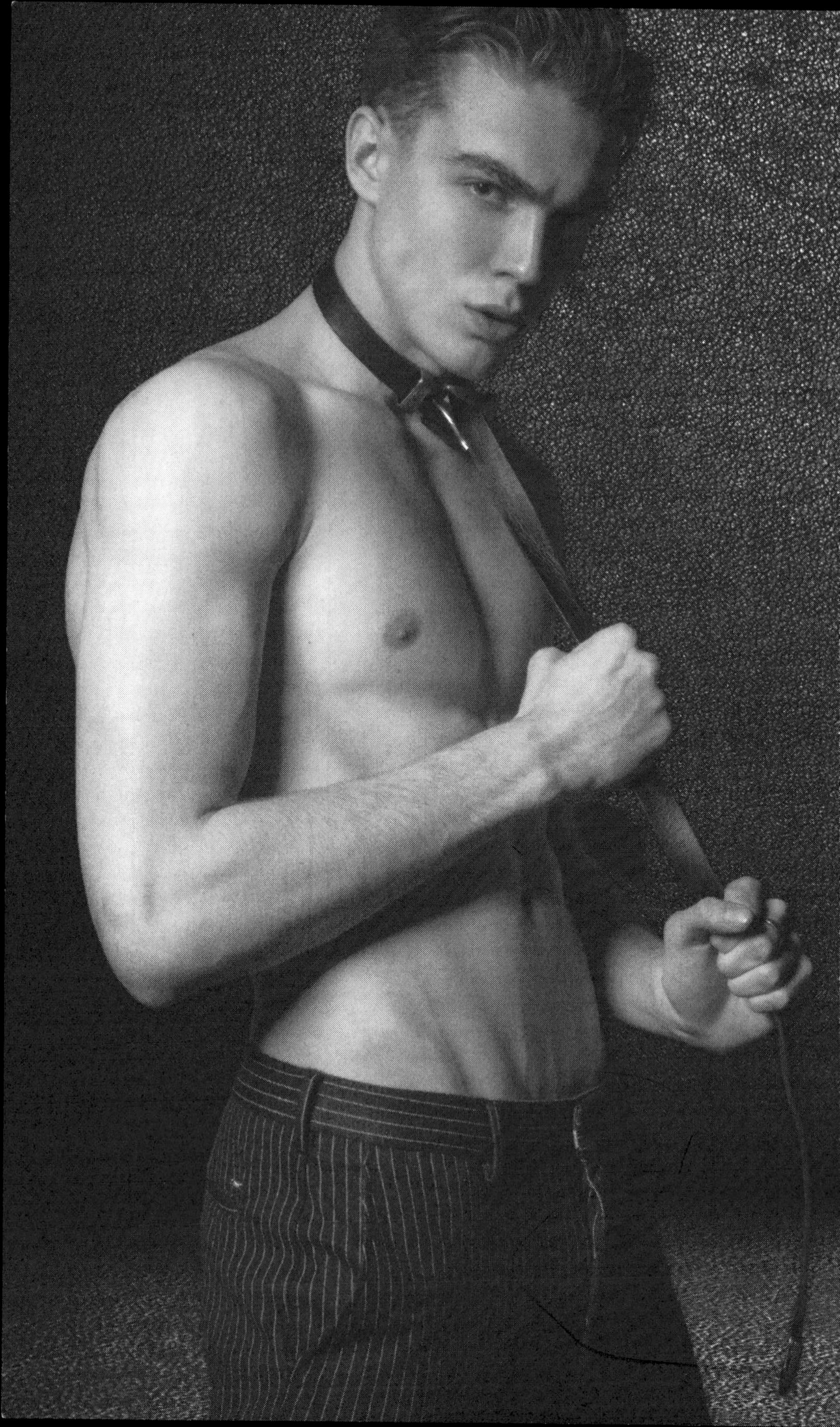

TWENTY-SEVEN
LIAM

When I woke up the second time, I was no longer in the SUV. Now, I was tied to a chair with my arms behind my back. I lifted my head and took in the room around me. It looked like a club but not Asha's club. It was dark. There were no windows to let in light. Neon signs hung on the walls, and the ceiling had a whole lighting assembly for dancing. Tables and booths were scattered about. A stage and deejay booth were off to one side.

I rolled my head, making my neck crack. I let out a groan as I waited for whatever was to come. In the meantime, I tried to figure out who in the hell had taken me and why they hadn't just killed me. If they were holding me, it was because they wanted something from me. But what? I couldn't think of anyone who'd want me though. Unless it was Asha's stepfather, Gio. *Why would he want me?* Maybe he found out about my relationship with Asha, and he was pissed she was sleeping with me for free.

A door opened somewhere in the club and slammed shut loudly. It sounded like a big, metal door. The sound echoed in the empty club like a gym door would. I heard their footsteps, but I couldn't see them as they walked up from behind me.

"Time to go," a man said as he fiddled with my restraints.

"Go where?" I asked, my voice dry and raspy.

"You'll see."

My wrists were freed. He grabbed me by the back of my hoodie and jerked me to my feet. The sudden movement made my head pound and my body scream in response. The man kept his hand on my back, guiding me to the back of the club and through a door. The bright light behind it made my eyes hurt. The man made a turn and pushed me up a flight of stairs. At the top was another door. He opened it and shuffled me through. I tripped but managed to catch myself. When I looked up, I found we were in an office. One wall was nothing but windows with a view of the club below.

"I think it's about time we got to know one another," another man said, stealing my attention from the club.

I turned my head and found him sitting behind a big oak desk in the center of the room. The man looked oddly familiar. He had light-colored hair and blue eyes. He was tall and built, but the wrinkles around his eyes told me he was probably in his late forties.

"I'm Nicolai Reznikov, Asha's father," he said as I was urged down into a chair across from him. "And you must be Liam Hastings, the boyfriend."

A puff of air left my lips. "Not anymore. She broke up with me today."

The man ignored me and sat taller in his seat. "Tell me what you know about my daughter."

"I know everything about Asha. Probably more than you do."

"Enlighten me."

"I know she's a good person. She's beautiful and kind, even though she wants everyone to think she's mean and untouchable. And she hates you for abandoning her and leaving her to fend for herself. I know her stepdad forced her into sex work. Asha's been made to strip, fuck men, and perform like a trained monkey. I also know her stepdad, the one you left her with, has not only beaten and abused her, but also raped her. And I know she's in the hospital right now because she tried to kill herself."

He absorbed everything I said. I watched as more and more anger painted his face. His once pale skin had turned to a red, almost purple color. His jaw clenched. "I thought she liked Gio. I thought she picked him over me."

I snorted. "You couldn't be more wrong. She tried killing herself because of him. Well, and I guess I may have contributed to that too."

"How so?"

I stared down at my hands, wishing my nervous mouth would've kept quiet. The last damn thing I needed was to be spouting off to some powerful mobster about how I had a hand in his daughter's attempted suicide. Or suicide because she may be dead. The idea of Asha not making it made me want to vomit. If she wasn't in this world, I didn't want to be either. I didn't care if it was a toxic as fuck attitude. She was mine, and I was hers. It was that simple.

"Asha and her friends used to pick on me. She and I got paired up for this school assignment. Asha and I got close. She brought me into her inner circle, and I was sure it was all going to be a joke. So, while I was there, I uncovered some of their dirty, little secrets. I typed it all up into an article I could publish in the school paper if I ever needed to. But someone stole the paper off my computer and released it without my knowledge. Asha thought I did it. She felt I'd fucked her over. I tried telling her that it wasn't me, but she didn't believe me. Then today, after school, she overdosed. Another guy and I found her. We called 9-1-1 and stayed with her until they took her away. I was on my way to the hospital when your men grabbed me." I paused and exhaled. "What do you want from me anyway? And why have your men been following me all week? I need to get to Asha. I should make sure she's OK."

"I want my daughter back, Liam. I thought she chose Gio. I believed she wanted nothing to do with me. That was why I left her alone. I didn't abandon her. I love her. I was so shocked when I sent some men into Gio's club to see what he was up to. They reported back that my very own daughter was working in the club. I want Gio dead. I want my daughter away from him and that life, and I want any man who has hurt her to die."

"Good! Me too! I've been trying to figure out how to get her away from him ever since I found out, but I think the only way is for me to kill him."

Nico leaned forward. I saw the seriousness etched on his face. It made the lines around his eyes become more prominent. "You're supposed to be her boyfriend. You're supposed to protect her."

My back straightened. "I didn't know about any of this until a few days ago! You're her father. You should've protected her," I threw back.

"You're the reason she's lying in a hospital bed right now. And if she dies, someone will pay," he said, pointing at me. "You have two choices."

I waited.

"You can either go kill Gio, get him out of my daughter's life for good...or you can kill yourself for pushing her to her breaking point. The choice is yours." He pulled out a gun and set it on his desk between us.

For a moment, I thought about it. Not so much killing myself, but killing Gio—how I could do it, how I could get away with it. I knew it would only take a second for one of Nico's men to snap my neck and end it all. But Gio needed to be out of Asha's life first. I didn't care if I died. I only cared about Asha and making sure she lived the best life possible. My hellcat deserved that much.

"I'll do it. I'll kill Gio."

Nico almost smiled as he nodded. He pushed the gun closer to me. I reached out and took it. I'd gone shooting many times with my dad, brother, and Uncle Mike over the years. I knew how to handle a weapon and was a damn good shot.

"I trust you won't let me down." He opened his desk drawer and tossed down a cheap, burner phone. "Call when it's done. I'll expect your call before sunrise."

I nodded as I stood. "I won't disappoint you, sir. And just so you know, I love Asha. I want her as happy as you do." I started for the door.

"Oh, and, Liam?" he said before I left.

I paused and looked back at him. "If I have to send a man after Gio, I'll send one for you too for not keeping your word. You understand, don't you?"

I swallowed and nodded. "Yes, sir."

I pulled the door open and thundered down the steps.

When I exited the club, I was surprised to find a man dressed in black, waiting by the SUV. He opened the back door, and I climbed inside. Moments later, he was behind the wheel, driving me somewhere. I didn't know if he was taking me back home or to Gio. Either way, it didn't matter. I'd take care of Gio, and since I had a gun, I figured it'd be easy. Point and shoot.

How hard could it be to kill the asshole who was hurting your girl? I didn't have to get creative and figure out how to kill him with my bare hands. It would be quick. He wouldn't even see it coming.

The SUV stopped outside of my house. I got out and strode up the drive to my car. I glanced back at the SUV, but it was gone. I stared at my house. It was still dark inside. Time was on my side.

I slid behind the wheel and slammed the door shut, but I was suddenly hit with the seriousness of what I was about to do. I was on my way to *kill* someone.

I tried to envision how it would play out. I already knew Gio wasn't home. I figured that only left the club. I had to get him alone. I couldn't just march into a busy club filled with drug dealers and start firing. I'd be dead for sure. I hoped I'd be able to go in and ask for a private chat. I assumed he'd probably clear out a room in the club or maybe take me to his office. From there, I could tell him everything I wanted to. Even if I wouldn't be allowed to leave after getting the job done, at least Asha would be safe. That was the silver lining.

I twisted the key in the ignition, and my car roared to life. I took a few deep breaths and shifted into reverse, starting down the drive. As

I made my way toward the club, my hands shook with nerves. My stomach was doing flips. I was worrying myself sick. But it was kill or be killed, and I wanted Asha safe if she survived. I wanted her to have the life she deserved. I needed her happy. And taking out Gio was the only thing standing between her and her happily ever after.

In a way, it felt as if my whole life had been leading up to this moment. I suddenly had a purpose. I wasn't just put on Earth to float around from this to that. I was put on here to save Asha, to be her saving grace. And I would not fail.

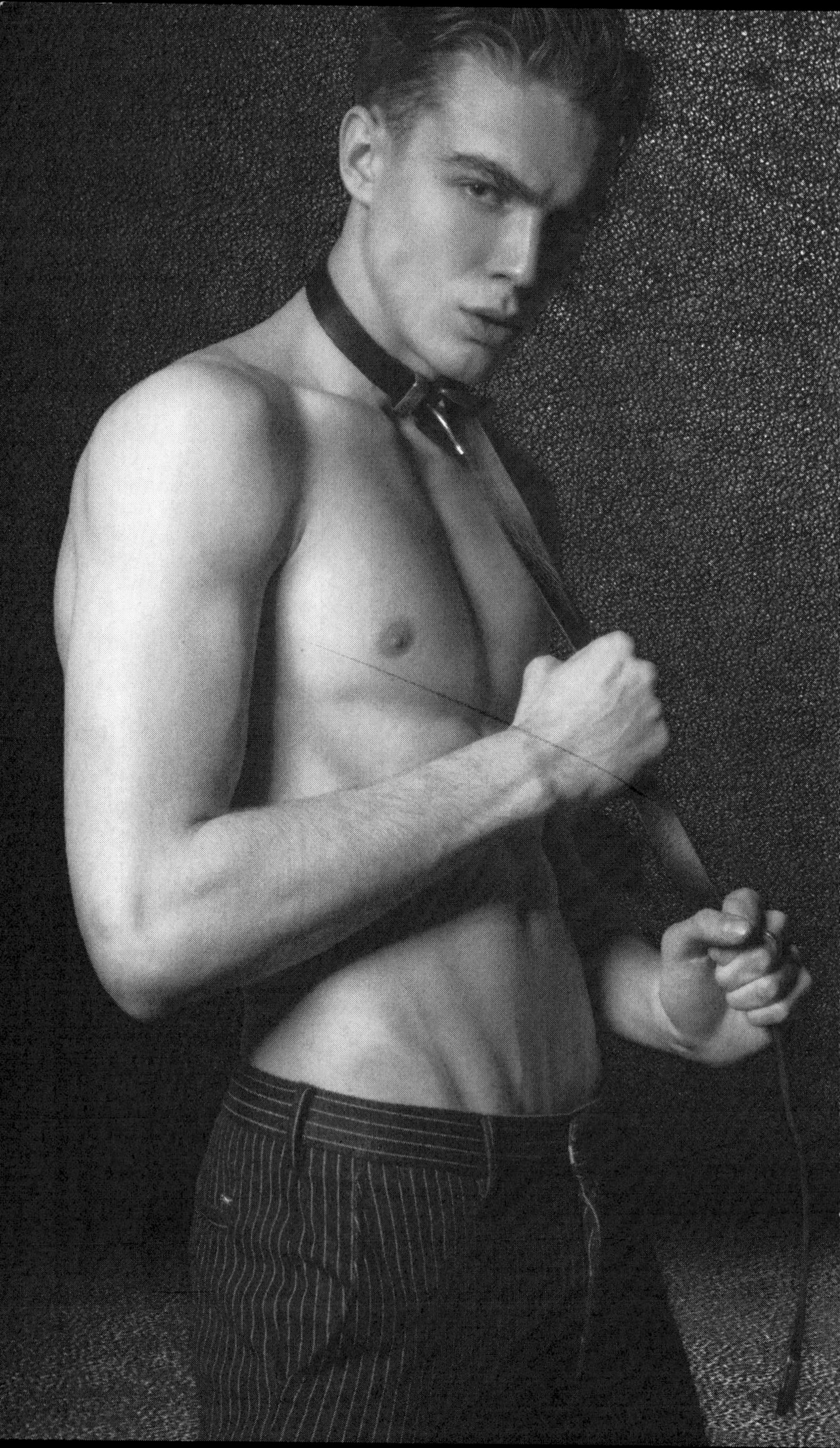

TWENTY-EIGHT
LIAM

I parked my car a few blocks away from the club I'd never planned to visit again. With a heavy sigh, I got out and sauntered through the darkness, my leather gloves on. Once I was at my destination, I stared at the building, trying to talk myself into going in.

My nerves had suddenly vanished. It was time to get the job done, and I was ready. I had everything I needed. I had a gun and the desire. My heart had been ripped out of my chest when I saw Asha lying in bed and covered in vomit. I knew I was part of the reason she'd done it, but I also knew the main reason was her stepdad and his club. There was no use being afraid anymore. I didn't have a life without her. If she pulled through, she'd wake to find Gio gone and her life her own again.

As I stood, surveying the building, I noticed the CLOSED sign light up. A few girls stumbled out, barely dressed and tucking their money into their pockets while moving toward their cars. I guessed the place was already cleared out for the night, so I climbed out of the car and jogged to the door. I pushed through and headed down the stairs and into the club, which smelled of bleach.

It was dark and quiet, but I heard people talking in the back rooms. I kept to the shadows, so I wouldn't be seen as I tried to figure out where Gio was. He wasn't on the main floor. I remembered seeing a door the night Asha took me to the private room. I was betting on that being his office. I headed down the hallway, past the four private rooms, to the door at the end of the hall. It opened easily and led me into another hallway. I followed it to yet one more door which opened into an office.

I shut myself inside and decided to hide in the closet as I waited. Things were unfolding perfectly. I didn't have to worry about a club full of people. I didn't have to seek him head-on and ask for a private meeting. Now I just needed him to come back to his office and sit at his desk where I could sneak out and end him before he even caught on. I didn't care if he saw it coming. I wasn't trying to scare the life out of him or force an apology. All I wanted was him dead and Asha to be mine.

The door to the office opened, and I listened and waited.

"Bend over the desk," Gio demanded loudly.

His belt buckle clanked followed by the sound of his zipper being lowered. Then he let out a low moan. "Yes, that's it, you fucking whore. You like that, don't you? You like it when Daddy punishes you."

The girl never made a peep, but he did enough grunting and moaning for the both of them. His desk screeched across the floor as he thrusted into her. I heard smacking sounds and wasn't sure if she was smacking him or if he was smacking her, but it was loud and made a chill run up my spine. I couldn't stop my mind from going to a dark place, a place where it wasn't just some girl bent over for him. It was Asha. I wondered if he talked to her that way. If he hit her.

I knew without a doubt he did, and rage boiled in my stomach.

Eventually, I knew it was over when he let out a grunting sound and the noises stopped. I eased the gun from my waistband and held it firmly in front of me.

"Get the fuck out," Gio told the woman.

She was sniffling and whimpering, and I had no doubt she was crying. The door clicked closed, and then the desk chair squeaked. I grabbed the doorknob and twisted it slowly, quietly. When it was no longer latched, I pushed it open with the toe of my shoe and exited the closet as I brought the gun up, aiming it at the side of his head.

He was sitting in his desk chair and had just lit a cigarette. Smoke encircled him as he slowly spun and looked my way.

"Well, did you enjoy the show?" he asked, an amused grin on his face.

I didn't respond. I just kept the gun trained on him as I slowly inched closer.

"What the fuck are you even doing here with that thing? Let me guess, you came to kill me?"

I only nodded, not wanting to break my concentration.

"Who sent you?" He glared at me.

"I came on my own. For her."

His brows rose. "*Her*? I know you don't mean my whore of a stepdaughter."

"Did you know she tried to kill herself today? I found her. She was in bed. She overdosed. I had to call an ambulance. I don't even know if she's alive right now. But it doesn't really matter one way or another for you, because you're already dead."

He let out a bitter laugh. "You think you have what it takes to kill me? And for what? A whore? I'll tell ya what kid, how much does she mean to you? Would a grand work?" He studied me. "No, of course not. Ten?"

I didn't flinch.

"Fine, twenty. Twenty grand to turn and walk out of here right now."

I ground my teeth, and my jaw flexed.

"Wait a minute. I know you. You're that kid who came in here before. You paid for a private dance, and she sucked you off then you fucked her."

He knew about that?

He nodded and smiled. "Yeah, I know everything that happens in my club. There are cameras everywhere. You're on camera right now." He took a drag of his cigarette. "So you know if I come up dead, they'll know right where to go. And that's only if you actually make it out of here alive. With my men out there, you probably won't even make it out of this office. You'd have to burn this entire place to the ground to be free and without witness."

"I know I might not make it out, and I'm willing to die if it means killing you." I cocked the gun. "Does she even mean anything to you?"

He snorted. "Asha is nothing but a warm hole to sink my dick in and fill with as much come as she can hold. She's trash. Not worthy of anything but to be treated like the whore she is."

My hands trembled in anger. "Don't you regret any of it?"

"I regret not fucking her sooner. She's a hot, little piece of ass. I'll give you that. I can see where a kid like you would be confused. She's beautiful. She sucks dick like a fucking angel. And her pussy is golden, tight, wet, and warm. I don't regret burying myself in her tight ass." He moaned. "The sounds I was able wring out of her. Did she tell you about me fucking her perfect, little ass? How she fought me and begged me to stop? She screamed until she couldn't anymore."

He took his eyes off me to put out his cigarette, and I seized my opportunity. I used every bit of anger, rage, and hate I had in me. I thought about how much I loved Asha, about how she'd worked herself beneath my skin, and how I'd promised to do anything to protect her. Then I squeezed the trigger. The gunfire was fast and loud. So quick I almost couldn't process it myself. One minute, Gio was in front of me, and the next, he slumped back in his chair, a hole in his forehead and blood splattered all over the wall behind him.

My heart hammered away in my chest. I was filled with adrenaline. Ragged breaths whooshed in and out of my lungs as my mind raced.

I did it. I killed Gio. I saved Asha.

But I needed to get out of there. Quickly, I went to the bar behind his desk and started dumping the alcohol out. On him. On the curtains, carpet, anywhere I could. I snagged his lighter and flipped it open, staring at the dancing flame.

"For you, hellcat," I said softly, dropping the Zippo lighter onto Gio's body.

His suit caught quick, the flames eating their way over his body.

"Thanks for the tip, prick." It took me a moment to drag my gaze from him before I was racing for the door, the flames having caught fast.

I pushed my way back into the club in a hurry. I forgot to be quiet. My only thought was getting out. When I busted through the door leading into the club, Gio's men spun around. It was no wonder they hadn't heard the gunshot. The loud bass from the club's music system was still thundering along.

I froze as they took me in. Their eyes traveled from mine to the gun in my hand.

"Get him!" one of them yelled.

I quickly jumped to the side, crashing into some chairs. I hit the edge of a table, and it flipped onto its side, giving me something to crouch behind. I knew I couldn't hide in any of the private rooms. There I'd be trapped. I was going to have to fight my way out. I propped the gun up on the edge of the table and fired off a couple shots. Someone yelled before a round of return fire filled the air around me.

I lay on my stomach and peeked around the table, noticing a few of Gio's men were behind tables like me while one was trying to sneak up on me. I aimed the gun and fired, hitting him in the head. The man fell flat on his back. I took my opportunity and ran. I fired anywhere and everywhere I could as I dashed for the door.

They returned fire, but their bullets missed. I shoved my way through the door. Before I could run up the steps, another shot filled my ears, and a burning sensation bloomed in my arm. I glanced down as I ran up the steps. Blood was starting to spread across the sleeve of my gray hoodie.

I didn't have time to examine it though. I grabbed a mop handle and barred the door. There weren't windows down there. They'd all fucking die. I made it up the stairs and exited the door into the night air. My gaze zeroed in on two large, metal bars propped against a dumpster. I quickly snagged them and shoved one into the door handle, effectively locking the men inside in the event they managed to break through my other barrier. I was still pissed off, so I sprinted to the front and barred the doors there too.

They could burn for all I fucking cared. Smoke was already billowing out in thick, black clouds from the cracks in the ground floor windows.

Fuck them all.

I spun and pushed myself to run faster, harder. I didn't stop until I got to my car even though I was lightheaded and dizzy. I jumped behind the wheel, turned the key, shifted into drive, and stomped on the gas after tossing the gun onto the passenger seat. I executed a quick U-turn and went in the opposite direction. My gaze went to the rearview mirror. No one exited the club amid the flames licking the night sky like a dying serpent.

I drove fast until I decided I was far enough away to slow to normal speed. When I did that, I dug the phone from my pocket and called Nico.

He didn't speak, but I could tell he'd picked up.

"It's done," I said in a shaky voice.

"Meet me. One hour. I'll text you the address."

I dropped the phone onto my lap. Moments later, it chimed with a text. I drove to the location and parked by the docks. While I waited, I took out my phone and sent Asha one last message.

I knew I was probably going to die. I'd done Nico's dirty work. Now it was time for him to get rid of the evidence. I was a part of that mess for him. With me gone, he'd have nothing to tie him to the crime I'd just committed.

LIAM: Get better, beautiful, and don't you ever try doing something like that again. Your life is your own

now. Live it. Enjoy it. Cherish it. And never forget me. I love you, hellcat.

I sent a few quick messages to my friends and family. telling them I loved them as well. I even managed to tell Sofia that I forgave her. It wasn't completely the truth, but she might as well get forgiveness since I wouldn't be around to make her feel guilty. When I was done, I shut off the phone and waited. It wasn't long before the headlights on the black SUV cut through the darkness.

It was time.

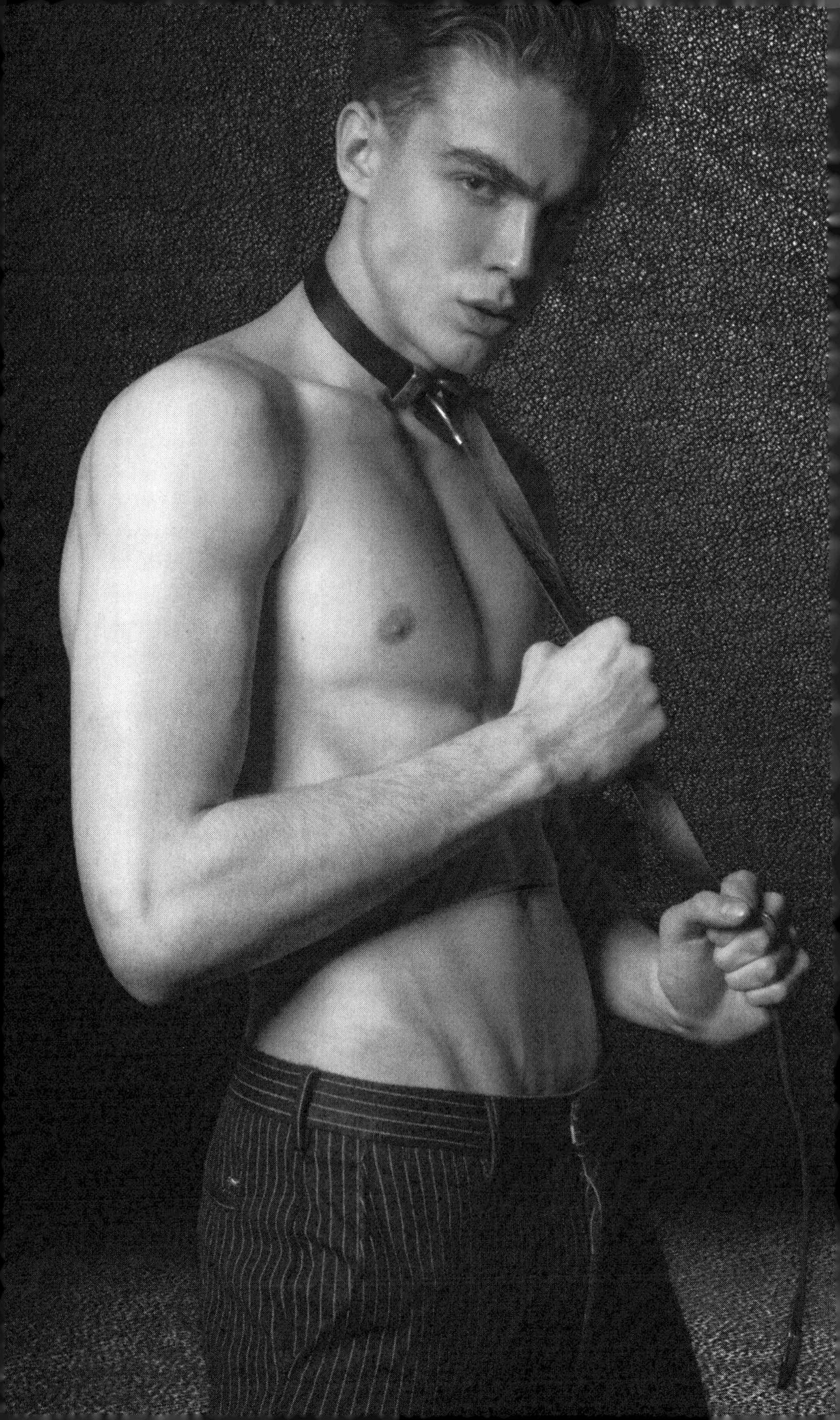

TWENTY-NINE
LIAM

The vehicle came to a stop near me. I stepped out of my car, ready to meet my maker. The driver got out first. He was a big man who stood at least six and a half feet tall. He looked big in his black pants and coat, but I knew from his facial structure he was all muscle. He wasn't fat. He was toned and could probably survive getting ran over with a Mack truck.

"Weapon and phone on the hood," he ordered in a deep voice.

I did as he asked and set the items on the hood of the SUV.

"Any more weapons on you?" He surveyed me with his dark eyes.

I patted my pockets to appease him. "Nope."

He took the phone and gun and got back inside the SUV. A second later, the back door opened and Nico emerged. He strode over to me slowly, casually.

"How is it that an eighteen-year-old kid managed to do what grown men have tried and failed countless times?" he asked, looking amused as he tucked his hands into his pants pockets.

I shrugged. "Maybe they didn't have the right motivation," I answered, staring into his eyes.

He was a mere few inches taller than me, but his presence

demanded respect. He barked out a loud laugh as he considered my answer.

"Have you heard anything about Asha?" I had to know before he killed me and threw me into Lake Michigan. I needed to know I'd died for something, that it was all worth it.

He nodded. "She's fine. She had her stomach pumped and will be in the hospital overnight to get fluids. They want to keep a close watch, but she's going to be OK."

A sigh of relief escaped my lips. My body finally thawed. She was alive and OK. She was free from Gio and the shit life she'd been forced to live. Finally, I could die happy, knowing she'd go off and do great things, living the life she'd always deserved.

"So, did you start the fire at Gio's club?" Nico asked, looking down at me with a glint to his eye.

My brows pulled together. "Yes." No sense denying it.

He nodded.

"Nice touch, kid. Destroy the evidence. I couldn't have done it any better myself." he said, proudly. "And you killed a great deal of his men. No survivors from what my intel has gathered."

"I'd do it all over again... for her." I sucked in a long breath and prepared myself for the answer to my next question. "So, what happens now?"

"Well, to be honest, I was planning on killing you—all in name of destroying the evidence of course. But now, I'm not so sure. How much do you love my daughter?" One hand came out of his pocket, and he rubbed it across his jaw.

"I'd do anything for her. I already killed for her," I pointed out.

Nico nodded as he thought about my words. "I'll let you live on one condition."

"What's that?" I held my breath, waiting for the hammer to fall.

"If I call, you must come and do my bidding. A kid like you who everyone underestimates could come in handy. You'll be my own little, secret weapon. Nobody will see you coming. You have a lot of potential, and I want to turn you into something great."

"And what happens if someone finds out I killed Gio?"

He chuckled. "No need to worry about that. If you work for me, you have my protection. Not to mention the Bratva will be behind you. You know about the Russian mob, right?"

I didn't really, but I nodded. "And what exactly will you want me to do?"

Nico offered up an evil smile with a dark glint in his eye. "Half the fun in life is the unknown. So, what do you say?"

I thought it over, but what choice did I really have? It was either do Nico's occasional dirty work or die. "All right," I agreed.

He smiled as he shook my hand. "Pleasure doing business with you, son. Welcome to the family."

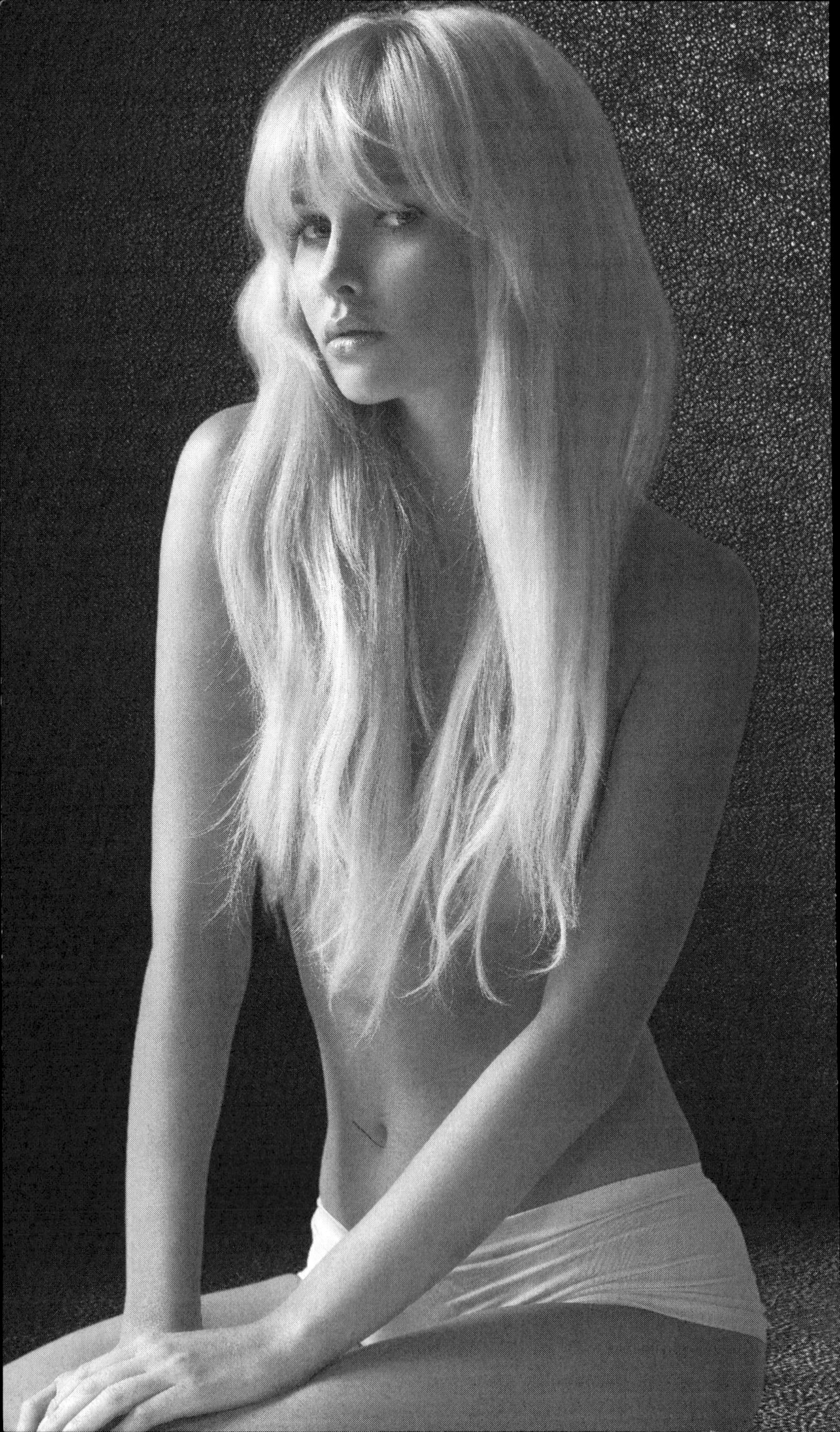

THIRTY
ASHA

I felt like death. My entire body was filled with pain. There was a burning in my throat making it feel like it was on fire. Every muscle in my chest ached like I'd never worked out in my life. I opened my eyes, and the brightness of the room blinded me.

Where was I?

My bedroom never got that much light, but it was the last place I remembered being.

"Asha?" my mother cried softly beside me.

I pried my eyes open again and turned to find her sitting next to me. Then I realized where I was. I was in the hospital.

Everything came rushing back. The day at school, having everyone turned against me, losing Liam, taking the pills.

"You're awake. Thank God," Mom cried, holding my hand in hers. "I'm so sorry, Asha. I had no idea," she sobbed as tears streaked down her cheeks.

"What? What's going on, Mom?"

She forced herself to calm down. "I came home last night and f-found your letter. I panicked. I didn't know what was going on. You weren't home, but you left that letter. I called every hospital until I found you. Lucas was here. He filled me in, said he and a boy named Liam found you unconscious and covered in vomit. Lucas said they pumped your stomach when you got here." She dabbed her eyes with a tissue. "Why didn't you tell me what was going on, Asha? I-I didn't know it was that bad. I would've tried to help you. *Help us.*" The tears started to reform.

I shook my head slightly. "Gio said he'd kill you. He said he'd sell me for good. I... I was scared," I confessed, my own tears overfilling my eyes and rolling down my cheeks.

"Things weren't good between me and him for a long time. He called me names, hit me, but I never thought he'd touch you. H-He made me do things too sometimes. Told me if I didn't, he'd hurt you. I-I had no idea he already had." She shook her head and attempted to dry her eyes, her words coming out as a garbled mess. "I promise, Asha. From now on, you're my top priority. I will be better. I'll take care of you. I'll protect you. You'll never have to worry about that again."

My tears turned to happy sobs. "You can't promise that, Mom. As soon as Gio finds out—"

"No, Asha. He's gone."

"What?" I asked, confused, my brows drawing together. "How?"

She grabbed the remote off the table and turned on the TV. "Sometimes, the Lord works in mysterious ways. We're free, honey."

I turned my attention from her to the TV and watched the news play out. It was video of Gio's club. Apparently, it had caught fire and burned. The flames had been extinguished, and uniformed men were carrying out body bags. The headline on the screen read: **Giovanni Valetti, local crime boss, confirmed dead**

More tears formed in my eyes. I couldn't make them stop. I was crying for the girl I used to be and the woman I was now, a free woman who could live however she wanted. I wept out of happiness, excitement, and fear. Fear because I figured Liam had something to do with it.

"I spoke to your father a bit ago. He wants to get together and talk. I-I think it'll be a good thing."

There was too much to try wrap my mind around at the moment, so I focused on one thing. The most important thing. Liam.

"Mom, do you have my phone?"

She dug around in her purse until she found it. When she handed it over, I read over the texts Liam had sent, and I was instantly worried. I immediately wrote back.

ASHA: I'm so sorry, Liam. I don't know what I was thinking. I'm fine. Please come to me. I need you.

I gave him a few minutes to respond, but I was too impatient and ended up calling. The phone rang until it went to voicemail.

"Hey, it's Liam. Sorry I missed your call. Leave a message, and I'll call ya back."

"Liam, it's Asha. I'm so sorry. For everything. Please, call me back. Or text me. Come to the hospital. *Something*. I just want to know you're OK."

I hung up, more afraid than ever. Liam always picked up whenever I called. If he wasn't answering, there was a reason. I couldn't believe Lucas and Liam were the ones who'd found me. I couldn't fathom why the two of them were together. I felt horrible for leaving Liam to find me that way. I hoped seeing me half dead wasn't what caused him to run out and set fire to Gio's club. I was so worried about him getting caught. But then again, it was Gio. *Would anyone really care to investigate?* The police had been after him for years. If it wasn't for the cops he had in his pocket, he would've been caught long ago. Hopefully, the police didn't question it and just took it for what it was. A miracle.

And hopefully, Liam wasn't one of the bodies being hauled out. My heart wouldn't be able to take it if he were gone.

I WAS RELEASED the next day. Mom had stayed with me all night. She helped me to get dressed. I was fine, but I felt weak and sore all over for reasons I couldn't understand. The drive home was slow and quiet. She seemed to be giving me time to wrap my head around all that had changed. When she turned into the drive, the usual unease settled over me. I tried to remind myself Gio was gone. He wasn't waiting for me to come home so he could whisk me away and force me to go to work.

She parked, and the two of us got out and slowly walked through the front door. I paused in the entryway and took in the space. Something about it just felt different. The atmosphere didn't feel as heavy.

"Go on and lie down, hon. I had the sheets changed, so it's all ready for you. I'll make some lunch and bring it up later," she said, going into the kitchen.

I started toward the stairs but stopped in the threshold of Gio's office. The room was empty, as was his desk. Papers were scattered across the top. Out of curiosity, I walked over and picked up the stack. I started flipping through them. There was a different man on each page. It listed their contact information along with their bids.

What were they bidding on?

When I got to the last page, I found several pictures of me. There was my school yearbook photo and a few of me Gio had snapped at the club of me stripping and working in the private rooms. He was planning to sell me.

I sighed as I shook my head and dropped the stack back onto his desk, vowing to get the information into the hands of the right people. I'd turn them over to police or maybe even my father. I was overwhelmed and tired, so I went up to my room and fell into bed. I tried calling Liam again. When that failed, I sent him a text.

ASHA: I'm home. Please come over or call. I need to know you're OK.

I dropped my cell onto the mattress, and my eyes closed. But they opened almost instantly when I heard Lucas's voice.

"Asha?"

"Hey," I said, as he perched on the edge of my bed.

He leaned in and gave me a hug. "I'm so glad you're OK. You fucking scared the shit out of me," he breathed out.

"I'm sorry."

"Don't you ever do that to me again. Fuck, I thought you were dead."

He eased back, and I realized he was no longer looking at me sitting in front of him. He was lost to the memory of finding me.

"Your body was limp and so fucking white. You had puke all over you. You looked dead. I thought I'd lost you."

I clasped his hand in mine. "I really am sorry. I was... just in a bad place. All I wanted was to sleep, escape it all for a little while."

"I understand that, but next time, just answer your phone and talk it out. Don't eat a bottle of sleeping pills. I swear, if you pull something like that again and you don't die, I will kill you myself," he said with a small smirk.

I grinned sadly. "Deal."

Lucas crawled up in my bed beside me and held my hand while we both stared off into space, reflecting on the last couple days.

"Have you talked to Liam yet?"

"Not yet. I've called and texted, but he's not answering. I guess I shouldn't be surprised since I didn't believe him and then you guys kicked his ass. He's probably done with me."

"Nah," Lucas said softly. "I saw the way he looked at you. He'll come around. Just give him some time. He's probably trying to get the image of your nearly dead body out of his mind."

Guilt filled me for doing what I'd done. "You think he'll forgive me?"

"That depends. Are *you* going to forgive him for the article?"

"I already have," I admitted.

"Then I'm sure he'll come around soon. I'll talk to him if you want."

"How are the two of you even on speaking terms after you beat his ass?"

Lucas shrugged. "Dudes are like that. We can fight and then be friends five minutes later."

"So, you two are friends now?"

He laughed. "Yeah, I guess so. Although, I haven't seen him since we found you. He's a good guy. I see how much he cares about you. He treats you better than I ever did. I think that's the most I can ask for. I really am sorry for being a douchebag. And you don't have to believe me, but I didn't have sex with Tiffany. But I did do...*things*...with other people," he admitted sheepishly.

"The blowjob?" I asked.

"Among other things. I'm sorry. No matter how much I tried to convince myself it didn't count, I know it was cheating."

I smiled. "It's OK. I wasn't always a bowl of sunshine. Let's just move on."

Silenced filled the room and eventually, I drifted off to sleep.

"Asha, will you come downstairs please?" Mom asked, gently shaking my hip.

Groggily, I blinked my eyes opened and found my room growing dark. Lucas was gone.

I sat up and rubbed the sleep from my eyes. "What's going on?"

"Just... come down." She headed back downstairs.

I forced myself to get up. I relieved myself in the bathroom before exiting my room and shuffling downstairs. As I eased down the steps, my gaze moved past the railing where my mother was standing next to my father and Liam.

Liam looked rough. His hair was a mess. His face was bruised, and he had a busted lip. Dark circles rimmed his green eyes, like he'd gone days without sleeping. Even though I felt nearly dead, I took off running for him. His lips quirked up in a grin and he opened his arms, crushing me against his chest. His scent settled around me, and tears filled my eyes.

"Thank God you're OK. I was so worried," I mumbled, sobbing.

His hand cupped my cheek. "*You* were worried. Imagine how I felt."

"I'm sorry I scared you. I love you. I didn't. I mean... I wasn't thinking clearly. Do you hate me?"

He smiled and said, "Never, hellcat. I love you too. And I need you to know, I never wrote anything about *you* in that article. I did write about the others. But Sofia added the stuff about you and the club after Andy and Max told her about seeing you there. She's the one who printed the article. I was never going to hurt you. Please forgive me."

I cupped his cheek. "I know you didn't do it, so there's nothing to forgive."

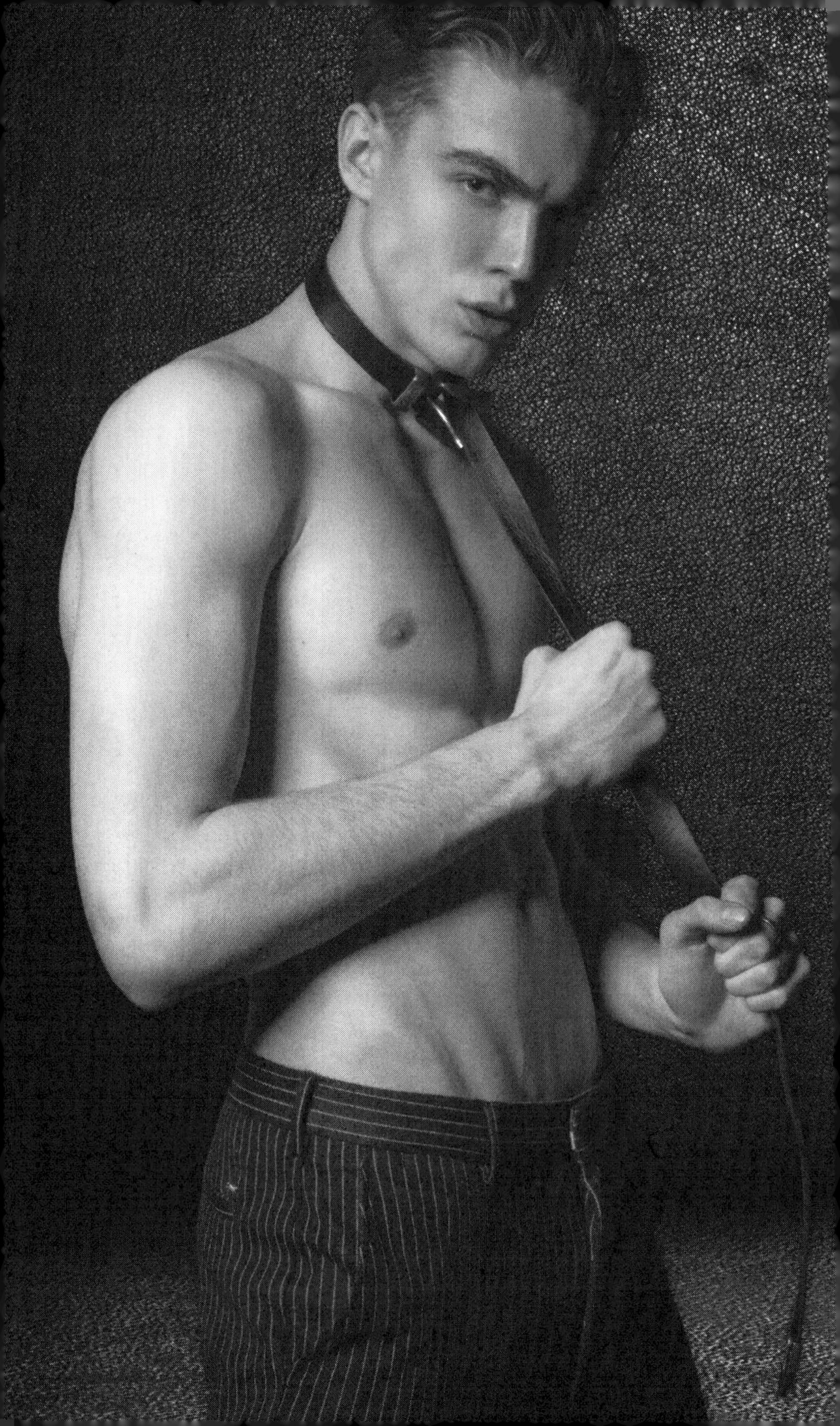

THIRTY-ONE
LIAM

"You got yourself a good guy here, Asha," Nico said as the four of us sat around the table in the dining room, having dinner.

Asha's cheeks blushed a light pink color. "I know," she said, reaching under the table and planting her hand on my thigh.

"I don't know what I would've done if you hadn't found her, Liam. Thank you for being a good friend and checking on her," her mom said.

"Don't mention it," I said, finishing my bite of pot roast.

"Well," Nico said, wiping his mouth. "If you'd like, I could take a look at those papers now."

"Oh, yes." Asha's mom pushed away from the table. "I'm going to show your father to the office."

"Oh, Dad," Asha said, stopping them from walking out. "There's a stack of papers on Gio's desk you might find interesting too."

He nodded before walking out and leaving us alone.

Asha turned to face me. "Are you expected home tonight?"

"My parents are gone, so...no."

"Want to stay here, with me?"

"Your mom won't care?"

"I have a feeling she won't even notice," she said, standing and taking my hand in hers.

"What was on Gio's desk?" I asked as I followed her up to her room.

"A stack of offers. Gio was trying to sell me. He was actually taking bids."

"I wonder why? I mean, from a business standpoint, he'd make more in the long run keeping you locked up in the club."

"My mother admitted she'd been in contact with my dad. Maybe Gio knew and was making plans to take them down or something. Either way, it doesn't matter now. He's gone, and I'm here with you, safe."

I closed the door to her bedroom and spun her around, pressing her back against it. "I don't know about safe," I said, kissing her as I pressed my chest against hers.

She wrapped her arms around my neck and deepened our kiss.

"Don't ever do that to me again," I whispered against her lips.

"I won't," she promised.

She felt good pressed against me, especially after thinking I'd never hold her again. My dick grew hard from our kiss, but I didn't want to push her too far. She'd just gotten out of the hospital, so I eased back and peered into her blue eyes which were darkening with need.

"Oh no, you don't. You aren't getting off that easy," she said, pushing against my chest and forcing me to walk backward to her bed.

I took a seat on the edge of the bed, and she stepped between my legs, pressing her lips to mine.

My hands found her hips and then drifted around to squeeze her ass.

"Make love to me, Liam," she whispered against my lips.

I picked her up and laid her on the mattress next to me before gently rolling on top of her. So much for letting her rest.

Our kisses grew more passionate as we worked to strip one

another of our clothing. Finally, there was nothing between us, and I was able to slide inside. Her hot, tight body felt like home.

After a few minutes of being inside her, her muscles tightened around me. It made me thrust into her deeper and harder until she shattered around me. When her moans and cries had quieted, I flipped us over.

"Show me what you got, hellcat."

She offered a sexy grin before lifting herself up and lowering back down. My hands firmly gripped her hips while she rocked against me, giving me a nice little show of her perky tits bouncing and jiggling in front of my face. Leaning forward, I caught her nipple in my mouth. I bit lightly while flicking my tongue against it. It made her hips move faster. She threw her head back, moaning and calling out my name. When she came undone on my dick, I felt like I was about to explode at any minute. But I wasn't ready to let it go yet. I wanted that moment to last forever.

I rolled us again until I was back on top. I thrusted into her as hard as I could. "Say it."

"Liam," she breathed out my name.

"Louder," I ordered, knowing that hearing her moan my name would push me over the edge.

"Liam," she said it in a breathy moan which made my body tighten as my release threatened me until it erupted.

I rode out every last wave of my orgasm and pumped into her until I had nothing left to give. Finally, I came to a stop on top of her.

She cradled my head against her chest, and I listened to the way her heart pounded. Neither of us moved until we'd regained control of our bodies. When our hearts and breathing slowed and when I could feel my limbs again, I rolled off of her and held her to me. I listened to her deep, even breathing and wondered if she'd fallen asleep, but then she spoke.

"You did it, didn't you?"

"Did what?"

"Killed Gio." She fingered the bandage on my arm. After I'd agreed to work for Nico, he'd taken me to get patched up at his club.

I squeezed her a little closer at the mention of his name. "I told you I'd save you."

"You shouldn't have done that, Liam. What if he'd hurt you? What if you get caught?"

"I'm not worried about that and neither should you. I thought you were dead, Asha. There was no point in living without you, so if I'd died, at least I would've died doing something good. He was evil, and he needed taken out, not only to save you, but to save countless other women and children. I'd do it all over again. He's gone. Your life is yours again."

She kissed my chest lightly. I knew it was her way of saying thank you. The two of us lay in bed until we finally got up to take shower. Her shower was just as lavish as the rest of the house. It was a big, walk in unit with a glass door. The showerhead sprayed at all angles, and there was plenty of room for both of us to clean off at the same time. After washing, I yanked her against me, and my lips found hers. I shuffled us around until her back was against the white tiled wall. Her arms wound around my neck, welcoming my kiss. After several minutes of holding her naked body against mine, my cock came alive again. I picked her up and held her to the wall while I tenderly stroked inside her.

The rest of the night was spent with me buried inside her until we were both sated and slept. When we woke in the morning, we spent our time the same way instead of going to school. After the last few days, we both deserved a break.

Our time together passed by in a flash, and before I was ready, it was time to go home. My parents were due back, and I knew they'd notice my absence.

Asha walked me out and gave me a long kiss that would have to last me until morning. Eventually, we pulled apart, and I climbed behind the wheel to go home.

I greeted both my parents with my head ducked and hood up

when I came in, but I went straight to my room and called Asha. We had a Netflix date planned, and I couldn't think of a better way to spend the night.

～

IN THE MORNING, I got dressed for school and drove to pick up Asha. On my way, my phone rang. I answered without looking since I was driving. I figured it was Max or Andy, demanding to know what the hell was going on. I was surprised to hear Nico's voice on the other end of the line instead.

"I have a job for you, son. Why don't you drop by my office after school?"

I swallowed the fear bubbling up with his request. I knew the day would come when he'd call, but I hadn't expected it to be so soon.

"OK," I agreed, knowing I didn't have a choice. I had to honor our deal.

I thought about telling Asha about the mess I'd found myself in by killing Gio and getting mixed up with her father, but I decided against it. Her life was just starting to come together. I didn't want to ruin it already. I figured I could tell her when the time came that I had to.

As soon as I pulled into her drive, Asha rushed out the door. She jumped into the passenger seat and leaned over, pressing her lips to mine.

"Good morning," she said with a wide smile.

"It is now, hellcat," I replied, shifting into gear and driving us to school.

I parked. Just like last time we showed up together, everyone was staring. We strolled hand in hand up the sidewalk where both our groups of friends were—hers on the left and mine to the right of the door.

Her friends gathered around us. They were all happy and excited to see her back at school. Apparently, Lucas had filled them in and given me all the credit for saving her, so they were just as thrilled to see me. They welcomed me back into their group. I released Asha's hand and marched over to my friends.

"Hey, look who's back on top," Max said with a grin.

I smiled and glanced past them to Sofia.

She swallowed hard, looking ashamed. "I'm so glad everything is OK." She rushed to give me a hug. "I really am sorry about that shit. I don't know what I was thinking."

I hugged her back. "Yeah, I think we've all had that problem the last few days."

"So, we're cool?" she asked, stepping back.

"We're cool."

Sofia nervously glanced at Asha. "Can I talk to you for a second?"

Asha's brow wrinkled, but she stepped closer.

Sofia fidgeted with her sleeves. "I just wanted to say I'm sorry for adding the stuff about you to the article, for judging you, for...everything."

Asha inhaled deeply and then gave Sofia a genuine smile. "It's all good. Water under the bridge."

Sofia breathed a sigh of relief and turned her attention back to me. "So, what now? You go back to your cool friends and we only see you after school?"

"Nope, actually," I said, turning to face Asha and the rest of them. "I'd like to bring in a few new members."

Asha beamed and sauntered to my side. "All in favor?" She raised her hand.

I followed suit, and everyone else did too, one by one. The group welcomed them in with open arms.

Somehow, I'd managed to bridge the gap between the elite crew and the scholarship kids. We all strutted into the building together. Hudson and the guys were already deep in conversation about football, video games, and cars. Jude and Lucas were eyeing Sofia with interest. When I moved to follow everyone, Asha held me back. I halted and turned to her.

"I love you."

I smiled. "I love you too, hellcat. Forever." I yanked her against me and kissed her long and hard for the whole school to see.

"And ever," she added, before her mouth found mine again.

My senior year had been a total fuck fest. I'd started the year on the bottom, and I'd fought my way to the top in just a matter of months. I'd had my ass beaten, my heart broken, nearly gotten myself killed, and thought I'd lost it all. But I'd do it all over again if it meant getting my hellcat. She was worth all the pain, hurt, and shit I'd gone through. I was her saving grace, and she was the key to my undoing.

She'd been living in hell until me, and I'd walked through the fire to get to her. I didn't know where we were going, but I knew we were going there together. In the end, it was all that mattered.

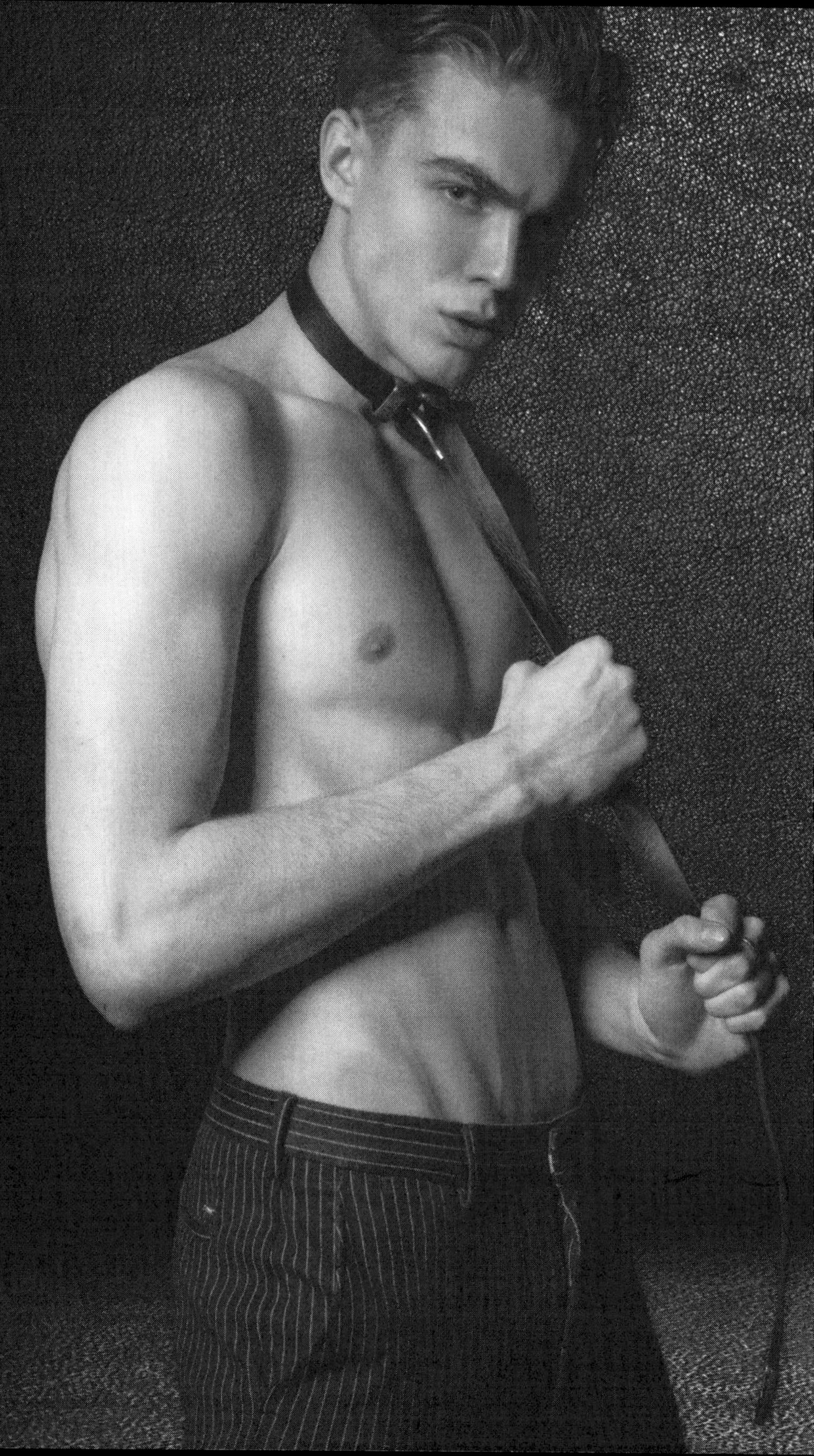

EPILOGUE PART I

LIAM

"Paul O'Keef." Nico pushed a folder toward me.

I reached out and took it, opening it to find a photo of a man with dark hair in a suit slipping into a car.

"He put in a bid for Asha. I want him dead. In fact..." He pushed a fat manilla envelope at me.

I opened it to find a thick stack of hundred-dollar bills.

"I want them all dead. Every single person who touched her. Who thought about her. Or who bid on her. Each hit pays a minimum of fifty thousand. Half up front. Half when the job's done." Nico leaned back in his seat and surveyed me with cool eyes.

"OK."

"That's it? No begging me to let you be free?"

I crinkled my brows at him. "No. They hurt her or wanted to. They deserve to die. I'm probably saving more lives than I'm taking."

I wasn't sure at what point in my life I'd become completely calm with the idea of killing someone, but it had happened in a matter of days it seemed. There was no anxiety in my chest. Only quiet rage, simmering as I thought over the evil living in these men's hearts.

"Love does crazy things to a man," Nico said, nodding his head at me.

"Or maybe it does sane things to crazy men."

He smiled. "I like that. Hell, I like you, kid. I think we're going to have a good relationship together. Someday, I'll need someone to take over for me. Prove yourself and you may find yourself in this spot. What do you think about that?"

I licked my lips. I'd never considered such a life, but the possibility was very real and staring me in the face. Something had snapped inside me ever since Asha. I rather liked the guy I was becoming.

"I might consider it."

Nico let out a laugh and slid a gun to me. Shiny. Black. Silenced.

"A gift from me to you. It's yours. Name her. Keep her close. And take out any fuckers who displease you. Within reason, of course."

"Of course," I said, taking the pistol and looking it over. A Glock. My favorite to shoot whenever I went out with my dad, brother, and Uncle Mike.

"I want to teach you a few things before you head out. I think you'll like them."

"OK." I tucked the gun away and stared back at him.

"Sometimes, it's more fun to be creative." He got up and gestured for me to follow him.

I wandered behind him until we came to a set of doors. He pulled them open and stepped inside. The room lit up, displaying hundreds of weapons. Everything from guns to knives to swords to rope and various odds and ends like grenades and launchers. There was even a flamethrower on the wall.

"Choking someone can be fun." He nodded to the rope hanging on the wall. "Of course, you could always just bring them back here and let Sergei teach you a few things. He does so enjoy disembowelment and torture."

"You guys do that?"

"We do it all." Nico shot me a dark smile. "I want you trained. In the art of knives. Guns. Rope. Death. You'll be my death dealer. My right hand. That's where I see you, Liam. Right here." He patted his side. "My daughter loves you, and so do I. You did me proud with Valetti and his men. You're in, and the only way out is death."

I knew this. I accepted it. It was an easy exchange when it came to Asha.

"How many will I be killing?" I asked.

"However many it takes to teach them a lesson. My men are gathering information on everyone who needs to be dealt with. So far, we're at eight, but the folder was thick. Think you can handle it?"

Eight. Eight more people at minimum were going to die by my hand. But for Asha, I'd take out the world.

"Eight won't be a problem," I said softly.

"That's what I thought. Let's get started, shall we?"

I nodded.

I was staring down the rest of my life. Ironic how things never went to plan.

But it would be worth it. In the end, all the fuckers would pay. No one touched my girl and got away with it.

I wasn't just Liam Hasting, scholarship kid anymore.

I was Liam Hastings, hitman to the biggest crime boss this side of the country.

I was Liam Hastings, the guy willing to kill for his girl.

Funny how a class project and a girl had turned me into a killer.

I was pretty OK with that because Asha Blake was worth everything. Even my soul.

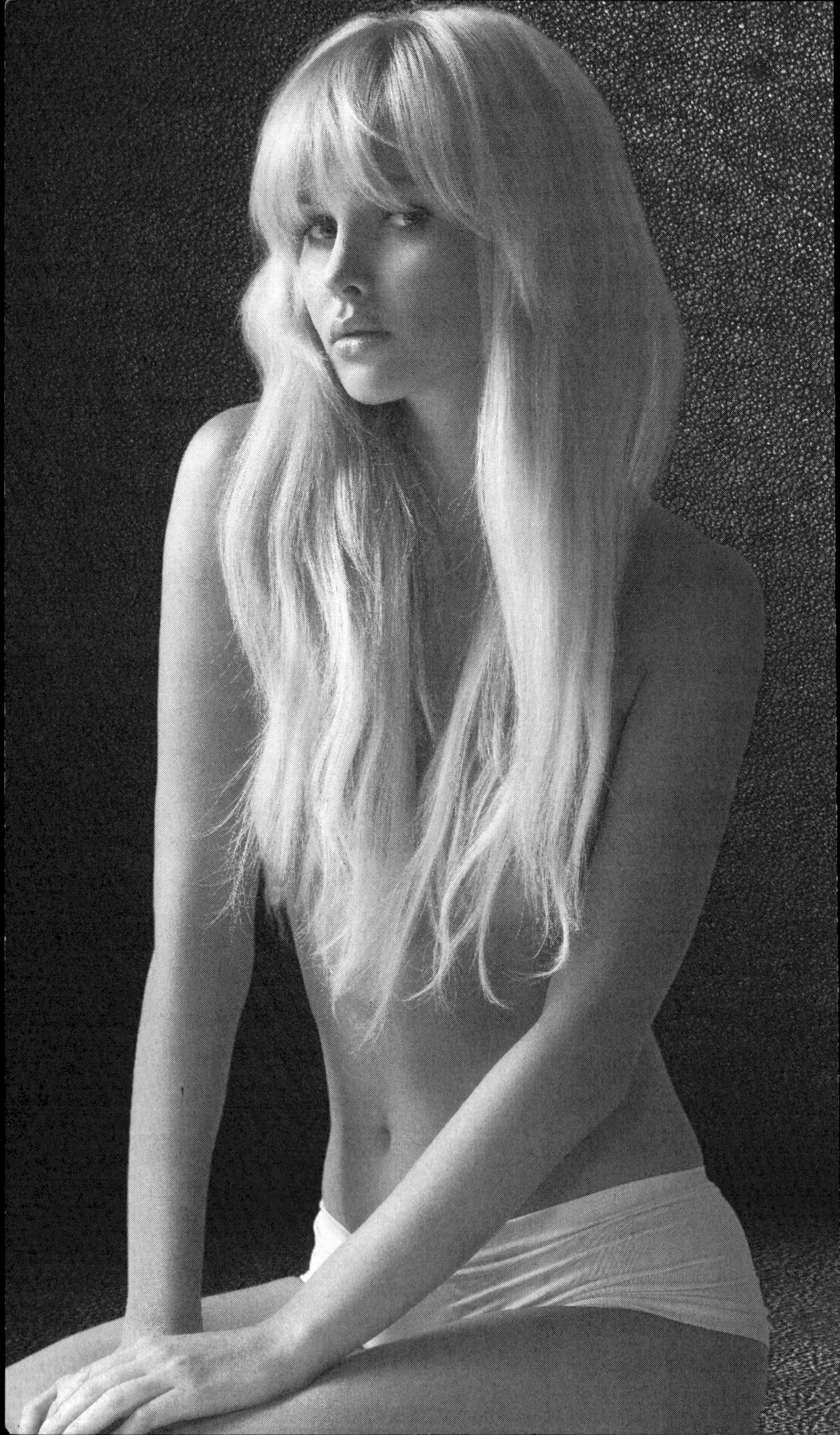

EPILOGUE PART II
ASHA: YEARS LATER

I let out a soft hum of contentment as warm arms encircled my waist while I stared out at the lake from my balcony, the moonlight dancing on the gentle waves.

"Miss me?" Liam's soft voice called out as his lips skimmed along my collarbone and up my neck.

"Mm, yes," I said, turning in his arms to get a good look at him.

Liam had been muscular in high school, but it all changed after graduation. He'd grown taller. Broader. His muscles were thicker, and his boyish good looks faded into the sexiness of manhood.

We'd gone to college. We'd graduated. I'd gotten my degree in clothing design, and he'd gotten a business degree. I was in the middle of starting my own fashion line while he worked for my dad.

I knew what Liam did. Mostly. He never spoke about it, but I knew my dad's business, and I'd seen Liam come back to our home late in the night with blood on his hands. Whenever I'd ask him about it, he'd only scrub harder, his body tense. I also knew the men who came up missing. Many were ones who'd harmed me years ago. I never asked him about that part, but I didn't have to.

I'd be lying if I said I didn't feel guilty about having a hand in it.

If I had my way, Liam would be doing what he loved, which was photography. He'd be traveling the world, taking photos, smiling. Not that he didn't still do photographs, it just wasn't his career.

"Liam?"

"Hellcat." He studied me.

"Are you happy?"

"Of course, baby. Why do you ask?" He reached out and thumbed my bottom lip. "Is something wrong?"

I took his hand and led him to the bed, pulling him down beside me. "I don't want you to work for my dad anymore. I want you to do photography and all the other things you love doing. I feel like you getting wrapped up with my dad is all my fault."

"None of what I do is your fault. I chose to do it, OK? Don't ever think otherwise. I promise you, I'm happy. I get to come home to my beautiful wife. I get to kiss her." He pressed his lips to mine. "Touch her." His hand swept up my bare thigh as his lips skimmed across my jaw. "Love her." He pushed me to my back and hovered over me. "Trust me when I say, I'm exactly where I need to be. I'm happy. In fact. . ." His hand moved beneath my nightdress before his fingers found my heat over my panties. "I was thinking maybe it's time we add to our happy, little family."

My pulse thundered in my ears. I'd been wanting a baby since the day he got down on one knee after college graduation two years ago and proposed to me in front of our families. His family had welcomed me into theirs with open arms. In fact, I spent a lot of time with his mom and sister, Lisa. We met weekly to catch lunch and shop. I was Auntie Ash to Lisa's little ones, and I'd be lying if I said my heart wasn't desperate to have a tiny Liam running around. My own mom had remarried my dad. Every Sunday night, we had dinner with them. I'd sit and talk with my mom over a glass of wine while Liam headed off to my dad's study with him. Everything was good, but it wasn't complete.

"Really?" I breathed out.

"I've been thinking about it a lot lately. I think we're ready." He kissed along my neck.

I angled my head for him, butterflies taking flight in my belly. After all these years, he still made me feel like it was the first time.

"Me too," I said breathlessly as he worked my panties down my thighs without breaking his lips away from my skin. I shimmied out of them the rest of the way as he chuckled against me. "I can stop taking my pill."

"Do it." He ran his tongue along my collarbone. "For now, we can practice."

My heart soared.

"Sofia told me today her and the guys are trying." I raked my fingers through my husband's hair and let out a soft moan as he pushed a finger into my hot center and rubbed my clit the way I liked with his thumb.

"Well, we certainly can't let them beat us, now can we?" He planted a kiss on my lips as he pushed another finger into my molten center.

I let out a gasp, goosebumps coursing over my skin.

"I hate it when they win."

He laughed softly, his fingers working me over until I was clenching around them, riding out my orgasm.

"That's a good girl," he praised, sounding pleased as he withdrew from me.

A moment later, he had my nightdress off and stood naked over me, his thick cock at my entrance as he sucked the sensitive flesh of my breasts before drawing a hardened peak into his mouth to tease.

"Please," I moaned, my fingers in his hair.

"Tell me you want it."

"I want it, Liam. All of it."

"How much?" He growled, playfully nipping at a nipple.

"So much."

He laughed. "You don't sound very convincing."

I let out a snarl and flipped him over so I was straddling him.

"There's my hellcat," he growled his approval as he gripped my hips.

I slid onto his thickness, letting out a moan of contentment. His hands tightened on my waist as I started to move on him, his dick buried to the hilt inside my heat.

"Come on my cock, hellcat. Show me how much you want it."

I whimpered, picking up my pace.

His hips thrust up to meet my movements, his cock hitting all the right places. I threw my head back, milking his cock as I came hard. He followed a moment later, filling me with his hot release.

I collapsed against his chest, and he trailed his fingers tenderly along my skin.

"I love you so fucking much," he whispered, his voice thick.

"Promise?"

"I swear it, hellcat. I'd do anything in this world and the next for you." He placed a fierce kiss on the top of my head and held me tight.

I buried my face in his neck and smiled. This was the life I'd always wanted, and he'd given it to me. The guy I'd tormented. The one I'd teased and taunted and hurt.

But he'd seen something in me I'd failed to see in myself. He'd saved me and continued to do it every day.

I knew it all those years ago. There was just something about Liam Hastings. Even when I was barely breathing, he was there to breathe life into me. And now, we were heading off on another adventure together.

I never imagined getting my happy ending with my soulmate, but there I was, wrapped in his strong arms, planning the next step in our journey together.

Every agonizing step I'd taken before him led me to all these moments with him.

This was happiness. This...was us.

And I wouldn't change a damn thing.

The End

Thank you for reading Barely Breathing. Please consider leaving your review!

**Do you want more stories from Acadia Prep? How about a reverse harem with Lucas, Jude, Hudson and a very special girl?
Barely Alive is coming soon!
Join K.G. Reuss's Renegade Readers on Facebook and get updates on upcoming books:
https://www.facebook.com/groups/streetteamkgreuss**

ABOUT THE AUTHOR

Known mostly for being strange, USA Today bestselling author K.G. Reuss knows what it takes to wear the crown of town weirdo. A cemetery creeper and ghost enthusiast, K.G. spends most of her time toeing the line between imagination and forced adulthood.

After a stint in college in Iowa, K.G. moved back to her home in Michigan to work in emergency medicine. She's currently raising three small ghouls and is married to a vampire overlord (not really but maybe he could be someday).

K.G. is the author of The Everlasting Chronicles series, Emissary of the Devil series, The Chronicles of Winterset series, The Middle Road (with co-author CM Lally) Black Falls High series and Seven Minutes in Heaven with a ridiculous amount of other series set to be released.

Sign up for her newsletter to stay updated on all the things happening in her freakishly ghoulish world.

http://eepurl.com/c2qQWP

Come join the Facebook group!

facebook.com/groups/streetteamkgreuss

Like TikTok? Find bonus content and book trailers on K.G.'s TikTok!

https://www.tiktok.com/@kgreuss

ALSO BY K.G. REUSS

Emissary of the Devil: Testimony of the Damned

Emissary of the Devil: Testimony of the Blessed

Emissary of the Devil: Gospel of the Fallen

The Everlasting Chronicles: Dead Silence

The Everlasting Chronicles: Shadow Song

The Everlasting Chronicles: Grave Secrets

The Everlasting Chronicles: Soul Bound

The Chronicles of Winterset: Oracle

The Chronicles of Winterset: Tempest

Black Falls High: In Ruins

Black Falls High: In Silence

Black Falls High: In Pieces, A Novella

Black Falls High: In Chaos

Hard Pass

Kings of Bolten: Dirty Little Secrets

Barely Breathing

The Middle Road

Seven Minutes in Heaven

Printed in Great Britain
by Amazon